CAROL
and the
Belles

Chautona Havig

Chautona Havig lives in a small, remote town in California's Mojave Desert with her husband and eight of her nine children. When not writing, she enjoys paper crafting, sewing, and trying to finish educating her remaining three children so she can retire from home education.

Edited by: Haug Editing
Fonts: Adobe Devanagari, Jacoba, Copperplate Gothic, Alex Brush
Cover photos: sonjarose/thinkstock.com, Rido franz/thinkstock.com, Kamil Makniac/thinkstock.com, Oksana_Alekseeva/thinkstock.com, gl0ck/thinkstock.com
Cover art by: Chautona Havig

The events and people in this book are purely fictional, and any resemblance to actual people is purely coincidental. I'd love to meet them!

Connect with Me Online:
Twitter: https://twitter.com/Chautona
Facebook: https://www.facebook.com/justhewriteescape
My blog: http://chautona.com/chautona/blog/
My newsletter (sign up for news of FREE eBook offers): http://chautona.com/chautona/newsletter

Dedication

Odessa

This book seriously would not have been possible without the help of my amazing niece, Odessa. Married to a Romanian and living on the Danube, just across from Ukraine, she has insight into Romanian culture that really gave life to this book and made Carol come alive. Where I failed—that's completely my fault. I did my best to take the answers she sent to my endless questions and translate them into an accurate portrayal of a Romanian in the USA.

Thanks to the wonder of the Internet and the connectivity provided by Facebook, I sent question after question—some pretty silly ones, too. "Do they have marshmallows? If not, do they know what they are? What kinds of notebooks would they use to write a letter?"

Ever-patient, Odessa answered every single one, sometimes doing research to verify things I'd found.

I also spent hours listening to interviews with Romanians trying to get the broken English just right. I'm sure I failed. Especially since I softened that broken English the more Carol spoke and then had it become worse again in emotionally charged or flustered situations. It seemed logical. One other thing you'll note is that when not actually speaking, Carol's perspective uses unbroken English. I did this because it would be difficult to read a book written in first-person perspective with *that* much broken English. Those thoughts and narratives would have been written in Romanian and then translated to English, so that's how I wrote those—for clarity rather than as if Carol spoke, thought *and* wrote only in English.

So, Odessa, thank you for blessing this silly aunt with all your help. Thank you for helping me make Carol's character the rich person I'd envisioned.

Escapeables

I also want to thank my "Escapeables"—that fabulous group of super-heroes who read faster than a "speeding bullet," helped me rewrite sentences into something more "powerful than a locomotive," and who helped me tell this "tall tale" in almost a single write. You're amazing people. The emails, the board posts, and the Facebook messages you sent me—from the "This is awesome" to the "I can't stand him" ones—they helped make this book into something I'm really proud of. I thank you.

Dear reader, if you saw quotes or announcements about this book on social media, it's likely because one of these amazing people took time out of his or her day to share for me. I am truly blessed.

1

I'll never get off this plane. The thought didn't appear just once or even twice. Passengers pulled suitcases down from overhead bins, collected e-readers, tablets, headphones, pillows, coats—an endless array of paraphernalia designed to keep me stuck on the plane forever.

The little girl with a couple dozen braids all over her head who had whined her way across the Atlantic—driving everyone in earshot a little crazy—had continued her journey with us from JFK to Rockland and now bounced in the aisle ahead, chanting in a little sing-song voice, "I'm gonna see Grannnnn-maaaa." It would have been—well no, it *was*—quite adorable. But it would have been more adorable had she not performed the same sing-songy dance demanding that we get *off* the plane just an hour earlier.

The view from the window didn't show much about this Rockland. After twenty years of addressing envelopes to the USA—to a pen pal who had become a good friend—I wanted to see it. Waiting, even as I crept a little closer to the door that would let me onto the jet way and into the airport, proved tedious in the extreme.

He'd promised he'd be waiting in baggage claim—holding a sign with my name. After baggage claim we would go have pasties—some kind of meat sandwich of British origin, he'd said—and walk in the park for a while so I could stretch my legs. That American idiom didn't make sense to my Romanian sensibilities. It had taken a Google search for me to understand it. But Google assured me that it only meant "get a little exercise after being immobile for a while," and who could argue with the chance to walk and talk with an old friend who is also a new one?

The moment my turn came, I bolted through the doorway. Exhaustion dissolved in the wake of eagerness. As a boy, I'd dreamed of meeting the American who wrote me every month. At nine, I imagined us playing football and watching an American baseball game—with hot dogs. For some reason, I was obsessed with the idea of eating hot dogs at an American ballgame.

As a teenager, that dream changed. We still played football, but by then I was confident that we were good enough to impress the girls. Michal had described his track meets, swim meets, and basketball games. He won trophies, and from the way he described the girls at his school and their excitement over what he accomplished, I doubt I would have been disappointed.

By the time I arrived there, the baggage claim area teemed with weary passengers waiting for their luggage. The turnstile for our flight hadn't even turned on yet, and the woman closest to me complained to the man with her that it would be a good fifteen minutes more. That's all I needed to hear.

Across the way, near the doors, a line of people stood holding placards. Jones, Frank, Abdi. I couldn't see the man holding mine at first, but I saw my name. It is impossible to move through the airport with speed—especially when everyone around you is determined not to move at all. A large group of teenagers, students who had been on my plane, blocked my view of Michal. But when I finally made it through them, the person standing there wasn't my friend—wasn't Michal. Instead, a tall, tanned woman with the longest legs I'd ever seen stood there, her eyes darting around the immense space in the hopes of seeing... me?

But she looked right past me—irritation in her eyes when I blocked her view. *He must have sent someone for him—maybe work prevented...*

My staring must have made her uncomfortable. She flicked hair—curly, brown hair that hung nearly to her waist—over her shoulder and dropped her eyes. It's embarrassing to admit that I was annoyed I hadn't seen the color. But a moment later, she looked up again, and this time they flashed at me—anger. Brown eyes, too.

Strange how disappointment can fizzle into intrigue when things change—while not for the *better*—in exciting ways. As much as I wanted to meet Michal—get to know him—this woman with my name on her little white square of paper fascinated me.

She spoke first. "Can I help you?"

"That's me." I pointed to the paper. "Did Michal send you?"

Okay, so the guy with the killer eyes and shoulders—since when did shoulders impress me anyway?—might have been fascinating, but I was looking for a woman. She'd be about thirty-four, and my mind pictured her as killer gorgeous.

We'd never exchanged pictures. Well, I'd sent one with my initial letter, but Carol had never sent me one of her, and we'd never exchanged them since—just didn't seem like something she could do. Maybe she didn't want to. I didn't know, which means I didn't know exactly what to expect, but all the pictures of Romanian women that I'd Googled were beyond beautiful.

So when Mr. I'm-gonna-stare-at-you-and-distract-you wouldn't *stop* staring, I got a bit... *torqued.* "Can I *help* you?"

The guy pointed to the paper. "That's me. Did Michal send you?"

Oooooh boy! Okay, so I admit that I looked around for a minute. I mean, it seemed like a joke, and Carol had always said she liked practical jokes. But the man's earnest expression just killed that thought. So, I did the only thing I could. I gave him—that pronoun just didn't fit my two-decade-old mental picture—the best sheepish grin ever bestowed on a confused man and said, "Uhhh... Hi... I *am* Michal."

Even as I spoke, every letter whizzed through my memory—every single one. I knew many by heart. We'd been such silly kids, writing about the differences in our lives, about being afraid of making fools of ourselves in school or with the other kids—even dreaming about hopping on a plane and visiting. *And yet, here he is—and he's not a* she! *How did that happen?*

Clearly, Carol—the name still threw me—didn't understand. I could see it in his eyes, the way he shifted the jacket from one arm to the other, the way he blinked—several times. "I think problem is my English—is not so good." He frowned as he added, "How you say...?" Insert totally adorable pause. "I don't understand."

I fumbled through my purse for my wallet and presented him with my driver's license. What else would prove that the woman standing there was the woman he'd come to meet? He looked just as confused as I was. "See— that's me. Michal Hargrave."

When the guy blinked again, in my nervousness, I almost offered eye drops from my purse. How rude would that have been? Carol stared at me, disbelieving. "You are Michal? I write you from Constanţa?" The once-over he gave me sent my cheeks flaming. "But you are woman."

"Romania, yeah." About that point, curiosity overrode courtesy and I blurted out, "Sorry, I thought *you* were a woman. I mean, Carol! Your name's Carol, right? Carol Stefan? Or!" Understanding hit me just as he opened his mouth to speak. "It's backwards, isn't it? Some Romanian thing. You're Stefan Carol."

"No..." His hands fumbled with a front pocket in the duffel bag he had slung over one arm. He fished out his passport and handed it to me. "See—Carol Stefan."

Before I could try to work out how I'd been writing to a *man*—well, originally a boy—all these years, the annoying baggage carousel buzzer went off. Baggage, I could deal with. "Hey, looks like your suitcases are coming."

"Is there a trolley—for carrying? I have many—too many for carrying."

Finally, something I knew how to do. Solving problems is my job. With Carol set and ready to go, in less than five minutes, I was out the door and on my way to get my car—a perfect opportunity to call my best friend and get help while Carol grabbed his. As usual, it went to voice mail, and as usual, I left a frantic message begging her to return my call. Crystal, with incredible dependability, called back before I made it to the shuttle. "Is she there? Can't you find her? Wha—"

"Stop. Please. Crisis."

"Oh, no. You don't like her." Crystal groaned and started throwing out a million ideas of how we could get Carol wrapped up in business he'd come for, and I'd hardly have to see him—except she kept calling him a her.

"Stop!" Thank the Lord for friends who get you—who know you're not trying to be a jerk when you're panicked.

"What? What's wrong with you?"

Cleansing breath, hand covering the phone as much as possible to fade the noise around me... go! "Okay, so Carol is a he—like a guy. Like, he's a crazy good-looking—why does that even matter?" That thought stopped all others until I shook myself and refocused. "Crystal, my pen pal is a *he*!"

"No way. Carol? Like C-a-r-o-l? Not double Rs and Ls?"

"Saw it on the passport. Apparently he expected me to be a guy too."

"Well... Michal is really close to a guy's spelling, and it's not a very common girl's name. That makes more sense to me than Carol-the-man."

Look, I wanted to go on trying to figure out how this had happened— I did. But I had bigger problems. "Crystal, the *party*! I've got a houseful of women coming tomorrow night. I seriously doubt Mr. Masculine over here is going to be interested in a mani-pedi party with six of my closest friends!"

"I'll call the guys. We'll fix this. You call Lloyd and get him there. Your boyfriend is definitely going to want to be at this party. Did you get a picture of him?"

"How?! I was staring at him like some crazy lunatic."

"That's redundant, Michal."

Stunned into silence, seconds ticked past until laughter overtook me. "Okay, you got me. How you can say the most normal things and make them hilarious, I'll never understand, but thanks. You're right. I'll get a picture and put it on Instagram as soon as I get him to the park."

"You're still going?"

"Of course! He needs food and some exercise before I stick him in my car for another hour." But the question hung there—taunting. "You think I shouldn't?"

"Not until you talk to Lloyd."

The question made no sense. Lloyd isn't the kind of boyfriend who gets all upset if I talk to other guys. So why would he care if I took a friend—one I hardly know—to get some food and walk around the park? But Crystal's kind of a relational genius. So, when she asks a question like that, we all just kind of nod and do it—except on days when I get rebellious.

Who knew this would be one of those days?

Michal—

September in Rockland is one of my favorite sights. The City Park has a fabulous array of trees, and Carol arrived at just the right time to see the beginning of the change. We walked under amber canopies and talked. At first, awkward silences and rushed attempts to break them threatened any chance of a real friendship. But then a thought occurred to me. No matter who had stepped up and claimed to be my friend from Romania, that same awkwardness would be there—the unfamiliar encroaching on us until we pushed it aside. And Carol and I had something *to* talk about. I needed to seize the opportunity.

"So you thought I was a man…"

Red crept up his neck as he nodded. "Is foolish thought, now, but Michal sounds like boy…" He shrugged. "My *doamnă* says you are American boy. I pick your letter because you talk about the sports."

Well, sports… I'd forgotten that. We had more to talk about there too. "I picked you because of your name too—and sports. Another girl who was a tomboy. What more could I want?" The question refused to go away, so I just asked it. "Are there a lot of guys named Carol in Romania?"

"Is common—not as common as Gheorghe, Ioan, or Constantin. We have two kings who are Carol." As if I'd given him permission to ask, he turned the question on me. "There are many girls named Michal?"

And there went my hopes of justifying myself. I didn't know any other girls named Michal. "No... it's from the Bible—David's wife? She got mad at him for dancing? Anyway, guys named Michael have an E in their names." Spelling it out didn't seem to help him much, but he tried.

"So we have interesting dilemma. I came to meet my friend and she is he—"

"He is she, you mean. I'm a she."

"Yes, is true. I get the words..." Carol shrugged and sent me a sidelong smile. "My friends will be the surprise."

"Friends!" How I'd already forgotten the party, my promise for a picture—everything—who knew? "Look, can I get a picture? I have friends all stalking my Instagram account for an update. They're going to be shocked when they see me with a cute—" Okay, just push me through the concrete and spread leaves over me. I wanted to die. Instead, I swallowed the lump in my throat and tried again. "—guy."

Carol didn't seem to think anything of it. We took half a dozen selfies before I decided one was good enough. That, on the other hand, definitely confused him. "Is camera not work?"

"Oh, it worked. But see..." I shoved the screen at him and showed the crooked smile that I hated, the one where I blinked—six rejects before the perfect picture of us. "This one's perfect."

He flipped back to the crooked smile and pointed. "This one too is perfect."

Of you, maybe.

My Instagram account went crazy—proof that Crystal had given the others a heads-up to watch for my picture of me with Carol. *Bet you didn't tell them about him, either. Sly... very sly.*

While retrieving the car, I'd revamped my plans, and those had begun with the guy who brought Carol here in the first place—Ralph Myner. Well, actually, I think some guy named Zain had done the bulk of it, but HearthLand is Myner's baby. Me, I've never been tempted to move out into the country and raise chickens or vegetables. But, Myner had quite the community built up already. And now they wanted Carol's art guild in Romania to provide their gift store with handmade artisan crafts. So, he kind of has a vested interest in Carol, too.

That's why I had decided to let Myner know about my plans for the afternoon. There was just one problem. I'd forgotten to mention it to Carol. "So... do you want to walk around downtown or just get on the road? I zipped an email to Ralph. He's going to pick you up in Brunswick later, so you could come meet my parents..."

It's as if just asking the question opened a floodgate. Carol had a million questions of his own—what was in the pasties we'd eaten? Where could we get "fro-yo"? Would my parents be upset when they found out their daughter had been writing a boy instead of a girl?

That one got me thinking. "Do you remember when I asked if you wanted to do email instead of snail mail?"

Confusion wrinkled his forehead. "I do not—what is snail—?"

"Sorry—regular mail. Like we did—*do*!"

"Oh, yes. I thought you would not wish to keep writing. My mentor says to me, 'No one writes in the old way. Everything is with the computers.'" Carol's smile told me what he'd say before he spoke. "But you say no—that you are happy. You don't want to be like that movie—"

"*You've Got Mail.*" Embarrassment washed over me. "Totally embarrassing now that you're a guy. Wow."

"I have not seen," he said as some measure of reassurance. "Is no reason to be embarrass."

It wasn't what he said—the words were simple enough. It was just how he said them. There wasn't any attempt at chivalry. He genuinely didn't want me to feel awkward. I could sense it. That kind of thing is usually a deliberate move—not always insincere or anything—just deliberate. Carol's wasn't. Probably some kind of Romanian charm.

He seemed uncertain. It showed in the way his hands shifted. Carol needed reassurance. "I was so relieved. It's kind of a ritual for me—writing you. I take my stationery to a coffee shop, put on my headphones, and write. I try to imagine you're sitting opposite me and just 'talk' to you on paper."

"I do that too—pretend you are there. But you were always man and we—" He ducked his head.

Could anything be more charming? A guy trying to hide his chagrin? "What? It can't be worse than the silly things I've done."

Carol's eyes—man, I swear he could see right through me. "We try to convince the girls to like us." His laughter rang out, and an elderly couple on a bench smiled at us. "You might not like that—trying to ask a girl for date."

"Um, no. And I don't think my boyfriend would like it either." Again, things grew awkward. I moved toward the gazebo. "Come see this. I wrote one here too."

He pointed to the little bench on one side. "There?"

"Yep. The one when my grandpa Colbert died." Okay, I didn't mean to, but it happened again—like every time I talked about him. My voice cracked. And before I knew what happened, these arms—*his* arms— wrapped around and held me.

"I am sorry, Michal." He looked and sounded so awkward—helpless. But he did it.

Don't know how long we stood there, and I don't really care. I'd been missing Grandpa as we walked through the park just like Grandpa and I had so many times. And well, it destroyed the last remnants of that awkwardness. Gone—in the space of a timeless hug and the forging of a deeper friendship.

Carol—

The pictures on the HearthLand website didn't do justice to the little town out in the country. Rather than the more primitive community I'd envisioned, this place seemed modern. Windmills—every building had one. The town square had little to offer—just a couple of stores near the corners, but anyone could see the potential.

Ralph, the man who had brought me to America, who had made this trip possible, pulled up in front of a house and grinned. "We're here." He pointed to a dog. "That's Gertie. She's a gentle dog. Won't bother you." The moment he stepped out of the truck, Ralph began talking to the animal. "Hey, girl. I brought home a guest. This is Stefan."

It wasn't the first time Ralph had called me by my last name. I didn't want to be rude and correct him—especially if he did it deliberately. In school, we used our last name first. Even Michal had mentioned something about it in her letters once or twice, but I couldn't remember what. Instead, I offered my hand to the dog. She growled. "The dog—is bite?"

With an apologetic gesture, Ralph insisted the dog was friendly. "She's never even growled that I know of. You must remind her of someone, but I can't imagine who…"

Gertie growled again—growled and snapped. Me? I jumped back and decided to leave her alone.

"Gertie!" Ralph stepped between the dog and me. "Go find Rory. Go!"

Before I could stop him, Ralph began trying to unload my enormous suitcases—the ones full of merchandise for their store. "These—are—heavy!" His groan snapped me out of my stupor.

"Yes," I insisted as I took one from him. "I carry."

His protest sounded a bit weak, but he made it anyway. "I can help."

Offending my host would be a poor beginning, so I pulled out my personal duffel bag and passed it to him. "Take this one, please. I carry these."

It wasn't easy to hoist one suitcase under each arm and follow Ralph up the steps and into the house. Muscles strained as I held onto them through a mini-tour of the house, but thankfully, Ralph suggested unloading the big suitcases into the basement before the upstairs tour. My relief didn't last long. It occurred to me that carrying them down a long flight of steep steps would be a pain, especially since I would then have to turn around and carry them back up when we put them in the store.

As we worked, Ralph talked about the town, the basement, the community center, repacking. The store wasn't ready for us to put stuff in there. I had to stifle a smile when he said, "We can unpack them later and carry them over in smaller boxes, too. Less likely to get banged up that way."

And more easily carried by you. You want to help, but you are not the young, strong man you once were.

Upstairs, he took me to a room—much larger than I'd expected—with a view of the back and side of the house and a bathroom just across the hall. The entire way, Ralph talked—explaining everything. "Feel free to move things around. We don't have satellite TV or anything, but we do have Internet, so you can stream on a laptop or tablet or something." He started to drop the duffel on the bed, but I managed to stop him just in time.

"The plane is dirty. Still it is on the bag—the dirt. It ruin the blanket."

Ralph began to argue but didn't. He brought a towel from the bathroom and spread it across the window seat. "Here. Set it here until you get it emptied." He pointed out the empty drawers in the bureau and the hangers and the space heater in the closet. "In case you get cold. We're still getting wood ready for the winter. Found quite a few trees down from last year's tornado, so we dragged them up and started cutting and splitting. Most are dry. We're not ready to start the stoves yet, though."

"I see." The words were almost a lie. I understood most of what Ralph said and little of what he meant—something that had happened too often in the past twelve hours.

With Ralph gone, it didn't take long to unpack. I hadn't brought much. Most of the luggage space I'd reserved for all the pieces I wanted to show these Americans—jewelry, hand-blown bowls and candlesticks, carved puzzle boxes. Not much hung in the closet when I finished. I needed

17

a suit, but the director of the guild had insisted I could get a better suit for the price in Rockland.

Michal's face appeared in my thoughts as I washed up and jogged downstairs. Perhaps she'd help me find one. Somehow shopping with Michal seemed like might be more fun than simple suit shopping.

Ralph and another man—Zain Kadir, the man who had helped me make my arrangements, if I guessed correctly— discussed an email mix up just as I entered the living room. Such an awkward moment, but I made myself step into the room smiling. "Hello, I am—"

"Stefan! Yes. So good to meet you. I'm Zain. We've been corresponding."

If you are Zain and not Kadir, why am I "Stefan"?

"—need to get a move on if we're going to show him any of the town. I just felt the dip." My confusion must have shown, because Ralph laughed and tried to explain. "It's what I call that moment when you can sense the sun going down. Ignore me. I'm a bit odd at times."

"He's a lot odd a lot of the time!" Zain argued. "But he's right. It will be dark soon."

Gertie waited on the porch with a wag for Ralph—and a growl for me. I tried to act ambivalent, in hopes that the dog would decide I wasn't worth the hassle of a chewed ankle. That thought also gave me an idea. "Should I give dog food? Special food for trust?"

"Maybe if she doesn't warm up in a day or two. She's had a rough month, so it might just be more unfamiliarity. Poor girl."

Most of what Ralph said made sense, but the man spoke so quickly that I began to doubt my translation skills. "You have much buildings. I thought still it would be very..." When the word didn't come, I shrugged. "I don't remember how you say. The same."

"Oh, undeveloped?" Zain nodded. "We've done more this year than should be possible. Our contractor had to hire two extra crews for the job. I thought he'd be laying everyone off soon, but we're starting another housing settlement over that way—just as soon as we get a road made."

"The houses here so close to the town. Why those so far?"

As the men explained, each in excited tones and rapid speech, I just watched and tried to follow their words, but most of the time they made no sense. Still, the idea of small, close-knit neighborhoods sounded familiar and cozy. "It is like that in Romania. In Constanța there are neighborhoods—little towns in the city. You have wise decision."

They described a restaurant they had planned—a home-style place of different cuisine— my excitement grew. Such a fine idea. But the wood cook stove made me nervous. "It will be too hot? In summer?" The words sounded too critical even as I spoke them. "I like!" I insisted. "You make food artisan. Is great idea. Even when hot, people will eat?"

Whatever Zain said next was drowned out by the frantic words of a woman who burst through a door and raced across the yard. She apologized but dragged the men toward the door. It sounded as if someone was hurt. Ralph apologized, but I waved them off. I could not help, and a bit of time alone sounded like a piece of heaven right then.

Michal—

Nerves will be the death of me—seriously. And meeting old friends who are new friends pulled out this weird sort of maternal instinct in me. Carol was supposed to be driving his rental car to my condo. Yeah. Insane, right?

"Lloyd? Lloyd!" That guy could disappear so fast...

"Sorry. Just setting up the chocolate fountain."

Forgiven. "What side of the road do Romanians drive on?"

He paused mid-stride and spun in place. "Since they were never invaded by England, my vote is the right side. I think I read that somewhere." Even as he spoke, Lloyd pulled out his phone to verify his answer. "Yep..." I must have looked as unsettled as I felt, because he pulled me close, held me for a moment, and promised that Carol would be just fine driving on American roads. "He has a phone, so if he gets lost..."

After a quick kiss, with hands over my ears, I rushed to the kitchen calling, "I don't want to hear thaaat..."

Crystal burst into my apartment with a "Welcome to America" banner and a bottle of wine. "I figured being European, he might like it."

I, on the other hand, struggled to keep my opinion regarding the empty calories of alcoholic beverages to myself and instead, focused on stalking the door and checking my phone with almost relentless dedication.

I have a few serious faults—don't we all? Mine is definitely being too opinionated about things like wine and stuff and being snarky when nervous—snarky is a bad one, I'm afraid.

Two more of my friends—both women, of course—showed up before Carol finally knocked on the door. Can I just say that it's hard to call a man "Carol" without seeing that extra R and L in your mind? Trust me. It is. It's an American thing. Romanians probably have a hard time imagining a woman named Carol—it doesn't end in A.

Yeah… in the past twenty-four hours, I'd done a lot of research on Romanian naming practices, and let's just say that they have it made over there. Almost every woman's name ends in A. Genius. You know before you meet someone if it's a man or a woman. Except for Carmen (and a couple of others). Over here, Carmen might be a guy singer that people love— even if it is spelled differently. Over there… a woman. But otherwise, it's an easy bet that you won't be introduced to "Jordan" or "Terry" or "Robin" or "Taylor" and be shocked to discover that your long-time pen pal is actually a man… or a woman, depending on situation. Yeah. Carol too—that wouldn't happen over there. Lucky dogs.

As Crystal dug through the cupboards for the wine glasses, I filled the sink with water and soap. Let's just say my glasses don't get enough use to pull them out of the cupboard without a quick rinse, okay? If it weren't for friends who are really into the celebration of wine as a good gift from the Lord, I wouldn't own them. It may be—not arguing that—but it's also a good gift of calories I can't afford with my workout regimen, too. So I leave that blessing to them and enjoy my sparkling water with a "shot" of grapefruit juice. Win-win, right?

Therese—the friend who had always mocked me for my silly obsession with my pen pal thing—called out, "Hey, Michal. I think he's here!" A second later she added, "Whoa… this guy is cute—way hot!"

And so sparked an idea. That would be another fault of mine. If I'm going to confess them, it just makes sense to be thorough. Some people thrive on minding their own business, and I thrive on "fixing" things—even if it's none of my business. I've looked for a twelve-step program on that, but so far, no luck.

Poor Carol—he was totally out of his element. The guy stepped into the room expecting I-don't-know-what, and my friends bombarded him with their questions, their compliments, their *flirting*. Oh, yeah. I've never seen any of them—Crystal especially—quite so... *forward* in their attempts to be friendly to a guy. It would have been comical if Carol hadn't looked so panicked.

Lloyd draped an arm around my shoulder and murmured, "Every guy's dream and he looks ready to puke."

His aftershave—something he only wears for me on occasions like this—sent my senses zinging. But it probably wouldn't be in good taste to give a public display of exactly how much I like it, so I opted to deflect. "Why did you all have to decide to take off for the lake, anyway?"

"Because *you* said this was an all-girl's night. How often do guys get a Saturday night free to be stupid without their girlfriends judging?"

Okay, he had a point. You can't fault a guy for wanting to spend time somewhere where he can belch and his buddies think it's funny. Or maybe you can, but it helps if you show appreciation for him doing it *away* from you. So, I kissed his cheek, paused, gave his lips a once-over—and another—and went to save Carol—or at least throw him a lifeline.

"Okay! I guess everyone here knows Carol now." He stepped forward and took the hand I offered him. "So let's do some introductions." At the panicked look on his face, I added, "You don't have to remember names—"

Crystal nearly bolted from the room calling, "You've got those sticker name tags in your room!"

Best idea ever—trust me. Carol nearly sagged in relief as I explained what she meant. With everyone speaking at breakneck speed, each one trying to make him feel welcome, the room buzzed until even I wanted to wave my grannie's undies in surrender! Note that I said my grannie's undies—not my granny undies. Big difference. Literally.

I snatched the stickers from Crystal, almost before she could offer them, and began scribbling names. "This is Therese. She's from my church.

She's a teacher at Brunswick Christian Academy." I turned to one of the guys to give Carol a bit of a break from the flood of females and patted his arm. "This is Trent. He loves kayaking. Do you like that kind of thing? I thought maybe he could take you out once before it gets too cold."

Trent graciously suggested that they go the next day, but Carol shook his head. "I am sorry, but the man I stay with, Ralph Myner, is having party tomorrow. I would like to go," he assured me—why *me*, I don't know. "But if some other day is good, I would like very much."

"We'll make it happen."

All around the room, Wendy, Felicity, Jenn, Robb, and the others wound up with stickers on them and assurances that Carol was just aching to spend time with each and every one. Somehow, I doubted it. But, who can complain about that kind of welcome for a friend or that friend's amazing graciousness? Apparently, I can because all I could think of was, *Man, let him breathe!*

As if that wasn't bad enough, well, my friends started begging me to set them up with him. Okay, for that, I can't blame them. The guy is seriously good-looking, absolutely charming, and just shy enough to be endearing without being awkward. If I wasn't so happy with my own boyfriend, I might have been just as eager to get him to notice me—that way, I mean—spend one-on-one time with *me*. Then again, I could spend all the time with him that I wanted—it's why he pushed for the chance to be his artisan guild's "ambassador" to the HearthLand thing.

Yeah. That. Since when does a sustainable community—*intentional* community, anyway—have gift shops and stuff like that? I mean, it's all good for Carol and his group, but it seems a bit incongruous—okay, a *lot* incongruous—for people who are trying to be eco-conscious and stuff to be so touristy, too. Lloyd said I was just doing my devil's advocate thing. He was probably right, but it still bugged me.

"—he'd want to have lunch on Monday? You've got that meeting, right?"

Crystal's voice jerked me from my critical thoughts and brought me back to the present. "Huh?"

"Carol. If we don't get him taken for Monday, Jenn's going to get her talons into him."

"That's not fair. She's a nice girl…" Conscience demanded I amend that statement—at least to myself. *Desperate for a guy, but really nice in every other respect.*

"He's your friend. She's waiting right there—hovering. She's going to do it…"

The sad thing is that Crystal was right. I glanced at her and realized she might be interested as well, but her offer was truly for Carol's benefit rather than hers. It settled things in my book. "Hey, Carol," when he moved to my side, I continued. "Crystal here really is into art. She has all kinds of amazing pieces—not just sculpture or paintings, but the kind of stuff your guild does."

A glance at Jenn told me I'd made the right decision. Guilt made me promise to get her at least one date with him.

Carol—

Confusion. If one word could describe the party at Michal's house, it would be confusion. Three names stood out to me: Michal, of course, Lloyd, and Crystal. There was another woman I'd never forget, but her hair covered her nametag. Michal had mentioned Lloyd often. Looking back, I should have known that he was something more than just a friend.

Crystal wasn't like the others. Where many of the women tried *too* hard to make me feel welcome, Crystal actually managed to succeed. So, when Michal called me over, explained about her Monday meeting, and asked me to go to lunch with Crystal instead, how could I refuse?

"Is kind of you to offer. I would enjoy if not too much trouble?"

The woman's smile reassured me—in several ways. These women liked my accent. They left no doubt of it. And, if I had been too obtuse to notice, their half-whispered comments could have been heard by a half-deaf person. At least Crystal didn't make me feel like a circus animal.

"Should I pick you up at HearthLand, or would you like to meet somewhere? Dolman? Fairbury?"

All my life, it seemed, I'd read about this magical place—Fairbury. Several times a year, the quaint little town appeared in one of Michal's letters. I started to suggest that, when a flash of disappointment in Michal's eyes stopped me. "I would say Fairbury…" I was right. The minute I said it, that flash came again. "But through Michal's eyes I read about it all these years. I would much like to *see* it with her first. Maybe here—in Brunswick?" Close by, I heard someone echo my pronunciation and giggle.

"Let's meet at Hipsters," Crystal suggested. "Do you have a phone?"

I pulled out the iPhone Ralph had given me. "I left my mobile in Constanța. Ralph say she will give me one to use."

After an amused smirk at Michal—what I'd said now, I couldn't imagine—Crystal tapped her mobile to mine and instantly her contact information appeared. "Just text me, and I'll reply with an address and everything." She peered over my mobile and grinned. "Good. It has Google Maps—GPS."

"*Da.* It has the GPS." I typed a quick note into the mobile. THANK YOU FOR INVITATION. I COME @ WHAT TIME?

When she smiled, at that moment I realized how beautiful Michal's friend is—not just a pretty face, but a kind heart. I've always treasured people with kind hearts. The little boy in me craves that kindness—the kindness I rarely saw as a child.

"Let's meet at one, okay? Then we won't be hogging a table during the lunch rush. I have a feeling I'm going to enjoy talking with you."

A glance at Michal is all I needed to know I'd done the right thing. She wanted me to spend time with her friend. How could I say no?

3

Carol—

Music pulsated around us as we ate. I'd begun to dread the idea of lunch with Michal's friend, but once we were seated and perusing the menu, Crystal began to ask questions. At first, they were the usual ones, how long was my flight, did I like HearthLand, and how long would I stay? But they changed when she asked about my work.

"So you make jewelry?"

"Silver work, yes. But is more than the necklace or ring. I make much with the silver. Pen casing, medals, ornament for the Christmas tree."

"Do you enjoy it?" She ducked her head and took a sip of her coffee, embarrassed. That embarrassment took an attractive woman and made her beautiful in ways you can't see in a magazine photo. "That sounds so rude aloud."

"Is... how you say..." The struggle to find the right word—a frustration by non-native speakers the world over. "*Vai de capul meu!*"

"Well, you could say that," Crystal joked. "But now I don't know how or what to say."

"Is mean, 'Oh, my head.'"

"Oh, your head hurts trying to find the right word?"

"*Da!* Yes! You are correct. I try to say your question is..." Again, the word eluded me.

Crystal swirled a fry in ketchup before she winked and asked, "Brilliant? Stupid? Ridiculous? Um... reasonable?"

"Yes! The reasonable. It *is reasonable question.*" The definition—one of my tutor's contextual definitions, anyway—of reasonable clicked and I added, "It make sense."

She waited. I tried not to stare. She smiled. I smiled back. Just as panic that I'd missed some important social cue set in, she leaned forward and asked, "Well... are you going to tell me? Or is it some Romanian national secret?"

"Is what secret?"

"If you like making silver things."

When you are passionate about something—when that thing creates an ache in your soul because of the sheer beauty of what it is—keeping it to yourself is either imperative or impossible. When asked, I find it impossible. I tried not to monopolize the conversation—that word is a favorite. Monopolize. It has a fascinating sound and the meaning is so rich. I love monopolize—as a word. Probably not so good in practice. But I found myself talking—a lot.

Something about Crystal's personality reminded me of Michal's letters. In person, Michal seemed more... intense. But in her letters, while her driven personality came through, she seemed a little more carefree. Crystal blended both characteristics well. She must have noticed my distraction, because she asked if I was "okay." Americans seemed to do that a lot when I didn't speak. "Am good, yes. I wondered..."

Again, she swirled a fry in the ketchup, but this time she didn't eat. She just swirled. "Carol, you can ask me pretty much anything. If I can't answer it, I'll tell you."

"Is Michal always so... intense?" I waited for confirmation that I'd used the right word before continuing. "Is just that she seemed... what is word? Frantic? At the party, I mean."

"Well, she *acted* frantic, but that was because she was stressed out."

"Yes! The stress. This is word."

Her laughter caused a few people to look our way, but Crystal didn't seem to notice or care. "That would be because she *was* stressed. You see, she'd planned this big party for you with *all* our friends—our *girl*friends. And then here comes this guy, and…"

"And that might be…" Flustered, again, the words failed me.

"Awkward."

"Right. Is awkward to be only man at the party."

Her eyes sparkled in the light of the window before she said, "Some men would consider that a dream come true."

It tempted me—the idea to pretend not to understand her joke, but I wanted to tease back. I wanted to see if I could make an American laugh. "Yes, and Michal rides a bicycle as fast and as far as she can. She calls *that* fun. She would think Tour de France dream come true. Is what I call crazy."

Disappointment filled me as Crystal cocked her head and mused, "You make people underestimate you." Laughter bubbled over. "And you're so right. She *is* crazy. She barely gets me in the gym door." Crystal leaned forward and whispered, "It only works when she reminds me that I pay good money for that membership." Her finger beckoned me closer, and I obliged. "Shhh… don't tell."

In Romania, if a woman did those things—especially the *way* Crystal did them—I would consider it flirting, but I didn't see that in her eyes or her smile. We were co-conspirators in some secret plot that we didn't even know. It was nice. And, it opened up the side of me I don't usually share with people I don't know. "I didn't understand why Michal wanted us to do this." A question in her eyes I met with a shrug and an attempt to explain. "Is inconvenience for you to come out just because she couldn't, isn't it? I could stay at HearthLand and help Ralph. But now…" It was my turn to swirl a fry as an excuse not to look at her. "Now I am glad. Thank you for coming."

Crystal snitched a fry from my plate and ate it before she replied, "Just be careful if Michal suggests spending time with Jenn. She's a great girl— Jenn that is." The woman frowned as her words jumbled. Even I knew she was saying things all wrong. "I mean, Michal is too! Anyway, just be careful with Jenn. She's nice, she's sweet, but she's a bit… *desperate* for a guy, and she tends to take friendly gestures too seriously."

The words struck fear into the deepest corners of my heart. "You think Michal will wish this?"

"She might—if meetings come up again or something. I'll try to talk her out of it, though."

"*Da.* Please, *please* do. It sounds, this idea, horrifying." I blinked, unsure of what I'd actually said. "Is right word?"

She nodded. "Unfortunately, yes. It's exactly the right word."

"Why is unfortunately?"

"Because…" Crystal signaled the server—wanted the check. "Like I said. Jenn is a great girl—really."

You, like Shakespeare said, protest too much.

Michal—

A long meeting—longest our organization has endured in ages—ended at four-fifteen, and my boss, fabulous man that he is, insisted I go home early. "*We got the grant. You worked hard for it, so go home and put your feet up, take a bubble bath, go out to eat… something.*"

So, lounging on the couch, the "treasure chest" of letters and stationery spread out around me, I reread Carol's letters, trying to find some hint that he had given himself away. "Problem is," I informed my cat, Mr. Miniver, "he's always mixed up his genders in speech. I bet he did give himself away, but I just brushed it off as nothing." He jumped up on the couch, scattering letters, of course, and rubbed my leg with his head.

Mr. Miniver has always enjoyed draping himself across my lap when new letters come. It's like he reads them, too and has an opinion. Once, he even slapped the page and gave Carol a "high five" when he read that Carol got a special commission for a wedding set—four pieces plus a tiara for the bride. So sprawling across my workspace didn't exactly surprise me, but it's harder to read when your cat decides to slap a leg across the exact portion of the letter you're reading.

Still found nothing. Seeing *how* the mix up had happened wasn't difficult. But how it continued... I'd have to leave that up to childishness, language barrier, and the propensity of humans to read what they expect to rather than what is actually there. If you have any doubt that this is a true phenomenon, simply read Facebook or message boards—or Christmas letters!

Seriously! I can read the same letter as my cousin Janice, and to hear her tell it, our "perfect cousin" Marla said that her kids were better than Marla's—*in the letter.* I didn't get that out of it—not even close. We read the same letter but our personalities and insecurities—our *strengths* and weaknesses—affect how we translate the words. I'm telling you, we see and read what we *think* is in there half the time.

Crystal zinged me a text while she exited her car and seconds later, burst through my front door. "You're home! I saw your car as I passed and zipped in. How'd it go?"

"We got it."

Crystal isn't the "do the happy dance" kind of woman. She's more the quiet boil over with joy—like the "smoke" from dry ice. Just slowly fill the room with her happiness until no one can see anything else. But right then, she did a half-Charleston/half-shimmy before plopping down on the other end of my ridiculously large couch. "What *are* you doing?"

"Trying to figure out how I missed Carol's *gender.*"

"Which one goes first?" Before I could answer, Crystal found the pile with letter *numero uno* right on top. "Never mind. Got it." She read.

"Dear Michal in the USA,

I was happy to choose your letter to be pen pal for me. My teacher, Doamnă Spalding, says you live in the middle of America. She is from Florida. She help me understand parts of letter for the words I do not know.

Yes, I like to play the sports. I like football, like you. Doamnă Spalding say you call it soccer in USA. I also like to run. I must run many times. But I run so I am not late to the school. I also like to swim. I do not swim in the pool like you. I swim in ocean when I can sneak away.

I do not have pets. I live in orphanage. There is not enough food for the children. We cannot feed dogs or cats too. I have pretend that a dog that follows me sometimes is my dog. I call him Dracul so the other children will not play with him. Is so they do not make him hurt.

Yes, I have the friend. His name is Constantin. She is friend when other boys cannot play. They say many mean things to him if she talks to me, so I must only talk if they are gone."

Crystal's voice broke there. "What a sad letter. So lonely sounding."

My frustration boiled over into an accusation. "How many times have you read those, and *now* you think his life was sad?" Even before she said something, a suspicion I'd had for years confirmed itself. "You never read them."

"I did!" she protested. "I... skimmed." When she received no understanding reply, Crystal shrugged and began to apologize. "It's—I'm sorry. But, c'mon. It's like a grandma expecting everyone to think every single, solitary photo—all 400 taken in the span of 20 seconds—is uniquely amazing. You read one, you read 'em all—or so it seemed." She picked up the next letter. "Obviously, I was wrong."

"Sure were." That's when her face changed, and I knew what it meant. "Dooon't..."

"Seriously, Michal. Go for a run. You're getting all worked up over the fact that your life-long friend happens to be an entertaining, charming, and scary good-looking *guy*."

"And, if I didn't have a boyfriend with whom I've shared a four-year relationship, that might appeal to me."

"And that's what makes it perfect! Lloyd knows you're practically married to him, so there's no reason to be jealous, and you won't have to have any of those awkward, 'Am I attracted, or is he just a friend...?' questions. It's perfect."

They were too—her words. They were perfect—exactly what I needed to hear. And, her earlier words also spoke volumes to me. I did need that run. Without even bothering to reply, I jumped up and raced for my exercise pants, shirt, and jacket. Probably wouldn't need the jacket, but if I don't bring it, an arctic wind invariably appears to mock and torment me. I suspect he's in Murphy's pocket.

By the time I arrived back in the living room to tie on my shoes, Crystal had curled up with a stack of the letters and appeared to be reading each one multiple times. One look at her, and an idea formed. Carol was supposed to stay at least through Christmas—maybe longer if things worked out. Everyone already *wanted* a chance to go out with him. Why not capitalize on that?

I could introduce him to several of my girlfriends—get him to take them out one at a time. Maybe… just maybe, he'd find one he really liked. Crystal's silky, honey-colored hair draping over one cheek as it always did, combined with the memory of why she rarely dated, gave me hope that she might be just the woman for him. *Like a combination, "Welcome to America" and Christmas present all in one.*

Her eyes lifted to meet my gaze. "Good run?"

"Yeah. Thanks. Sorry for being so difficult."

"No worries." She shook the stack of letters in her hand for effect as she added, "And if it makes you feel any better, with the way he jumbles the pronouns, and you both just assume things, I think anyone would have thought he was a she."

4

Carol—

When Mirela brought the idea of selling our work—our *art*—in a community in the United States, we were ecstatic. We've received some recognition over the years, but most people who find us want what Mirela calls "rock bottom" wholesale prices that give us barely enough to eat. She will not agree, and she fights when artisans become so desperate to sell their work that they give it away. *"We must not devalue our work, because if we do not value it, no one else will."*

Some people leave—go to work in factories or try to sell enough online to make a living. Etsy is a gift to people like me—a lifeline. But those of us who value art for more than what it can give us, those of us who value art for what it will give the person who buys it, we stay. We stay and create. We create because *not* to create starves us more than not to have money for food.

I have an advantage over most. I've never known a comfortable life. My country is poor—most Romanians do not have wealth like Americans. We know what true poverty is. But, beyond that, having been an orphan during one of the worst, if not *the* worst times in Romanian history for orphans, I know how to survive without food, without clothes, without adequate shelter. It made me strong. And that strength carries me when nothing else but my faith can.

I stood in the little space that was to become HearthLand's "finest" gift shop and closed my eyes. Questions fired at me at speeds too fast to translate, much less respond. The vision of what this store could be transported me to a place of happiness as it formed until it took on a life of its own. "If store is a success, artists work here sometimes—how you say when you work so people can see?"

"Demonstrate?"

"*Da!*" The vision blossomed. I pointed to the bowed-out window and climbed up there to show what I meant. "This window, it is perfect. The artist, she work here making his pottery or his carvings. People stand outside or right there—" I pointed to where Ralph stood. "—to watch him. Will give reason for people to come—people who don't want gift today. They see it made; they like it. They buy it."

"So you'd use that window for demonstrations rather than display?" Ralph glanced toward Zain as if waiting for the man's opinion.

The answer didn't come for so long that nerves set in. I didn't know if I'd explained well—used the proper words. As Zain's head began to shake, discouragement set in. They couldn't see it. Or perhaps, Americans don't enjoy the same things Romanians do.

"I don't know why I didn't think of it—I mean, I did, but the window. That's genius."

Excitement filled my heart, but Ralph's words dashed those ideas again. "If you're sure..."

Zain lacked my reticence in addressing Ralph's uncertainty. "You don't like it?"

"No, I love it. I just assumed..." That must have been when my confusion and dismay clicked with Ralph. "Oh! Stefan, I didn't mean that I didn't like it. I'm just usually the one with the very bad ideas, and I wanted to do this. This is perfect."

Buoyed by the excitement in Ralph's tone, I wandered through the space, talking about all the things we could do with it. Some items weren't worth shipping. Ioan's large carved wood pieces—the furniture. "It would cost less to bring him here. He works in window or maybe workroom somewhere, builds the bigger pieces, and goes home. The customers see process. You have inventory. Everyone wins for not so much money."

"Could we do that with the glass blower?"

He would be disappointed. "The furnace is big—very large. You need much space for the tools. Glory hole and annealer—very large." The room we stood in might be large enough. But people couldn't come in or watch, and there wouldn't be a place for the glass or any other art. "And is very expensive. To buy this would be... how you say?"

"Cost prohibitive." Zain nodded, agreeing. "But, we could rent the materials, I bet. He could bring his smaller tools—his favorites—but we could rent the big stuff for say a month. Surely, he could make enough during that time to cover the cost of shipping the same amount of stuff here. We'd have less breakage, so we'd come out ahead, wouldn't we?"

Despite the confusing questions, my confidence grew. "I will ask. You can find what is cost for rent?"

Ralph interrupted before Zain could respond. "We still don't have a place—"

But Zain already had ideas. "We could do it at the restaurant. There's all that space at one end of the kitchen. We could do it there. With the glass to separate people, there would be protection. I don't think we'd have insurance issues with it then."

At that, the men began talking about insurance and liability—things I thought I understood but didn't quite. I measured for display cases and shelving, drew sketches and made plans, and as I worked, something changed in the way I saw this place—this community.

They'd welcomed me here as a "neighbor." Every person, aside from a couple of little boys, had accepted me as part of their community without hesitation. Never have I felt so connected to people so quickly. I try to, but I don't trust easily. Years in a Romanian orphanage will do that to you.

After the fall of Nicolai Ceausescu, things did get a little better— eventually. Some of the children went to foster homes. I did not. But unlike many orphans, I had school—thanks to a church in America that heard about us on television. They sent workers and teachers to come help. I was sent to a regular school with the other children. Then I was sent to apprentice with Ioan—to be a wood carver. That was the first time I felt the joy of community. I felt it again in this place.

Zain's voice ripped me from thoughts of the past. "Everything okay, Stefan?"

"Yes. I was just think of how I never feel at home, but here I feel at home. This is wonderful place you have. I am blessed to come. When Mirela say we have opportunity to come, I did not wish to. My home is Constanṭa. But then she say Rockland, and…"

"And your friend is here."

Zain said in few words what I didn't have enough to express. "Yes. But is better than I think. I meet friend *and* find new place where I am feel at home." Tears choked me as I added, "I never imagine…"

A gift from Michal arrived with the mail one morning. Ralph brought it into the kitchen and set it next to my sketchbook. "That looks pretty…" He tapped the swirling vine I'd sketched. The loose infinity symbol with leaves and crystals might be the best I've ever done—if I could make it look good.

"Thank you. I think I like, too. Is—"

"That almost looks like an infinity symbol—the way it flows in a figure eight." Ralph traced it with his finger. "Yeah. I love the subtlety of it."

Sometimes the words take time to translate, but the tone, the wonder, the admiration—those things are easy to comprehend. As an artist, I value people who understand my work. "That was what I attempt to do. I am glad I am succeed."

He moved away to the refrigerator and pulled out the soup left over from the previous night's dinner. "Hungry?"

He must have decided I was, because before I could answer, two bowls appeared on the counter. I think he murmured a question about toast, but the wrappers fell away from the package at that moment, and a leather bound book dropped into my hands. Long leather straps bound it in a knot in front.

"Is that a journal? Gorgeous."

"Is very nice." The opening page had writing on it—Michal's familiar penmanship. Short—the message was short, but oh so like her.

Carol,

I saw this as I walked past a gift store today, and I realized that we'll be talking about your adventures here in America, but you won't have a record of them. So I bought it. I thought maybe you'd like to write down what you did, where you went, who you met, and how you feel about all of it. A Selphy printer is on its way to my house. I thought you might like to add photos too, so save room if you start writing before Friday.

So glad to get to know you even better,
Michal

At that moment, Rory burst through the door looking for Gertie and asking for a snack. He always seemed to be eating, but he was small. "Hello, Rory."

He just looked at me, nodded, and mumbled, "Hey." Immediately, he turned back to Ralph and added, "Oh, and crackers? I really need crackers. Mom's out."

Watching the interchange sparked the first entry into the journal. A pencil wouldn't work—wouldn't last. Words written in ink stain your heart as well as the page. Pencil is too easy to erase—to hide what was true in that moment. A trip to Ralph's office to retrieve one of the many pens he kept in a cup there remedied that problem. Soup waited for me when I returned. "Thank you. Also I can make food. Is not necessary to serve."

"It's my pleasure," he insisted. "Garlic toast?" Again, without asking, he passed the plate of bread and sat down. "Whatcha gonna write in that?"

"Michal says I should... how you say... write the *experiences*. I think I will."

Rory burst through the door. "Forgot water! Can I have a bottle?"

"Sure, son, but—" He was out the door before Ralph could finish speaking. "That boy…"

And so began my first entry.

The boys do not like me, but they do not like each other either. The small one, Rory, wears glasses that fall down his nose and clothes that always look just a little too big. The dog and Rory go everywhere together, and I suspect the boy confides in the dog, much as I did a few street dogs as a boy myself. The fact that the dog—Gertie—doesn't like me seems to be why Rory is wary.

He watches me. Everywhere I go, if he's home, he watches and writes down what he observes in a small notebook. I think he pretends to be a detective on an important case, but Ralph tells me he is a comedian—always writing down jokes.

Andre is different. He's sullen, angry, terrified. I recognize myself in him, too. If I knew his mother better, I'd talk to her and explain what I think is going through her son's head. I can see she doesn't know what to do with him. She thinks she's failing. She's not. He loves and respects her, although he doesn't always show it. He rarely shows it. But I see it in his eyes. I see something else in them, too—pain. Something about her makes him feel guilty. I wish I knew what it was.

I will keep trying to make friends. For Rory, I think I only need to convince Gertie that I am not an enemy. Then he will like me—trust me. Andre, on the other hand, I will have to earn his trust, but I can't do that until I learn what he is so afraid of. Maybe Ralph knows.

Before I took my first bite, I looked up at Ralph. "Do you know why Andre is afraid?"

"No, why?"

An odd question—I shrugged. "I thought you might know."

"Oh! Sorry, it sounded like you were being Socratic. Um, I'm not really sure. He is probably just ticked off about having to leave his old home for here. I don't think he's afraid."

Telling people about my past has always been difficult. Most don't want to hear it, and those who do want to hear more than I am comfortable sharing. But these people had welcomed me, and I thought I could help. "I think he is very scare." The word sounded wrong. "Very *scared*. Is right?"

"Yes, it's scared," Ralph assured me. "Why do you think he's so afraid?"

"He is like me when I was boy. I see it in his eyes."

"Maybe you should talk to his mother."

Though the suggestion did make sense, acting on it would be difficult. People don't always appreciate interference in their children's upbringing—particularly from near strangers. "I might. I will wait, though. You are correct. He is new, and the new fears people. If still he is like this in a few weeks, then I will speak."

Ralph's approval cut deep. I was a coward, and I knew it. *You know that's not it. Why let him continue like this? You would have liked someone to help you, wouldn't you?*

5

Michal—

Friday night is standing date night. We'd missed it last week, with Carol's arrival and all, so I tried to make it a little extra special—romantic. I even bought wine and put a glass in front of my spot. I wouldn't pour much in, of course, but it would show Lloyd that I did appreciate him.

The key turned in the lock just a moment after he rang the bell—as always. My mom had a *thing* about him owning that key, but it had come in handy too many times for me to feel guilty about giving the guy I'd be marrying someday access to my apartment. She saw it as access to my bed. I suppose, if you want to look at it in the worst possible light, that's true, but honestly, the only way he *didn't* have access—technically speaking—is if I didn't ever let him in the apartment.

Which is probably her preferred option as well.

Don't get me wrong. Mom loves Lloyd. She just doesn't love that he hasn't put a ring on my finger. He tried once, okay? Mom doesn't know that. But it was when Grandpa Colbert died, and it just wasn't the right time. We've been busy since—no time to plan and execute a wedding and honeymoon—and I think he has the idea I want time for an elaborate wedding. Regardless, we have our whole lives ahead of us. What's the rush?

Arms around my waist did hint that there might be other reasons to rush. "Mmm..." There's something magical about turning slowly in a man's arms—or at least in Lloyd's. Something in his hands around my waist makes me go all weak at the knees, and his aftershave doesn't hurt. "Hey... you put on your aftershave. Did you go home first?"

"I knew I'd be stubbly..." The faint whoosh of his breath on my cheek mingled with the softness of his chin sent my senses in a dizzy circle.

"Well, I like it."

My favorite kisses are the ones that take forever to happen. That anticipation that comes as Lloyd's lips get closer and closer while he murmurs random things—killer. "Did you know...?" The lips grew closer and my toes tingled. "...that a Seattle doctor says kissing actually offers similar benefits to meditation?"

Sometimes, you just can't wait another second, you know? And well, I happen to know that Lloyd loves it when I let my lips walk over his as I talk. "Then I say we do a little meditation." So for the better part of a minute or three Lloyd and I...*meditated.* So what? As long as Mom doesn't have to watch it, and as long as we keep it mostly G-rated, what's the big deal?

Lloyd broke away first. I tried not to cry. "Smells good."

"Thought I'd make up for last week. You know I love that oven cordon bleu."

"What's Carol up to tonight?"

It couldn't have been a better segue if I'd planned it. "Actually, I don't know. His phone went to voicemail when I called. But, I did have an idea..."

His hand slipped around my waist once more and he sent shivers down my spine as he murmured, "I get nervous when you say that."

"You're killing me here, Lloyd." His smile told me I'd said just the right thing. Perfect timing for my plan, too. "What if we did a double date tomorrow night? Are you busy?"

He pulled the chicken from the oven as we talked and loaded our plates for me. That's just the awesome kind of guy Lloyd is. I make him dinner, and he serves me. Bet he does the dishes too. #Luckiestgirlontheplanet. "I thought we'd just watch that movie you've been wanting to see, so we could do that afterward. What do you have in mind?"

Double that hashtag. "Just maybe dinner and a movie. I was thinking Therese."

"Not Crystal?" His eyebrows rose. "I was sure she'd be your top choice."

You know me well, my love. You know me well. As Lloyd pulled out my chair, I tried to explain. "She is. I think she'd be perfect for him, and maybe if he found someone, he'd want to stay, you know? It would be so great. But just because I like her for him doesn't mean he will. He needs options. Three or four women, to get a feel for who he likes."

Lloyd prayed and grabbed the parmesan before he responded. That told me he wasn't as excited about this idea as I was. "If you're sure…"

"I won't try to take him on all our dates, Lloyd! I promise. Just a few to introduce him to a couple of the girls, so he can really get to know them. Then it's up to him. Okay?"

The minute he nodded, mouth full of food and reaching for the wine, I grabbed my phone and zipped Therese a text. IF CAROL'S FREE, WANT TO DOUBLE UP WITH LLOYD AND ME TOMORROW NIGHT?

Her reply came before I could take a sip of my inch of wine. YEAH! TELL ME HE'S FREE. LIE IF NECESSARY.

Like an idiot, I started to send another text message, but something in Lloyd's expression stopped me. *You're just being rude. This is* his *time. At least wait until he has to go to the bathroom or something.* The fact that he smiled when I set down the phone hinted that I'd made the right decision. "So, how was the clinic today?"

"Four stitches, three food poisonings—don't eat at Tristan's for a couple of weeks—and a woman almost seven months pregnant who didn't know it."

"How does that even happen?"

He shrugged. "It does more often than you'd think. I mean, I didn't see it until I felt her stomach. The foot was right there. But until she was flat on her back, it just didn't show."

"And no periods?"

"She's forty-five. She said she thought she was entering menopause or something." He stared at his plate. "She'll be retired by the time her child graduates from college."

Okay, that just freaked me out a little. Probably because Lloyd sounded a bit panicked at the idea of being retired when kids graduated from college. I'd always thought it sounded reasonable. Older parents are often more patient. I read a study on it somewhere. Then again, Lloyd is pushing thirty-nine. He and his ex-*strife* thankfully split before they had kids. So if men have biological clocks, his must be nearing the alarm stage. And, as I said, that thought freaked *me* out a little.

Time for a subject change. "No assault wounds? No Ebola or hanta?"

"Those aren't even in the same league, but no. Just a bunch of helicopter moms who don't understand that their darlings can heal without super glue on a superficial cut, who want antibiotics for a head cold that is almost over, and who flip out at a one degree temperature. Don't people know that temperatures, generally speaking, are helping the body?"

"Pharmaceutical companies have ensured that people forget that."

Look, Lloyd's discussions of his days at work are usually comical. They feature nurses who flirt with him in the most ridiculous ways, nurses who make his life miserable because he doesn't return the flirting, and nurses who are old enough to try to set him up with their granddaughters, nieces, cousins removed a time or two—anyone. Last week it was a church pianist who had been inveigled into visiting the Urgent Care clinic on the pretext of returning a Bible left at church. The moment that nurse introduced the pianist, the poor woman realized what had happened and nearly puked on Lloyd's shoes.

So the night's slim pickings left me jittery. I didn't want him to ask about *my* work, but he would if I didn't come up with something else and fast.

Too late. Just as I opened my mouth to say something, Lloyd asked, "How'd work go for you today?"

"Fine…" That wouldn't work, and I knew it. No one reads me as well as Lloyd—except maybe Carol in a letter. I still didn't know if he could do that in person or not, but man, in a letter, he always knew when I was hiding something or troubled or whatever, and wrote back immediately to ask. "They're balking on the Romanian orphan project."

"That doesn't sound fine to me."

"I have one more shot, but I don't know if it'd help or hurt."

The slow nod told me he'd read my mind. "Carol. He can either help them see how bad it is—or at least was—or he can be proof that it's not a problem anymore because he's doing so well."

"But he's *not!* He has a pseudo family with this artist guild, and he has a church he attends, but he's so *alone* there. He says it's hard to make friends—that the old days still haunt him. People reject orphans there. If they know, he's still an outcast in so many ways. He says some orphanages are better, but it's not what it should be. I want to help with that."

"I know it's close to your heart, Michal, but there are so many needs. They can't do it all. Not agreeing to this one isn't saying that it doesn't matter. It's saying that—"

"I know, okay?" Jumping down Lloyd's throat about this wasn't fair, but I did. I let him have it. "Just because they can't see how horrible it was for Carol, just because *Carol* hid most of it from me, doesn't mean I didn't see it. You can piece together so much of what *did* happen by what he didn't say. He was lonely, scared, and hungry. They *abused* him, Lloyd. And a lot of the girls that were with him ended up as prostitutes. They just shove them out on the streets at eighteen with no clue how to provide for themselves. They don't know how to cook—"

"—or do laundry. I know." Something in his voice soothed me— cracked the shell I'd begun to hide under. "They don't know basic life skills or how to make a living." He stood, skirted the table, hunkered down on his heels, and gazed into my eyes. When I blinked back tears, he kissed my cheek. "I've heard it a dozen times—a year, at least. So maybe that's the problem." He stood at the corner of the table and gazed down at me. "Maybe *they've* heard it too much at the office, too. Maybe they *do* need to hear it from him."

Lloyd excused himself to the restroom—which totally explained why he'd gotten up and kissed me. That's just not a Lloyd thing, you know? And I did what any loving girlfriend would do. I used the spare minutes to call Carol. Thankfully, he answered this time. "Hey, it's me. Look, Lloyd and I are going out to eat and to see a movie tomorrow night. Therese is coming with us, too. Would you like to join us? We were thinking Rockland. Better movie choices there."

"Um..."

Panic set in as I heard the uncertainty in his voice. I just *had* to get him to agree. "It'd be great if you could come. Therese will feel awkward there with just the two of us. I promise to pick a great restaurant..."

"Um..."

My heart sank, and then an idea presented itself. "Look, if you're busy, I understand. But otherwise, we'd really like to take you." Even as I spoke, I bought four movie tickets online so I could use it as an excuse. "I've got these movie tickets that'll just go to waste..."

"Yes, that would be nice. Am I to meet you somewhere, or...?"

Lloyd seated himself across from me with one eyebrow definitely *trying* to rise. Poor guy never could manage it, no matter how hard he tried. "I'll text you details. Great! Can't wait to see you. I want to ask you about talking to my work about the orphanages in Romania, too."

"Is not a pleasant subject."

"That's why I want you. They'll hear it better coming from you."

The moment he agreed, I disconnected the call, grinning. "Done and done. And you only lost twelve seconds with me. Not too shabby."

"That was the slow tap of each of your fingers on the table. I couldn't figure out what I was supposed to get from that."

It was there, that edge to his voice when he was peeved about something. I considered my choice to call and decided it was worth it. You know, sometimes people need to get over themselves. Twelve seconds isn't much time to lose when you were the one who got up from the table in the first place. So, I smiled, took a bite of chicken, and then asked, "How about a nice walk after dinner? It was raining leaves in the park earlier today."

"Do I get to kiss you under a shower of them?"

That's my Lloyd. "You'd better."

Carol—

Therese has the vocabulary of an Oxford scholar and absolutely no intention of using it unless under duress. The upside of it was that I didn't have to try to decipher the meanings of most of the things she said. Only when she chose to try to impress me—those thirty-two second bursts of time before she decided that I had no clue what she meant—did I hear anything that didn't sound like utter nonsense.

The restaurant couldn't have been more elegant. I had a suspicion that it had been chosen to impress me—likely by Therese—but Lloyd and Michal talked about it as if they visited often.

Seated opposite my "date" had distinct advantages. The first was, of course, that I didn't have to converse with her for long periods. This is an advantage because to listen in one language, translate into your native language, then formulate a reply and translate once more before speaking is exhausting—exhilarating at times, but also exhausting. It happens quickly—so quickly, I think, that people forget it's happening, but it is. Translating Therese's conversation almost seemed like adding a third language to the mix.

"So are you enjoying your stay in Rockland so far? How's the store coming? Is it everything you hoped for?"

Michal's questions reminded me of our letters, and the awkwardness that I had felt just melted into a pool of ink I could work with. "I am like very much. There is much work to do, but is good work—wholesome. 'Artistry in the ordinary.' That is what HearthLand is."

"Will you stay past Christmas or...?"

"If still they want me, I will stay as long as visa says is okay."

Her smile—all the years I'd imagined Michal's smile, it had been just like that—but where I'd seen the joyous abandon, I'd never expected such beauty. Lloyd gave her a look that I recognized. I'd seen it in friends, people at church. Love.

"That's great news! Isn't it, Lloyd?! Carol could stay through the winter—see spring. I bet spring at HearthLand is amazing—all the little chicks and green things trying to grow. I can't wait!"

Speaking of changes in HearthLand reminded me of something Ralph had said. "They are having—are have…"

"Having is correct," Lloyd assured me.

"Yes. They are having great opening. All stores."

This excited Therese, and with that excitement came clarity. I understood her for almost the first time. "Really? I thought it was all just farming and, like, outhouses or something. They're actually going to have stores? What kind?"

Michal winked at me and answered before I could. "Pretty sure you'd find the finest seeds there—and probably the best manure in the country. The general store probably carries high fashion like overalls and rubber boots or something—you know, for mucking that manure…"

It may have been rude. I don't know. But the look of utter disgust and disappointment mingling on Therese's lovely face produced such a comical effect, I couldn't help but laugh. Michal and Lloyd joined me, which did make me feel a bit better about it. The little pout on Therese's lips was, however, surprisingly attractive. I took pity and explained all I remembered.

"There are those things." One word tripped me up before I continued. "But I think manure is free—gift of nature?" When they laughed, I continued. "They have store with variety—food, tools, soap and candles."

"A general store," Michal repeated. "See, I was right!"

"Is called 'Hearth & Pantry'. Ralph say it mean that it carries what we need for everything in house or for food."

Lloyd snickered that time. "Self-explanatory name, then."

With the dirty looks that the women gave him, I suspected his words were meant to mock me. I chose to ignore it. "Yes, it is. There is also what Zain call 'candy-store-slash-bakery.' Is like a store in Fairbury."

"There's going to be a Confectionary in HearthLand? Really?" Therese almost bounced as she spoke. "I'm *so* visiting you all the time."

"Don't leave me behind—two sweet things at once. Carol and candy!"

My suspicions were confirmed with that statement. If he could have, I think Lloyd would have insisted they leave. I became desperate to change the subject—for his sake. "Then there is plant shop." As hard as I tried, I couldn't remember the name of the business selling indoor greenhouse styled planters disguised as furniture. "Is furniture—to grow plants in. Tables, shelves, lamps—you harvest lettuce from lounge. Not necessary to go outside in rain to get salad."

"Wow!" Michal gave Lloyd a look I recognized from my days in the guild shop. It meant, "We need to buy one."

"Yes, and the gift shop. This is my job. I am almost done filling with things from Romania. Is beautiful building... how you say...?" I struggled to remember the word Ralph used. "Begins with R I think—for old wood and—"

"Rustic!" Therese gave me an enormous grin. "Right?"

"Is right! Yes. Rustic. Like old barn inside—big beams and shelves made of old wood. Josh Roth did design. His is next store—studio?" I shrugged. "Is a place to buy the furniture and materials for house— curtains and cloth for the tables."

"Oh, wow! I've seen that in a couple of magazines," Michal told Therese. "This guy is seriously good. He's going to be the new Pottery Barn—but better. It's so homey and fresh without being cutesy or cluttery. I've already added a new category to my budget to replace pieces I have that I hate with his stuff. They featured this hand-hewn table? WOW. We're talking seriously amazing."

Therese joined in Michal's excitement with an idea of her own. "Oh! I have that money my dad gave me to furnish my new house! I wonder if it's enough to do a room or two. If you like it, I *know* I will."

I felt like a salesman who had made his first big sale. Pride welled up inside. People would make this community successful—people like these new friends. A glance at Michal, the smile she gave only to me... My enthusiasm bubbled over. I think much of what I said was incomprehensible, but Michal managed to translate.

"Then there is restaurant—is not like this." I took in the elegance around me—the ivory tablecloths, the gold flatware, the candles and the glittering chandelier. "Is more..." I winked at Therese—something that in retrospect, may not have been wise. "Rustic. For families. Long tables where everyone sits together. There are few big round ones in corners for special things, but if still you just come for eating, you sit at table."

"Oh! Family style!" Therese leaned forward. "I love those. What kind of food is it? All American? Country?"

"All kinds—Mexican, Chinese..." I grinned and attempted a country accent. "Down home cooking."

I think the ladies swooned, and if the look on Lloyd's face meant what I thought it did, I was right. Michal found her voice first. "Oh, man. You're going to drive my friends crazy between your *real* accent and that one. I won't get to spend any time with you at all!"

Oh, if she could have seen Lloyd's face. It almost screamed, "That's fine with me." But it changed immediately, and shame filled it. I gave him a smile and a look to say, "Aren't they ridiculous?" I think he got it, because he laughed and nodded.

"I say I will try to make Romanian meal—just simple meal of *mămăligă* and pork sausage. Maybe *Salată de roșii* too.

"What's that?" Therese cocked her head like a curious puppy. "Sounds like something rose?"

"Is tomato salad. But *roșii* does mean red—like rose." I gave a weak smile and added, "I do not recommend you come to the meal. I am not cook good." After a moment of reflection, I changed that. "I am not *good* cook. But Ralph say, 'People will like because is authentic. You must do this.' So I will."

Questions flew like snowballs in winter—one after the other. I had no time to make my own because I had to dodge so many so quickly. After a moment, I threw up my hands and said, "I don't know. Ralph is in charge of restaurant. If you want food, you call him. She will get. She is strong..." The word seemed wrong.

"Finish the sentence," Michal suggested. "We'll help you find the right word."

"—strong to make restaurant success."

She squeezed my hand. I think Lloyd wanted to squeeze my neck. "Determined. *He's* determined to make the restaurant *a* success."

I couldn't help but laugh. People always corrected my he and she. The words made no sense to me. I tried—and sometimes I got it right. But if I had to use both in the same sentence... as Ralph kept saying, 'All bets are off.'"

Lloyd spoke up. "We need to be going if we're going to get to the cinema on time."

Therese almost beamed. "I'll ride with Carol so he doesn't get lost."

So you can flirt. I see it in your eyes. But it's somewhat enchanting how hard you try to hide it. I pulled out my wallet as I reached for the ticket.

"Oh, we've got it," Michal assured me.

"I cannot take lovely woman to dinner and ask friends to pay. Ralph gives me the salary. I can afford—"

Lloyd came to my rescue, and once again, I felt as if we understood each other. Having a friendship with this man wouldn't be easy until he realized that Michal didn't care about me—not like he cared about her. "Your portion is..." His eyes scanned the bill, "Seventy-five. That includes tip."

"Lloyd!"

"It's a guy thing, Mickey. Just accept it."

It was the first time I'd heard anyone call her that. I'd always read it as "Mike-ee" but he said it like the mouse from Disneyland. I pulled out the money and passed it to Lloyd. "Thank you. Is a good feeling to give the gift like this."

"Seriously, Michal," Therese murmured—any lower and I couldn't have heard it. "If you talk him into asking out anyone else, I'll never speak to you again. He's perfect."

Oh, how I wanted to laugh—to howl at the ridiculousness of her words. I saw what she did not. She was charmed by an unusual accent, a face that she found attractive, a polite gesture. But when she got to know me, she wouldn't like me. I knew this because I could only be polite about the inanity of her conversation for so long. Eventually my true feelings would show. And then she would be hurt. I prayed that it didn't have to happen.

Michal—

Conferences are the bane of a doctor's existence. I'd learned that in the three and a half years—almost four, actually—that I'd dated Lloyd. He's a smart guy—dedicated. He wants to learn everything he can, so ten percent of his post-taxes dollars goes to furthering his education. He can do a lot of that at conferences. So, almost every quarter, he packs his bags for some place—usually Las Vegas, Miami, San Diego. Chicago—every year. Like clockwork. I think Chicago is like the Mecca of medical conferences or something.

We have a routine—tradition, I like to call it. I drive him, we get one last bit of time together, and I pick him up. At drop-off, I always park and walk him in. We take our time, linger. It's the last we'll see each other for at least seventy-two hours, so we might as well enjoy it.

I know, crazy, right? We're talking three days like it's three months or years. It's not that we're that attached at the hip or anything. We're more... independent than that. But Frank Welk, one of our elders at The Assembly where we go to church, told us that if we were serious about our relationship, we'd make the extra time to invest in each other at times like that. So we do. It can't hurt, right? And honestly, there's something stirring in those dizzying feelings that come with a goodbye kiss. That alone is worth it.

Hand in hand, we strolled from the parking garage, across the breezeway, and into the airport. "One of these days," Lloyd began.

"We need to get me a room, and I need to go with you."

He squeezed my hand and chuckled as he pulled me around a pillar to get out of the way of a motorized luggage cart barreling toward us. His gray eyes—man I love the crazy things they do to me when he looks at me like that. "I say that often, don't I?"

"About every time."

The sight of one of the doctors in his practice just ten feet ahead froze the kiss I'd begun to work up to. "Looks like Malinda is already here."

He glanced that way and back at me. "Probably should go then. I think our seats are together."

When Malinda looked our way, I waved. She's a nice woman—overly intellectual, if you know what I mean, but nice. Her patients love her because she gives them confidence that she knows what she's doing. Lloyd's patients love him because he's kind and reassuring. Both get the job done, but in different ways. I've never told him this, but I'd prefer Malinda's style myself. Is that bad? Probably. But it is what it is.

A tap of her watch hinted that Malinda had grown impatient. I kissed Lloyd—just a quick, disappointing, "See you when you get home," kiss—and waved once more. "Be safe…"

"You going to do something with the girls tonight?"

"No… I promised Carol I'd help out over at HearthLand. We're taste-testing some Mexican food for dinner, and I think they said something about a bonfire."

Lloyd stiffened and I hugged him once more. "I won't let anyone get burned. I promise."

"That's not—"

Another glare from Malinda told me it was *really* time to go, so I just cut him off with another brief kiss and strolled back toward the front entrance. "Have a good time. Learn how to keep me alive!"

A text appeared minutes later. I LOVE YOU. SORRY MALINDA IS BEING SO DIFFICULT.

Texting and walking is nearly as dangerous as texting and driving. I almost plowed over two old ladies with bags large enough to do some serious damage. They scolded me until the double, automatic sliding doors sucked them into the airport. But the message finally made it into my phone and off of my screen. SHE'S NOT BEING DIFFICULT. SHE'S BEING RESPONSIBLE. BE NICE TO HER. THAT BREAK UP WITH JEFF REALLY TOOK IT OUT OF HER.

Okay, so I loved getting a text back saying how right I was. Let's face it. Humans like to be right—especially with people who rarely admit that they're wrong. We all have our failings. Lloyd's is that he is careful not to do anything until he can be 100% right It's just who he is. He accepts my faults—all two of them? Yeah. Let's go with that. And I accept his.

I also tried *not* to allow my elation to erupt when I climbed into my car and took off toward Dolman—and HearthLand. Setting up stores and eating amazing Mexican food sounded better than a flight and a stuffy conference any day. I mean, it may be stereotypical and all, but I really do picture those conferences full of people with ties on, stethoscopes around their necks, and speaking in medical puns. C'mon. You know they all debate whether Valium is effective at high altitudes or not. They have to.

I hadn't been super impressed with the idea of HearthLand when I first heard about it. But, after listening to Carol talk about all its advantages and disadvantages, it grew on me. No, I wasn't really into candlelight and oil lamps. Wind power is great. I'm all for it. But I don't mind being "on grid" either. I love farm fresh eggs, but if I have to buy them from the store, then so be it. Same is true of fruit and vegetables. No one *wants* to coat their salad with pesticides as an alternative to fattening dressing. But we wash and we go on with our lives.

No, what first appealed to me was the intentionality of it all. People *choosing* to do without one thing in order to gain another—that I get. It's like exercise. I choose to avoid empty-calorie foods and sedentary activities like playing games on my phone, in favor of nutrient rich foods and jogging or a good workout. In the health department, even a leisurely ride on a coaster bike is better than Candy Crush. Sure, there are no calories and it doesn't rot your teeth, but does it *help* your body? That's debatable. And I err on the "choose something else" side. Lloyd doesn't always agree, by the way. He considers mental health as equally important and thinks games like that, in moderation, as with all candy, to be very good for brain function. Who's right? I don't know. But I'll still take a stroll down the street first.

So no, I wasn't eager to embrace a *life* at HearthLand when I arrived, but when you see it, when you walk the streets and *feel* the community—nothing can compare. I had a false picture of these people. I saw everyone as using composting toilets and raising their own rabbits for meat while wearing shapeless clothing in drab colors. It took me ten minutes to figure out that some were there for the philosophy of the place rather than a prescribed lifestyle.

Carol introduced me to everyone—Ralph, Zain, Savannah, Delores, and the sweetest old lady I've ever met—Janie. I could have moved there tomorrow just to be Janie's neighbor. As we walked away, I pulled him close and murmured, "How can you stand it?"

"What?" I swear he looked at his feet. "Something is wrong..."

"I mean—" Okay, there I cracked up. I know it's rude, I know you're not supposed to, but I did. I just let loose and howled a bit. I think Carol was less than amused. "Sorry. I mean, how do you not go crazy with how wonderful these people are? That Janie—"

"Janie is wonderful woman. She make me feel like I live here always."

"I see why." As I inhaled the fresh, clean air and gazed around me once more, I almost hated to ask, but we had gathered to work, after all. "So what do we do first?"

Carol had warned me there'd be a lot of work to do—that he couldn't spend too much time just exploring with me, but Ralph, the man in charge, insisted that he walk me out to the brook—about a mile or so away. "The work will wait," Ralph insisted. "Take her out there."

So he led me out there with all the eagerness of a little boy sharing his secret hideout. I learned something about him that I'd never discovered in his letters—sunflower seeds. The moment we started walking, he pulled a handful from his pocket and offered them to me. I hoped I wouldn't offend him, but I declined. Apparently it didn't, because he just popped a bunch in his mouth and munched as we walked. He pointed out where there would be a Christmas tree lot, where some guy named Justin raised wheat, and where there would be a new community.

Look, my work with humanitarian organizations means that I see a lot of people living in rural areas—rarely is it pretty. HearthLand seemed to take the idealized version of those lives and make it a reality.

But it was more than that. The Lord is a genius with nature's paintbrush, and He'd used it liberally over every inch of the countryside. Awed—I walked across that meadow to the brook just enthralled by the feeling that I'd stepped into God's studio and watched Him at work.

Okay, now I just sound like Carol. He's more poetic than I've ever been. It's hard to see in the letters sometimes—the language barrier, I think. But the way he phrases things shows it. And as we walked, I saw it again. He pointed out things that reminded him of home, and in them I heard longing that unsettled me. I didn't want to think of him missing Romania. I wanted him to stay here.

"Is like the Apusei Mountains in Transylvania—but not as rich. The colors there they are so..." His head shook. "What is the thing that says much color?"

"Vivid?"

"*Da!* Is so vivid—like is not even real. It aches the soul and squeezes the heart." His hand swept the view before us. "This is beautiful. But is not taking breath away like some places at home."

"Breathtaking," I whispered. Our eyes met and a smile grew between us—one that tethered us together in that moment. Wow. Further proof that Carol rubs off on me or something. "Tethered us together." Oh, well. It's nice to know I can grow.

Carol sighed—a deep exhale of emotion. "This is right word. Breathtaking."

The expression of love and longing on his face, in his eyes, on his lips—if he ever looked at a woman that way, the look alone would steal her heart.

It took more effort than I would have expected to drag Carol from the little grove of trees near the brook. Only the reminder that we had a long night of work ahead of us diverted his attention—his *heart*—from the area that sparked such thoughts of home. It wasn't even *like* the area he lived in. His is on the Black Sea. It's more Mediterranean. According to Google, to find that rich, vivid feel that is more like Appalachia, you had to go to the Transylvanian mountains far away from Constanța.

Twice in our letters I'd asked a question, but never had the answers really satisfied me, so halfway back to the town, I asked again. "So Transylvania really exists?" Okay, I knew that geographically speaking, it did. But Americans hear it and immediately think of vampires, and it just makes everything seem so… fictional. I wanted to hear him talk about it in his charming Romanian accent. I wanted to hear him make it real for me.

"Yes, but the Count read the Twilight books and move to Washington."

Tell me why I just assumed he wouldn't know about the Twilight books! I mean, one minute he's just astounded over free refills like they're an intergalactic phenomenon, and the next he's talking American vampires like he's #TeamBella's founder.

"Very funny."

"Yes, is amusing. I am comedian as side job. You should hear my knock-knock joke."

I couldn't resist. His laughing eyes, the twitch of his upper lip. I just couldn't. "Okay, okay. Knock. Knock…"

Crickets. Seriously. He didn't say a word. Even after a few repeats, he still said nothing. When I threw up my hands in exasperation he leaned close and murmured, "I'm not supposed to talk to strangers."

I think something got lost in the translation. Or maybe Romanians have quirky senses of humor—kind of like my dad's favorite British cartoon. The one that depicts a couple looking at used cars and the salesman says, "So, want to take it for a push around the block?" Yeah. Like I said, people have quirky senses of humor sometimes. So why did I laugh? I mean, I cracked up like it was the funniest thing ever.

He looked like a naughty kid who'd just pulled one over on the adults. He could be a comedian just with his expressions. No one would care that his jokes didn't make sense or weren't funny. The expressions would do it.

"Okay…" I gasped. "Let's get star—" My phone rang. I held it up to show Carol and almost missed the flicker of disappointment in his eyes. He must have assumed Lloyd would need me to leave or something. "Hey, Lloyd. Make it okay?"

"Yeah, but there's a problem here. I thought I should get your input on it before I made a decision."

"Let me have it." Carol's eyes widened, but I rubbed his arm as an "everything's okay" gesture. It seemed to work.

"—lost her reservation. They don't have any rooms. The nearest one is a really iffy place, and the more decent ones are an expensive cab ride away."

"That's terrible! What are they going to do to make up for it? Want me to talk to them?" As soon as I asked, I figured that had to be it. Lloyd's a pushover. He's a sweetheart who doesn't want to make waves. I don't like it either, but I can do it if someone's being taken advantage of. Malinda clearly was.

"They've already booked her a free weekend whenever she likes. But they were able to move me around a bit and put me in a suite with a bedroom. How would you feel about her sleeping in the bedroom there and me taking the other bed? I mean, she'd have a lock on her door…"

"Genius! That's great. At least they're trying. She shouldn't be out anything for this."

Lloyd sounded relieved—relieved and a bit put out, which I totally didn't get. "Well, if you're sure…"

"You've got privacy there. Or she does. Anyway, it's not that much different than side by side rooms or anything, right? Just get a good night's sleep and learn great stuff at that conference. I'll pick you up on Sunday afternoon."

As I pocketed the phone, Carol stared at me—genuine shock in his face. "She is okay?"

"Yeah—mix up at the hotel. He's fine." Relief filled Carol's face until I added, "A friend lost her reservation. He's got to share a room with Malinda."

His face scrunched up as he tried to follow. "Malinda is man who works with him?"

"No…" His confusion had an adorable quality I wasn't quite prepared for. Who knew lifelong pen pals could be so enchanting? "She's a woman—a colleague. They've got separate bedrooms." And that's when I got a little defensive. "There's nothing wrong with it."

Carol shrugged and turned away. We'd made it to the gift shop before he said, "I am not used to see all, what you say—not jealous. Women I know would scream and say, 'Not with my man. No!' You are not angry."

"I trust him."

Something about him said he didn't believe me—didn't believe me or thought I was in denial, maybe. I thought about trying to explain and decided against it. If Lloyd wanted to cheat on me, he wouldn't call and tell me he was setting it up. I may be naïve in some people's eyes, but Lloyd's not *stupid.*

7

Carol—

Therese and Michal came through the door of the gift shop just minutes after we opened. Unfortunately—and fortunately, I suppose—I already had a couple asking questions about carved puzzle boxes. It's not easy to give your full attention to someone when others compete for it, and the snippets of their conversation distracted me from my demonstration of how the box worked.

I should have known it would make the man determined to show off his superior deductive reasoning skills. After about five minutes, and several more customers crowding into the shop and around the man, his wife—or girlfriend, I didn't know which—insisted they buy it before he wasted the entire day trying to solve it. A hundred fifty dollars later, I'd made the first sale. I'd also won one third of the guild's pool. I said a puzzle box would sell first.

A hand-blown vase captured Michal's attention. Her favorite color—blue. A-symmetrical. While Therese pointed to fluted bowls and hand-carved jewelry boxes, always with an eye to ensuring I heard her compliment everything she touched, Michal came back to the same piece repeatedly.

"I think Crystal should buy this. It's so *her.*"

"Her?" Therese left the display of jewelry and moved to study it.

"Really? Looks more like you to me. She likes order. That's not orderly."

I suspect that several shoppers approached me. I don't know for sure, because I found myself hanging on each word, aching to know if Michal loved it or only saw it as something Crystal would appreciate. Considering it wasn't even my artwork, it made little sense. Why would I care?

"I do love it. I mean, can't you see it on the buffet by my table? Of course, it'd look better if everything wasn't crammed in there! Still, it's amazing. But Crystal likes things that have a true artistic look to them. This doesn't look like a pretty glass vase. It's art."

Who could argue? Certainly not me. Therese nodded with that slow, hesitant movement that meant she wanted to agree but still didn't understand. Why do people do that? Why not just say, "Oh, I hadn't thought of that. I'm sure you're right"? Why pretend to understand what moves someone *else's* soul?

"I like this better." Therese picked up a giant fluted bowl. A *heavy*, giant fluted bowl. Although it would probably insult or offend her, I had to step forward and take it from her. "Heavy—more than it looks."

"Wow, yeah! I thought it would be light. It looks so delicate."

"Looks are the deceiving—like beautiful woman who seems fragile but stands strong against life."

Those would be the wrong words to say, but I realized that too late. I think Therese swooned. Her hand grabbed Michal's arm and she leaned close. It sounded like she whispered, "Could he be more perfect?" Surely not. But something in Michal's eyes hinted that maybe she had—hinted that Michal might even agree. I'll never admit it to anyone, but I think *I* swooned at the look in Michal's eyes. If it hadn't been for a customer asking to purchase the bowl I still held in my arms, who knows how long we would have stood there staring at each other, unspeaking.

"Yes, of course." How did I ever concentrate enough to wrap that box? With one ear on everything Michal said, I fumbled through the strange variety packing materials to find a box that would fit. HearthLand reused packing boxes and materials collected from all over the area in keeping with their philosophy of life, but it did make wrapping less simple than a stack of uniform boxes and a roll of bubble wrap. As I passed the sealed box—tied with jute string, of course—I asked them to come again. "Bring your box. We will fill with something beautiful again."

The sigh behind me hinted I'd said something right. A muffled, "Ouch," on the other hand, hinted that Michal had tried to shush her friend. If it wasn't rude to cheer...

Therese's hand wrapped around my arm—or tried. I then was treated to raptures about the size of my biceps. I wished, for the first time ever, that I had muscles the size and strength of a spaghetti noodle. She, on the other hand, asked what piece of "art" would best suit her.

I've always believed you could learn much about people by observing their friends. I didn't quite know what to think of Michal in that light. Therese is a lovely girl—truly. She's kind—compassionate even. But the word that comes to mind when you spend much time with her is shallow. My eyes traveled to a bowl of about twelve inches wide and an inch deep.

I guess my face showed my thoughts. Or perhaps it was the way I couldn't help but look at Therese again—at the bowl again—but Michal covered a snicker with a cough. I had to say something, so I just murmured something like, "I think is difficult to... how you say?"

"Determine?"

"*Da!* Is difficult to determine if you not know someone."

A few more customers came in the shop, and Michal suggested that she and Therese leave before it got too crowded in the store. "Besides, we're not going to buy anything, so let's get out and let him work. We'll go carve a pumpkin."

Why do the most innocent of statements often sound ridiculously funny? Had I not been trying *not* to laugh, I am certain I would have felt properly ashamed of myself.

"Get out of here."

The pottery pitcher I'd hefted to shift for a more pleasing display nearly crashed into a blown-glass chess set as I whirled in place. "Ralph!"

"Sorry." He stepped forward, anxious for the fate of the chess set as well. "I thought you saw me heading in." Ralph stepped forward and took the pitcher from my arms. "I came to relieve you. Go find your friends and go dancing."

I'd heard the music—strange stuff I could only imagine was some kind of folk music that Americans must know how to dance to. I certainly didn't. "Um—"

My uncertainty must have been visible because Ralph tried to reassure me. "Don't worry. None of us know how to square dance around here. But there's a caller, and he'll tell you what to do."

Just then, Michal opened the door and beckoned. "C'mon! Ralph says you can dance with us. I've always wanted to learn how to square dance."

At least I'd be making a fool of myself in the company of a couple of pretty women—one of them a friend. Who could object to that? *Me. I could.*

"Okay, but I don't know what is the square dancing."

"It's probably similar to some of the Romanian folk dances. A lot of those older dances are similar in one way or another," Therese assured me.

So we walked, three abreast, along a sidewalk meant for two and maybe a small child. Men passed—envious men. Time with Michal notwithstanding, I'd have given anything to trade with any one of them as long as it meant I could hide somewhere until the band had finished.

All cars had been removed from the square, and at one end, they'd erected a stage. How did I miss that? A band played at the back of the stage, dancers spun in slow circles at the front, weaving in and out, and a man in a cowboy hat stood at a microphone calling out orders. Each time he said to do something, the dancers seamlessly followed the command.

In the street, though—a different story all together. People ran into each other, laughing even as they apologized. A man turned the wrong way right in front of us. A woman did something—whatever it was, however, was *not* the "do-si-do" she was ordered to do by the man with the straw hat at the mic. Again, the people around her gave her encouraging waves and

66

thumbs-ups and kept dancing.

"See—it's easy. Just follow what the caller says. No one knows what they're doing. It's just fun!" Before Therese could drag me to the floor—kicking and screaming might have been preferable—a man appeared and asked her to dance. I grinned, took Michal's hand, and wove through the dancers to a semi-empty spot. Therese and her new partner followed.

I've never decided if the daggers were for him or for me.

We all discovered that I have a brilliant skill for square dancing—in reverse. Every move I made—every one. Backwards. He told us to swing our partners left. I went right. He said to promenade. I knocked over the lemonade. Mortification, thy name is Carol. I also now know why learning anything about Shakespeare would help me in life—rewriting his quotes to fit me. It's hard enough for native English speakers. For those of us who know just enough to butcher the language, it's torture. However, it makes me feel sufficiently educated in English to be able to quote Shakespeare to my purpose.

Michal had to wash off her legs. Me, I needed to stay a sticky mess. But Therese's dance partner seemed a little less than thrilled with his choice, and I decided to try to cut in. Apparently, that isn't "done" in square dancing, but he didn't seem to mind. Therese *definitely* didn't mind. So, I proceeded to mortify her. The good news: there was no more lemonade to drench her with. If there had been, well, I make no promises.

"Have to make lot of apologies, lot of them," I admitted. "I understand if now you do not wish—"

"Are you kidding?! I stepped on that guy's feet and slammed into him so much that he was glad to get rid of me. Between you going backwards and me flubbing it, I bet we're perfect for each other."

For some reason, those words embarrassed her. I just shrugged and tried following the other dancers again—and that's when I realized my mistake. I'd been following those on stage and it kept me from paying attention to those closest. To avoid people, I did the opposite of what I should but it just meant that we crashed rather than avoided the collision. "I think I know the right step now."

I confess, I will never be a champion or professional square dancer, but I did manage to finish the dance without knocking over anything or anyone else. I even managed to help Therese not to step on anyone or anything—or so she says. I think it may have been an excuse to hug me. That sounds arrogant. It is what it is, though.

Michal came back and murmured something to Therese. *She wishes to leave. Did I offend?* I had to apologize—to try. "Sorry, I am—about the lemonade. I destroy, very well, the fun for you. Please forgive me."

"Oh, it's not that, really!" Michal hugged me.

Why can one hug be so awkward and another so delightful?

"There are still *lots* of people, Michal!" Therese turned to me. "She always wants to go first—to avoid the traffic. The only time she endures traffic is for Lloyd and his trips. Then, even the rush hour madness won't keep her from wading through the muck of steel and exhaust."

Michal rolled her eyes. "It's going to be a nightmare getting out of here. I don't want to be trapped on that road forever." She took my arm and led me toward the parking area. "So, are you free Monday afternoon? I thought we could go looking for that suit you said you wanted to buy. You have meetings scheduled in the next few weeks, right?"

I don't remember what I said—how we even got to her car. I don't remember saying goodnight—only waving as the car crept through the field and onto Hearthfield Way. A perky "beep-beep" signaled their departure, but still I stood staring. Ralph appeared minutes later—at least, I think it was minutes later.

"That Michal is something..."

"And I am much too happy to spend time with a woman who is in relationship with other man."

Ralph folded his arms over his chest and stared at me. The more he stared, the more uncomfortable I became, but at last he said, "You've been friends for years. There's nothing wrong with wanting to spend more time with her."

"This is true only if my heart does not sing when she say we spend Monday afternoon together."

8

Michal—

When I arrived at the Brookside Mall, Carol was just sitting on a bench—utterly relaxed. He watched the shoppers—few that there were—with a curious but lazy eye. But when he saw me, he lit up like the proverbial yuletide tree. For a fleeting moment, I wondered if Lloyd ever did that. The question—ridiculous. Of course, he did. I'd seen it.

Look, Carol is a lot more...*expressive* than either Lloyd or me. His emotions play out across his face like a movie screen. Once in a while, it's in a foreign language, and there are no subtitles, but you still know that he's feeling *something.*

"Hey! You're early!"

"I finish with errands for Ralph and still there is time before you come. So I watch."

A people watcher. I knew that. He'd told me in his letters so many times. How had I forgotten? Nothing about him was different from what he'd shared in them, but everything *seemed* new. Okay, so I wanted to know too, all right? I had to ask. "Hey, Carol?"

"Yes?" His eyes hinted at concern, but all I had to do was smile and loop my arm through his and the little line between his eyebrows—how had I not noticed how bushy they were?—disappeared.

"Am I different from my letters?"

He didn't even have to think about it. Immediately, he nodded. "Yes. Very."

Look, I wasn't surprised. Would you be? Letters are for pouring out your heart and soul. People just don't do that while walking through a mall or sitting at a restaurant with a couple of friends. And that thought explained it all. We'd always just communicated alone—just him. Just me. And since he'd arrived, we'd spent almost no time together—just the two of us.

I eyed him as we walked—hesitating. Did I really want to know? Yeah. Who wouldn't? "So what's different? I won't be offended," I explained before he could resist.

"I write to boy who is great athlete—always with the girls. I write to boy who has lots of girlfriends. I write to man who runs the marathon, eats the good food, and is dedicated to helping orphans—like me." His smile— man, he'd make a woman fall for him just with that one asset—disarmed me. "You are *not* that man."

"I could say the same about you! Do you know how mortified I am that I sent you all those stickers? Pink hearts? Unicorns? Flowers? BFF?"

That one stopped the laughter that had half the people around us curious and watching. "What is the BFF? I look online once when I remember. It only say that BF is boyfriend. Then Internet connection die. Weeks later, still I forget to look."

As I dragged him toward Brooks Brothers, I explained the American propensity to exaggerate everything for emphasis. "It stands for 'Best Friends Forever'. Girls say it all the time—and sometimes change that 'forever' friend more often than they change their bed sheets."

"So I am not best friend forever." He pulled out his wallet, and beneath an ID card, he removed a well-worn sticker—a heart, pink. BFF in giant bubble letters—you could still make out the outline. "I should give back?"

"I can't believe you kept that! You lost all the letters when your stuff was stolen! How—"

"I always keep in wallet." He handed it to me. "See? Is fade, but…"

That just made no sense, okay? I mean, what guy keeps a heart with BFF from some other guy in his wallet? None I know of. "But why?"

His hand, I think it shook as he pulled a worn picture from the wallet. I recognized it immediately. "You *kept* that in your wallet, too? Not with the letters? But why?"

He pointed to the store. "Is that—?"

So, I had to grin at that one—tease him. "Oh, no you don't. I want the answer." I've never seen anything more adorable than Carol, beet red and stammering. Just watching him made me up my resolve to find a good woman for him. All he needed was a little encouragement and someone a little less... *desperate* than Therese. I love Therese to pieces. She's really a sweet girl. But she gets her self-worth from a man, and when she doesn't have a boyfriend, it's a bit pathetic. Hate to say it about my own friend, but the truth is the truth. At that moment, I realized that I have a couple of friends like that. I needed to remember to take time to send notes of encouragement—to compliment them on their strengths. Yeah. That went in my phone reminders so fast Carol was probably crazy confused.

"I was read your letter when sticker fell out. Boys were come in the room, so I hide sticker in pocket." He shot me this sweet apologetic look before he said, "I hide in book later. Then someone find—lots of places. But when I get wallet, I put in picture to keep safe. Sticker, too. It refuse to disappear—hide to keep me from embarrass. In my wallet, no one sees. Still it is there after many years, but is hard to read now." His thumb rubbed a small smudge of dirt from the faded and worn picture. It was kind of proof that as much as he treasured the sticker, the photo meant more to him. "This is almost wash many times."

I wanted it—the sticker, I mean. It was so tempting just to keep the dumb thing. After all, he'd offered it back to me, but I couldn't do that to him. I just couldn't. As much as he'd been embarrassed by it, he also proved it meant something to him. "Well, I should be mad that you were embarrassed by my incredibly thoughtful and expensive gift, but since you kept it all this time—even when people might mock you..."

He didn't even hesitate. The crackled sticker with its faded and worn face slid back beneath his ID just as he stood before a gray suit I knew would look fabulous on him. "This, I like."

I nodded. "You should totally try that on. The color would be great. Oh, and look at this gray over here—a lot of brown in this one. It's fabulous." After that, well... let's just say I doubt he'll ever ask my help for shopping again. Each suit looked better than the last, until I finally just shrugged and assured him that no matter what he chose, he'd knock the women dead.

"I think," he said to the man assisting us, "I should stick to jeans and shirt. They will kick me out of country if I kill women with suit."

His features—so serious. Carol looked genuinely panicked at the thought. I tried to explain—to give him other idioms to consider. He just shook his head and refused to purchase a suit until both the sales associate and I were a bit frantic in our attempts to reassure him. Then, in an instant, he grinned and winked.

"I get you."

What else could I do? I whacked him with my purse and corrected his English. "Got—you *got* us. Jerk."

"I—"

"Teasing!"

After a few chuckles and a snicker or two, he pointed to the blue suit that was a perfect middle ground between sapphire and navy. "I like this one. Mirela say to get two pants and three shirts."

"Excellent choice." It was, really... but what else could the associate have said?

As we left the store, Carol said, "Can we find restaurant somewhere? I am hungry and need opinions from you."

"Yes! You know how women love to give opinions. There's a Red Lobst—no... you're probably used to amazing seafood. How about we go with Red Robin? Doesn't get much more American than that."

Carol—

Music pulsed around us—loud, I thought, for midday at a restaurant. Michal suggested burgers, so I chose one with mushrooms and Swiss cheese. As soon as the server had disappeared with our orders, I pulled a piece of paper from my pocket and laid it out for her. "These are where I must go—to San Francisco, Cleveland, Dallas, and Chicago—maybe Seattle."

She took the tentative dates and entered them in some app on her mobile. A minute later, she nodded slowly. "Okay, so it looks like if you go to Chicago between October fifteenth and seventeenth, that's the best airfare—only ninety-three dollars round trip. I don't think you'll get better than that. But if you go earlier or later, it almost doubles—stupid airlines."

This we had learned in planning my trip to America. If I flew on one day, it could be twenty-four hundred dollars. But if I flew the day before or after, that price would be eleven hundred. Considering the baggage I also had to pay for, we chose to fly on the best day. She shoved her mobile at me, and I tried to scroll to see the options.

"Oh, here. Sorry." After that, she began speaking so quickly, planning so many different itineraries, that soon everything swirled in a haze that left me feeling like I'd stepped into a room of marijuana smoke.

At last, she pushed the mobile across the table again. "See... it's this one here. It leaves at a good time—actually. I could take you that day. It'll be cheaper if you keep your rental here for just those days."

"Yes, I lease rental for month by month." Relief washed over me as I realized my tongue worked again. A beautiful woman—one who knows you better than you know yourself in some ways—she is a dangerous creature to a man's heart.

"Want me to book this? I mean, these seats go fast."

I choked again, but this time she heard me. Her eyes grew concerned, but somehow I spat out, *"Da."*

"Okay! We have one of these down. So the next one is Cleveland—wait. No..." She scribbled a few things out on the paper and frowned.

"Ugh. You're going to be gone for a full two weeks. That stinks." When I didn't respond right away, she moved to my side of the table and showed me.

"Is my job," I reminded her. "Is why I come to see America—to see you. To do—"

"I know, I know. But I don't have to like it!" She nudged me—one of those ones you see in films where a teenage boy wants to act casual to hide his true feelings. A glance at her as her fingers tapped and slid along the screen told me it's not what *she* meant. *Unfortunately.* The thought produced instant guilt. *I must find a priest. It's been too long already, and now I hope that a woman—practically engaged to her boyfriend—will notice me instead. It is stealing.* I amended that thought. *Or rather, I am tempted to steal. I* want *to steal.*

"Carol!"

Michal's voice ripped me from my thoughts. "Sorry, I lose the thought train."

"Train of thought," she said as she smiled. "Look what I found. If you switch these two dates, you shave off three hundred dollars and two days from your trip."

Without hesitation, I pulled out my mobile and dialed the number for the store in San Francisco. Our food arrived while I spoke to the manager, but it was worth the risk of a cold burger. "He says yes. Can you reserve tickets?"

"I'll book it now." She took my mobile, and while hers loaded information, she entered the same information into mine. Back and forth, her fingers flew even as her own food grew cold. "Eat a fry. They're great. Can you pass the catsup?"

"Um..."

Without taking her eyes from the mobile, she reached across me for an upside down bottle—the ketchup. I could have sworn she said catsup. Apparently, it's a pronunciation thing. I gave her an apologetic smile and pointed to the mobile. "I have reservation?"

"Yep!" Michal slid mine the entire three inches that separated us and concentrated on her burger.

With the lingering scent of her perfume, the nearness of her, and the delightful realization that she'd sounded almost put out that I'd be gone for two weeks, I never tasted the food. She asked how I liked it. The words, "Is very good," slipped out before I could stop them. *Another one for the priest.* Before I could dismiss the idea again, I grabbed the mobile and searched for a church.

"What are you looking for now?"

Again, the words slipped out faster than I could stop them. "A confessional."

Carol—

Whoever invented the GPS—the kind available to the average man or woman—deserves the Nobel Peace Prize for reducing road rage. I am convinced that without it, I might have managed to plow my rental vehicle into the nearest street lamp without the slightest hesitation. There were tiny streets everywhere—each dead ended if you turned wrong. Dahlia Place—not Dahlia Court or Dahlia Street—all of which existed off the main parkway—Meadowview Parkway. Just for the curious, I will relieve your curiosity. There is no meadow to view.

But then, as you finally turn onto Dahlia Place, six thousand condominiums or town homes—I've yet to discover the difference between them—mock you from a parking-less area designed to ensure maximum tickets from the local constabulary. I know this because I received one within minutes of exiting my vehicle and trying to find the right number.

The mobile in my pocket buzzed with a text from Jenn. FINDING IT OK? IT'S TRICKY IF UR NOT USED 2 IT.

Truer words, or however that saying goes. I didn't want to admit I couldn't find it. She might come out, and a man should go to the door. I believe this. It shows respect. It might not have been a "real" date, but I believed that I should treat Michal's friends well. It's only right. She asked me to take Jenn out. At first, I thought it was so I could make friends. That was before I realized she only set me up with women. Then again, I guess it makes sense that a woman would have more female friends than male.

After scanning the area again, I sent back the vaguest response I could think of. I'M HERE. COMING TO THE DOOR NOW.

A passing man pointed to the right building for me. "Upstairs—to the left of the garages. That one right there—can you see it?"

"Thank you. Is one with circle in window?"

He glanced over his shoulder mumbling, "Circle—oh! The dream catcher. Yeah. That's Jenn's place." He let me get a couple of steps away before he said, "Jenn's a nice girl—a really *nice* girl. She's not going to—" The look I shot him shut the man's vile accusations down before he could finish. "Whatever. Just warning you. Some guy is gonna get himself arrested for assault just trying to get some..." After a moment's hesitation he added, "*Attention.*"

"She will not worry for me. I do not care for her *attention.*"

Only after I made it halfway up the stairs did I realize his confused expression and subsequent nod, and his, "Ooooh... gotcha," meant that he thought I was gay. I didn't care. If it kept him from thinking vile things about a girl who sounded chaste and lovely, it was worth the misunderstanding.

I must say, however, when she opened the door and her cleavage said hello before she had a chance to speak, I considered revising my suppositions. "Jenn?" Mortification flooded my face, turning it what I could only imagine to be a gruesome shade of borscht. "I'm sorry. The faces are hard to remember—so many people that night."

"No problem! I get it. I can't imagine how confusing it must have been—especially after finding out Michal is a girl! Was that, like, freaky?"

"I was the confusion." I stepped aside to let her out. "We should go? The reservation is soon."

By the time we were seated at the restaurant, perusing menus and discussing the various options, I had once again revised my opinion of Jenn. While I did have to be very careful where I looked, she was just as sweet and lovely as the man had unintentionally implied. I sensed a bit of desperation—a deep desire to be understood by someone. Of course, that someone probably needed to be a man, too.

"So how long are you staying? Michal keeps giving vague answers. Do you have to go back to Romania right away, or are you here on a visa or..."

"I have the temporary business visa—six months. Then I must go home."

"Oh."

I'm not sure why those words didn't stop me. The disappointment in her eyes, tone, and even the way she moved her fingers ripped ideas I'd been forming in my heart and molded them into words. "I like it here—at HearthLand. Ralph has create such fine community. If still I think is wonderful—if still I feel at home there—when is time to go, then I ask for extension. Then I file for resident visa."

"So you might stay?!" At that moment, I saw how truly beautiful Jenn is. It's not what my English tutor called a "Classic beauty." Hers is more like an actress who, because of the many camera angles used to showcase it, turns an unusual face into an exotic one.

"I hope very much to do that. I must learn more. Can I work for guild in Romania and live here? I don't know, but I will learn all what I need to make wise decision."

The server came and took our order. I wasn't ready, so I asked for the server's suggestion and ordered that. Such things can be either a way to taste incredible food or a way to ensure you starve all night. Once we were alone again, Jenn asked a question no one had yet asked me.

"What is the one thing you like *and* dislike most about America/Rockland/HearthLand—any of them?"

Answering the question wouldn't be easy. I could barely articulate my thoughts and questions in Romanian, much less English. After several fumbles about churches and just as many failed attempts, I groaned. "*Vai de capul meu.*"

"What's that mean?"

Unfortunately, I winked at her before I realized she might mistake it for flirting. "Oh, my head."

"Is it that big of a difference? Your church from Ralph's?"

The question helped immensely. Suddenly, the words flowed as if I'd never struggled at all. "Is not real church—but is. That is how Zain describe it. He say, 'We *are* the church. We gather here in His name to worship and learn. Is not what you find in building in town, but works for us.'"

"Oh, like a Bible study or something—or Life Groups."

The words felt like they should make sense, but they didn't. A half-shrug/half-nod worked, though. "In Constanţa, I go to Orthodox—Romanian Orthodox, but is Eastern."

"What's the difference between Eastern Orthodox and Catholic? I've never understood that."

I didn't know how to answer. I didn't know much about Roman Catholics. One difference jumped out, though. "Oh—the priest she can be marry before she is become priest. I think the Catholic must all be celibate always?"

"Well, Catholics can become a priest if his wife dies or something—I think. I saw that in a movie once." Jenn sighed. "So you're a lot like Catholics."

The sigh gave her away. She didn't like the idea of a Catholic—and presumably an Orthodox—boyfriend. I tried not to show my elation. "I think, yes."

Michal—

The phone rang at 9:53. It seemed promising. After all, it wasn't early. They must have had a good time for him to drop her off that late, right?

"Hey, Jenn. How'd it go?"

"Well *I* had a great time. I think he even flirted with me a bit."

My heart swam to the bottom of my stomach and locked itself there. "Buuuuttt…"

"But he's like a Catholic. Do you *know* what they believe?"

Okay, so I *do* know a lot of what Catholics believe and I don't. And I agree with some and don't with others. I mean, if I agreed with everything, I'd be a Catholic, right? And if Baptists believed everything Pentecostals believe, they would be Pentecostals. It's the nature of the game. You can't agree with everyone. And, if I'm honest with myself, before I met Carol in person, I might have sounded exactly like Jenn. I'm not saying I'm proud of that, but there you have it.

Despite the theological differences between us, I knew that Carol placed his faith in Jesus—that Jesus' shed blood and resurrection alone saves. We'd talked about it over the years. So whatever else he believes that I *don't* wasn't my particular focus. And hearing that snotty, "Do you *know*" as if they were devil worshipers or something, just got to me.

"Do *you*?"

Jenn stumbled—stammered. "Uh—" After a few inane comments about confession and penance, she threw in. "They *worship* Mary—and like, don't even let their priests get *married!* I mean, Paul talks about how bad that is—the people who 'forbid to marry.'" Before I could interject— could say the words that might destroy a friendship—Jenn added, "Well, actually, his church allows guys already married to become priests. So that's a little better. Still, they *forbid* it after they're priests. What about 'it's better to marry than burn'?"

"I think you might want to study up on what he actually believes. And, maybe check out what kind of church *options* are there?"

"Are you saying you—?"

Okay, so I lost it. Look, I didn't even know why I was defending a faith I didn't completely agree with, but I was. I felt like Carol's character and heart was being attacked, and I whipped out both verbal pistols and emptied their chambers into the conversation. "I'm saying that there's a lot of judgment in your voice about something you admit you haven't even looked into yet. We both know what happened when *I* did that a year ago. I got blasted—pretty sure by you—for shredding the church's singles program for being too shallow."

"That's hardly parallel—"

"I agree. That was much less serious than essentially questioning a man's salvation based solely upon incomplete information about what—almost, anyway—the only church he has available to him teaches." I heard the sniffle. I heard the defensiveness well up in her staccato stammers, and I did the most mature thing I could think of. "Yeah. Gotta go. Sorry to set you up with such a loser. Bye."

I disconnected. In less than two minutes, I'd have a slew of texts—ten at the least—telling me what a horrible friend I was. Then five minutes later, I'd have a dozen more—from all of our friends as they asked me why I'd gone off on her. Oh, yeah. I seriously hate drama. Despise it. To top it off, I just threw a drama stink bomb into a room filled with my friends. And at that moment, I didn't even care.

Carol picked up just as I expected it to go to voicemail. "Hey! How'd it go?"

"Um... Go? Oh, I pull over on side of road before answering. This is why it takes much time to answer."

"No, no... but I'm glad you're smart about that. No, I meant your date..." Waiting for his reply—harder than you can imagine.

"The dinner was good. We talk about much things. He doesn't like my church. I don't think he wishes to do again."

Look, anytime you try to set people up, it's not even a 50/50 proposition as to whether or not it'll work. You get maybe thirty-five to forty percent odds—at best. I just needed to assure him that I wouldn't ask him to try again. Yeah. That's it. "Well, if she made that obvious then I won't ask you to spend much time alone with her. I'm sorry. I didn't know she'd be offensive."

"I have not the offense," Carol began. His words, as they often did, jumbled, sputtered, jerked forward, and died. "Is only that I have no wish to make uncomfortable your friend—and you."

The topic gave me an excuse to ask a question that had formed while talking to Jenn. I knew the basics of Carol's faith. We'd written of it several times. And yeah, it might have been an awkward time to bring it up, but sometimes you just have to jump in when you have the guts to do it. So I did. "Can I ask a personal question?"

"Yes…" Before I could ask, he sighed. "You miss the star falling. So beautiful."

"Oh! You saw a shooting star? Make a wish!"

Carol fumbled. "Wish?"

"Yes! Think of something you want to happen—to come true—and wish for it. But don't tell me!"

"I know what is make wish—blow out candles on cake. But why—"

"The magic is disappearing. Make the stupid wish!" Okay, so in the tender moments between friends category, that response didn't even hit the scoreboard. But I heard Carol say "*Va doresc numai bucurie si fericire.*"

"What was that?"

"Is my wish. I cannot tell you or it will not come true. You want it to come true. Trust me."

Who could argue with that? Okay, and so maybe I prayed and asked the Lord to grant Carol's wish—to give him the desire of his heart. I suspected that it might have to do with staying in America, and well, I wanted that too.

"Michal?"

"Yeah?"

"Some evening, do you think we could walk through HearthLand meadow and watch the moon on the water of the brook?"

You should save that one for one of your dates. Still, if I go, I get to see it, and *I have an excuse to suggest it. Win-win!* "You name the day and I'll be there."

Only the faint click-click of Carol's turn signal broke the companionable silence that filled the miles between us until Carol said, "Can you feel it?"

"What?"

"The amazement. I am in America. All the times I wish I could go to your house, knock on your door, ask for advice—now I can do! You tell me about StoryLand. I can go. You tell me about big maze in gardens. I can go. You tell me about big lake with little village that is like old Vienna. I can see this. Is childhood dream—come true." I started to reply when I heard him whisper, "I already got long-time wish. To ask more is greedy."

I'd never planned to admit it to him—even when I thought he was a she—but I heard myself blurting out my own childhood confession. "I used to talk to you, you know. I'd be upset because Mom said no to my sleepover plans or made me babysit my little brother—by the way, Micaiah is dying to meet you. When he was little, he used to try to make me mad by saying you weren't real."

"I should be glad to meet him. But you did not finish story. You say you talk to me. How?"

"I just did. I'd be in my room all ticked off about something, and I'd just, like, pour out my heart to you—tell you everything. You were my best friend—always said what I wanted you to say." Then, I mortified myself and giggled. "You always took my side."

"I think you play me very well. This I would do." He cleared his throat. "I should get home. Police just pass me and slow down to look in window."

"Okay... well, sorry you didn't have more fun. I just appreciate you trying. That was nice of you."

"Is a pleasure. Goodnight, Michal."

After a few seconds of staring at a disconnected phone, I jumped up and retrieved my running shoes and jacket. That's the great thing about coming home from work and pulling on yoga pants and a t-shirt. You don't have to change if you get the sudden urge for a run after talking to a childhood friend who is everything you hoped and nothing like you imagined. I know it doesn't make sense. But neither did anything that had happened since I stepped into the airport that day.

10

Carol—

I couldn't help but keep writing to Michal. As awkward as it felt, it's really the only way I knew how to communicate with her. My life in Romania—night and day compared to living in America. But, on the other hand, it's not. At the core of everything, life is the same. People try to make a living, have relationships, and make sense of this thing we call life.

So, one morning I seated myself at a picnic table in Ralph's yard while the others worked around me. Justin is a farmer. He grows "heirloom wheat," and in the mornings, he often helps Ralph and Annie milk the cows. Annie, she's amazing. She worked everywhere in HearthLand. One minute she was making cheese or soap, and another she'd be out in the gardens or the greenhouse. Annie spent lots of time in that greenhouse. There was a secret surrounding her. What it was, I didn't really know, but she'd tell me someday. I saw it when she had to stop herself from saying something. She didn't like that, so one day soon, I'd know what she was reluctant to say now.

So as they worked that morning and many other mornings, I wrote. Those letters contained things I'd never admitted to her—things I thought would make someone as deeply religious as she was reject me. I wrote things I wished weren't true of me.

Most people have family, a home, memories of special occasions, or something that remains constant in their lives. Christmas mornings, family reunions, festivals, a grandparent, a parent, a sibling—a friend. I had a friend. I had a girl, one I thought was a boy, who wrote me letters most months. She got me through my worst year of school, my first real crush, my lonely years. Her words (and the stamps she sent to keep me writing once that class had ended) anchored me to the one constant that wasn't negative in my life. Just knowing that a girl across the ocean had a mother who wrote to the Romanian embassy to purchase stamps for her to send me—it made such a difference in my life.

So when I wrote, I left out the things I knew might shock, offend, or distance her. I didn't tell about my troubled years—years I tried to numb the pain in my life with things like sex, pornography, excessive alcohol, drugs—pain. But in that beautiful place, the place they call HearthLand, I found the strength to write it—even if I never shared it with her.

Michal,

Do you remember when I am sixteen? I wrote of the apprentice who came to orphanage to find someone to train? I never tell you that he say no first. He saw through me—through my pain. He saw boy who is broken and trouble. He saw drug-addicted boy who steal and do unspeakable things to get the drugs or buy vodka to try to numb pain and loneliness. But the director of orphanage take him into office and talk for long time. I am rebellious and stubborn. I will not take help. Director say he will call police if he find me stealing again. At that time, I do not care because I think I am too clever to be caught again. I have made all stupid mistake. I am arrogant.

When he come out of office, Ioan say he will take me on trial. I learn that he too was orphan after Soviet occupation. He is plan to help other orphan now that communist regime is truly gone. He say it will be me as long as I do not steal and do not work when high. Is right word? High? He say I must not be drunk either.

I wanted to write about it. I wanted to tell you, to ask you to pray. You are boy who prays, I think. But words will not come. You will stop the writing. This is when I go to church for first time—just me. Not on holiday or because someone say I must. I talk to priest. He make me so anger! He tell me, "Carol, you are God's child. You have been claimed by God. You shame Him. Confess. Do your penance. Keep coming and learning. God will change you."

I do not want change. I do not return. I am scared. I am lonely. But still if I do not, I may not learn very well the job Ioan say he will teach me.

Before I could continue, Ralph sat down across from me and pushed a cup of coffee to my side of the table. "Everything okay? You look… pained."

"Is much pain." My hand trembled just a little as I hesitated, trembled as it hovered over the paper. I pushed it in front of him in a silent gesture—a request to read—but he didn't look at it—not at first. His eyes watched mine as if waiting for more. So, I explained why I was writing it in the first place. "I am here with Michal and want to tell her things I am afraid to say."

"Falling for her, are you?"

I will not insult anyone's intelligence by pretending I didn't know I admired her. I will not pretend that I didn't know how much she affected me. But the way Ralph put it, "falling for her," struck my heart with a well-aimed arrow of truth. "I think I am, but is not what I mean." I nodded at the paper. "Read it." My words sounded demanding. "Please."

Perspiration covered all of me, disgusting as that is to admit, by the time Ralph pushed the paper back to my side of the table. "You are afraid to say this? Why?"

"She is religious woman—deeply. She is like you. I hide this from her because I do not want to lose her as friend. But maybe now, now that she know me and know I am not this man anymore, is not so bad. But I wonder. I do not know. I do not like the secrets."

"Secrets have a way of burning into our soul and scarring us, don't they? Secrets designed to bring joy are delightful. Secrets designed to hide truth bear the weight of guilt—even on the one who is not guilty sometimes."

I thought I understood him. The words sounded wise and true. I had kept secrets that crushed me with guilt that wasn't mine. I knew things from my days in the orphanage—things children should not know. That knowledge—and the misguided feeling that I should have been able to prevent it—sometimes crushed my heart. But the secrets I kept from Michal were personal—my sins against myself. They didn't involve her, but the guilt of hiding that an ugly part of my life once existed overrode that.

"You think she will read and learn all what I did. You think she does that and still she will be a friend?"

Ralph's hands—odd hands. Not old, worn, calloused hands of a man who has worked with them all his life, but neither were they soft hands of a priest or a doctor. The hands wrapped around his cup and he inhaled a long whiff of roasted goodness before he said, "Stefan, her faith has taught her something more important than following rules and 'being good.' Her faith has taught her the value of forgiveness—because she needs it too. We all do."

I hesitated for just a moment before I nodded. "I should post it."

He climbed from the table and beckoned me to follow. "C'mon. I'll get you an envelope—a stamp. Annie's probably got something for us to do in there."

Michal—

To say I wasn't surprised when a call from my brother came is a gross understatement. I mean, c'mon. It had been two and a half months since I got the last one—the one when I told him Carol was coming. Now I don't want to give the impression that I don't love my brother. I do. He's the sweetest kid, really. I was twelve when he was born—yeah. Just old enough to really enjoy the baby part, which most kids don't get, but also just old enough to hate having our whole family disrupted. Fortunately, he was cute, a laid-back baby, and always happy. Not much has changed—

including the baby part.

When they did the whole birth-order thing and said "the baby of the family" tends to be a bit spoiled? Yeah. They modeled it after Micaiah. And yeah, I wasn't too happy that my already hard name to explain had yet another "M" Bible name that no one knew about. I read a book when I was little once—about a girl named Wallis who was named after Wallis Simpson. She's the gal that Edward the something of England abdicated the throne for and the George that Colin Firth got to play—the one with the stutter—took over for. I digress.

Anyway, I don't remember anything about the book except that the girl's name was Wallis, and I loved her. She knew what it was like to have a guy's name and not be a guy. But then we have Micaiah. Not Malachi, Not Micah. Micaiah. Some obscure prophet who, as it turns out, was pretty cool. Truth-teller, even at his own peril. And, well, as it turns out, *our* Micaiah is just like him. Sometimes, that's not such a good thing. Sometimes it ticks me off, frankly. Just because something may be true (or in your opinion it is), doesn't mean you have to say it.

Micaiah does.

Where was I? Oh, the call. I saw his name on my screen and well... *thud.* "Hey, bro."

"What's up?"

For someone who is really into truth, you'd think he wouldn't play the polite game. But he does. Still haven't figured that one out. "Not much." In case this was about my love life, I threw in some bait. "Lloyd and I have a date tonight—"

"On a Monday night?"

"I've been busy a lot—with work and Carol—"

"Oh! Forgot about her. How's that going?"

See, he's a good kid. I like him a lot and love him to death. "Well, you must not have talked to Mom in the past few weeks. Carol is a he. Apparently it's common enough over there."

"Whoa—he's your age, right? You 'met' in like the fourth grade or something?"

Great. I knew where this was going. "Yep."

"Competition for the dud. Awesome."

Why I protested, who knows. Habit, I guess. "He's not a *dud!*"

"He's a dude without enough to make him worth that E."

"You liked him at first."

"Yeah!" Micaiah growled at something—probably his cat—and continued as if he hadn't interrupted his own conversation. "Back when he was just a nice guy from your church. Now that he's Mr. I'm-too-busy-and-boring-to-commit-thank-Jesus, I'm just glad he *is.*"

"You do know we're planning marriage, right? It's on the agenda for our lives?" I wouldn't like where he took it if I let that stand, so I preempted his answer with a different question. "So how's school?"

"Not going this semester. Figured I'd work at the rock-climbing place to get my skills up to par for spring. I will probably do spring, though. Educate the brains during the week and work out the body between classes and on weekends."

"You could have been graduated by now."

"And your point is?"

"How do you expect to go anywhere—?" I cut myself off. If I pushed too much, Micaiah would just go talk to someone else about his problem. Oh, he had a problem. There was no doubt about that. He never called unless he wanted to hang out—which he didn't, or he'd have asked already—or if something was bugging him. "So what's up with you?"

"What would you say if I told you I got a girl pregnant?"

"Oh, you've *got* to be kidding me. You *know*—"

"I didn't."

And this is why he calls. Because if he showed up at my doorstep and pulled that, I'd beat him to a pulp. He may have fifty pounds on me and some seriously wide shoulders—the kind that make women cross their ankles like a prim princess when they hold an infant like him—but I'm a better athlete and he knows it. I have majorly impressive kickboxing skills, and I'm not afraid to use them.

"Okay, so now that you've thrown the, 'See, it could be worse,' scenario at me, what's up?"

"I think I'm in love."

I waited for the punchline. *Five… four… three… two… one…* Oh. He was serious. "Who is she?"

And the floodgates exploded. Look, 'Caiah has had his fair share of crushes. Haven't we all? But I've never heard him talk about a girl like this. He talked about wanting to be something amazing for *her* rather than how she made *him* feel—although, I heard that too. He told me about her family and about how her father owned the rock-climbing place. That's when the light bulb went off.

"So are you in love with… Ella? Elle?"

"Elle, yeah."

"Or," I continued, "Are you in love with her family's business."

"Never mind."

A smile grew before I could stop it—before I could keep it from my voice. "Oh, no. I want to meet her."

"You'll torture me—tell her about how I streaked through church diaperless or something. I still don't believe I did that."

"The only reason you can doubt it is because everyone didn't have cellphones with great cameras back then. If it happened today, you'd be an Internet sensation—the church streak."

"Maybe I should become a Luddite."

He does this—he throws these one-line zingers out of nowhere, and the words themselves aren't even that funny—mildly humorous, but not really funny. But the way he says it… man. Bet this Elle loves him for his humor first—followed closely by blue eyes that change shades based on his emotions and a crazy curl he lets grow over his forehead for that reason. Girls really dig that curl.

"Maybe you should let me take you guys out to dinner. I could bring Carol. You could meet him. It'd be fun."

"Tomorrow?"

"Sorry, he's on his way to Chicago for a meeting. What about…" I checked my Google Calendar and nodded. "Tuesday. Can you do

Tuesday—not this one coming up. The next one? I have to pick him up at the airport anyway."

"Torture—you're cruel. Doing this on purpose. But I'll wait until then. Just for you."

"Hey, 'Caiah?"

"Yeah?"

"Love you, buddy."

With a snort of protest, he hung up. He pretends that he hates it when I call him buddy—that it's too immature or something. But he loves it. And well, even if he didn't, it's the duty of sisters to torture their little brothers as often as possible. Just call it payback for those blow-out diapers that still haunt me in my nightmares.

Michal—

While Carol was gone, my usual routine fell back into place. I got up, jogged, got ready for work, went to work, came home, hung out with Lloyd on the nights he was free, and then I kicked it back into overdrive with a run each night.

It should have been good. Really. I had a great life and seriously, the world's best friends. My boyfriend was the most *comfortable* friend I've ever had—going to be a fabulous husband someday—an awesome family, a great condo, and my dream job. The last time I remember being discontented was when the dealership I wanted to buy from didn't have, and claimed they couldn't get, the car I wanted in the color I wanted. Considering I wanted simple, boring silver, it's not like it should have been a big deal. That's it. Major first-world problems here.

So when I found myself dissatisfied by Wednesday afternoon I couldn't understand it. And stupidly, Carol being the difference never came to mind. So, instead of moping around feeling antsy and discontented over nothing, I decided to do something about it. My plan: twofold. I'd ramp up my pet project at work—have it all ready for the board to consider the minute Carol returned from his trip, *and* I'd show a little appreciation to the man who loved me unconditionally. I mean, c'mon. Sometimes we get so comfortable in our relationships that we take them for granted. I treasured the comfortableness, but I didn't want to abuse it.

The solution? I showed up at his office during the "only death or dismemberment can interrupt" hour at his clinic. Look, Lloyd works long, focused hours. He interacts personally with each patient until that person is comfortable—and sometimes that becomes a bit of a counseling session rather than just a checkup for diabetes meds. But I didn't just show up to say hi, give him a kiss, and wish him well. No. I brought a picnic with all his favorite comfort foods—chicken noodle soup from this incredible diner we found a few months ago, hot grilled cheese sandwiches from the sandwich shop down the street from him, and coffee from The Kosher Cup. No, we're not Jewish or Messianic, but they make some seriously great coffee. There's something about making sure there are no unclean bugs in your coffee brew that must really affect flavor or quality or something.

So there I was, with all those different bags of food in a cute picnic basket, waltzing into the clinic. Almost literally, I might add. I half-skipped, half-grape vined through the room. And, as a result, the staff waved me through. They like me—and not just because I brought a dozen pastries from the shop next to The Kosher Cup.

The door flung open with ease as I cried, "Surprise!" Instead of a stunned and thrilled boyfriend, I found Malinda and Lloyd standing in the middle of his office, wrapped in each other's arms. "Oh, no! What happened?"

Malinda clung to him even more. And this is why you never do the superficial judging thing. I'd seen it once before—Malinda crushed when a patient died that she thought she could save. I just knew she'd lost someone—prayed it wasn't the little boy with cystic fibrosis. His treatment had really looked promising—a chance at a longer life than most.

Lloyd just shook his head and mouthed, "Sorry."

With a quick point to the basket and a whispered, "There's enough for two. Try to get her to eat," I hurried out of the office.

At the front, the office manager asked if everything was okay. "No... something's up with Malinda. If you could reschedule as many of her patients as possible, I think it would be best."

"Oh, no. I bet her article got rejected again. It's really wearing on her. Yeah, I'll take care of that. Thanks, Michal. You're a good girlfriend."

Who wouldn't leave feeling like she'd conquered the world?

Crazy part? My whole day went like that. I went to my favorite cafe for lunch—and the line was so far out the door that I just gave up and went to a deli across the street. It turned out to be seriously the best chicken and prosciutto anyone has ever made. At work, I wanted to prepare my presentation for the orphanage project. But instead, a man representing one of Rockland's most wealthy citizens appeared without an appointment with a request to ask a few questions. After an impromptu presentation by yours truly, he left with a five-figure check on my desk to be used "at my discretion." Um, hello! It could be the first step to funding that orphanage project! Everything went "wrong" and turned out fabulously right. I still can't believe it.

But, the cherry on top of all of that goodness was a letter from Carol—sent from Chicago. Have you ever read something so heartbreaking that your physical heart actually hurt—constricted with empathetic pain? Reading about Carol's past—the things he hid from me because he feared losing what I suspect was his only real friend—one he never expected to meet, and one who couldn't really *be* a friend—it just hurt. But, as with everything, there was so much joy in it for me. He trusted me now. He had faith now—faith to keep him from trying to numb pain with things that are only temporary and always bring further pain. And, there was that tiny bit of me that loved that he hadn't stopped writing.

A glance at the clock gave me ten minutes before I would have to have an overnight package in the outgoing bin. Time to write—no routine, no pretty paper, no *handwritten* note. But sometimes content is more important than packaging or process. Okay, it always is, but I love my rituals. People make fun of me for them, but I couldn't care less what they think.

Carol,
I just received your letter, and I cannot tell you how much it means to

me that you felt comfortable sharing something so very personal. My first response is to assure you that I wouldn't have rejected you. But that isn't the point, is it? The point is that God was faithful, even when I didn't know what wasn't my "need to know" thing at the time.

This letter is the last in a line of "disappointments" in a day of blessings. Why do I say disappointment when I actually squealed when it arrived? Because I was just sitting here thinking, "I want to share my day with Carol. He would totally get how cool everything going wrong and then into right again is!" And then the mail arrives and here's your letter. I'm so happy that you thought to send it to my work! Thank you!

At the six minute mark, I mentioned wanting to get together with him and Micaiah and slipped it into an overnight envelope. A quick Internet search provided an address. By the time I dashed it to the outgoing bin, I had less than thirty-seconds to spare. And the UPS guy walked in... early. If I'd been late, things would not have been pretty.

"Best day of my life—started out so stinky, too!"

Okay, so the clichéd "Girls can't even go to the bathroom by themselves" has kind of kept up with the times. While I showered after my run, I chatted with Crystal—over the phone, of course. She, on the other hand, didn't appreciate my enthusiasm for *all* of my day.

"Michal, I'm going to say it. It's been a long time since I have, so you can't say I'm nagging. You know I love Lloyd, but *why* are you with him?"

"Because, I love him too—obviously more than you. He's perfect for me. You know it. We get each other. I tell you this every time you find a new reason to question the wisdom of us." I allowed the water to beat on my face while waiting for her to reply. She didn't. Water off, an invigorating towel rub proved even more relaxing for my protesting muscles. "What is it this time?"

"I want you happy—head-over-heels-in-love happy. I just don't see that."

Sometimes a well-timed joke can diffuse tension. I tried it. "If I didn't know he wasn't your type, I might be suspicious—and a little jealous."

"That's just it, Mickey. I don't think you *would* be jealous. That's the problem."

Okay, that's a new one. The jealous girlfriend is someone that *everyone* despises—even her best friends most of the time. It's immature, it's pathetic, and it's annoying as anything. You know, the whole, "You looked at that girl passing our table!" And the guy says, "Um, yeah. She's our server, and I want more coffee." Crazy, right?

So when Crystal's Argument 2.1 against Lloyd turned out to be caused by her shock that I *wasn't* jealous when I found him in the arms of another woman... I can't even think that with a straight face. It's so crazy funny. Lloyd and Malinda. At least *I* think it's funny. I'm pretty sure Malinda would take off Crystal's head for suggesting it.

"—have even a bit of a twinge! But you're over there slathering lotion on your legs—"

"How'd you know that?"

Crystal's laughter told me she wasn't too concerned about the Lloyd thing. Big relief right there. She's my best friend. I hate it when we disagree. "It's what you do, and besides, I can hear you slapping it onto your legs. It's like your version of smacking gum." She paused before she continued, and *that* made me nervous. "It's just that you're *too* calm. You sound like you're thrilled that he ignored your romantic gesture in favor of holding another woman. I know she was upset," Crystal insisted. "But it's still, at the very least, unprofessional. But you act like it's the greatest thing that your boyfriend is brushing you off for another woman."

"It's not like he didn't call as soon as he could to thank me for bringing food and for understanding. She'd gotten rejected—again."

"Which any jerk—and I'm not saying he is one. I know better. It's something any jerk would do to keep his woman strung along while he messes around with someone else. Don't you see? I'm concerned because you are so stagnant in your relationship that you're fine with this!"

"I wouldn't be fine with it if it *meant* anything to him. I'd be more upset if he didn't comfort any coworker when another dream died."

"But that's what I mean. He can comfort another woman in other ways than holding her while his girlfriend watches. He didn't even have the decency to move away."

"Because he wasn't doing anything wrong!" I started to protest further—to insist she had misrepresented the situation—when Crystal threw another accusation at me. This one I didn't know how to or even if I should respond.

"Just think about this. If Carol had been standing there holding another woman, would you be so perfectly fine with it? He's just a friend you hardly know in 'real life,' but I bet if you brought *him* lunch and he expected you to leave it for some girl he was wrapped up with, you wouldn't be quite so forgiving—so *embracing* of the situation. And you're not even interested in *him* that way. So, c'mon!"

Um, ouch.

It's strange how things can totally throw you off your game that you never would have imagined. I mean, Carol hadn't been a part of my daily life for years, so why was I so annoyed by him being gone for so long? Lloyd didn't seem to understand either. "Can't say, Michal. You're probably just worried about a guy in a strange place or something."

That earned him a kiss. I mean, if a guy figures you out before you can, he totally deserves recognition for it. And besides, we hadn't had much time together lately, so it was probably more of an excuse to have a quick make-out session with my guy. No... Lloyd didn't seem to mind at all when I dropped the remote and slid my hand up his scruffy face. "Hey..."

His lips teased the corner of my mouth as he threw in his usual tidbit. "You know..." My heart spun in dizzying circles until I almost missed this one. "...you can burn double your metabolic rate if you kiss just right."

I pulled away and issued a challenge. "Prove it." And he did—boy, did he. I think all the commercials ended while we kicked our metabolisms into overdrive. "Missed you…"

"Well, between work, conferences, and Carol, we've both been busy."

The way he said "Carol" rubbed me wrong. It sounded familiar—uncomfortably and irritably familiar, but I couldn't figure out why at first. Then when he asked how Micaiah was, it hit me. He said their names exactly the same way—with a kind of cross between condescension and mild irritation. Then again, Lloyd always hated my devotion to my brother. He said I don't just mother him. He always insisted that I sss*mother* him.

It's probably that. He just thinks I'm going to tick off Carol. And he's right. When a man is alone in a strange country, his only friend—or at least I was—shouldn't alienate him with her hovering. I'm like a helicopter mom with the guys in my life. Sheesh!

"You know what?" I said. "I think it'll be good for Micaiah and Carol when I introduce them. They'll have something to talk about—how I smother them with my over-involvement."

"You're introducing Carol to Micaiah?"

"Yeah! We're going to The Diner in Fairbury when Carol gets back. I've written about it so much that I thought it might be fun. We can walk around the lake and—"

Lloyd cut me off—very unusual for him. He's usually the epitome of gentleman, but Lloyd really hates that diner. "Sounds delightful."

"You're a terrible liar." His kiss took me off-guard. Unsettled me, but I knew exactly what he wanted to hear, and I gave it to him. "But you're a great kisser."

"I stick with my strong points…"

His next words came out of the field left of left field. "You know, relationships always have their awkward or difficult parts. I'm just thankful that we're committed to working stuff out."

My mind screamed, *"Huh???? Where'd that come from?"* but I managed to stammer, "Yeah. Well, if you're not committed to the relationship, then why are you in it?"

Thankfully, it worked. Lloyd beamed, grabbed the remote, and flipped the channel to the eleven o'clock news—a signal that he'd have to go home soon. In one of my rare "need space" moments, I wasn't sorry.

"Oh," Lloyd interjected at the first commercial. He pulled me close, just the way I like it, and chuckled. "You'll never believe what Doris said at the office today."

The grandmotherly nurse probably should have retired a decade or two ago, but she seriously was the best nurse I'd ever met. Besides, Lloyd inherited her from the last doctor at the clinic, and he's a bit afraid of her.

"I'll bite. What?"

"She asked when we were getting married. I told her we'd talked about it, but we're waiting until we're settled and ready for that step."

"Best line you ever came up with. I have diffused so many nosy questions with it." I expected him to beam at my approval. He just snickered.

"Exactly what I expected. Instead, she said, 'Most people who wait until they're ready to get married or have children, never do. Either the day never comes, or they find that when they are ready, there's no one to marry or they can't conceive.'"

Where did that come from? I wanted to ask, but something in Lloyd's tone rattled me a bit. I *almost* expected an impromptu proposal, and I should admit that I would have refused—not permanently, but I would have insisted he ask again after thinking about it, instead of reacting to someone who couldn't possibly understand modern sensibilities.

When Lloyd proposed after Grandpa Colbert got sick—right before he died—it just wasn't the right time. I didn't know what was up or down, so I said no. We agreed to revisit it later. And we do talk about it as if it's a given. Once in a while, one of us sees a house that intrigues us or whatever. So far, neither one of us has liked the same one. I figure if we ever do, we'll both propose spontaneously on the spot. It's become kind of my dream proposal. How cool would that be?

Anyway, after that, I was so unnerved by everything that I just kicked him out and went to bed. Last thing I saw before I fell asleep was a text from him. I LOVE YOU.

12

Carol—

They chose the wrong person to send to America. It was a kind gesture—a generous one even—but I knew nothing about trying to sell my or anyone else's work. I could tell you what it is, why it is unique, why I love it, how people use it in their lives. I just do not know how to try to convince someone to buy it—especially in a language I am only moderately fluent in. Each city seemed worse than the last. My highlights of each day were trying different foods, swimming in the hotel pool, talking with Michal, and collapsing in an exhausted heap on the bed at the end of the day. Of course, Michal's overnighted letter almost wiped the stress completely from that day.

I love people. They energize me. So I hadn't expected that part of travel to be a problem, but by the time Michal pulled up to the curb of the terminal, I was, as she says, "peopled out." I think she guessed, because she pulled out her mobile and offered to cancel with Micaiah. In America, is it a sin that I didn't confess that I'd forgotten the dinner she'd planned? I'll have to ask the priest. I did, though—forget, that is.

When Michal texts, her fingers fly across the keys with a bit of a bounce—just like when she jogs up and down the stairs or rushes up to meet you. Even her voice has that hint of a lilt to it when she is excited. All that fizzled into limp movements as her thumbs slid back and forth across the screen. And I couldn't stand seeing her so visibly disappointed.

"I am well. I need only the restroom and to wash my face." A quick rub of my chin prompted me to add, "I also need shaving, but is no time. Sorry."

When a woman like Michal turns and looks at you—cocoa-colored eyes made darker by emotion—it does things to a man. If I hadn't been half in love with her then, that look alone would have done it. As it was, I knew what she'd say before she spoke. "You should skip shaving more often. It looks *good* on you."

And if that wasn't torture enough, she followed it with a gentle slide of her hand along my jaw. It lingered there for a moment—right up to the moment when some guy blew a whistle and ordered us from the curb. "I think he would wish you to leave now."

"I'm goin'… I'm goin'." How we missed the giant shuttle behind us as she shot into traffic, no one will ever be able to explain. It defied some law of physics. It had to.

As much as I wanted to spend time with them, as interesting as Micaiah sounded, by the time she merged onto the Rockland Loop, I had begun to regret agreeing to go. *Should have asked Ralph to come.* And when a new barrage of questions began as she wove through traffic and off the Loop again, all I could do was attempt to answer with semi-intelligible phrases.

"What about a series of gift stores? You could donate a portion of sales to orphanages in Romania! People love to buy something when they think they're getting two things for the price of one."

"This, I cannot say. The things aren't mine to make decision."

"Well, they'd just have to agree to put their things in those stores. So, no one would be out anything they didn't choose to be."

How do you explain to a woman who is passionate about helping people like you—or rather, like who you *used* to be? How do you tell her that her idea is admirable but impractical? That the money made would be insignificant after administrative costs? That question gave me an idea.

"We should ask business person—for the money—if it is profitable.

If we can pay for the buildings and the people to run stores, and people to manage charity side, and still we can make profit, then is good idea. I don't know who can I ask for advice."

In the space of time that it took to shatter her new dreams of saving the orphans of Romania, Michal had pulled off the Loop and onto side streets. A small house—two houses in one, it seemed—had an old, once yellow, Volkswagen parked in the narrow driveway. "This is Micaiah's duplex. Hang on, I'll get him."

She bolted from the car before I could offer to go myself. From the front seat, I found myself watching her, hair bouncing and tumbling around her shoulders and nearly to her waist as she jogged to the front. Two knocks—Michal didn't even give him time to respond—and she burst through the door. Quiet enveloped me. Not even the hum of the engine penetrated the cocoon of peace. No questions, no need to interact. Slow, deliberate inhales and exhales helped breathe out the guilt.

You couldn't wait to get back to see her—another man's girlfriend—and now you only wish that she would go away. It's wrong, Carol Stefan. So very wrong.

The sight of her hanging on a man's arm as they strolled from the little house spun my heart in dizzy circles. *You want her to hang on you like that. Well, she can't. He's her brother. Lloyd is practically her fiancé. You are a friend. Show yourself to be a true one.*

The door flung open and Michal nearly jerked me from the car. "Carol, this is my brother, Micaiah. He's heard about you since he was born!"

"And I hear of little brother who is cute and funny even as infant." I winked at her and held out a hand. When he laughed as he shook it, I suspected I might have made a new friend.

"She used to *love* to brag about her friend in Romania who wrote such good letters and beat up the kids at school who teased...*her.* If she only knew..." The man gave me such a deep, penetrating look. I worried about what it might mean. Maybe we wouldn't be friends after all.

"I think..." He crawled in the back seat, slid to the middle, and buckled a lap belt across his middle. A guy that tall can lean forward and drape his arms comfortably over each of the front seats—which he did. "I think I like him."

"Is good thing that I like you, too."

Michal—

Okay, so this was supposed to be about me meeting 'Caiah's girlfriend—um... whatshername. And, of course, it occurred to me that I'd better remember before I have to say something that shows I paid attention. Oops.

Unfortunately, the name appeared in my head and belched from my lips before I could stop myself. "Elle."

"Um... yeah..."

"I don't know where she lives." Okay, so pride falls heaviest in fall. That's my excuse, and I'm sticking to it.

Micaiah tapped Carol's shoulder. "Has she been this ditzy all day?"

"I do not know. I have only seen her this hour—and a half." He glanced my way. "Have you been the ditzy? And what is it? Is it good?"

Dead silence counted down from a beat of three before the car erupted in laughter. Micaiah wheezed before saying, "I totally bought it. Good one, Carol. I officially like you."

"You already said that, 'Caiah."

"No..." He shoved Carol's shoulder. "I said I *thought* I liked him. Now I do. Playing up that language barrier thing to get you like that. Good one."

Carol's laughter filled the car again. "I did not think I could put you off like that. It work-*ed.* I always forget the 'd' sound."

We tried not to laugh again. Really. But who wouldn't? And Carol, he thought we were laughing at the way he tended to leave everything singular and in present tense. I managed *not* to sideswipe a sandwich truck as I choked out, "It's not that. You said, 'put you off'. That means irritate you or make you disgusted. I think you mean 'put one over' on us. Fool us. Trick us."

"Yes. This is the one. 'Put one over.' I try to make joke that my tutor say is good one. And I have the epic fail."

I didn't have the heart to tell him that no one said 'epic fail' anymore. Let's face it. It's cute coming from a guy like Carol with that accent and those eyes. Those eyes killed me, you know. *He's going to break half my friends' hearts.*

Of course, that's when I realized that I'd circled a block—twice. "Micaiah! Where do I go for Elle?"

"Like I said… ditzy. We talked about this. She had to take someone else's shift tonight."

Sometimes, no matter what you do, you can't do anything right. "Right. Sorry. It's been a long day." Lame excuse, but sometimes…sometimes they're the best ones because they're the only ones. "So, The Diner. Let's go."

How many times has my family driven to Fairbury for a concert in the park or an old movie at The Fox? How many times did the trip seem to take forever when I was a kid? And this time we'd hardly turned off onto the highway when it seemed as if I pulled up in front of The Diner. By that time, Carol and Micaiah were discussing American vs. European football. I swear, I thought Micaiah would recruit Carol on the spot.

It took until we had been seated, had our orders taken, and I'd listened to yet another debate on whether the World Cup or the Super Bowl was more exciting, before I decided I couldn't take any more. I mean, I'm a crazed sports fan. I watch both and cheer until I'm hoarse, but I just wasn't feeling it. So, I changed the subject. "I have tentative approval on a project. There won't be time for this year, but next…"

"The orphan project?" When I gave Micaiah a disbelieving look, he did that whole rolling of the eyes thing he does when he thinks he's being clever. "You think I don't listen when Mom goes on and on about your amazing responsible skills and how you're making a difference in the world while I'm just wasting my potential."

"Okay, well yeah. We can't do it this year—not enough time—but we *can* get it set up. And with Carol for contacts, we're going to have an awesome chance at a fabulous program."

Thankfully, Carol asked about it. I didn't want to have to *try* to get him interested. As it was, the director of our organization was concerned about offending Romanians with our attempts to help.

"What is program? In Romania?"

I don't even remember them bringing our food. I think we ignored Micaiah too. For the next forty minutes, until my brother *insisted* we walk the town or something, to give the table up for others, I tried to explain my vision for a program that incorporated the best of all the sponsorship programs out there—maximum benefit to the children with minimal overhead.

We buttoned up coats and stuffed our hands in our pockets as the cold air blasted us the moment we stepped outside. A tiny part of me wished that Micaiah wasn't there. I wanted to share this place with Carol by myself.

"So let me bullet point this for him, Mickey. What you want is a program where American families—"

"Or churches, businesses, clubs—anyone, really."

"Fine. Where Americans—"

Had to interrupt again. "I want to make it international as soon as possible. I am sure churches in England and Australia—Canada, all over the globe, they're going to want to help too."

"Shut up and let me break down the bones of it for him, will you?"

The confusion on Carol's face—priceless. I mean, seriously hysterical. And, of course, I couldn't stop laughing once I realized that first 'Caiah had mentioned bullets and now he was talking bones. It had to be an idiomatic nightmare for the poor guy. But I choked back more laughter, smiled, and let him talk. Sisters do that sometimes. Not often, so note it. It happened.

"Thank you. Okay... so *people*—in groups and individually—will 'sponsor' a child in an orphanage." Before I could blurt out the general orphanage sponsorship, he added it in on his own. Should have known he'd actually be listening. "Others will be pooled together to sponsor entire orphanages if that's what they want. Some people provide clothes, education, and trips to the zoo or whatever. Others provide beds, heat, and teachers. Am I right so far?"

"Yes."

Carol asked a question before Micaiah could continue. "Did you say you will buy from Romania for orphans?"

"That's what she said. It's brilliant, actually. I mean, so often Americans buy stuff and ship it over. Talk about a waste of money in shipping and a wasted opportunity to help the other country's economy. I know we want to help our own, too, but is it really worth it if we're wasting dollars?" Micaiah pushed us into The Confectionary. "Go get your chocolate fix. I'm going to run into The Grind and grab one of their coffees—best ever."

"Bring me back a latte, will you? Double shot no cream." Yes, I asked if Carol wanted anything, but he just shook his head. He seemed a bit out of it, but his next question explained it all.

"Why you wish to do this, Michal? Why is so important?"

But the bubbly teen behind the counter interrupted us. "What can I get you? We have a few specials today. There's a Caramel Fudge Pumpkin Sundae…" Yeah, I heard every word in capitals. I thought she must have been practicing for a play or something. Each word so very clearly enunciated and emphasized. "And then there are our famous pumpkin delight truffles."

Nope. Not a play. She just wanted to use up that ice cream. Pushing with emphasis. Nice. I bought both. I'd be jogging double for a week to make up for the calories. But a splurge with an old-slash-new friend— sometimes that's more important.

Carol chose the sundae too and laughed about eating ice cream with already half-frozen fingers. But the minute we stepped outside, he asked again. "Why?"

"I've wanted to do it for years—ever since I was about oh… ten or twelve years old. I knew how hard your life was, and it bugged me that we couldn't do anything about it. Then when you came, and you weren't the broken little girl I always imagined, I reread every letter. Our conversations about how poor your country is, your ideas for making things better—it all made my dream fall into place. So, I pitched it while I had the opportunity. And even though they were against it at first, they're going to *do* it."

He took another bite of the sundae and sighed. "I cannot eat—too much food. My stomach is revolting." A frown appeared as his eyebrows drew together in confusion. "Is revolt? Both, they sound right."

"Well, that's because you can say that line a dozen ways and make it mean different things and the same—both."

"English is crazy language. I will never learn it." He tossed his ice cream—longing lingered as his eyes followed it down into the garbage can. I couldn't decide if he liked it that much or if a lifetime of never being able to get enough to eat scolded him. But his next words cleared it up. "Such a waste. I knew I should not buy. I am sorry."

"It's okay. Everyone has eyes bigger than their stomachs sometimes. It's usually Thanksgiving, you know? Or Christmas." I shook my head. "No, Thanksgiving. You know, the one with all the food that the family brings and expects you to take a giant spoonful of everything?"

"Yes. You write about it in your letters. I think, 'They must be rich—so much food. They send me stamps. I have very rich friend.'"

Some things you learn are hard to share. Sometimes you just don't want to deal with it all. But I remember the day I learned that TV and movies warped our minds about what rich really is. I used to think we were average—maybe even a little under average. But reading about Carol digging in garbage cans for any scrap that someone might have thrown out had cured me. Reading about him wearing all his clothes to bed—all two sets. Reading about him trying to curl up with one of the littler boys to protect the kid from the cruelty of bullies and from freezing to death—how that kept him warmer too. The little boys didn't like it—didn't want to be touched. But they needed the warmth too.

"You taught me that, Carol. *You* taught me that food whenever I'm hungry—or even when I'm not—clothes that keep me warm, and a clean, comfortable home means I *am* rich. Even if everything isn't very nice, it's *there.* I'm rich and I know it because of you."

He took my hand—held it as we wandered back toward The Grind. "You teach me that being poor has no shame. Only shame is when you have something to share and don't. You teach me that God gives the blessings to everyone. Only you must look for the blessings sometimes." Micaiah strode toward us like a man on a mission and totally ruined the moment. But not before Carol added, "And I learn from you that blessings you must search to find are most precious." I think he choked up for a second before asking, "Is right word? Precious?"

"Definitely the right word." I couldn't help it. He looked like a little boy who had received the highest praise possible. So I kissed his cheek. It seemed like a European kind of thing to do.

13

Carol—

HearthLand had something about it—a richness in relationships and lives. Those people work hard, but they never seem to make it *look* like work. It's much like when I create. It feeds me. It's *work*, but it feels more like play.

Inspiration surrounded me. Inside the house, on a walk with Janie, the wise, aged woman who watched over HearthLand with a motherly eye, and even as I drove down Hearthfield Way. Just sitting on Lavonne's porch, talking. She worried about her son, Andre. I told her he would be fine if she kept being the wonderful mother she was. She told me her story. I told her mine.

They teased me, these new friends of mine. Where they zipped down the road as fast as they could, I liked to roll along, foot off the gas pedal most of the time, and just *be* in the moment. Golden fields stretched around me—flat stretches of grasses and gentle rolling hills. Trees—everywhere. Leaves swirled from branches in lazy circles until a breeze would come along. Then they'd shower down as if an artist tried to paint a literal representation of "Autumn Rain."

Constanţa doesn't have the fields and the trees of many colors. It's a port—a big one—on the coast of the Black Sea. Many people there but little open space like I saw between HearthLand and Rockland. Flying over different states in America—so open and empty. It's a different world for me. Sure, trees change colors in Constanța, but not like here. Like I told Michal once, most of that kind of autumn glory is inland.

The inspiration I gained from HearthLand made my art better. The pieces I designed held deeper richness than anything I'd created at home. I wanted to say it was just the locale—the beauty around me. It wasn't.

I had come to America to represent my guild and forge a working relationship between us and the people of HearthLand. I had come to meet my childhood "pen pal" and take our friendship to a new level. And I had done all of that, in ways I'd never imagined. My childhood friend stole my heart, and she didn't know it. Her *boyfriend* didn't know it, thank heaven.

She treated me like a little brother—teasing, laughing, trying to make my time in America so incredible that I'd never want to leave. I couldn't tell her she didn't need to try. I hadn't wanted to leave after the first two weeks. How I'd stay, I didn't know.

Janie, the wise older woman she was, discovered my secret before anyone else. While I'd admitted to Ralph that I found it hard to think of Michal as just a friend, Janie saw deep into my heart. She saw just how deeply I'd fallen in love with another man's almost-fiancée.

We sat on her porch steps and watched the boys try to build the shell of a cart that would coast down the hill. Rory's father had promised to find a way to attach wheels to it if they built something that could withstand the bouncing and jostling over the ground. That's when she asked.

"Is your friend married, Stefan?"

At times like that, I found it tempting to ask why they chose to call me Stefan instead of my first name. Mirela thought it was because it was a business relationship—trying to show me respect and friendship at the same time—leave off mister but defer to my surname. It made as much sense as anything, I suppose.

"No, Michal is have boyfriend, but not married—not engaged to be marry."

"And you love her."

Shame filled me. When you have years of immorality behind you, it is hard not to see everything related to relationships as wrong if there is even the slightest chance it could be. I am an emotional man. I cry. And I did.

Janie's fragile arms—I could break them if I wasn't careful—tried to hold and comfort me. "Is very wrong of me, I know."

"It's not, Stefan. It isn't. She isn't married, and even if she were, you can't help who you love. You can only help what you *do* about that love."

"And this is problem I have. She is think of me as brother—good friend. I wait for the touch on my face or the hug. I hold my breath and do not let myself pray that she hold my hand again. But the prayer, it is in my heart anyway."

But her protest—loud enough to make the boys look our way as they tried to see if I was harming her—insisted I did no wrong. "She isn't *married*, Stefan. She hasn't made that commitment yet."

"I will not steal other man's love. I want to try. I won't." Hands wringing, heart weeping—I needed out of there, but I couldn't do it. I couldn't just walk away from a woman who was trying to help me.

"You're such an honorable man. A fool," she added with a pat on my cheek, "but a truly honorable man."

If you only knew who I once was, you would not say that.

Before I had to find a way to respond, Rory called out to me. "Can you help us? This screw won't go in!"

"Go, Stefan. The boys need you more. I'll pray that the Lord will guide all of you."

These people prayed so much. If you sneezed, they prayed that you would get well soon. If you looked confused, they prayed for wisdom for you. If you wanted something you couldn't afford, they prayed that God would provide the money. They prayed for *everything.* And I wanted to learn that.

The boys really had done an amazing job with their project. Everything looked perfect to my inexperienced eyes. "What is problem with car?"

"This screw. It has to be there. I can't make it work. It just slides right out!"

Andre's near-panic seemed excessive for the simple loss of a screw, but what did I know? I'd never built anything like it. Then I saw the problem. The screw went all the way through and out the other side. It wouldn't hold that way. And it looked like they'd used a smaller screw than drill bit.

"We need other kind of screw—with back piece. What you call the thing that fit on back... do you know what I mean?"

"A bolt!" Rory jumped up and ran down the road toward his house without another word.

"I think he knows what you mean. A bolt and a nut?" Andre nodded as he examined his project. "Yeah... that'll work. I ran out of screws, so I used this one. It went all the way through."

"Is small for hole." I guess my explanation made sense, because he nodded and began sanding the area around the hole while he waited.

"You're not bad at this. Want to help us figure out how to support the bottom? I think the boards should go this way..." He turned over the little car looking cart and showed how he wanted to put boards lengthwise down the bottom. "But Rory says across it—like a bed. I think it'll just break with all the weight in one spot."

The solution made perfect sense to me, but before I could suggest doing both, my mobile rang. I listened to Michal's latest spiel on how I should go out with her friend Piper. "She is friend from party? Is she short hair or long?"

"Short, spiky blond hair—like a better Meg Ryan cut—aaand you have no clue what that means. Um... Who cares? You know who she is now. She hinted that she's feeling left out. You took out Jen and Crystal and Therese. So what do you say? Lloyd and I can go with you guys if you like, but I think he'd like it if we had a night in."

You want this for tonight? Why so sudden? Why not tomorrow or even Friday? Why now?

She answered as if she could hear my thoughts. "I'd suggest on Friday, but she works weekends. She's a deejay for parties."

"Send me the number. I will call and ask. Tomorrow is good?

Monday?"

"Either." Michal cleared her throat. "There's one other thing..."

Why do those words strike fear in my heart every time? Americans say this all the time, and it always feels so ominous—as if someone is going to tell you that you have a month to live. Not sure how, but I managed to choke out, "And what is that?" without my voice cracking or hesitating.

"Can we meet to talk about an idea I have for doing something for your orphanage this Christmas?"

Can we meet? Can we sit together and talk? Can you do something for children who need so much? Can you let me watch your eyes, the way you move your hands, hear the inflections in your voice? Somehow, I managed to say a simple, "Yes. This is good idea. I can come for lunch any day this week. We talk."

Michal—

Ever feel like your life is absolutely perfect until a call comes in to mess it all up? Yeah. Micaiah did that to me. He waited for a few days after our date, you know. Just long enough to give me that false sense that all was well. When I saw his name on my phone, I grinned and punched it. "Hey! Did Elle come up with another date for us?"

"Yeah... she said that Greg owes her now, so whenever we want to go we can." I didn't even get to ask about the weekend when he added, "So are you dumping Lloyd or not?"

"Huh?" Let's face it. Most people lose all hope of eloquence when they're cornered like that.

"You heard me. After seeing you guys walking around holding hands, you kissing him—"

Had to protest that one. "Hey! His *cheek!* I kissed his cheek. Sheesh, 'Caiah! He's like another brother. I'd have kissed *your* cheek right then. So, yeah. So what?"

"Except he's *not* your brother."

Way to state the obvious, bro. Way to state the obvious. "But he knows I'm with Lloyd. He didn't take it to mean anything. I *have* a boyfriend, and Carol understands that."

Look, Micaiah isn't exactly known for his astute observations, so when he said, "If he understands it now, he won't when he falls that much more in love with you."

"He's not—"

Silence. It didn't surprise me. Micaiah has always been a "hanger upper," as my mom calls it.

It was early for a lunch break, but I had to get some exercise—move around. So I kicked off my heels and grabbed my slip-on walkers. The inventor who designs a pair of heels that feel like you're walking on clouds like those shoes—his greatest of grandchildren will be set for their lives. Man, I love those shoes.

Of course, I didn't make it to the corner before my frustration reached the boiling point. He'd never be able to answer—not at eleven-thirty in the morning, but I couldn't help but call and rant at Lloyd's voice mail.

"Just got a call from 'Caiah. He asked when I was dumping you! Can you believe that? We've been together for *four* years and I'm just going to dump you because my childhood pen pal isn't female? He actually thought me kissing Carol's cheek *meant* something." Yeah, I got a few strange looks from passersby. I tried to be incensed about it, but hey. I know that I'd have been just as curious as anyone. I try not to be a hypocrite.

"I can't decide if I should be disgusted that he doesn't know the difference between a *kiss* and a peck on the cheek or thrilled that he might be more chaste than I've imagined. I *told* him you wouldn't care—that you know I am fully committed to you and our relationship. He knows I love *you*. It makes me so *mad!* Who does he think he is?"

That's about where I lost steam. I think it's because I realized that I hadn't actually *said* I loved Lloyd in that particular conversation. It was implied—sure. But Micaiah can be a bit... what's the British term? Yeah.

Thick about stuff like that.

Fortunately for my self-induced, anger-riddled adrenaline rush, I remembered one more little tidbit my interfering brother had lobbed at me. "And he is under some stupid delusion that Carol either *is* or *will be* in love with me. How stupid is that? I can't wait for him to get out of the teen years. Didn't you once say it takes men until like twenty-five or twenty-six? Well... yeah. I don't think I can take four more years of this. Anyway, love you. I'll rant more later."

A text came through from Micaiah. JUST THINK @ IT, K? IT'S NOT NICE 2 LEAD CAROL ON WHEN HE NOS HE CAN'T HAVE U.

"Text-speak." The bane of my existence. 'Caiah can't even stay consistent with it. Sometimes he writes OK. Others, K. Sometimes he spells out to. Others he doesn't. What is up with that? And the @ symbol for about. Where did that even come from? No one I know does that. And he doesn't do it all the time—just enough to drive me to seriously consider a Luddite commune. I won't even address "nos." Really? *Really?*

Then I remembered how much my friend Piper wanted to go out with Carol. So, I set it up. Carol actually sounded a little excited about it. Less than fifteen minutes after my brother's stupid text, I sent back one of my own. FOR A GUY SO "IN LOVE" WITH ME, HE SURE IS EXCITED ABOUT HIS DATE WITH PIPER BROWNE.

Ha. Take that, you little pipsqueak. Yeah. I went there... pipsqueak. Sometimes the old slang is just so much better. I decided right then that I might try to revive the twenties' and thirties' slang. Everything else retro is popular. Why not their slang? I put a reminder in Evernote to make a list of new slang terms—new to me, anyway—and blissfully walked into my favorite coffee shop for a tuna on rye and a coffee. Turned out to be a pretty decent morning after all.

14

Carol—

One problem with taking a girl out on a date in a foreign country is that you don't really know what people like. I suspect that is even true of just a different city, or in America, different state. I thought a restaurant would be safe, but when I mentioned it to Ralph and his nephew, Harlan couldn't stop laughing. Explanations go a long way to rectify misunderstandings. Apparently restaurants are great date ideas, but no matter how much people rave about how amazing "Chick-fil-a" is, don't plan to take your date there. It's an insult, or something like that. I suggested a picnic in the park that afternoon, but Ralph's nephew, Harlan, shut that down as well.

"It's too cold. Save that for spring." Then he turned to his uncle and said, "There. I just gave him a reason to get that extended visa you were talking about. He needs to stay for a date in the park with a picnic basket and one of his friend's friends. Done."

But Ralph surprised me with his response. "I thought you'd be taking out Lavonne—or even Annie. They both seem to like you."

And I thought you were in love with Annie. Strange... How to answer that one eluded me. Lavonne is an amazing woman—beautiful, dedicated worker, devoted mother. I could see really enjoying spending time with her. There was just one little problem. She could never be Michal. Was it right

119

to go out with someone, when I was in love with someone else? I did with Michal's friends, of course. Still, she had to know I wasn't really interested in any of them. The way she talked about it felt as though it was a way to ensure no one felt left out. She hadn't asked me to go out with the same woman twice, so it only made sense. And... there were only three to go, if I remembered that night correctly. Surely *one* of those women had a boyfriend!

"I would not wish to give false impression—is right words?"

Harlan nodded. "Yeah, if you're not interested, don't ask her."

"I am the interested. This is not correct. I am *interested*. But I do not think very much it is good to... how you say..." But I couldn't. I didn't know how to say that, no matter how interested I was, I wasn't going to let anyone know it, because interested in someone isn't the same as desiring to develop a relationship. It didn't take a saint to know that it wasn't right to explore a relationship when all I wanted is to make someone else's boyfriend go away.

And that was the real problem. Lloyd. He was a good man. He was careful of Michal—treated her wonderfully. If he was unkind or selfish, I could wish her away from him, but how could I justify wishing for someone's relationship to die when it was a *good* one?

"Well, if you are just interested in being Lavonne's friend, why not just say so?" Harlan looked at his uncle for support. "Right? He can invite Lavonne and Andre out for mini golf or something—bowling. Just as friends. She could use that kind of 'out.'"

It sounded fun. I would take just Andre even, but Ralph had suggested that it wouldn't be wise to take him anywhere alone. Why it never occurred to me to take the boy's mom, I'll never know. "I will ask for Saturday. Thank you."

But as I turned to call Piper and see what she thought of trying the Pho Bowl in Ferndale that had been mentioned a couple of times, I swear Harlan murmured, "And if he happens to decide that she's a better candidate than he thought, all the better."

"So I know you went out with Jenn, Therese...and Crystal?" Piper waved her spoon around until I expected a noodle to fly off and plaster itself to my head like a mummy's wrapping.

"Yes, and a girl named Piper. He is very intelligent woman who likes to take the long walks along the lake and movies on cold winter nights." With a wink, I added, "And he think that our friend Michal has crazy in the head for all the exercise he does."

Saying just the right thing when you feel like you've hurt someone is one of life's most wonderful, free gifts. She lit up at that. I knew she thought I hadn't been listening, and it was *partly* true. Some of what she said made no sense to me. The woman spoke with such speed—like the auctioneer on a TV program I saw in a hotel room in Seattle. Half the time I didn't have a clue what she said, so I worked to find words that I could pull out. That helped me decipher what she meant. I was a little uncertain about the "crazy for exercising so much" bit, but I thought that's what she meant.

Piper is a beautiful woman—except when she smiles. I usually think that a smile makes everyone more attractive, but something about Piper's mouth and teeth just becomes all you can see. The amazing thing is that when she smiles, her entire personality becomes enlivened. I think she knows about her mouth, so she reigns in her personality, and then you don't see the real her. And the real Piper is so much more interesting than the restrained version.

In my experience, complimenting a woman implies more interest than I intended, but I had to do it. Someone needed to tell her that she should be herself. "You have the engaging smile. When you relax, you show very well the genuine you."

She brushed it off as nothing, but something in her changed. I watched her slowly relax into that person I'd seen when she grinned at my exercising comment. And, she picked up the question that began the whole conversation. "So I'm the last of the unattacheds... I'm surprised that Crystal went, though. She doesn't date."

"I think she is go with me because Michal ask." The words sounded all wrong, even to my confused ears. But Piper acted as if she understood what I meant.

"Probably." She twirled a noodle on her spoon and gave me a funny look. "Had you heard? The guys are all calling us 'Carol's Belles'…" When I blinked, she added, "You know, like the song."

I didn't know it—not at first. But she tapped a few things onto her mobile and presto! Music I loved filled our little space of the Asian restaurant. The incongruity amused me, but at least she took my smile for recognition rather than mockery. "This song I know. Is beautiful song. Is called in the English, 'Carol of the Bells?' Why are you bells?"

"No, no. Belles—like Southern belles… debutantes…" Her eyebrows drew together in a unibrow that would have pleased even the vilest of villains. "Like beautiful, unmarried women at a dance or something."

"I see." Of course, I didn't. But I would. Google is amazing. Before I went to sleep that night, I would understand, and that's all that mattered.

"So… whose turn is next? Didn't you go out with Crystal first?"

The future in Rockland stretched out before me. Once or twice a week I'd be out with one of the "Belles." And the whole time I'd be wishing I was with Michal. It couldn't happen. *You cannot treat Lloyd, Michal, or their friends like that. If you agree to the date, then be the date.*

And something interesting happened when I decided to focus on Piper—I found myself enjoying it. The art of conversation is something I appreciate, because so few, including myself, have mastered it. Piper had. She knew exactly how to ask questions that didn't feel like a police interrogation. She knew how to share enough of herself without dominating the conversation. Like a Russian bottle dancer, she balanced every aspect with grace and contagious energy.

Empty bowls brought a server to our table with the check. Before I could pick it up, her hand covered mine. "Look, I know you didn't want to do this. I could feel it—at first. Let me get the check."

Embarrassment flooded me. I thought I'd been polite, at least. "No, no. I am happy you agree to come. I have great time with you." The server took the check—and my cash. Piper didn't protest. "I plan to ask if we can walk, maybe around lake in Fairbury. Talk." I stared at my hands as if they'd give me the words that would make her agree. Strange how I hadn't wanted to go on the date at first and by that point, I wanted her to spend *more* time with me.

"Do you really want to go, or are you just being polite?" When I convinced her that I meant it, she stood and held out her hand. "Then let's go. But you'd better ask me out again, or I won't believe you."

"Is date."

Michal—

The best part of Carol's dates was what I called our "debrief" sessions. I'd call and eventually get him to spill everything. It always took a long time—first with him talking about how much he loved life in HearthLand—who knew a guy could get so into milking cows and working in greenhouses? After a long ramble about what was up with the contacts he'd made or when the next shipment of stuff from Romania would go out, I'd manage to weasel out how he chose what he'd do on a date, and finally he'd tell me all about the date. So far, his recounting had hinted that he didn't really enjoy himself, so when he talked about his date with Piper, I couldn't help but get excited.

"So you finally had *fun*. That's great! Are you going out again?"

"She make me promise to ask again—after I go out with other belles."

Ouch—instant dry throat, you know? I choked, sputtered. I swear Carol laughed at me. I hadn't meant for him to find out about our friends' nickname for my project. How mortifying—for both of us! "I…"

"I have to type into the Google for a search. I am very much, the disappointed."

So, have you ever gotten the feeling that you're getting set up to be pranked? That's just how his tone sounded. "Disappointed… how?"

"Your belles don't wear the dresses—big bell-shape dresses like in the pictures. No rippling fabric on the top or bottom."

Look, I know what he *said*, but it sounded like he expected ruffles across the girls' chests and butts. It was just something in the way he phrased it. And I lost it. I tried not to laugh at him. C'mon, it's just mean to laugh at someone for his inability to speak a second language fluently—especially one like English. But when Carol started cracking up with me, I got it.

"Carol, next time I see you, I'm gonna get you."

"Dare you."

It was such an all-American thing that it took me a second to figure out why it sounded so crazy adorable. Then it hit me—the accent. Carol shouldn't be able to pull these kinds of things over on me. I'd have to get him for it.

"You're on. Okay. So what was so great about Piper? I wasn't even sure you'd like her."

"He is intelligent woman—fun. When he has not self-conscious, he is very much the fun person."

It was difficult to follow all of that, but I got the gist. Self-conscious equals awkward. And he's right. Piper is always trying to be serious so she won't smile. But she's a lot of fun when she lets go and just *is*. "Yeah, I get what you mean. So who's next, then?"

"Jenn will not wish to go out with me again. This leaves only Crystal and Therese. But Piper say that Crystal does not much date—date much?"

"Right. It's date much." That's when I had a decision to make—let Carol stay confused about Crystal's decision or tell him and explain it to her later. She'd understand. She's not exactly *hiding* her reasons. She just didn't broadcast them, either. "Look, Crystal isn't *against* dating or anything. It's kind of the opposite."

I heard it. He didn't say anything at all, but his interest became obvious just by the way he became quieter. I hadn't noticed his breathing, but the *lack* of it came through the phone. Then he asked. "Is acceptable for you to tell me?"

"Yeah. She won't care. It'll probably make her feel less freaked out if you guys go out again." Dead silence. Then it hit me. Duh. I'm supposed to be telling him about this thing with Crystal. "Anyway, sorry. So Crystal went through this phase a few years ago. She's always wanted to be the soccer mom type—work from home while the kids are at school and then be a total Pinterest mom when they're home. Well, she was twenty-nine and hadn't been on a date in like *years*. At least two. So, she got a bit desperate and went out with any guy who asked. You've seen her, she gets asked a lot."

"Yes, she is beautiful woman."

I wondered if he meant it. So far he'd found all my friends—even Therese—attractive in some way. Was it because he was just being polite, or did he really think it? I never did manage to bring myself to ask. If he said he was just being polite, then if he ever complimented *me* on anything, I wouldn't believe him. So I chose to live in ignorant bliss.

"I think she went out with like thirty guys in the space of three months. I kid you not; a few times, she had two dates on the same night."

Sometimes it's hard to predict what another person's reaction will be to something, but Carol's, "That is—wow," was a bit all-American for a Romanian dude.

"I know, right? So anyway, a couple of us tried to talk to her, but she really didn't listen. We're talking desperate here. It's so not like her, too. She's one of the most self-confident women I know. But she had a mini-midlife crisis before she even got to mid-life or something."

I can't remember exactly what Carol said—something about how it didn't sound like the girl he'd met, I think. But whatever it was, he sounded confused and almost a little hurt. That didn't make sense. Then he asked the question I needed him to. "So what makes the change for her?"

"We have this friend, Grace. She's just amazing. When she butts into our lives, we know we should listen. So she like prayed for I don't know how long… weeks. Then she invited Crystal over, made one of her famous pot pies, and waited."

I heard it in his voice—eagerness. Curiosity. "She wait? Why?"

"Because sometimes if you just give people time, they'll talk of their own accord. And she did. Crystal explained everything. Told Grace about how she just wanted to be married. How she wanted a husband and family. And then Grace said something so amazing..."

I didn't realize I'd stopped talking. Not until Carol asked, "Michal? Did are you disconnect?"

"No, sorry. I kind of got lost in memories. It was so good for me at the time, too. I'd just broken up with a boyfriend who I'd always known wouldn't work out, and I'd met Lloyd. Man, I liked him, but Lloyd was just recently divorced. He didn't want to jump right into dating. I could tell."

"Is wise decision to let the heart heal."

"That's just what I told him when he confessed that he *wanted* to ask me out but knew he shouldn't! We are so alike sometimes. It's freaky." I was so excited about yet another connection with Carol that I almost forgot about Crystal's story. "Oh—Crystal. Right. Anyway, Grace told her that she needed to learn to be satisfied only with Jesus. That until Jesus could fill her with contentment, she'd never find what she was looking for—even if she *did* meet the right man."

He asked me to repeat it—twice. I didn't know if he really liked what Grace had said or if he thought it was stupid. But then his low, rumbly half-murmur, half-whisper came through the airwaves and made a home in an unused cupboard of my heart. "This is speak to my heart. To have that kind of trust..." A sigh, a groan, and then another sigh. "Michal, this I need to hear as child when I miss my mother so much it hurt to cry—when it hurt because the tears won't come." He swallowed so hard I heard it through the phone. "I need to hear this now when I am torn between home in Romania and HearthLand."

"Oh, Carol..."

"Is beautiful thought," he insisted. "So she decid—ed not to date until she finds the contentment?"

It was so cute to hear him catch little nuances of the English language and correct them himself. He wanted so much to learn it well. "That's right. She decided not to date until she could be truly *content* if she never marries.

I think she's there. I mean, she still has that *desire,* but she is in a good place. She'll accept the life she *has* with thanksgiving if the Lord never brings the right man. She wasn't there even last year."

He said he had to go. "I will call tomorrow. I am glad you tell me. I am glad you ask me to take Piper out. Piper is very nice belle."

"Carol?"

"Yes?"

"I'm so sorry you didn't know Jesus then. I'm so sorry you didn't know He could take the pieces of your heart and make something beautiful and strong again. I'm so sorry I didn't know how to share that with you."

His sob wrenched my heart. "Is good. God knows when is best. He becomes my Father when I need one most. This is good."

"Car—" The phone went dead before I finished saying his name. I don't know when the tears began, but they fell until I couldn't breathe anymore. The mental image of a cold, scared, hungry Carol curled up in one of those horrible orphanage beds, crying for his mother, ripped at my heart. *Lord, he just needs someone to love—someone to show him the love he missed all those years. I know You are enough. I just want everything for him.*

That quiet voice of the Lord—the one that takes His words from our memories and whispers them into our hearts—spoke to me then. *"I have loved you with an everlasting love; Therefore, I have drawn you with lovingkindness. Again I will build you, and you shall be rebuilt."*

Never have I clung to a verse more in my life. I knew the Lord loved Carol more than I ever could—more than anyone ever could. Through His lovingkindness, He had already drawn Carol out of such a horrible past. Even now, the Lord was rebuilding him. I sat there, Mr. Miniver on my lap, tears coursing down my cheeks—tears of joy and gratitude for the Lord's love and mercy.

15

Carol—

Michal's words had wormed their way into my heart as I listened to Crystal's story. Oh, how I wanted that kind of contentment. A lifetime of having little-to-nothing teaches gratitude. Had you asked me if I was content *before* coming to America, I would have been adamant. Of course! I had a job, a way to earn money. I didn't make *much*, but it was enough. Then came the opportunity to come to Rockland—to meet Michal. I remember the guilt I felt for being bothered by a noisy child on the plane. It's not as if noise is unfamiliar to me. I would have told you I was utterly content. I would have lied.

Michal was the source of my discontent, of course. I had considered my unexpected attraction to her to be just that—unexpected and just attraction. It was a lie. I fell more in love with her every day. She was not *available*. But I still found myself thinking of her, praying for her, and wrestling with my thoughts. And that's where the lie came in. I thought my unease had to do with her unavailability—the *dishonor* of allowing myself to care for another man's near-fiancée. It wasn't. That conversation with Michal proved it to me. I was *discontent* with the idea that I could never tell her how I felt—could never hope to capture her heart. I think mine cracked that day.

I did not do the wise thing and focus immediately on trusting that

God had better plans for my life. This is not an easy concept for me. When you've lived through the death of both of your parents, the loss of that kind of loving home, and then the brutality that was life in a Romanian orphanage as a very small child, you must make a conscious effort to remember that God is there and He *does* care.

I also did not do the *honorable* thing and pray for her happiness. I did not focus on how to encourage her in her relationship with Lloyd. I couldn't. I didn't even want to want to do that. I'm not sure that makes sense to anyone but me, but it's the truth.

What I did instead was call Crystal immediately. The mobile rang so long, I expected it to go to voice mail, but she must have a way to decide how long it could ring or something, because she answered it just as I was about to give up.

"Hey! Carol! Sorry it took so long. I was blow drying my hair and didn't hear the phone at first."

"It ring so long, I think you are turn off the voice mail."

"I set it up so it'll go thirty seconds before switching to voice mail. It probably sounds like forever on your end, but if I could get a whole minute, I would. I always leave my phone in the randomest places. It's hard to find it sometimes."

Right then, I made a mental note to ask Ralph how to do that. It would be helpful while working. Sometimes I use my elbow to try to answer it, and half the time, it gets pushed off the table. I'm so glad he bought that heavy-duty case for it. Surely, I'd have broken it by now.

"I call to see if you would like to do something soon. I do not know what for here is best, but…"

"That would be awesome!" My stomach flopped a bit at the genuine excitement in her voice. But when she added, "I want to hear all about your dates!" the uncertainty fizzled.

"There is not much to tell."

"So it's my turn, is it? How do you feel about being Michal's little pet project?" She hesitated, but before I could answer, she added, "She means well, but…"

When you've grown up using lies for survival, they come so naturally you often don't realize you've done it until it's out there. So when I said, "Is fine. I know she wish for me to like to be here—for me to stay," it took a minute to realize that I truly meant it.

"You're a good guy, Carol. Really. I don't know many guys who would put up with it—especially if what I suspect is true."

She let it hang there between us. I didn't know what to say. Did she know? That would be uncomfortable—or it could be, anyway.

"I would not go if I did not wish to. I too am stubborn—is right word? Stubborn? I am *Încăpățânate*. I do not yield if I do not wish."

"That's stubborn all right. You and Michal make an interesting pair, then. She's the most stubborn person I know. It's the only reason she's with Lloyd, if you ask me—too stubborn to admit they're more of a habit than a couple."

Those were not the kinds of words I needed to hear. I needed to hear how happy they were—how much in love. I needed to hear anything that would drive away the temptation to hope. "I think she is love him very much."

"I think she loves the illusion of who they are together. I don't know. Maybe not. You might be right. So, you called to ask me out? Why?"

The abrupt change of subject sent my mind whirling so fast I almost became dizzy. I sat on my bed and glanced around the room. Already it was like home to me—familiar. I had the first selfie Michal had taken of us sitting on the nightstand. Annie teased me about it when she cleaned my room, but I didn't care. Well, I didn't then. I might now.

"Because I think of you as friend already. I think, 'We will have fun again.'" At that moment, a new truth struck me and I added, "And I know now that if you do not wish to go, you will not go. You will not be just the politeness." It sounded wrong, even to my own ears, but nervousness always made my English worse.

"Then let's do it. I can't go anywhere tonight, but I'm free for the next few days—lunch or dinner either. We could go to one of the Rockland museums, if you like. Or maybe walk around Boutique Row—it's our version of Rodeo Drive or the Magnificent Mile. You'll love it. You might even find a store to take your jewelry!"

We settled for Wednesday afternoon—museum, dinner, and then a stroll through Rockland's famous "Boutique Row." I didn't really understand why it would be so wonderful, but even then, I knew it would likely turn out to be my favorite date.

The clock read 9:30 by the time I got off the mobile. A knock on the door told me I'd better hurry downstairs. I was right, too. I could see Andre's shoes from the top of the landing as I jogged downstairs. "I am coming. Is much fun today, yes?"

"Are you really taking us to Storyland?" The question didn't come in the form of eager words from an excited kid. They were more like a challenge—an accusation.

"If you do not wish to go, we can do something else…" Yes, I began to doubt the wisdom of Ralph's suggestion. Maybe it was too childish for a boy like Andre. "There is football game at university today, yes?"

He waited until we got out the door and down the steps before he asked his next question. "Why are you taking us? My mom's not for sale."

I don't know if it was the surprise that came with a boy thinking like that or if I truly didn't understand what he meant at first, but I think the shock I must have shown is what made him apologize. I'd never heard him apologize to anyone—not voluntarily.

"Sorry. I'm not used to people *asking* to spend time with me. Whatever. Let's go. Mom's ready." He gave me a look—one I couldn't interpret—and added, "She's fixing her makeup and stuff. Tell her she looks pretty, okay? She's nervous."

She's not the only one, Andre…

"… he went on the Lilipppttht. I do not remember how is said."

"Lilliputian ride? The one where weird mirrors make everything seem huge compared to you? That thing is so freaky!"

"He scream, and then Andre say, 'Mom, you are wuss. You scream like girl.'"

"Um... she is a girl."

It felt good just to let loose and laugh. "He... how you say...? Like a ball?"

"Rolled up? Balled up?"

"*Da!* Is like that. Hands over the ears. I tell her. I say, 'You do not see the fun if you cover the eyes! But he stay hide.'" For some inexplicable reason, I found myself sharing the whole story—even the part that still embarrassed me. "Andre is laugh. She give me wave from in front and scream, 'Put your arm around her. She is scare!' So I do it, and Lavonne... um... how you say, 'cannot move'?"

"She froze?"

"Yes! He froze. The ride, it stop, and the man come to help new people in little cars. But Lavonne, he cannot move. Man has to help me carry her from ride."

Crystal's laughter—it's a beautiful sound. You could hear it as we walked through the halls of the Pennsylvania Avenue museum. "I think that's one of the best first date stories I've ever heard. Are you going to ask her out again?"

Some questions are difficult to answer, not because of their complexity or because you don't *have* an answer. They're difficult because you don't *like* the answer. "I don't know. Maybe I go. Maybe instead I pray God brings good man to her. I don't know."

I stood in the "oval office" and stared at a replica of the desk American presidents have used for I didn't know how long. Was it George Washington's desk? I forgot to ask. I remembered Michal once writing that George Washington was the best president the United States has ever had because he didn't *do* anything. He left the country alone. I don't know if she was right, but I remembered reading it, and it made me wonder about it again.

One room had a replica of the signing of the Declaration of Independence. Romania has only regained independence in my lifetime.

My parents— I must have sucked in air, because Crystal took my hand and held it. My eyes met hers and I whispered, "Thank you."

"It's a bit overwhelming for Americans when we really think about it. With your independence so recent…"

I think I cried. I don't remember. I remember rambling about the price of freedom and overthrowing tyranny. "My parents die in revolution. The *doamnă* at my *orfelinatul* say he is not know why. I think he think they are loyal to Ceaușescu. I do not think this. I think they protest and are shot. I remember *Mamica* kiss me when she leave me with old woman. I do not know woman. He is probably neighbor. *Tata* and *Mamica* they do not come home. Old woman take me to the *orfelinatul* outside Constanța and say, 'His parents have die in revolution. He is yours to have the responsibility.'"

After that, I couldn't see anything else in the museum. Crystal sensed it and urged me to take her to eat early. "We'll miss the rush that way. Then we can still do some real shopping. I want your input on a cool sweater for Michal. It's not really a color she wears much, but I think it would look fabulous on her."

Rain beat down on us as we stepped from the museum. The car was half a block down and across the street in a parking garage. We ran, umbrella over our heads and doing little to shield us from the downpour, dashing across the street with speed that I never knew women could achieve in heels like Crystal's. Our laughter echoed in the half-empty parking garage as we arrived at my car. When I unlocked her door and opened it for her, a pang of disappointment hit me. *I should be attracted to her. This is where I should tell her that she is beautiful with raindrops on her hair and coat. I should kiss her and lose myself in the wonder that is love. Instead, I smile, hand her the closed umbrella and admonish her not to get the water all over her clothes. Whoever wrote that love is pain told a terrible truth.*

Crystal didn't notice, or if she did, she said nothing. Instead, she told me funny stories about Michal's first date, their prom night, and the college boyfriend that Michal found making out with a college professor in their third year. "Yeah, that one was brutal. It's one thing to have a disastrous first date or a prom where everything is so perfect it's boring, but what a kick in the gut to catch your professor and your boyfriend backstage after his theater class. She still doesn't know if she got an A because she earned it or because Professor Strout was afraid of being reported."

"I do not know that he take the class in theater. I thought Michal say he is 'dismal failure' in high school play."

It took a couple of minutes before Crystal could explain. She had to direct me through traffic, down a side street, and back onto Waterbrook Drive so we could avoid a traffic jam first. "She was. I really thought she'd do it too—take another class or two in college just because she's stubborn that way. She won't let anything get her down. But she never did." A gasp. Wide eyes. Crystal turned to me and gripped my arm. "I bet that creep Daniel told her not to—talked her out of it *so he could have a safe place to meet that 'hussy of a professor,'* like my grandma called her*!* Oh, wow. I never realized that's what it must have been. That's crazy."

"The Michal I think I know would hear 'do not do this' and decide she must." It was truer than even Michal probably wanted to admit. Crystal agreed.

"That's how I know her too, but it's the only way she wouldn't do it—if he convinced her that he'd be embarrassed or something. Oh!" She pointed to a sign ahead. "Pull in there. The restaurant is behind that hotel. It's faster to go through this way."

I waited until we were seated—until our drink order was taken, and then I made my confession. "Michal write me those stories—the first date with Terry Hopkins and how the braces get stuck together when she try to kiss her, the prom where her 'friend' Crystal was the date and he is disappointment because he cannot kiss Crystal goodnight. She say, 'Prom night should end with kiss.' She never tell me about professor and boyfriend, though. I wonder why."

"It must sound weird now—all those stories you thought were about a guy are really about a girl." Crystal's eyes widened and she nearly spewed her drink across the table. Instead, she choked it down and then coughed until it went down the right way. "You thought she wanted to kiss *me!* That's so funny!"

It's an unusual thing to have something to reminisce over with a new friend. I knew so many of Crystal's stories of Michal, and yet I'd never been there. She sounded apologetic when she brought up Michal and Lloyd's first date. At first, I thought she'd figured out my secret, but then she confessed her true opinion.

"I really like Lloyd. He's a great guy. I mean, if I wasn't sworn off men right now, I'd easily fall in love with him myself—if he were available, of course. But I never see that...*something* I want to see in her. I guess that's selfish, though, isn't it?"

She handed me the perfect opportunity to confess that I knew about her dating situation. So, I seized it and ran with it. "She tell me about your decision. She say, 'Crystal is wait for contentment in Jesus. Then she date.'" My hands gripped the bench I sat on and held it until I couldn't feel my fingers, but I made myself meet her gaze. "You are wise."

I think she did understand then. I saw compassion, understanding, *strength* in her eyes. She brushed a piece of hair from her face with the kind of grace and elegance that usually belongs in a movie—in one of those scenes where that simple action works its way into a man's heart and grows into love.

She said only five words. "I'll pray for you, Carol."

16

Carol—

The Hearth & Pantry—HearthLand's "general store" as Ralph called it. I had a crate of milk quarts for it. Annie didn't need to be carrying those things if I could help. So, with my mobile propped between the jars, I carried it out of the house, still talking to Michal about my date with Crystal. "Then we go walk down the Boutique Row. The rain, it stop while we shop. I tell her, I say, 'This is a gift from God.'" The memory of her smile made me wish, not for the first time, that I could learn to care for her. "She say, 'I need to write that down.'"

"Yeah, I bet she loved that. She doesn't do a lot of journaling—writing of any kind, really. But I got her a small journal last year—about half the size of most you see. I thought she might use it for Bible study notes or something, but she writes down one special thing about each day. Almost like a gratitude journal, but not. It's more like learning to observe the little things."

"Is nice idea. I should write the observations in the journal you give me." It seemed like the best time, so I told her about my conversation with Crystal. "I tell her we talk about how she not date. So, then she talk about your first date. Is funny story when I remember that I think you are boy with big crush on girl when I read about it." I had to set down the box to open the door to the Hearth & Pantry, so I talked louder. "The Boutique

Row is beautiful place. I enjoy very much the shops."

"They have so much character. I just love those old buildings. And they keep it up so nice. Are the Christmas decorations up yet?"

"Some shops they have the decorations. One bookstore man say, 'I will not decorate until after the midnight on Thanksgiving. I will not take away from the holiday.' Crystal look pleased by that."

Ramiro came forward to help me with the box. I took the mobile and nodded my thanks, while Michal laughed and shared a few of Crystal's more extreme rants against the encroachment of Christmas on other holidays. "She doesn't even *like* Halloween that much. She thinks it's gotten too icky. But man, when you can pick up candy for the trick-or-treaters and then pivot in the aisle to grab candy canes, she has a point, you know?"

I didn't know. I had no clue. But Ramiro nodded as if everything Michal said made perfect sense. "I am sorry. I do not understand. I hope very soon to, though. Crystal say she will take me to see stores where Thanksgiving holiday is ignore."

"Oh... so you're going out with her again?"

This time, Ramiro raised an eyebrow and smirked. I knew what he thought. I didn't know how to explain without making the conversation any more complicated than it already was. Instead, I saw some of the candles she'd asked me about and changed the subject. "Do still you want the candles from the farm? The ones in the jars? Again, Ramiro has them in the store."

"Please! That would be great. I'll pay you for them... what, Thursday? Are we still doing lunch and then a tour of my office? I tried to get Lloyd to come with us, but he has a group practice meeting."

With three of the candles in hand, I moved to the register to pay for them as I assured her she wouldn't be without her candles for long. "I will come Thursday. I will bring the candles and candy from The Confectionary. Is your favorite, yes?"

"You're the best. Oh! Gotta go. Boss needs me. Bye!"

The mobile went dead in my hand. "I think he is gone."

"Wow, man. You are one hot item around here. Every time I speak to you, you have *another* date. Maybe I should send my little brother with you to learn some moves or something."

"I only have the date because he is ask. He thinks I am too much alone. I tell her, I say, 'I have new friends in the HearthLand. I talk to you every day. I do not need more dates. Still he is—what is word? It mean won't stop the trying."

"Determined?"

It's so nice when people understand me. I'd go crazy otherwise. Sometimes the words come quickly, and other times, they elude me until I want to pound something in frustration. "*Da*! That is word. He is determine I will not be alone when I am not with her."

The snicker—I knew what it meant. Before he could tell me or apologize, I asked. "Which is the way? He is determine or *she* is?"

"She. She and her go together and he and him do." Ramiro handed me a receipt to sign—I could pay when Michal paid for them. While I did, he frowned. "Why do you sign your last name first? I know Ralph and Zain have wondered about that. Is it a Romanian thing?"

I decided it was time to explain. At first, I didn't understand if it was an American thing or not. Sometimes I heard Americans call others just by their last name. But by the time I realized that they really did think my name was Stefan, I didn't know how to correct them without being rude. "Is not last name. I am Carol Stefan. I do not remember the last name when I am taken to orphanage. I am too small. I tell them, 'My *tata* is Stefan.' So they give me my *tata*'s name as surname."

Ramiro stepped back for a second as if my words physically shoved him. "Why didn't you say anything? I—I'm sorry. I've never seen a guy with your name spelled the way yours is."

"Carol is name of two of our kings. Is good name."

I must have sounded defensive, because Ramiro began apologizing. Stopping him didn't prove easy. He wanted to call Ralph, but that just sounded even more awkward to me. So, I just shrugged and tried to pull the subject back to Michal and her friends. "Do you know her friends call the girls, 'Carol's Belles'? I do not know what this mean at first. But now is funny."

"Oh! Like 'The Carol of the Bells.' Good one." His hands stopped moving, his eyes searching my face for something. "You know she's just trying to set you up, right? She's trying to get you a girlfriend. She probably thinks you'll stay longer if you meet someone."

I hadn't realized it—not at first. But it had become readily apparent after each phone call where she wanted to know every detail—every second and how I *felt* about it. Even Lloyd had joked about her turning it into a therapy session the last time he'd been there.

"Yes, this I know. But he is friend—good friend. *She*— " I winked as I saw Ramiro's head shake. "—she is reason I stop doing the bad things as young man. I think, 'My friend Michal will be the disappointment with me. I will not do this.'" A smile grew before I could stop it. "Of course, that is when I think she is he." My lungs nearly exploded while I waited for Ramiro to nod—to show I had said the words correctly this time. "I cannot say no."

"But you can!" Ramiro's voice, overloud for the store, dropped again. "You don't have to do this unless you want to, and it seems to me that you'd rather—"

Ramiro cut himself off, and I knew why. He was going to say I would rather go out with *her* instead. He realized how much that must hurt me, I believe. And he was correct, of course. His concern bothered me, though. It was only a matter of time before he decided to say something to someone. And someone would eventually tell the right person, who would then say something to Michal. I'd seen it already in some of the conversations between Michal's friends.

So, I said what I wanted to be true—what was *almost* true. "Of courses, I *can* say no. I can. Michal would be understanding. I will not do this, though. Michal knows me. She maybe knows that one of these women has something..." I didn't know how to express it. "Something I cannot see? And she is my friend. If I can make friend happy, I will do this."

The walk back to Ralph's house, with a little shopping bag of candles in one hand and the crate in another, sent my mind whirling in multiple directions. Ramiro had poked at something I'd wrestled with since the second date. In the kitchen, Annie made something. She did that often—worked in his kitchen. And when he wasn't home, she'd clean the house. How many times had I seen him grab a cloth and a spray bottle to go clean something and return almost perplexed? He *knew* she did it, but he never seemed to grasp why. Their relationship perplexed *me!*

I just dropped off the empty crate and hurried up to my room. I could write it down. Maybe it would help to show her if it became awkward. I could write better on paper than I could explain—even if I had to translate it again in my broken English. When I realized *all* I wanted to write, I knew I'd *have* to write in Romanian. To try to write it in English would give away much more than I was comfortable sharing.

I love this place. I love the people and their connections. I think Michal knows this better than I realized. It's why she keeps setting me up on these dates. And of course, if she asks, I cannot say no. She is my friend. For years, she has done so much to give me hope—a deeper connection with any person that I've had since Mamica died. I can do this for her. So she asks me, "Can you take out so-and-so again?" and I do.

The hardest part is that I think the girls like me. I treat them well. Jenn is uncomfortable with my faith, but even she likes me. She wishes I were a Baptist—or something other than 'Catholic.' To her, Orthodox is the same as Roman Catholic, and Roman Catholic is bad. Crystal understands me. She has told Michal that she thinks I am only going out with these girls to please Michal. She is an astute woman. But Michal was sure that I enjoyed it—that I wanted to find a girlfriend as much as she did. She told Crystal, "Oh, no. That can't be it. He doesn't always like the girl, but I can tell he likes the process." But Crystal argued. She said, "He will call and ask me out, and I'll think it's just him until I talk to you and realize you put him up to it—again. You need to stop, Michal." As Crystal told me that, I flushed so deeply I thought she'd say something. But she just held my hand, smiled, and led me into another store. Why cannot I fall in love with Crystal? Why does my heart not listen to my head? Ralph said in their church meeting last week that love is a choice. I don't believe it. If love is a choice, why cannot I choose to love who I wish? Why does my heart love the one I know it shouldn't?

How can I tell either of them that I go because she asks and I cannot say no? It would be wonderful if some other woman could drive thoughts and feelings for Michal out of my mind—out of my heart. It is a terrible thing to love someone who is not free for you to love. So, I work every day. I try to be the loving brother *to her. I fail. Brothers do not remember the way their sisters laugh at a joke or touch their faces. A brother would not be thankful for a crowded elevator because it allows him the opportunity to inhale the scent of his sister's hair.*

Yes, I try to treat her as I would want some man to treat my sister. But my heart calls me a liar. I do not want her for my sister, and I cannot have her as my sweetheart. So another crack fractures another piece of my heart.

Michal—

The shrimp linguine bake filled the kitchen with tantalizing scents just as I heard Lloyd's key in the lock. *Timing couldn't be better. Yes!*

"In here. Dinner just came out of the oven!"

Hands around my waist. Chin on my shoulder. The way his lips brushed my jaw—*man, I love this guy.* "Smells amazing." His lips tickled my ear.

Okay, I love it when he does that. "Yeah. Crystal—"

"No... I was talking about you, but that's not too bad either."

He loves me. It's the little things, you know? The little things show it. The looks, the small remembrances, the moments when you realize that you can be one hundred percent *you* around this person. That defined Lloyd.

Lettuce and gang abandoned on the counter, I turned to wrap my arms around his neck. Our kiss sent tingles through my lips. "Hungry?"

"That's a dangerous question, but yeah. I'd like to eat." He loosened his tie. "I brought a change of clothes. Be right back."

As I tossed the salad, I gave him an update on Carol's latest news. "Hey! Guess what? The Romanian stuff is selling like hotcakes!"

"Yeah?" Lloyd's voice was too loud for my room. He had to be in the guest bath. That meant I didn't have to shout as loud—a blessing when the walls are stupid thin.

"Yeah. The stuff is flying off the shelves. And the new shipment—the one they sent by boat? It docked in New York last week. Isn't that fabulous? They've already sold out of so much stuff. And he's making jewelry round the clock it seems."

Lloyd met me at the table and took the dish from me. "I thought he was going out every other night. How can he be doing both?"

"Well, you know what I mean. He's just making stuff left and right. Hang on…" I dashed for my phone. "Look at this." No matter how many times I'd seen it that day, the slave bracelet still astounded me. "I love this thing. I've never liked them, but this is amazing."

His response shouldn't have been a surprise, but it was. "Should I ask him to save it for me for your Christmas present?"

Okay, I still don't know whether I'm more surprised that I said no, or at the look of relief in Lloyd's eyes. I stared, trying to figure it out—even as he prayed over the food. *What is it? Do you already have my present?* The idea of a repeat proposal occurred to me, but the look on Lloyd's face didn't show it. I didn't know *what* was up.

He spoke between mouthfuls. "So what are they going to do?"

"They're going to start bringing over the craftsmen one at a time. I think the potter is coming first. They're still working on the glass blower, but the carver…"

Dinner revolved around Carol and the upcoming Thanksgiving fundraiser. Our organization has found that for the kind of work we do, having a big fundraiser near Thanksgiving sparks people's generosity much more than Christmas does. Christmas is the time for reminders of last-minute gift and/or tax deductions.

You know, Lloyd's used to my rambles like that. But Even someone as understanding as Lloyd would get tired of work discussions or my rambles about my friend. It was *our* time, and as usual, I got caught up in excitement over a new project. Thankfully, I know just how to make it up to him. I mean, he's a guy. People say guys aren't the "touchy, feely" sorts. I say that's garbage. Let your lips do the touching and the feeling and they're *really* into it.

Don't believe me? Look, anytime I try to get emotional about things, he turns it into a massive make out session. There's a reason I limit my emotional vulnerability with him. Which, if you think about it, is kind of bizarre since he does know me so well. You'd think he'd get that. He's not quite perfect, but he's so close, I overlook the rest, you know? Overlook it and leave baring my soul to friends. I don't want to resent him for turning my vulnerable moments into something merely physical.

We settled for a movie—after I cleared the table and loaded the dishwasher. You know, sometimes I get why people say we're too boring. But, they also aren't around when we're supposed to be watching *Inception* and end up making out on the couch instead. And, yeah. The irony isn't lost on me—complaining about him turning everything physical and then making up to him with a make-out session. Yeah. I know.

"Your lips are scary weapons, Michal…"

Yeah… it might be time to start considering something permanent. Moments like that remind me that there are reasons to actually get married rather than just spend a few years talking about it.

17

Michal—

Soft music, gentle lighting, people milling about creating a low din—hallmarks of the *beginning* of a successful fundraiser. Of course, without Lloyd there I wouldn't feel like I succeeded at anything. He'd been there for the first. And, if I had my way, he'd be there for the last.

A few women nearby began making comments that made the new arrival sound like the only piece of chocolate left in Fairbury's Confectionary. Even without turning to look, I knew it had to be Carol. But look, Carol in a suit is one thing. Carol in a *tux* is a much more dangerous dude. But as our eyes met, I sensed it. Something had happened—something good.

"Hey! What's up? You beat Lloyd."

The second I saw relief wash over him, I dragged him to the corner of the room. "Okay. Spill it."

"What is spill? I should go get a cloth to dry?"

I almost fell for it. The guy can make the most obvious jokes seem serious. "Okay, now you have to talk about life in the orphanage for that—and what we can do to help. Maybe explain the apprenticeship idea."

If I'd thought he would object, I couldn't have been more wrong. He nodded and then grinned. "I have talk with Ralph again. He is promise to let me have upstairs of community center if I will stay. He will put small kitchen in one of the rooms."

"That's great! And aren't there a couple of bedrooms there? You could totally have a place for the other guild artists, too!"

Of course, before we could talk about it anymore, half a dozen people showed up to be introduced. I think that's when I realized what a "people person" Carol is. He comes off as reserved—shy even. You'd think he'd be a total introvert, but he comes alive when people talk to him. They asked about the program, about his life there. I nearly choked one woman.

"So, how did your adoptive parents deal with things like RAD? Isn't it pretty serious? You seem so well-adjusted; they must have done a lot of intensive therapy or..."

Carol blinked, confused. "I do not know what is RAD. My parents die in revolution."

The woman—then I remembered her name. Paulson. She came to any fundraiser that had even the most remote Christian connections and grilled the coordinators on theology, use of funds—anything. I think she thinks she's some kind of one-woman charity watchdog organization. Anyway, she kind of went off on both of us.

"So he isn't an American, Miss Hargrave? You expect people to donate to a—"

"I expect nothing, Mrs. Paulson. If helping Romanian orphans isn't what God has called you to do, then I would hope you wouldn't. As for Carol, having lived most of his life in an orphanage, he is uniquely suited to give accurate insights into the actual needs there. Excuse us. We have a few things to discuss about tonight's event. I'm sure you understand."

"Well—"

Look, with people like that, you have to act like they've done you a favor and move. So, we did—closer to the podium. "Sorry about that. That woman's spiritual gift is annoying the body of Christ."

"I think very hard I would pray for new gift."

Okay, that killer smile of his—totally makes sense why all my friends were crushing on him. It's like junior high all over again, but now we're actually *allowed* to date. Even I had to remind myself that I had a great boyfriend that I loved when he did stuff like that.

"So what did Ralph suggest? Extended work visa or residential?"

"He say I have to have extended visa because I have no family here to sponsor me. Will take years of wait in Romania for residential. He offer me official job. Zain make the paperwork for me yesterday so I can apply. Then I start residential process."

"Aaaaannnd? Will you?"

He pulled out a manila envelope and passed it to me.

For the record, I didn't even need to open the envelope. Trust me. Didn't need to at *all*. The excited look in his eyes, the smile he couldn't possibly repress despite his pathetic attempts at trying—all of it told me he'd already done it. And sure enough, the second I pulled out the duplicate copies of his forms, I lost it. Even knowing it was coming, I totally lost it.

I think the whole room heard me squeal. I know most of them saw me hug him—kiss his cheek. Then I saw him—Lloyd. He crossed the room with a look on his face that I've never seen. Confusion? Anger? Caution? A bunch of possibilities presented themselves, but I couldn't figure it out.

It doesn't always matter if you understand something right away. I mean, he hugged me, kissed me longer than he's ever done in front of our friends or in public, and wrapped an arm around my waist. "So what are we celebrating besides the new project?"

"Carol's staying! Isn't that fabulous? We'll be able to shamelessly use him for all our promotional needs."

Some other expression chiseled itself into his face, but this time I knew what it was. Resolve.

Carol—

Americans have a unique way of raising money. They spend thousands of dollars on an "event" to raise more money. It's an "investment" into the cause. Our guild does things quite differently. When we need money to rent a space or something for an exhibit, we have an outdoor show so people can see what we do. They buy, we pool our money, we rent the space, and we make more money. Michal says it's the same thing. I don't quite understand, but throughout the night, she'd text me the latest in donations, and every time she'd add, AND WE HAVEN'T EVEN MADE OUR PRESENTATION YET. I think it was meant to imply that once people had relaxed, were happy and fed, and heard how amazing her idea was, they'd be even more inclined to give.

I don't like to criticize, but I have to wonder why the same people wouldn't read a letter, see the need, and send a check. That seems to me a much more efficient way to raise money than the elaborate affair she'd planned. However, the dinner and power point show was, at least for everyone else there, much more entertaining than a letter.

Those power point slides cut deep every time I forgot to ignore the giant screen behind the lectern at one end of the room. I didn't know where she'd gotten the pictures, but they were both horribly accurate and unfortunately outdated. I remembered things being that bad. They were. But it had improved much by the time I left. Fifteen years later, things weren't anything like the old days. Much still needed to change, it's true. But the stark, cold, harsh institutions had slowly improved.

Anger began to rise within me as I watched those pictures rotate one after the other. *They are exploiting the past for today's gain. It is wrong. How I can I explain the changes without making Michal appear to be dishonest. She cannot know what has happened.*

A man stepped up to the lectern. I expected the images to cease—or at least become warped with his body blocking part of them, but the images remained undistorted...each one shifting every ten to fifteen seconds. He called Michal to the front, talking about her dedication to this project and how she would share her inspiration. I just listened—listened and prayed I would not say something rude. They meant well, these people. But with each passing second, the feeling of betrayal intensified.

Michal's voice filled the room—rich, warm, emotional. The Michal I'd seen in my letters. She thanked everyone for coming, but instead of laying out her plan for her new project, she looked my way, smiled, and launched into a story. Our story.

"Picture it—nine years old. Fourth grade. It's a Monday morning, and we learn we're going to be writing to kids in Romania as a pen pal project. We're allowed to bring a picture to school to include with our letter. I, of course, had just received back my school pictures. You know, those things they schedule for mid-morning—right after recess, when you look like you've been dragged from bed by a hurricane?"

A slow ripple of quiet laughter filled the room. One man with unruly locks that looked like static and curls had conspired to give him the world's most memorable hairstyle of all shouted, "Don't you know it!"

That quick flip of her hair over her shoulder. How had I been in America long enough to see that as a familiar gesture? She leaned forward and gripped the lectern. "Yeah. So my mom gave me this picture of me from little league—in summer. When I was nine. You know, and my hair is short for the heat? Curling all around the edge of the hat, but let's face it. I looked like a shaggy boy. So off my letter signed, *Michal* went to Romania. I got a reply from a sweet 'girl.'" She made air quotes with hyper-exaggerated gestures. "A sweet *girl* named Carol."

Emotion filled her voice. A lump rose in my throat as I watched her struggle to choke back tears. "I cried when I got that first letter. I don't think Carol knows that. I doubt I ever told him. Yes. *Him.* Imagine my surprise when I arrived at the airport a couple of months ago, ready to take her to meet all my friends for a girls' night, and she's a *he!*"

Again, the room erupted in laughter, but this time they all stared at me. I shrugged. "What can I say? A man will do anything to get to know beautiful woman."

She beamed at me before continuing. "Can you imagine what our letters were like? He was always saying just the right thing. Sometimes a joke, sometimes something so poetic it made my heart ache. Carol has such an artist's soul."

Right there, Lloyd's stiffened and his fists balled up at his sides.

"But sprinkled among stories about how he wrote the best short story

149

or how he dominated the 'football' game, were rare and insightful glimpses into a life that I couldn't imagine. I cried over those letters. I cried over a Romanian orphan whose only friend wouldn't speak to him if anyone else was around. Orphans are outcasts in Romania—especially those of Roma descent. Hearing him exult because someone dropped a packet of sausages—and him eating them *raw* because he had no way to cook them. It broke my heart."

Emotions welled up in me. I had meant to send entertaining and joyful stories. I had no idea that she would be so distraught over what I saw as good fortune. My arms ached to hold her as she struggled with pain-laced emotions. Emotions I had caused.

"But I just learned recently how much he kept from me. Years of things he feared would make me reject him. The things these kids have to do to survive are appalling."

Statistics flew. The seventy-thousand-plus "orphans" in the Romanian system. The tens of thousands more on the streets. How many of those orphans actually have parents—some who visit the child once a year or so. The homelessness. The drugs. The terrible fact that prostitution is preferable to the fate that many face—exported out of the country as sex slaves.

I glanced at my hands, stunned that they didn't shake. Every finger hung straight and steady, but my entire body shook inside as I listened to her talk about the babies who were never rocked, never held. I wept for the little boy I had once been—the things I'd done to survive. All without shedding a tear.

A new picture appeared—one that hadn't been a part of the carousel of photos before. It showed aid workers coming in after the revolution, and Michal spoke of the changes that took place after the fall of Ceaușescu. One by one, she showed changes—such as the school I'd attended, children being adopted by Americans and Europeans.

"Many improvements have been made over the past twenty years. *Many.* But there are still tens of thousands of 'orphans'—unadoptable children because their families will not release them or raise them—

150

roaming the streets and selling themselves to eat. There are still babies living in hospitals until the age of two before being transferred to places like this."

The photo changed to a picture of my old orphanage. My heart constricted as I stared at one of the windows—the one I'd often looked out of at night while trying to write my letters to her. All the anger I'd felt melted as I realized what she'd done. She showed the old and the first round of improvements—prove the money won't be wasted. It was a brilliant idea.

"These children are fed, clothed, but not loved. The psychological trauma and physical abuse at the hands of people inside and outside the system is almost irreparable in some of these children. Others are aged out at eighteen. They have very little education, no training, no life skills, and often don't even know the basics of good hygiene. These are the children we're asking you to support."

And the plan unfolded. Apprenticeships, week-long workshops on basics that, had I not had the blessing of a supportive church in America, I would have needed. Her plan had expanded far beyond anything I could have imagined. It was thorough, comprehensive, and probably impossible. People wouldn't have the time or money to do all that was involved.

"—the most important part of this plan is the way the money is distributed. We will be sure to purchase needed supplies from vendors in Romania—preferably from as many individuals or small businesses as we can. This helps the local economy, and hopefully we can slowly change the bias against orphans if they see love demonstrated *through* the locals instead of from outside the country."

Her boss wandered through the audience allowing guests to ask questions. Some, he asked me to answer, but most were fielded to Michal. The flair she showed—steadfastness with a dash of zest, I heard Lloyd call it. It's a good description for her.

But when pledges started rolling in—some for different businesses, others anonymously—everything changed. Lloyd scribbled something on his program and made his way to the front. Michal beamed.

There were times I wondered about them as a couple. Most of the time they seemed deeply committed to each other—very much in love. Other times, though. They seemed... *there*. As if their love was for the relationship instead of each other. But the look on Michal's face right then spoke of love and joy.

"Isn't he handsome? This is my fabulous boyfriend, Lloyd, who was late due to some emergency at his office. What was it today? Did another toddler stick a tiny battery up his nose—those are scary things, folks—or did some guy come in with a cold—just certain he was dying? C'mon," she joked. "You know it's true. 'My nose is running. My brains are just dripping...'" Her nose wrinkled. We could see it even from across the room. "Never mind."

Lloyd took it in better humor than I would. I love to tease as much as the next person, but such public teasing felt a bit more like mockery. But then, somehow, I don't think she would have done it with me. So, maybe it was just a dynamic of their relationship that I couldn't understand.

Without taking his eyes from her, he passed her the program. Her eyes widened, her lips parted. No woman who has ever received any gift has ever looked more stunned or thrilled. Then Lloyd stunned me as well as the rest of the room. He dropped to one knee, took her hand, and, in front of all of us, asked her to marry him.

Noooooo that is not how to do it. Give her the gift of intimacy—of a cherished, private moment. This is cheap!

"I didn't bring a ring. I've been waiting for that moment—that perfect moment that would show you just how much you mean to me. And, this event, for something I know means so much to you seemed to say, 'Now. Now she'll know just how committed you are to her and all that is important to her."

She won't do it. You've put her in an impossible position. If she says no, she is an ungrateful person. If she says yes, did she mean it or was she trying to be gracious? How will you ever know?

How it happened, I've never understood. One moment she stood there shocked, the other she jerked him to his feet and flung her arms around him. In slow circles that twisted my heart and cracked it again, he spun her. "Well, is there an answer in that hug somewhere?"

"Yes! Sorry! I am just so happy. Yes!"

Their kiss—anyone who saw that kiss couldn't doubt their love. I had to turn away before someone saw *my* face. I knew—just as sure as I knew my feelings for her had grown from friendship to attraction and attraction to love—if anyone saw my expression, they'd learn my secret. *And it's a secret you must keep to yourself now. God will give you strength.*

Michal—

Nothing could have been more amazing than a proposal at the event. Does Lloyd know me or *what?* And the check? Five thousand dollars toward the orphan project. How cool is that? Of course, the next morning, he insisted on taking me shopping for a ring. That's just the kind of guy he is.

"I've had the money set aside for two years. It's time to spend it before I decide I want a vacation in Borneo instead." Or that's what he claimed. We both know he'd never do it, but it sounds nice and threatening, doesn't it?

So, we ended up on Boutique Row in Rockland. I wanted to go to the mall or some little store in Brunswick—keep the money local, you know? But, Lloyd has always tried to pamper me, and it would be a lot cooler to take our kids down the row and point out a store there than to wave at a little place in a strip mall and say, "That's where Daddy bought this ring."

Part of me protested the idea. I mean, it does sound a little arrogant—snooty, you know? But Lloyd is all about making memories and that's one of the things I love about him. I can't exactly say I love how he does that and then *complain* about how he does it. That's complicated and convoluted even for me.

Near the Row is Bridal Aisle—a street almost exclusively devoted to businesses catering to the wedding industry. If we didn't find anything in one place, surely the other…

Just in case you didn't know, shopping for rings when you thought you knew what you liked and then discover that you don't—unsettling at best. I have always been a big fan of the princess cut. But as I turned my hand in the light, imagining it in our engagement photos, our wedding photos, family photos for decades… Something just didn't sit well with me. "What do you think?"

Lloyd's arms slipped around my waist and his chin rested on my shoulder. "It's stunning, but my question is, 'What do *you* think?'"

I held it out, fingers splayed. "Maybe it's just bigger than I imagined."

"Well, I'm not buying you a cheap ring. You deserve the best."

The woman behind the counter beamed with an eagerness that hinted that she loved her job. "We have a number of quality rings with smaller settings if you think you'd like to try one. Or perhaps a different cut? Marquise, asscher, brilliant, pear…"

Lloyd requested a good princess cut in a smaller stone—in platinum. "Let's see what smaller looks like, but I don't want you to settle."

Three princess cuts later, I shook my head. "They're all pretty."

"But not what you want. Okay, so… oval?"

A man stepped up and the woman shifted to the left. He took my hand, turned it over in his, and flipped it back with a smoothness that almost felt… intimate. Lloyd sure didn't like it. But then the man nodded and walked away. The woman grinned. "That was Tobias. He'll be back." She leaned forward, glanced around her, and whispered only when she obviously felt as if no one was watching, "Every once in a while, he sees someone on the camera and comes out. When he does… it's magic."

I don't know for sure, but I think I heard Lloyd mutter, "It's creepy. That's what it is."

But less than two minutes later, Tobias showed up with a tray holding only three rings—none of which I would have chosen. But he looked like a kid who has created a grand scheme that he just *knew* would work.

"I have my guess…" Tobias whispered something to the woman.

"Let's see if I am finally wrong."

"I doubt it," she muttered. The woman's eyes met mine. "He's nailed every single one."

I could hear Lloyd's thoughts as if he shouted them. *It's easy when you almost never help a customer. You can stack the deck.*

I pulled out the first ring and slid it on my finger. It sparkled, shimmered, it looked like it belonged in a bridal magazine as "Timeless beauty." Lloyd murmured his approval, and I couldn't argue. "It is amazing, isn't it?"

A man walked into the store—business suit, polished shoes, sunglasses that cost more than my purse—and my mom has a *thing* for buying me a designer purse every Christmas. I know expensive purses!

Lloyd nodded a greeting. I smiled. The man apologized for interrupting, asked if we'd mind if he spoke to the saleswoman, and thanked us when we said yes. I got the feeling he was the kind of customer that they couldn't refuse. You know, the ones who spend a fortune in there.

I got the first part right.

Everything happened in a blur. The man reached into his jacket pocket, pulled something out, and murmured something to the woman as he showed it to her. Her hands trembled. Her voice shook. Just a whisper— I couldn't hear what she said. But she pulled out a gift bag, grabbed everything in sight, and began dumping it in the bag.

Then I heard him murmur, "There's no reason to be nervous. I have no intention of hurting anyone unless I have to."

She began to reach for the rings in the tray before us when the man stopped her. He turned to us. "Do you like the one on your finger, or would you prefer one of these?"

My jaw dropped. The politeness never left his voice, but his eyes grew hard and cold. "I am afraid you have to decide now. Which one do you prefer? I think the one on your hand is perfect for your fingers, but it's not my choice."

Suddenly, I hated the other two rings. I can't say why. I didn't even want to try them on. My other hand began working the ring off my finger as I nodded. "I like it, too." How did I ever choke out the words? They sounded so calm. Carefree—compared to how I felt, anyway.

"Then you should keep that one." As he took the bag of jewelry from the saleswoman, he added, "You should give them a discount—for the mental strain of this ordeal. Have a lovely day. Tell the officers I'm sorry they came out for nothing."

It happened in less than a minute, I think. No more than two. There were cases untouched, but he'd gotten what he came for, I suppose. Lloyd tried to run after him—to see where he went or something, but the minute the man stepped from the jewelry store, he vanished—gone. As I reached Lloyd's side, he whirled to face me. "He's gone! Where'd he go?"

Sirens screamed as police cars wove through the pedestrians on the Row's cobblestone streets. Cars aren't allowed there, but apparently cop cars are. That's when another thought hit me. "Where's the store security guard. He was there when we came in. He smiled at me."

Just inside the door, we saw him—the guard slumped over on the floor. He looked dead. Turns out, he'd been drugged—somehow. The police burst through the door, guns drawn. Did they really think that wouldn't get people killed? "Which way did he go?"

Lloyd stepped forward. "I ran out to get a license plate—not too smart in retrospect. I wasn't thinking. But I was only seconds behind him and he was nowhere—gone."

Another man walked in and shouted, "Check the roof!"

The saleswoman, between stress-induced tears, told what happened. I couldn't understand much, but the word detonator—that I got. Tobias stepped forward and asked what happened to the camera feeds. His eyes grew wide and his face went ashen as he saw the empty case.

Look, I just wanted out of there by that point. Who wouldn't? I pushed off the ring from my finger and begged Lloyd to take me home. A cop took our statements. Got our contact information. He asked the same questions a dozen ways. Finally, after I was ready to collapse in a fit of weeping that would have completely freaked out my fiancé—wow. That was the first time I'd ever thought of Lloyd that way. *Fiancé*. But just as I almost fell apart, the cop let us go.

If you want the truth, I just wanted to go home. But Lloyd was determined to find that ring. We went to every store in walking distance—two halfway across town. We argued, and we *never* argue. I wanted to go home and order something from Amazon. He wanted to try Tiffany & Co. Then… out of the blue… I said the last thing I ever imagined saying.

"I want the one from the first store. Think they're open yet?"

"I don't know!" Lloyd inhaled and exhaled slowly. His eyes met mine and all the crazy stubbornness dissolved. He pulled me close and murmured, "I'm so sorry. I don't know what got into me. I just wanted you to have a ring, and that guy ruined our day."

Is it weird that I kept thinking, *"We did a pretty good job of it without his help, too"*? All the arguments were sparked by some guy in a suit, and I was blaming us. I think that's when I felt the tear. Lloyd's not much of a crier, but he does occasionally have the frustrated tear or three. "I'm sorry, too. I knew you wanted a good day and I just kept trying to end it. Let's go back to the first store. Try again."

"Seriously? You want to go *back* there?" Lloyd pulled out in traffic, but I could see he didn't want to do it.

"I liked it. I don't like the other ones we've seen as much as that one. I mean, if you don't want to…" The concession nearly killed me, but I had to offer it. "That's fine. But it's the one I want and…" Thanks to a red light, I was able to kiss him back into good humor. "I'm dying to know if it's the one the guy thought I'd get."

That's how we ended up back in the store that was robbed only hours before. Okay, it was almost five hours, but still. I made jokes all the way, talking about how lightning probably strikes sooner in the same place than robberies by guys who look like James Bond rather than a thug from the 'hood'. Joked about how he'd have some great stories to tell at his next convention—if he could turn them into a medical joke, of course. I suspected he'd turn my desire to return to the scene of a crime into something psychiatric.

Tobias stood behind the counter in what was now a bustling store.

Seriously, they had people all over the place. It took me the better part of a minute to realize most were insurance adjusters or owners or something. Lloyd stepped up and spoke. "Is that ring still available? It's her favorite."

Tobias pulled a bag from beneath the counter—wrapped and ready to go. "I knew you'd be back. Debra went home, understandably, but I waited for you. It's been inventoried already, so I can handle the sale for you. It fit well, did it not?"

Have you ever been so speechless you shocked yourself? Yeah. That was me. Lloyd finally got a nod out of me and paid for the ring. There's something nice about being so out of it that you don't know what your fiancé paid for your engagement ring.

I'd thought it would be nice to have a fun story to tell our kids about how or where I got my engagement ring. Well, I have the most unique one I've ever heard. Ugh.

Carol—

Some things are always familiar no matter where you are, how old you are, or who you're with—or not. All my life I've gone to sleep with my hands behind my head and staring into the black abyss above me. Many of those years, I was cold, not enough blankets, hard pallet on the floor instead of a comfortable mattress like at Ralph's house. But there's something beautiful and peaceful in those still moments of the night—a pause before you slip into the space between days.

My mobile pulled me out of that space just as my eyes closed in slumber. Michal's name glowed brightly on the screen. Panic, fear, silent prayerful thoughts as I grabbed it and answered. "Michal? Everything is well?"

"Great! Wait... what time is it? Were you asleep?"

For me, to sleep is to dream. I hadn't begun to dream, so I justified saying, "No. I am in bed, but I do not sleep."

"Whew! Sorry. Lloyd just left and I *had* to tell you about my ring. I got an engagement ring today!"

And that was the first stab of a knife in my heart. "This is wonderful." For a moment, I imagined what it would be like to make Michal's wedding ring. But people don't wear silver wedding rings in America, do they? Then again, the idea of making her ring for some other man—even if she loved him—that would hurt.

She must have been talking as I ruminated over rings. Her next words stunned me. "—doing it right now. Hang on."

It took a moment, but I realized she meant she was sending a picture. And the ring—wow. Lloyd is a doctor. It makes sense that he'd be able to afford something impressive, and that ring was definitely impressive. "Is beautiful ring. The stone is magnificent." I sat up and stared at the screen again. "Is right word? Magnificent?"

"Yes! It is. Isn't it beautiful? Wait until you hear the story behind it. No one would believe me if I hadn't been on the evening news. So, we went into this jewelry store on the Row—first store we went into..."

As I listened to her story, I couldn't help but send a quick prayer of thanks that I hadn't used the word malevolent. I mixed those words up for so long that I never knew which one was right. Malevolent might better fit my thoughts, but it would have been insulting to say it.

Then the entire story slammed into my head—full force. "Wait. You say the man in suit, he rob you?"

"Yeah! He took a full gift bag full of jewelry. A whole case worth or more. It was crazy!"

"Is like story I hear on news in Cleveland. Man in suit rob jewelry store—say he will blow up store if they do not give him jewels."

"No way! Wait'll I tell Lloyd! This is so crazy. So, anyway, you're the jewelry expert. I want your honest opinion of the style on my hand. What do you think?"

Her fingers, the cut of the stone, the width of the band—nothing could have been more perfect in my mind. Well, that's a bit of a lie. I already had an idea of just what I'd want. But, aside from that, from any store, I don't see how there could be a ring that would suit her better.

"Michal, is *you,* this ring. You choose well." I swallowed the disappointment and hurt that I'd been keeping stuffed deep in my heart and added, "I am very happy for you. I hope you have many years together." *And I hope that lie isn't a sin. I'm not confessing it to the priest.*

19

Michal—

So much happened so quickly that it's hard to remember what order everything was in. And I like order, okay? I don't like surprises, I'm *not* spontaneous, and well… sometimes life doesn't cooperate. Like when you go ring shopping and live to tell about a bomb-threat robbery. Yeah. Still not over that one, okay?

But Sunday after church, Lloyd got Chinese and took me to his place. We *never* go to his place, so I knew it was going to be a serious talk. It's rare that he tries to control the conversation or any other part of our relationship, so when he does, I try to pay attention. I mean, it's serious then, right?

"So, Kung Pao?" After I nodded he added, "Lo mein or rice or both?"

My man knows me well. All those carbs… But you know, I was still in celebration mode. So, I did what any reckless new fiancée would do. I went for broke. "Let's have it all."

"And people say you wouldn't know spontaneous if it jumped out of a hat and sang to you."

Okay… eyebrows raised—check! Disbelieving look—check, check! "They say that…"

"Well, they would if they thought of it."

We usually sit opposite each other. Lloyd says he likes that he can see my eyes that way. I think it's because I'm a lefty and he's a righty, and as much as we like to hold hands, it's awkward, you know? Well, it is in his kitchen with the little table pushed up against the wall. And we never eat in his dining room. I wonder why? Maybe because we never eat *there?*

This time, he pulled out the table, sat beside me, and reached for my hand. "Now that we're getting married, we need to be more consistent with prayer, don't you think?"

Okay, nothing melts a Christian woman's heart like a man who offers to pray with her. There's something spiritually magical in that moment—romantic in a way that nothing else can be. And really, when you consider the bride to church analogy with Jesus, it's even more surreal in its beauty.

Of course, Lloyd is a bit stiff in his prayers. He's a private person, so when he prays aloud, it always sounds like a kid who has memorized his prayer for a play. But how beautiful is it that he'll do it anyway—even knowing how awkward he sounds?

The Wok has like the best Chinese food outside Beijing—or whatever city in China has the best. I'm not arrogant enough to think it's better than authentic food made in China, but I've eaten at a *lot* of restaurants and none come close. So a lunch of Chinese, after a prayer *with* my fiancé, with a new ring on my finger—what could be better?

When he finished eating, Lloyd cleared the table, put away the food, and ordered me away from the kitchen. He's so cute when he tries to be overbearing. It's um… futile. But it's completely adorable. I'd do the dishes later when he had to use the bathroom or something.

"Okay, so this took some doing, but I managed." Lloyd pulled a bag out from beside his couch and handed it to me. Pink polka dots. Mounds of tissue. The guy has a thing for tissue. I think it's because he feels guilty about the gift bag or something. And I don't know where he finds it, but he always finds the coolest ones. Lloyd is definitely a giver.

I wondered right then if it meant I should consider giving *him* more gifts. The whole "love languages" thing. I'd ask Elder Welk in our pre-marital counseling. That thought opened a floodgate of ideas. "You know, we should probably try to schedule pre-marital counseling now. It'd be easier than trying to do it closer to the wedding. What kind of wedding were you thinking of, anyway?"

"The kind that comes *after* you open your gift!"

Touché.

People can say what they want about our "boring" relationship. Just because we don't slobber all over each other in public doesn't mean it isn't real. And when your fiancé—man, I love that word—gives you a gift that is so *you* nothing could be more perfect, it just proves it all over again. Crystal wants sparks and fireworks for me. I want what I have. That utter confidence that the man I love loves me because he *knows* me and likes me anyway. That's huge. I've had the "just sparks" relationships. Those sparks die. And then what do you have but the ashes of something that fizzled when the moment was gone. We have embers, slow burning, but steady and always... ahem. Hot.

I pulled a planner from the bag—the latest hot item among stationery-o-files. I mean, c'mon. What woman who loves hand writing letters wouldn't love hand writing her wedding plans? It came with everything I could hope for—calendars, vendor lists, seating arrangement stickers—that's right. *Stickers.* I couldn't wait to show them to Carol. He'd get a kick out of it after carrying my puffy heart sticker around for a couple of decades.

"This—how did you know I wanted one of these? It's like the latest thing in the planner community. They featured the company on Paisley Duncan last week!"

"And you recorded it. I put a note in my phone for *when* and then I overnighted one from the thing that night. Right under your nose."

A suspicion arose in me. "The Kennedy kid... that was actually the Kennedy May company, wasn't it? He didn't have a 'paper cut' because he wasn't real."

"You assumed," Lloyd laughed, "and I didn't correct you."

After the first quick flip through, I started back at page one. "Oh dear."

He peered over my shoulder at the opening page. "I guess it's time, huh?" He reached for my purse and passed it to me, but I shook my head.

"No... I think I want a fountain pen for this. It's just so cool. I can't believe you bought this."

Okay, so the fountain pen had to wait for a few minutes—you know, until I managed to extricate myself from his arms. Then, of course, I had to choose which one. Navy ink, gray, black, chocolate. He had the most delicious chocolate ink in his wood Staedtler. I had to use it.

Lloyd's laughter filled his living room when I returned. "How'd I guess you'd choose that one?"

"Maybe because I bought it for you?"

"And if it wasn't a gift, I'd have given it to you by now." He took it, rolled it between his fingers, and presented it back to me with a flourish. "We'll be 'one' soon enough. My *pluma es su pluma...* or something like that."

"You're so gonna regret that." Of course, the minute I said it, I knew it was a lie. He wouldn't care. "Or you should."

In less than a minute, the opening page had our names written on the appropriate lines. The date line stood empty. "Okay... so when can you get off work? I mean, the foundation will let me do whatever I like, so it's really up to you."

A medical conference killed the June idea—it's his favorite. I'd never ask him to miss it. Besides, he and Malinda have had it planned for two years. The good thing is that I'd get to go this time—no need for another room. Well, if I wanted to. If it was *before* the wedding, I'd probably be too busy, and the expense would be kind of stupid—an extra room when we needed to save for a honeymoon.

"Too bad we didn't think of this back in August or September," I muttered. "Christmas week would have been perfect. Everyone's already in town, we'd get great deals on travel... unless you're planning on Australia or something."

"I suppose a month isn't really enough time?" Lloyd laughed at the panicked look I threw him. "Sorry, couldn't resist. Considering Laurel took thirteen months and still rushed like a madwoman the last six weeks, I know better than to suggest it."

Look, that kind of joking is funny, okay? It is. But there's just something about hearing how much your fiancé didn't like a long, drawn-out ordeal that makes you want to insist you can pull off a nice, simple, tasteful, but totally awesome wedding in thirty days plus tax. I just knew I couldn't do it, either. "What about May?"

"I can't leave for four days in June after being gone two weeks in May."

"Two weeks... nice!" At that moment, I realized he'd never tell me where we were going. And yeah... that didn't sit well with me. "Just a note: I want in on that planning. You know how much I—" Somehow, I managed to switch my thoughts from dislike to like mid-sentence, "*Love* planning that kind of thing."

Lloyd didn't even look up from his phone. "Nice try."

Argh! Now what? Stick to the plan right now. We need a date. That thought prompted a new question. "So... do you even want to think about this right now? We don't *have* to."

"But you have your new toy. I wouldn't have given it to you if I didn't want to talk about it, so stop feeling guilty, and try another month. Right now, I'm seeing September... well, January works, but I guess that's kind of a bit much, too."

Okay, I don't know what got into me—seriously, it was probably the most insane moment of my life. But those words really did push me over the edge. I took them as a challenge and accepted them without hesitation that time. "Let's do it. Ninth or the twenty-third?"

He didn't believe me—not at first. But after I sat there with pen poised for the better part of a minute, Lloyd shrugged. "The twenty-third gives us a bit more time—in case vendors don't cooperate."

Oh, how I wanted to write the ninth down. You have no idea. Instead, I forced myself to write *January 23*. Nothing has ever looked so beautiful to me. In an instant, I'd zipped a text to my mom and Micaiah. "They're not going to believe it." A new idea taunted me. "Bets on who texts back first. Loser has to schedule the counseling."

Lloyd chose Micaiah. *Cheater. He knows Mom will talk to Dad before she replies.*

The first page spread had bride's attendants on the left and groomsmen on the right. Lloyd stared at it for a moment and boom. He just rattled off half a dozen names. "Depending on how many you're having, of course. But that should give you plenty to work with. I'd say my brother, Doug, and yours should definitely be on there. The rest you can match to your friends so everything is comfortable."

How do men *do* that? In a dozen seconds—at the most—he'd worked out the largest group of people we'd ever consider to be a part of the wedding party and named them. I'd be wrestling over it for weeks. Or, rather, I would have been if I hadn't agreed to nine weeks of preparation. At that moment, I almost caved in and told him we'd never manage it.

"At least your bridesmaids will be able to really help. I heard my cousin Carissa say that every wedding she's been in was just token nothing. All photo ops—no real help. Brides don't even let the attendants do the shower anymore. They want it how they want it, so it's all a sham."

He had a point... if I had a larger wedding party, I could schluff off some of the grunt work to the attendants. Delegate. I'm great at delegation. "I have a good idea of who I want," I admitted at last. "But who goes where/what/how... that's going to be tricky."

"How so?"

Why did I bother? I should have known better. "Because Crystal has been my best friend since like the sixth grade. But you know Jenn, Therese, Piper, Lila... everyone will expect to be asked, and half of them will think *they* should be the maid of honor. And c'mon. Even my cousin, Haley, is going to expect it. Can't you hear her? "*I just assumed. I mean, we are* family. *I had no idea it meant so little to you.*"

"Ignore them. It's *your* day. Do it how you want. I think Crystal is a given, of course." Right then, Lloyd stiffened for just a moment and then sank back into the cushions with a self-satisfied smile on his face. Okay, it was more like the Cheshire Cat... but it's Lloyd's... whatever. You get what I mean. I just didn't know what *he'd* say.

"Knock out Kyle. He won't care. Then put Carol in wherever you like. He should escort whoever he's most comfortable with, so that should solve it."

"But you don't want Carol…" The most genius idea hit me the minute I said Carol's name. Mom's text came through just as I finished typing out a text to Carol. I passed it to Lloyd. "How is that?"

He read it aloud. "'*So, I've been thinking, and since you're my oldest friend, I want you to be my 'Man of Honor' in the wedding. Will you? Please say yes and save me a lot of heartache and even more hassle. January 23.*'" Lloyd nodded and passed it back. "That seems like a viable solution."

"And…" I couldn't stand how cool it was. "It means he'll *have* to stay through Christmas and beyond. By then, maybe he'll be ready to settle down here—maybe fall in love with Crystal or Piper."

"*Piper!*" Apparently I'd forgotten to stress how much fun they'd had. "You seriously think he'll fall for Piper? I mean, Crystal I get. She seems just about his type, but Piper?"

"They had fun, remember?"

"So would *I,* but that doesn't mean I'd want to *date* her!" Before I could protest, he threw out another thought. "And how will this work, anyway? Are you seriously going to have him escort a *guy* back down the aisle?"

Okay, so the one time I do something totally spontaneous and impulsive, I end up with a potential nightmare. I'd solved one problem and created another one. Way to go, Michal. But, a girl's gotta save face—even if it's just with her boy—I mean, *fiancé.*

"That's it. I'm only having two other girls. He can escort them down, and your guys can escort them back up the aisle again. He'll walk behind. So I have Crystal and my cousin. Done. You can have your brother and Micaiah. Done. Easy. Peasy. Lemon. Squeezy."

His eyes narrowed. "Have you been hanging out with Micaiah's old girlfriend again?"

"There's nothing wrong with Flynne. She's sweet. Micaiah let a good one go when he didn't fight for her."

Lloyd rolled his eyes—something he rarely does. "Well, I '*totes*' don't miss her '*awesalicious*' vernacular."

Okay... I had to give him that. Flynne can be a bit annoying. But she's sweet, and we got off the subject before he figured out that I'd been texting with her over the past month—just to see if she was still with her new boyfriend. Seemed she was. Drat it all.

"Got a pencil?"

Lloyd fumbled through a drawer in the kitchen and returned with a mechanical one with a too-short lead. "Best I can do."

"It'll work."

On the attendants' page, I added Carol, Crystal, and Haley. On the groomsmen page, I put Doug and Micaiah. Just looking at the name and numbers settled something for me. "We're going to keep it small and intimate. No more than a hundred-fifty people at the church. Everyone and their brother can come to the reception."

"Isn't that backwards? Don't most people try to pack out the church because it's cheap and then invite only the cream of the guests to the reception?" The distaste in Lloyd's tone... I'd never realized just how much he hated his first wedding until that moment. Now I knew it and knew why.

I kissed him—like, seriously gave every ounce of how I felt about him in one seemingly-endless lip lock. Crude, but that's exactly what it was. And then, with our lips less than a centimeter apart, I murmured, "Well, I want it this way. Small wedding, huge party. I'll let my folks pay for the wedding, and we can manage the reception. That way, you can have an open bar without them balking."

"If they don't want a bar, we don't have to have one."

And that, folks, is just one of the kabillion reasons I love that man.

20

Carol—

They call it culture shock—the assault of different norms on a newcomer to a country or locale. It happens even in Romania for me. The northern country is culturally different even from Constanța. Crystal once said it was equivalent of a hillbilly climbing out of a beat up old pickup truck in overalls and bare feet and stepping into a Park Avenue penthouse. I think she called it "*Mr. Deeds Goes to Town* on steroids." That fits, now that I've seen the movie.

Now take that difference, multiply it by a couple hundred, and that was exactly how I felt about coming to America. Ralph said it's because HearthLand isn't representative of American life. So I lived there and interacted outside the community with people who led more "normal" lives. Double culture shock. Whatever it was, it could become overwhelming. The wedding business—*that* was definitely overwhelming for me.

She wanted me in the wedding party. I'd never heard of a "man of honor." What did one do? But how do you say no to your best friend? Especially one who seems to need you? So, I did the only thing I could think of. I called Crystal and asked her to meet me for lunch Tuesday afternoon. My official invitation to be "man of honor" arrived minutes before I left—express mail, no less. Ralph and Annie were impressed.

I sat with the card in my hands, rereading it over and over, as if the more I read it the more sense it might make. Crystal arrived, and I stood to seat her—something I'd learned from Ralph. He always stood when Annie came in the room—unless she called out before she got there and told him not to. I kept forgetting to ask why he did it and why she stopped him sometimes.

"You're so polite, Carol. If there were more guys like you, America would be a better place."

If you're wondering if that confused me, the answer is a resounding, "Yes!" I just smiled, though. It seemed appropriate. After all, it sounded like a compliment.

The card in my hand captured her attention, and she pulled one from her purse. "Are you a groomsman? Cool! I'm a bridesmaid. I'm not sure who the maid of honor is—I think probably Michal's cousin, Haley."

Something about "maid of honor" sent a wave of uncertainty through me. Unsure how to handle it, I just passed my card to her. "This is what come after text. Is okay to show text?"

She couldn't hide her surprise. Crystal is probably one of the most imperturbable people you'll ever meet. Nothing fazes her. The card did. "You're *man* of honor? Like the movie?"

"This I do not know. I am not hear of man of honor. What is responsibility?"

"Well..." She read my card. She read hers. Mine again. Hers again. "I don't know. It looks like we're having a dinner on Friday. I suppose we'll all learn about it then? I mean, usually the maid of honor throws a shower and helps the bride get dre—" My panic must have shown, because she laughed and shook her head. "Yeah—not happening. I don't even know how we're supposed to walk down the aisle. Lloyd doesn't have a sister to be 'best sis' or anything." When I couldn't turn my face back to a nice, calm expression, she added with a bit of excessive haste, "But don't worry. This is Michal we're talking about. She's got it all planned already. I'm sure of it."

"Then is good. If she wants, I will do it. You will help me?" I sounded choppy, confused. Even terrified. "I should maybe watch the movie?" Even as I asked, my finger slid over the surface of my mobile, trying to find the title. Only one sounded close. "Is this one?"

Crystal swallowed hard. "That might not be such a good idea."

Something in her voice made me read the movie synopsis. *He tries to make her fall in love with him—to leave her fiancé? I can't watch this. I don't need any more temptation.* Aloud I just said, "This is correct. This I should not watch."

"Sorry, Carol. I shouldn't have brought it up."

The server came to take our order. I had no idea what I wanted. The restaurant advertised "down home cooking." Whatever that meant. Crystal finally ordered me their famous chicken fried steak with gravy. She also laughed when I asked if they were bringing beef or chicken or beef and chicken chopped together.

"You'll like it. I don't know anyone who doesn't. Even people who usually hate chicken fried steak love theirs. And their green beans are just amazing. It's not *good* for you food, but it's really good *food*."

Crystal got a text message with a picture of a dress. She passed it across the table. "Michal wants to know if I like it."

The dress looked beautiful to me—chiffon with one sleeve. Unique, but not too over the top. Chocolate brown—just like Michal's eyes. The thought brought a lump to my throat—one I almost couldn't swallow again. *She's going to be a beautiful bride, surrounded by beautiful women.*

That's when another idea made me blurt out a panicked question before I could stop myself. "She will not wish I wear dress…"

Michal—

Sweat pooled in the most disgusting places as I did cool down stretches after my run that Tuesday night. We'd sent out five requests to join our wedding party and received four yeses and a no—Haley had a

173

mission trip to Guatemala in January. I promise I forgot before I decided to do the wedding then. I didn't *grieve,* but it wasn't intentional, either.

Just as I peeled off my socks, the door banged open and Crystal stormed in the room. Look, Crystal is about as unflappable as they come. She can *get* riled up—no doubt about it. But she rarely *shows* it. She *never* yells or causes drama.

So when she started in on me before she even got the door shut, I knew things were going to get ugly. "Whoa... wait. I'm sitting here literally in my own body waste. I am *not* in the mood to get yelled at. So give me two minutes to get in the shower, and then you can come rant at me all you want."

Sometimes, you have to give an order like that and walk out. Usually, I try for basic courtesy. Ask someone to do something and let them agree. But that time, no way. I barely got the shower door closed behind me and the water turned on when the bathroom door slammed against the rubber thingie that keeps it from making holes in the wall. I guarantee she'd have put one there without it.

"What were you *thinking?* Carol as 'man of honor'? Are you nuts? The poor guy is so confused. He asked me what he's supposed to do. And let me tell you, when you texted me the picture of that dress, he about peed his pants right there in Mama's Kitchen. He seriously wondered if he'd be expected to *wear* one, too!"

Okay, that was seriously funny. I totally ticked her off more by laughing until I cried. I mean, c'mon! Carol is brilliant with his occasional self-deprecating jokes about not understanding something. I really thought at that moment that the whole thing had been a big joke they planned between them. The only problem was that Crystal didn't laugh.

"Wait, you're serious?"

"Duh! Michal, he's a guy!"

A new idea, one that really didn't fit her personality, prompted me to ask an uncomfortable question. "You're not offended that I didn't ask you, are you? This was a way to include Carol *and* deal with the awkwardness of wanting you as my maid of honor and having a cousin that would, as you well know, never let me live down not asking her."

"Of course, I'm not offended. I assumed you'd ask Haley for that very reason." Silence, broken only by the sound of water spraying against me and my shower surround, filled the room and mingled with steam and more than a little awkwardness.

"Yeah... instead, she's ticked because January is her month in—"

"Guatemala! Oh my goodness! How did you manage that?"

That's when I knew our friendship would be just fine. Only Crystal would understand just how thrilled I was not to have to deal with Haley's drama in the last weeks and days before a wedding. Seriously, I think having to deal with her is what took Lloyd so long to propose again. He saw the drama she caused over another cousin's wedding. Okay... that's not true, but it *felt* true at that moment.

"Total accident. I didn't remember. It was either January or September. And that is busy season for me. So when Lloyd half-dared me to go with January..."

"I knew it! I told Carol it had to be a dare, but he insisted you wouldn't. You don't make decisions, 'to fly on.'"

"To—oh! On the fly. Well, I did. I've been hyperventilating over it for the past forty-eight hours, but I don't regret it at all. We've waited a full two years after Grandpa died. I'm ready."

That silence came again—so awkward and uncomfortable that I began shaving my legs as an excuse not to get out and face her. But her voice came quiet, halting, hesitant. "Michal..."

"Hmm?" Just a note, but just saying "hmm?" or something like that, when you don't know where something is going, keeps you out of a world of trouble. Ask me how I know.

"You know I'm happy for you, right?"

That's my Crystal. She always puts others above her agenda. I knew something was coming—even suspected what it might be—but the way she stopped to support me meant the world to me. "I know. You've always been supportive of what I want—even when you think I'm wrong. I love that about you."

"Then I'm going to ask this one more time and then I'll try to keep it to myself after that. Are you *sure* that Lloyd is who you want? I know you love him," she added when I didn't reply. "I know it. And I believe with all my heart that you think he's the one for you, but I have to ask this because I can't shake the feeling that you're settling for what you *know* instead of embracing what—or who—you really want."

You'd have to be an idiot not to understand her. I just didn't want to talk about it. For twenty- years I'd written to a *girl* who was really my true best friend. Even more than Crystal. Then she turned out to be a he. Okay, so you knew that part. It's been mentioned a time or twenty. But look at it through my eyes—just once more.

Yeah, he was a handsome guy—charming. Yeah, I bet I could have gotten him interested in me. But why? We're from two different worlds. I couldn't guarantee he'd want to stay in America—to be a part of my world. And horribly selfish as it sounded, I wasn't leaving my family to move to Romania. I wouldn't do it, even if I did fall in love with him. And I already *was* in love with Lloyd. So it wasn't the kind of love Crystal thought we needed. Or, rather, she didn't *think* it was. It was good, and true, and honest. It was rich and wonderful. And it was mine.

I had to say something and had no clue as to what would make her understand. So, I did the safe thing. I promised to pray about it. And then I got a backbone. "But you should know, I have prayed about it—for *three* years. After the first anniversary of our first date, I started praying about whether Lloyd was right for me or not. I prayed for the Lord to show me if I should stay or say goodbye. Am I just supposed to throw everything I want away because some people don't see in Lloyd what I do?"

"No." The answer came almost before I finished speaking. "I'm sorry. I know it sounds... pushy. I know I've harped on it too much. I just had to make sure." Her voice broke as she added, "I know you'll both be very happy. That's the great thing about you guys. No matter what, you're committed to each other. It's beautiful."

As I turned off the water, she stepped out of the bathroom so I could dress in privacy. I pulled on sweats and a long-sleeved t-shirt, and as I did, I brought the discussion back to Carol as "Man of Honor."

"Soooooooooo... since you're not offended at not being maid of honor, and I didn't think you would be, what do you say about being assistant to the *man* of honor? He's going to need help."

"Are you sure about this? I know he's just doing it because you asked. Since Haley isn't going to be a problem, can't you give it to me or Piper... or *someone*? It's not like he can help you with your dress, and Lloyd is going to hate it."

"Lloyd approved the text I sent Carol before I sent it. He's all for it."

"I have a hard time imagining that."

Oh, Crystal. Not everyone thinks like you and the over-possessive boyfriends you've had in your life. Some guys are stronger than that. I didn't say it, though. Why hurt a friend just to prove a point? It's just not right. Instead, I just reminded her of one simple fact. "But I'm not *marrying* Carol. I'm marrying *him*. I said yes to *him*, and Lloyd knows it. It's really no big deal."

"Okay... whatever you say. I just had to point out that it is a bit awkward for the *two* men in your life. So what do I do to help?"

Something kept niggling at me. The joke that wasn't. Why did I keep thinking of it? Then, just as I stepped into the kitchen to pour me a glass of lemon water, the idea exploded in my brain. The *dress*. "Crystal!"

"What?!"

"A dress—for Carol. Well, not really, but I could have a theme with this. It could be awesome!"

"If you turn this into some kind of drag wedding, I'm out."

I swear I almost threw my cold water at her just for making such a bad joke. "Very *not* funny. No..." A slow smile overtook me from the tips of my toes to the top of my head. I think I probably looked like the Walmart smiley faces or something. "What is my mom's family all into?"

She looked confused for a moment. Me, I sipped my water and waited. I knew it would come to her. And it did. With horror filling every feature, she shook her head. "No, no, no... you wouldn't do that to him. You *wouldn't* put him in a kilt!"

Michal—

Who knew that the first time we'd ever have the "where are we having our holiday dinner" argument would be *before* we got married? Lloyd proposed the mature thing—a compromise. I agreed—with utmost maturity myself. Outwardly anyway. Inwardly, I seethed. It's not pretty, it's not what I want to say happened, but it's the truth.

Lloyd's compromise: "We're not yet married, so we each spend the holiday with our respective families and take up the discussion next June."

To a certain extent, I will admit, it did make sense. Okay? There. I said it. But c'mon. When you have a cousin like my cousin Haley and her inability *not* to project what would be truth in her life onto every other person in the world, you just don't want to show up, recently engaged, *without a fiancé.* Lloyd's family doesn't even eat turkey! They eat whatever gourmet thing his mother and new stepfather found on the Internet. They eat at *eight o'clock!* Why Lloyd didn't want to come to our house, have great food at four, rest up a bit, and then have what may be equally great food at eight, I do not know.

I even offered to get Mom to serve at two o'clock. Yeah… I was *that* desperate.

So there I stood in Mom's kitchen, trying to help with whatever menial tasks she'd entrust to me, and listening to my cousin drone on about being *sure* I was making the right choice. Her voice gets a bit nasal when she's being particularly nasty. This sounded like a bad French caricature. "I'm just *saying*. You really need to be careful. A man like that with one divorce under his belt already..." She dropped her voice into a whisper that only *half* the house could hear. "And hasn't his mother been married a few times?"

"A few..." *If I can call five a few then I won't have to confess to the sin of deception.*

"He hasn't had much of an *example* in that department, has he?"

So what's your excuse, Haley? I'm pretty sure your mother was a fine example of graciousness, tact, and that rare skill of knowing how to mind your own business. I didn't say it. I'm not even proud that I thought it like I might be sometimes. Let's just say Haley brings out the worst in me, and like all sinners, I've got a lot of "worst" for Jesus' blood to cover.

Just as I was about to suggest that I didn't care to discuss it any further, a brilliant rebuttal formed. "Well, I think I disagree, Haley. I think he's had a fine example of what he *doesn't* want in his life, and after making a similar mistake already, he has better insight into what it will take to make a successful marriage than most of us. Our commitment alone is enough."

I could see it coming even before Haley managed a perfect hair flip, reminiscent of the eighth grade. "Commitments are broken all the time these days. That's the problem."

"Well, we've discussed this over the last *four* years, and we both agree that if we marry, divorce is not an option."

My mother stepped into the conversation there. I really can't blame her. She expected to have dinner with her future son-in-law—to brag a little on his accomplishments and the way he treats me. Instead, she gets a daughter with a nice ring, a funny story, and not much else.

"Well, Haley does have a bit of a point, Michal. I know many people who made that statement about *their* marriages—people who are now married to *other* people."

Right now, I just have to ask... what is it with holidays and italics? It's like they're conversational table decor or something. I don't get it, but every holiday is like that—in our family anyway. Digression over.

I busied myself with chopping celery—likely much more than we'd ever need—and just let it all out. "Look, like I said, we've talked about this—for *four* years. We don't just mean, 'No matter what, we're not filing those papers.' What we mean is deeper, stronger. We're committed to more than just hanging in there for dear life."

"So what *do* you mean?" Mom's question came so fast, I almost felt slapped. Then I saw it—Haley's 'I'm going to blow this argument out of the water' expression. She preempted an attack.

Thanks, Mom. I forked over the celery and started in on the onions. Hey, at least if they made me mad enough to cry, I could blame it on the stupid things. "What we mean is that we're committed to taking every step we need so that the other person will have no desire to divorce. I won't let myself go. I won't take him for granted, I'll be sure to find ways to demonstrate how I care. I won't nag. I will serve, love, and respect him. I'll show it at every opportunity. I won't give him Biblical grounds for divorce. Not even a hint of an emotional affair. I won't allow myself that temptation because that will be my vow before the Lord on our wedding day. He'll do the same for me. He won't hit me, so I won't have an excuse to leave. He won't have an affair. I won't drive him away with petty jealousies."

"So divorce isn't an option because you're both committing to making it divorce *proof?*" Mom frowned. "But what if one of you doesn't? Some husbands just walk away from the Lord—mid-life crisis and things like that."

The answers flowed. It had to be a God thing. He's so good to us— helping us be "ready in season" so to speak. "But if you go into any marriage with that expectation, then you shouldn't bother marrying at all." A new idea nearly exploded in my brain. On a roll? Oh, yeah! "If love 'keeps no record of wrongs,' then how can we hold anticipated wrongs— ones that haven't actually happened yet—against someone?"

The front door seemed to explode with guests—Haley's parents, my great Uncle Elmer, who seriously looks like his last name should be Fudd, and a few random people I didn't know. Uncle Elmer is really good about ensuring that everyone he knows has somewhere to go on Thanksgiving, Christmas, Easter, Mother's and Father's Days, and every patriotic holiday known to Americans. He's quite the patriot, Uncle Elmer.

I had to bend to hug him, but he held fast for a moment. "I heard about your engagement. Congratulations. Where's Lloyd?"

"He's with his family today. We decided not to stress about whose family is where today. We'll have a lifetime of that."

"Wise decision. Very wise. And by the time the next gathering comes, the news will be old hat. No one will put him—" He coughed. "Pardon me. The lungs... they aren't what they used to be. No one will put him on the spot. And what about your friend? The girl from Romania? Where is she? You didn't leave her alone on Thanksgiving?"

All eyes turned my way—family, because we realized someone forgot to tell Uncle Elmer about Carol, and the others, because that's what you do when everyone stares. Micaiah found his voice first—you know, that brother of mine I hadn't seen since I arrived? Him. "Funny story. My sister has had a secret boyfriend for the past twenty years. He's so secret even *she* didn't know she had him."

"Ha. Very funny." I bopped 'Caiah with a mock Gibb's slap and slipped my arm through Uncle Elmer's. "You've got to hear this story. It's amazing, really...."

Three hours later, stuffed and waiting for my body to make room for pie, and after a long conversation with Lloyd about the coffee and spice rubbed lamb dinner he was about to consume, I sat down with my phone and zipped Carol a text message.

HOW WAS YOUR FIRST AMERICAN THANKSGIVING? TELL ME IT WAS FABULOUS AND I MIGHT FORGIVE YOU FOR NOT COMING TO MY PARENTS' HOUSE.

Carol—

Michal's text message arrived just as Ralph told one of the children to find the others downstairs. I showed the mobile to Annie. "I have time to send reply?"

"You've got five minutes. Go!"

Ralph's office gave me the privacy I craved. It's a strange thing how, even with the relative privacy of texting, I really wanted to be alone to formulate a reply. Once the door shut behind me, I leaned against Ralph's desk, reread the words, and began working on a response. It took three tries to get it right, and just as I did, Annie stuck her head in the door. "Invite her over for the leftover potluck tomorrow. We're going to roast marshmallows afterward."

Once more, I deleted the wrong text message and tried again. IS EXCITING. CHILDREN PLAY GAMES AND ARGUE. FAMILY TELL STORIES ABOUT OTHER HOLIDAYS. THE KITCHEN SMELLS. EVERYTHING IS PERFECT— I hesitated before deciding to write the words I most wanted to say. EXCEPT THAT YOU ARE NOT HERE. I SHOULD HAVE COME TO YOUR HOUSE. I THINK, "LLOYD WILL WANT FIRST THANKSGIVING WITH HIS FIANCEE," SO I DO NOT COME.

The message sent before I remembered Annie's invitation. YOU AND LLOYD ARE INVITED TO "LEFTOVER POTLUCK." IS FOR EATING ALL THE FOODS BEFORE THEY SPOIL. TOMORROW NIGHT. WE PLAY GAMES AND ROAST THE MARSHMALLOWS. WHAT ARE THE MARSHMALLOWS?

Her reply came before I finished. Reading about how Lloyd wasn't even there struck my heart. Perhaps it's easy for me to say—me who has no family—but how can a man not spend an important holiday like Thanksgiving with his fiancée? Did he expect her to go to his family? I wanted to ask, but it seemed rude. I'd ask Ralph, though. He's very helpful in explaining American customs.

And another reply followed immediately. I felt foolish as I read her explanation of marshmallows. I'd enjoyed them in chocolate. Annie likes to put handfuls in her cups. They swell up and over the rim sometimes, which makes for a messy drink, but the boys like it—they get mustaches. Andre pretends he's too "cool" for it—that he only does it to make baby Emma smile—but I see the joy in his face as he just relaxes and has fun.

Ralph's sister knocked and peered around the corner. "They're going to pray in just a moment. Would you like us to wait for you or...?"

"I come now. Thank you."

She hesitated and then turned to go, but something made her turn back again. "I'm glad you're here, Stefan. Ralph enjoys your company so much. It's nice to know he has a friend to talk to. Annie's a wonderful person, but a man just needs another man sometimes." She winked at me. "Even if he'll never admit it."

Michal's text message came just as I stepped into the kitchen. I'M COMING FOR SURE. I'LL ASK LLOYD LATER WHAT HE THINKS. DO I NEED TO LET YOU KNOW FIRST, OR...?

I've never done anything like it before, and as guilty as I still feel, I doubt I'll ever do it again, but as Ralph prayed a prayer of gratitude for such a rich life and wonderful family, I typed a semi-garbled text message under the table. Some of the words looked wrong before I sent it off—even to me. Thankfully, Michal was used to my broken English. Why should my texting be any different?

22

Carol—

Friendship in America is different for me. I wonder if it's the culture of this place, the fact that people are predisposed to like me here, or if I'm different somehow. I find it both easier to make friends and difficult to allow those friendships to grow stronger. Is it because I know I could be leaving? If the extended visa weren't approved, it would be even harder to leave.

I thought about asking Ralph about it, but he, Annie, and the others were busy preparing for the big potluck. We had chairs everywhere, people… *everywhere*. So I sat alone in his office while I waited for Michal and Lloyd, and I considered my blessings. That's what they do here. At home, our version of Thanksgiving is strongly rooted in the harvest. America's seems to be rooted in family, friends, and to a degree, the ease of their lives. There's nothing wrong with that, but it's different.

Family, I had none, although my new friends in HearthLand gave me a taste of what belonging to a family is like. Friends—I had them at home and here. Not as many at home, of course. The stigma against orphans is still strong in my country. But the guild members—they were my friends, and until I came to America, I would have said my family. I sense the difference now.

As daylight faded into twilight, I thought of Michal—of *our* friendship. How can someone be so exactly as you've known them on paper and yet so very different? I asked Savannah about that earlier that day, and she suggested that sometimes it's easier for people to open up on paper. "In a sense," she'd said, "every American lives a celebrity life online, and that sometimes encroaches on our private lives as well. We have our Pinterest-worthy table scapes, our carefully constructed Facebook statuses—stati— statuses." She frowned at that and asked if the plural of status was stati. Of course, we both found it funny that she asked the non-native speaker.

"But what you have to understand, Carol, is that we crave authenticity, even as we rush to put on our makeup before taking a selfie with the baby."

Was that the difference? Michal in person is exactly like Michal on paper. And she is vastly different. I pondered how that could be until a knock came on the door. She opened it and hopped inside. "Hi!"

"You are come." When Lloyd didn't follow, I rose. "Lloyd is waiting in kitchen?"

"Lloyd couldn't come."

The disappointment in her face, her voice, it cut me. They hadn't spent Thanksgiving day together, and while she talked about it as if it was a good decision, I felt it was wrong. My opinion, though? It didn't matter. What *Michal* wanted for her life—that mattered.

"—said to say hi, though. If there's any left, I might beg to take some home. For the first year *ever*, we had *no* leftovers. Weirdest thing. It's like God knew it, so He kept Lloyd home." She blushed—such a beautiful woman when she blushes. "…like He knew. *Duh!* Of course, He did. How cool is that? I was disappointed, but now I see His hand in everything."

The words made no sense. If God's hand were directly involved in the situation, wouldn't it have been just as easy to ensure enough food for Lloyd? He's done that before… back in Galilee. I'd just listened to the chapter on my mobile that morning. Bible apps are amazing!

"—would love to have some traditional Thanksgiving food. He's totally disappointed that he couldn't be here, but one of his patients went to the hospital—little guy, about nine. Lloyd is so conscientious about his patients, and this kid has been sick so much this year. They can't find what it is."

Shame seeped into my pores, worked its way through me, and lodged deep in my bones. I don't know how else to describe the slow, thorough *soaking* of shame that came over me as I listened to her. *She's not blind. She's not a fool. She is loyal and true. And he's a good man. So no more petty jealousies. Be the friend you expected to be when you thought she was a man.*

A knock sounded. Ralph's niece peered around the door and said, "We're going to pray if you want to join us."

Michal beckoned, and as soon as I got close enough, she grabbed my hand and pulled me through the door. She grabbed my hand—grabbed it and held it all through the prayer. I've prayed for forgiveness so many times since then. Forgiveness for not thinking of Lloyd and how he might feel about it. Forgiveness for reveling in a moment that wasn't mine to enjoy. Forgiveness for ignoring a time of prayer to live a moment stolen from a man who gave up his day off to support a patient and his family. There is nothing more beautiful in this world than God's forgiveness.

The moment Ralph said, "Amen," the entire house erupted in a cacophony of interactions. Children squealed, parents scolded, grandparents, aunts, uncles, neighbors—we all laughed and talked. It felt like a TV show—so surreal. But the most surreal part of all was its utter *realness.*

Under the small table in the corner of the living room, Michal nudged my foot with hers. Her eyes—so bright, shining, happy—they sparkled at me as she spoke. "I've never really wanted a *big* family. I mean, it was just me for so long, and then Micaiah came along. I'm used to small. But this…" Her eyes swept the room, and she leaned back in her chair as if not to miss a moment of it. "I could get used to this. Can you imagine? It's like *My Big, Fat, Greek Wedding* but *better!*"

What Greek weddings had to do with things, I couldn't imagine. But I resonated with her feelings. Children… would I ever have them? Closing my eyes and trying to imagine brought only images of little girls with Michal's eyes and dark hair—my hair.

"What do you think? Would Lloyd go for four or five kids? I could work from home—while they nap or in the evenings. He could take over when he got home so they got some real one-on-one time with him. Yeah..." Before I could even hope to answer, she sighed. "Then again... labor four times. AAAK!"

Savannah MacKenzie overheard her and laughed. "Every mother of one or twenty has said that, I'm sure. When I was in labor with Rory, I turned to my mom, and she says I got this possessed look in my eyes and shouted, 'I'm *never* doing this again. God's a sadist!'"

The entire room quieted as shocked eyes turned toward her. I wasn't confident on the translation, but from the context, it didn't sound good. Savannah laughed and said, "I was in labor, out of my mind with pain, and had only a vague idea of what I was saying. And yes, I do ask for forgiveness every time I think of it. Which is probably insulting since the Psalmist says He 'will remember their sins no more.'" She shrugged. "But I can't help it. The guilt..."

Shock morphed into embarrassed amusement, but I didn't know if they were embarrassed *that* they were amused or embarrassed for *her*.

The meal dissolved in a mixture of spilled cups, children crying that their favorite bite landed on the floor, laughter from parents over their children's malapropisms, and joy. I'd never felt joy like that. Sometimes I think I never will again. And that's okay. There are many kinds and sources of joy. Some you only need to experience once for it to leave its mark on you.

Michal and I had dish duty—well, we had it because Ralph's family wanted to go find a Christmas tree out in the woods and chop it down, and of course, half of HearthLand followed. So, we stayed behind to be with a couple of sleeping babies and decided to wash dishes. Looking back, I suppose saying we had "dish duty" is a bit dishonest.

"Carol?" Lost in my own thoughts, I didn't hear her. Michal responded by throwing a handful of suds at me. "Are you even listening?"

Diving for the suds failed me. Michal blocked with the skill and speed of a basketball player. I retaliated by grabbing the damp dishtowel and snapping it in her general direction. Then it happened. Her eyes lit up. She issued a silent challenge—and came to a dangerous conclusion. She really believed I wouldn't do it. That's all it took.

"You are on!" I paused mid-snap and frowned. "Is right? You are on?"

"It's totally right, and I totally don't be—"

The dishtowel snapped at her upper thigh. I raised an eyebrow—or rather, I hope it was just one. "You do not believe what? That I will do this?" The towel hit its mark again. "I think you are mistake."

Another handful of suds flew at me, but dodging soap bubbles is much easier than sidestepping a killer dishtowel snap. I gave the blob of dissolving bubbles an amused glance and turned back to her. Michal's eyes widened, and she backed away from me. "I—"

"Yes?" Oh, the delight that coursed through me at the sheer panic I saw in her eyes. I don't know why it was so thrilling. I'm not usually one who enjoys torturing people, but something about playing with her... and that answered everything. I stood still and stared at the towel. "We play—like children. We do not play as children. We play now. This is to me, unbelievable."

"Oh, Carol..." She stepped forward and a surge of uncertainty overtook me. I aimed the towel and prepared to snap. Her eyes widened. "Um... Carol."

"Prepare the surrender!"

Michal backed away again... backed and bolted. I ran for her, snapping the towel all the way through the living room, around the dining table, and back toward the sink. But where she dashed around the right side of the island, I tried to cut her off—and slipped on what was once a pile of fluffy bubbles on the floor. How could something so innocent produce such pain?

My feet slid out from under me. If I'm honest, I probably looked like one of those animals in a cartoon—where all the arms and legs fly everywhere but where they should be. My tail bone connected with the floor and my pride lay crushed beneath the now dampness of my backside.

"Oh! Wow. Are you okay?" Michal offered a helping hand.

In a film, I would have reached for her. She would have slipped. We'd have been a tangled mess of arms and legs until I kissed her. Then, magically, it would be a picture perfect moment with no awkwardness—no wet spot on my jeans, no hair in her mouth.

Instead, I just held that hand a moment longer than I should have. Another thing to confess. "Thank you."

"Well... you totally deserved it, but... Yeah. Can't have you passed out on the floor when they get back. They'll wonder what *really* was in that nog."

Note: Americans say all kinds of things that mean nothing to non-Americans. Just as I realized that, it occurred to me that Romanians probably do it too. I suppose that's the purpose of idioms. But sometimes, I think Michal only gave me half an idiom or something.

Going back to washing up actually proved awkward. I found it hard to speak. My heart lodged itself in my throat and refused to leave. So when she packed bubbles on my chin to turn me into "Santa", I just stood there. Sure, I grinned. But my heart wept.

How did I fall in love with another man's fiancée? It's so very wrong.

"Oh! I forgot. My office is having an ugly sweater party on December fifteenth. Lloyd says he probably can't come—it's at three o'clock, you know—but we thought since you were such a big part of this year's success, we really wanted you to come. Will you?"

"What is ugly party?" The idea—unfathomable.

She rinsed her hands, dried them on a towel, and faced me. "Okay, so like there are these Christmas sweaters that companies make every year. They make them because people buy them. People buy them because they're saps. So we have millions of these ridiculous sweaters that only old ladies and quirky personalities actually *like*. The American solution? Celebrate the awfulness!"

I had to quote a TV show right then. I loved it when the smart woman on the show listened with a blank look on her face and said, "What does that even mean?" So I said it. Michal laughed.

"It means I want you to go to a thrift store and buy a super cheap, ugly Christmas sweater. I could get one for you, but half the fun is finding the most awful one you can. One guy last year actually found one with that leg lamp from *A Christmas Story* on it!!! I think I'm going to deck mine out with tiny ornaments this year. Unless I find the one I really want."

Yes, you heard her yourself. Michal wanted me to purchase a sweater I'd never wear again—preferably one I'd never *want* to wear in the first place. She wanted it to be as ugly as possible. All I can say is, "God bless the USA."

"So you'll come?" The question appeared out of nowhere.

I answered before I could consider if I even should. "Um... yes. I will buy the ugly sweater at the store—the..."

"*Thrift* store. Tell Annie or Savvy what you need. They'll probably have good ideas."

"A thrift store. Yes. I will ask."

Our eyes met and held. She smiled. My heart ran laps inside my chest. Or maybe Michal just dribbled it with mad football skills. Me, I just dribbled like an old man. Have you ever been so happy you couldn't breathe? Maybe it wasn't that. Maybe it was the guilt that regularly tried to silence me.

If the sound of people singing hadn't pierced through the fog in my mind, I'm afraid I might have told her just how I felt. Instead, I found myself propelled through the house to the front door—to see the giant tree.

Help me, Heavenly Father. Help me.

23

Carol—

Michal's party when I first arrived in America had been a little uncomfortable—a stranger in a room full of close friends. However, I'd met some wonderful people there, and even though it resulted in a series of dates that sometimes I still didn't quite understand, I'd made friends on those dates. So, when I stepped into her condo that Saturday night, I didn't think things would be *too* awkward. I knew Crystal and had heard of Grace. Oh, but *meeting* Grace was delightful. Never have I met such a gracious woman. Her name suits her. Everything should have been just fine.

But when I saw printouts of tartan scarves and kilts spread across the coffee table, a sickening dread filled me. *How can I possibly say, "No, I will not wear this"?* Another glance at the table—a glance is all I could stomach—prompted yet another thought. *How can I say no? How can I say yes? Can I not wear a tuxedo and be done with it?*

Crystal sat on the couch, arms crossed over her chest, glaring at the pictures. "I feel like I got a bait and switch."

You don't have to know the meaning of an idiom to recognize the tone, the nuances of facial expression. I wanted to add my agreement, but I couldn't. Michal looked absolutely crushed. "Is what you really want?"

"You don't like it?" Her eyes held mine for a moment. My throat went dry and made it impossible for me to answer. Before I could find my voice, she scooped up the papers and dumped them in a basket beside the couch. "Okay, back to the first idea."

Don't ask why I did it. I can't say. Maybe it was the disappointment in her eyes, or the brave smile she put on as she flipped through an iPad. I just knew I needed at least to try to be supportive. I needed to give her that much.

So, I fished out the papers. "Do scarves come in other cloth—not so..." The word refused to come. "Like those curtain. You see through."

Grace nodded. "I see what you mean, Carol. That's a good idea. It would go a long way to making the gowns less... *heavy* looking."

Seeing the approval in Grace's expression gave me the encouragement I needed to move forward. If Michal wanted this for her wedding, I would help her with it. Crystal, on the other hand, seemed more opposed to it than ever.

"Are Lloyd, Doug, and Micaiah wearing kilts?" Something in her tone hinted that she knew the answer—decidedly in the negative.

Michal's face gave it away long before she shook her head. "I hadn't thought of it... and Lloyd definitely wouldn't, but the guys could. I just thought..."

Crystal didn't say a word—not another word. But she gave Grace a *look* that said something meaningful. Grace nodded. Michal sagged.

"Okay," she agreed. "You're right. I was just caught up in the idea of all the bride's attendants being in 'skirts.' But that's ridiculous. I'll get him a tux. It'll be good."

Before I could ask if she *really* was okay with the idea of no skirt for me, she moved onto "venue." It still amazes me how many things go into planning just one wedding. Grace volunteered to "take" the venue. She pulled out a small spiral notebook, clicked a pen, and began writing down every place the others mentioned. Me... my head spun.

"Is not church fine place to get marry? I thought..."

Six eyes stared at me. Crystal found her voice first and said, "Okay, he has a point. Do we even know if the church is available for the ceremony?"

Michal nodded. "Yep! Got word yesterday that we can have it and the fellowship hall, as long as we're not doing alcohol."

I couldn't imagine a wedding without alcohol, but the women acted as if the words made perfect sense. Before I could ask, Crystal suggested several new places, as did Michal. Every one of them sounded like hotels or restaurants to me. Surely, places like that would take months to have an opening.

There's such a fine line between asking questions to help you understand and not offending people by seeming to imply they're idiots. But after several more obvious hotel names ended up on Grace's list, the question nearly erupted from me without my consent. "I think I do not understand. I think you say that places will be reserve."

"Most will, yeah. Probably all, actually." Michal's disappointment oozed and coated each word. "But if we get on waiting lists, we might just be able to get in on a cancellation."

According to Ralph, HearthLand has had one wedding—in June. The restaurant wouldn't be large enough. The house that Lavonne lived in wouldn't be large enough. In January, tents would be impossible. So that left nothing but unusual places. "Have you think about rent empty house for weekend? Can you go to zoo?"

The ladies snickered. I suppose it was funny, but all I could think of was big meeting rooms in a place with good parking. Michal caught on first. "Oh! Wait, I see what you mean. We're looking at all the traditional places—places I call for events. We need to think outside the box."

I imagine Americans would find Romanian idioms impossible to understand too, but I really do not understand most American phrases. What boxes had to do with weddings, I couldn't imagine. And thoughts don't belong in boxes, so...

"What about some place in New Cheltenham? It's their least busy time of year. After Christmas and before spring... no one wants to walk around in the cold out there." Crystal slid her finger around her mobile as she spoke. "Some shops even close, don't they?"

The light came on in Michal's eyes. "That's a great idea! And there's that maze in Rockland. They have that dome now. We could do that. Or, what about one of those new buildings they're cutting up into lofts over in that area just outside The Crypt? Maybe one of those developers has the interior all cleaned up and utilities going—just not broken up yet. We could rent a *floor* or something!"

Crystal stopped scrolling through whatever page she'd gone to look at and stared. "Okay, that's just genius right there. Who do we know who has an in in real estate?"

It became my job to find a developer and see if he'd have a floor ready. It didn't seem likely to me. Why would a man risk his construction site? Americans, if one could believe American movies, were eager to sue over the slightest thing. A construction site seemed like a lawsuit waiting to happen. But, I agreed to call. It's the least I could do.

Grace agreed to contact everyone else on the list—and more. Crystal took the flowers—ivory roses and "chocolate tulips", whatever those were. And Michal assured everyone that she'd secure a caterer by the following Friday. My protest was drowned out by her utter confidence—right up until the moment when Grace pointed out that businesses would still be gearing up for Christmas parties and things. "Just be prepared to hear a lot of, 'We can't schedule an appointment until after Christmas' from the smaller places, and the bigger ones will be booked for six months."

After three yawns in succession, Crystal stood, grabbed her purse, and hugged all of us. "I'm dead. I'm going to go home and take care of this tomorrow or Monday. I don't know if we can get chocolate colored tulips in January, but if it's possible, I'll do it."

As if a cue for everyone to leave, Grace gathered her things as well. "Carol, I am so happy to meet you. I've heard about you for years, and now to have you sitting right here, helping us plan Michal's *wedding*. It's just a beautiful thing the Lord has done for us."

"Is true. I am very bless...*ed*. Is good to meet you, too. I look forward to meet your husband and the children."

I tried to go too. I made it almost to the door, but Michal stopped me. "Can we talk for a bit? I wanted to plan out that Christmas for your orphanage. My boss says I can use Lloyd's check for that, so we can buy anything you think it needs most. Blankets, mattresses, shoes, coats, a big Christmas dinner…" One of the women called out to her, and Michal took a moment to wave goodnight again.

Me, I watched her and tried to control my overwhelming emotions. *She wishes to provide an American Christmas for the* orfelinatul. *How do I know what to do—what to say? There are so many needs…*

As soon as her friends drove off into the night, Michal came to sit across from me on the couch. She pulled her legs up under her and leaned forward with eagerness that I recognized from her letters. This was the Michal who would never let anything get in the way of winning. The Michal who hurt for the hurting and fought to help them.

"Okay, I have a thousand to donate myself. That's six thousand. So what are we going to do? What do you think?"

The tears came before I could stop them. Many of the children in the *orfelinatul* do not cry. Years of crying in cribs and no one responding will do that. But I never learned to shut out the pain. People tell me it's good—that I should be happy I can empathize—but sometimes it's just embarrassing. Michal hugged me—hugged and held me as I tried to regain my composure. Then I struggled more—fighting the part of me that wanted to weep for hours so I wouldn't have to move. It's shameful of me.

"Please forgive. Your kindness…" I pulled away and wiped at my eyes with my sleeve.

"I love that you can cry. From what I've read…"

Mercifully, she didn't continue.

To distract myself, I pulled out my mobile and sent Ioan a text message with the question. "I ask Ioan what the *doamnă* say is biggest need."

"Great idea. Can you ask if they can suggest a reputable place to purchase the supplies? I have to have receipts and everything—for taxes."

With the question sent over the ocean on airwaves, I had no reason to stay. We couldn't proceed without answers, but I did stay. I stayed and we talked until the sun rose. We stood at her kitchen window and watched the sky turn a greenish yellow—then pink. Her hand reached for mine. And in that moment, when nothing but she, me, and the beautiful sunrise existed, my life felt perfect.

Right up until the moment she said, "Oh, I wish Lloyd were here to see this with us."

Michal—

Only a few times in my life have I ever felt like everything was just perfect—couldn't be any better. They have usually been followed by what felt like disasters. The first I remember was the summer I was eleven. Captain of the church softball team. Yeah! A kid! I rode high for twenty-four hours, until Mom and Dad sat me down and told me the news that Mom didn't have the flu, she had a baby "growing in her tummy." I was almost twelve and they went there. They've all been like this. Glorious moment followed by a crash.

So when that feeling came about a week after Thanksgiving—on a Monday, no less—I panicked. Seriously. I called Lloyd's office and made them drag him out of an exam room to promise me that he wasn't calling off the engagement or anything. Of course, the moment I did *that,* I realized I'd created my own "bad moment." He'd call it off because of my paranoia! But he didn't. That crazy guy thought it was cute. I blushed. "Hey... I'm sorry. I can't believe I did that."

"Insecurity is rarely an attractive thing in a woman, but uncharacteristic insecurity is definitely attractive in you. Consider yourself 'kissed until your toes curl,' and I'll take care of that after I get home."

"I'll hold you to that." My thumb tapped the disconnect button and my screen saver appeared—the two of us on a church skiing trip last winter. I'd just changed it out that morning since we were expecting the first good snowfall that night.

A knock jerked me out of my thoughts. Carol's face—his voice. I almost told him to go away. No joke. The moment I saw him, I wanted to cry. He'd tell me he couldn't be in my wedding because the state department had ordered him out of the country or something equally horrible. So, it's no wonder that instead of hello I said, "If you have bad news, just go away."

I don't know what's more embarrassing—knowing I actually *said* that, or realizing I forgot to apologize.

"I find man who say she maybe can rent you floor."

So help me, I could have kissed him. It's probably a good thing I was seated behind the desk or I might have, and well… if you'd ever seen Carol, you'd understand. He could curl a girl's toes just by smiling at her. A kiss… even a friendly one… wow. Didn't need to go there.

"No way! Really? Where? What's it like? Did you go or see pictures or—"

The confusion on his face, the *panic* in his eyes. So funny. "I see picture on the Internet. Is nice building. They have finish many floors. People live there already. But top floor is to be… how you say…"

"Oh! The penthouse?"

"*Da!* Is penthouse. Is for…" He hesitated, as if trying to remember something. Then I saw it. He was. "'Someone with more money than sense.'"

"That was totally Ralph. I love it. Not bad for a guy who seems like he's not too bad off himself. So tell me about it!"

He came around my desk and began searching. It took a couple of consultations with his phone, but he got it. I stared at actual photos and designer concepts of what can only be described as a "penthouse loft." They were going high end everything, of course. My chocolate tulips would look *fabulous* in there.

"And he'll rent it?"

"She say if you get the insurance for event and give him large deposit, she rent to you. She is like the idea that she makes money even before is finish…ed."

Carol's English improved the more he used it, but I found myself missing the broken phrases. Before I could say anything, he stiffened and moved to the other side of the desk. What made him do that, I could only guess, and while flattering, he'd made the right decision.

Look, I don't want to pretend that I couldn't be tempted. With a guy like Carol, I didn't need inducement at all. He's wonderful. Hey, if I hadn't met Lloyd and invested four years of my life in creating the perfect relationship with him, I'd be totally infatuated with Carol by now. So seeing him make deliberate movements to keep us at the platonic place we needed to be just proved that he was the amazing guy I'd always known him to be.

Yeah, yeah. My conscience did try to remind me that I also knew him as a "her" but whatever. The point remains. And, well, that brought me back to another pet project of mine. "So... are you bringing someone to the ugly sweater party?"

There is nothing charming about a guy who isn't interested in commitment—who acts like it's a four-letter word. But a guy who is uncertain about *what* he wants is pretty cute. Especially when he's flustered. Carol sputtered and finally managed to spit out his confusion. "I am not know—I *do* not know that I am... oh... I...*Vai de capul meu!*"

That phrase I knew. He said it every time he just couldn't make his brain work in English. It meant something like, "My head!" But before I could assure him it was all good, that he didn't have to bring anyone, my boss burst in the office.

"Sorry, Michal, but you've got to see this. Your James Bond robber—he struck again." He grabbed the remote and turned on the large TV we used for presentations. "This time someone in the store caught it on their cellphone. Look!"

And there he was—large as life. The same suit, the same quiet, unruffled man, the same everything. You wouldn't surprise me if you said my jaw rested on my chest or something. You see, I'd almost begun to believe it was a dream or that my mind had exaggerated it. I mean, why hadn't they caught the guy on cameras? Why weren't there more security guards? How did this guy manage to disable *everything* and slip away unseen? None of the things that *should* have been there *were*.

But before I could say a word, the news anchor began describing what she called a "Galahad thief." The first words were a blur, but she showed a still from the video—a perfect profile shot. "If anyone knows this man, the Rockland police would like to hear from you. While he has yet to harm anyone, the police insist that no one should take that as proof that he won't. More from Jennifer Nolton on that."

The camera switched to a press conference in progress where "Jennifer" filled us in on what had taken place. The chief of police stood at a lectern reading a prepared statement. "—confident that we will catch this man. His methods imply a high level of control and knowledge of each establishment he targets. Business owners should be wary of any man who visits their store more than twice in a short span of time. Keep your cameras in good working order. Try to hide them where possible. This latest hit in Brunswick was particularly easy for him, because only one of the cameras was functional—one that was easy to disable with a can of spray paint."

A ripple of chuckles and gasps rang out over the snapping cameras and shouted out questions. Me, I stared at the screen, my heart sinking with each passing second. "I think I know what store it was. A guy in my church owns one, and he's always saying, 'It's *Brunswick*, not Rockland" when people try to get him to update his security protocol." Then the police chief's words really struck home. "Wait, did he say this guy like cases the joint, or whatever it's called? He *disables* the systems somehow?"

My boss nodded. "That's what I got from it."

Look, the guy's good, okay? I stared at that TV screen, not even hearing half of what the reporters and anchors said. All I could think of, all I could say was, "They're never going to catch him. And someday someone will decide he won't hurt anyone—that the detonator is a fake or something. And then people are going to get hurt."

The words hadn't left my lips for more than a few seconds when the "breaking news" banner flashed across the screen. The anchor listened for a moment and made an announcement. "This just in, the Fairbury police have made an arrest in the case. We have a team en route to learn what we can, but I repeat. They believe they have caught the Galahad thief."

I swear, Carol wept. Not like huge crocodile tears or anything, but he wiped at his eyes. "I do not have worry that you go to the store and find all what you need and this man make it explode because it does not have all what *she* needs."

How like him—how very like Carol to be relieved that a billion to one shot—me ever seeing this thief again—couldn't happen again.

Yeah... I've definitely got to get you a great date for the party. You will make some woman deliriously happy. And it kills me to imagine you all alone. You have such great capacity to love.

As these and more thoughts filled my heart, I wrapped my arms around him and promised that the Lord would take care of all of us. What else *could* I say?

24

Carol—

America at Christmastime. Magical. Terrifying. No, really, it's both. When and where else can you go into a store and hear about someone's grandma being run over by reindeer one minute, and the birth of Jesus the next? On Rockland's subway, I heard parents explaining that Christmas was all about giving, but seconds later, they complained that their bonus checks were smaller this year. One woman in Walmart enjoyed a running monologue with her teenager about how materialistic everything had become—how commercial. And the whole time, she piled more stuff into her cart. That girl rolled her eyes at her mom and gave me an exasperated look. I could see her point.

But amid the dichotomy of ideals, magical moments sparkled like the lights on the enormous Christmas trees everywhere. The carolers singing by a red bucket on the corner. Snow at their feet, bundled in heavy coats, scarves, gloves, hats—they sang one song after another to the odd percussion of a bell. Santa Clauses—everywhere. Something about them made you feel safe and secure.

And why is that? Why did the mere sight of a red suit inspire cautious mothers to urge their children to go cuddle up on a strange man's lap? I don't know why. And maybe I'm naive, but it's part of the magic of the season, I think. Magic that for just a few weeks of the year, Americans embrace the wonderment of childhood again. They accept that a stranger *can* be kind.

Twice someone paid for my coffee at a coffee shop. When I asked Michal about it, she said someone was doing a "RAK." Random act of kindness. I made sure to pay for two extra cups too. I even stood in a corner and watched one. Seeing the sour look on one woman's face soften as the barista told her, "It's been paid for by someone. Happy Holidays!" Nothing could be more beautiful—at least not at that moment.

I fell in love with Christmas lights at night, with the music, with the gift bags and wrapped packages. I learned about mistletoe and even allowed myself to be caught by Janie a time or two. I loved it. I loved that it wasn't just a day or a week. Six full weeks of joy. Some celebrating just because it's the thing to do, others celebrating the birth of God incarnate—often with the same songs, the same traditions.

And the *money!* I'd never dreamed of so much money being spent on one holiday. The gift store in HearthLand sold out of almost everything. We restocked with the shipment from Romania. Most of that had already sold or been promised. I worked most of every day, trying to make enough jewelry to keep up with demand. Zain tried to get our potter and woodcarver to come over for the final two weeks—anything to get and keep *something* in the store. But we couldn't do it. So I worked faster.

Still, the party was coming and I had no date. I had no sweater. I chose to shop first. So with a list of the best thrift stores in Rockland, courtesy of Annie, I drove into the city, parked at the travel hub, and braved the subway to the stops she'd indicated. As I came up from the station and saw the sea of cars, I almost choked with gratitude that I'd listened to her.

Two streets down, one street over. A man with a sign said he was hungry. His hand trembled a little as I squatted beside him. "Do you have favorite sandwich? Turkey? Beef?"

"Anything is great. Thanks."

It's no fun to buy for yourself when you want to bless someone else, so I pressed him for an answer. "Please tell me what is sound good."

"Soup—or chili? They have a cheap bowl over there at that sandwich shop on the corner. Bless you."

Three steps away, a woman stopped me. "Don't do it."

Something about her tone and look made me nervous. "Is illegal to buy food for man?"

"No… But he doesn't really want it. He just wants you to give him money so he can buy drugs."

When I didn't walk away, she rolled her eyes and stormed away with a malevolent look in the man's direction. Me, I bought the chili, a sandwich, and cup of coffee. When I handed it to him I said, "Merry Christmas."

"Thanks. You too."

The exchange with the woman made me curious, though, so I called Annie. She'd lived on the streets. "Why is woman say that man with sign that says he is hungry does not want the food?"

Annie's sigh showed a wealth of knowledge about things that I understood—and didn't. I knew hunger. I knew having nowhere to live. I just didn't know those things in America.

"Carol, she's either run into a druggie who just wants a fix, or she's bought the lie that all homeless are that way because they're druggies." Her voice wavered as she asked, "So, what'd you do?"

I couldn't believe she asked that question. To me, there was only one answer. "I buy him sandwich, chili, and coffee."

"Why? She told you not to. Why did you do it any—oh. Right. I forgot you'd lived on the streets more or less."

Sometimes, you don't want to answer fully and truthfully. Sometimes, allowing people to be a little off sounds heavenly. But I couldn't do it. "Yes, I live on streets. I know hunger. But I give the food because we are told to give food to the hungry. The priest teaches us that Jesus says to do this for our fellow man is to do for Him. I—"

"That's true, Carol. But a lot of people think they have to judge whether the person is lying first. And I get why… I do. I just love that you did it regardless."

"Is because of what the priest's words stir in my heart." It took a lot of inner strength to share the rest of my thoughts, but somehow I managed. "He say is like to do for Jesus. So *not* to do feels to tell Jesus, 'No. You cannot have the food. You must stay hungry. I don't trust You. I don't believe you are the hunger.' So I do. I let God decide. Is His responsibility to judge. Is mine to obey."

Annie's voice hinted I'd get a hug when I got home. She has something in her tone that gives away her emotions *and* her intentions. I don't know how else to describe it. "I'm proud to know you, Carol. Now go find an ugly sweater."

"Maybe I buy two. Maybe I give one to hungry man so she is not cold." Even as I spoke and laughed, I reached the store. "I go in. Pray for me." Annie's laughter propelled me through that door.

Thrift stores in America—amazing. Some of the stuff in there was junk—even to my eyes. But people put that junk in baskets and hauled it around the store. Other stuff was nice. They fought over it sometimes. Racks of clothing—enough to clothe every orphan in Romania, it seemed.

I found a rack of sweaters. The sign said fifty cents. I couldn't believe how inexpensive they were. In summer—then I would have understood. But while everyone was cold? Why so cheap? But before I could call Annie back and ask, I saw it. Another rack actually *labeled*, "Ugly Christmas Sweaters." I'm no marketer, but that just seemed like a great way *not* to sell stuff.

Each sweater was more horrible than the last. One was a camouflage in red and green. One looked like a Santa suit top. Another one had snowflakes with cheerful wiggly button eyes. Snowflakes should not have eyes. One after the next, I flipped through the rack looking for the worst. The problem was that each one *was* worse than the last. I finally settled on one with a giant reindeer that had 3-D antlers and a red nose that lit up if you pressed it. It wasn't as horrible as some of the others, but I liked the light-up nose. I didn't know what the significance was, but I was sure it had one, and the best thing—I'd get to find out what it was.

The worst thing? When I pulled out two quarters and was told it would be, "Five thirty-five."

"Sweater is fifty cents? I see on the sign."

"Sorry." The woman's bored and slightly irritated tone hinted that she wasn't sorry at all. "All other sweaters are fifty cents. Ugly Christmas sweaters are five dollars. Add tax, it's five thirty-five."

In a daze, I passed a five dollar bill, accepted my bag, my receipt, and my fifteen cents change. Sometime after I passed the hungry man again, I thought to call Michal. "Why is ugly sweater more expensive than other sweaters?"

"More?" Michal sounded as confused as I was. "What do you mean?"

"The thrift store." My voice had gone from confused to insistent. It would be indignant soon if I didn't get a bit more control over myself. "Why are all sweaters fifty cents except ugly ones? They are five dollars."

"You're kidd... oh, no you're not. I can hear it in your tone. Wow. Well, I guess it makes sense. There's a market for them, and there aren't as many as the basic ones."

It was rude. I know it, and I'm sorry, but the words came out before I could stop them. "This is reasonable to you? It makes the sense? No..." My brain spun for a moment. "It make sense?"

"Close enough. And yeah. It's capitalism at its finest."

"I think I am socialist."

Those words are funny. I know this because Michal laughed until she had to go to the bathroom. I stood on a Rockland corner and tried to justify buying a cup of coffee that would cost more than the sweater I just purchased. By the time I had it in hand, I realized I'd been wrong. With the receipts laying on each one, I took a picture of the sweater next to my coffee cup and sent a short message. I LIE. I PAY MORE FOR COFFEE THAN SWEATER. I AM CAPITALIST—OR FOOLISH.

Carol—

Once I'd conquered the procurement of the party's uniform—

namely, that ugly sweater—I should have turned my attention to the little matter of a date. I'd been upset about it—at first. The idea of having to invite someone who offered no romantic interest for me on a date—something that has inherent romantic overtones—made me uncomfortable.

That's probably why I did it. It's probably why I put it off and put it off until I got the call from Michal about who she should put on the guest list. "I have to get it off to Sylvia ASAP." I think she mistook my stunned silence for playfulness. "Oh, let me guess. I know it's not Therese, or she would have called. Piper might not or she might. Hard to tell." Silence followed. "I'm going to go with Crystal, actually. Piper would want to know if she can get away with a red sweater with little teeny bows safety pinned on so she could buy something she'd wear again. Am I right? Crystal?"

I cleared my throat, choked, and cleared it again. "I am sorry, Michal. I forget to ask. The work it is busy and I forget."

"Oh! Sorry..."

I instantly wished she'd used Facetime. I'd gotten used to those in the evening after Lloyd left or before he arrived. Sometimes she called on lunch breaks. And, well, when you have learned to read people's expressions, it's hard to know what to think when you can't see them. "Is the date necessary? Is late to ask."

"Oh, you still have a few days. Crystal and Piper won't care. I think it might offend Therese, though."

Andre walked by the window just then, that dog Gertie on his heels. *At least she doesn't try to trim my fingers anymore.*

"Carol? You there?"

"Sorry. I am think. I will ask Lavonne. I think she would like party. First, I must see if her son is—will. I must see if Savannah can be there for him."

"Oh! Babysit. Good idea." Something in Michal's tone changed. "I hadn't heard you talk much about her. What's she like? I mean, from what I've seen she's great, but what's she *like*?"

She's not so much like you that I will find myself thinking of you too much, and she's not so different that I will find her wanting. I'm not proud of the thoughts that came. What a horrible thing—to imagine that I would think of anyone as a poor substitute for anyone else. I sat there dumbfounded. How do you answer a question like that?

"Carol? Are you okay? You seem out of sorts."

Out of sorts. I think it's my favorite American idiom. It makes so much sense to me. It was sorted and perfect and then it's all out—of sorts.

The words came, though. "I am well. I am think about things. Lavonne is good mother to her son. This shows the good character. She is kind to everyone and works hard. She too is know how to laugh. No, this is not right. She too knows how to laugh. Is better?"

"It's perfect, Carol. I'm going to miss your funny little twists of speech. You're getting so good at catching them now." Michal sighed. "I wish we could just have coffee and talk. Why does HearthLand have to be so far away?"

Sometimes I miss rhetorical questions. Translating can make you miss those nuances until you've already answered something like that. So I wasn't surprised at her giggle when I said, "Is because there is not enough land close to the farm by Fair—oh."

"You just made my day. Oh, and did you hear from Ioan?"

Suddenly, I had to get off the mobile. I needed to go—to get away. Every word, every question smothered. "We will meet Thursday for lunch? We will make decision then?" The second she said yes, I said a quick goodbye and hung up. A text message arrived. God forgive me, it went unanswered for hours.

Instead, I strolled across the road to Lavonne's house—what would one day be mine. How strange to think of that! Lavonne answered my knock with a smile on her lips and flour on her nose. I wanted to brush it off, but something about that seemed too personal—almost intimate. As much as I tried to convince myself it was because I'd be touching Lavonne, my heart called me a liar. *It's because you want that moment with* her. *You want it with Michal and you know you can't—or rather, shouldn't—have it.*

"Hey! Come in. Just making cookies. Andre was all into it until he found out we had to mix the dough first. Then he took off with Gertie to go find Rory." Her eyes rolled. "That kid."

She talked all the way back to the kitchen. Only when she stopped to smile at me did I finally speak. "He is fine boy."

Why couldn't I have fallen in love with Lavonne? She's a beautiful woman—happy, funny, *available*. Instead, I fell for another man's fiancée. *God help me… please help me.*

"You know what's so great about you? When you say that, I think you mean it. Usually people say stuff like, 'He's a good kid—deep down' or whatever."

I had to ask Ralph later what she meant by that—by "deep down"— but then I just said, "I like him. Maybe because he is remind me of me."

"Well, if he turns out half as great as you did, I'll be a happy mom." Her eyes dropped to the bowl in front of her. "And if that doesn't sound like crazy flirting, I don't know what does. Sorry. I meant it, though. It wasn't empty." The "empty" comment didn't make sense, but I got the gist of the rest—even between her broken starts and stops as she tried to cover her embarrassment.

"This is embarrassment for me, because I come to ask favor."

"Oh, sure!" Relief—you could see it in her eyes, the way she stood, the way her hands no longer gripped the spoon as if she was preparing to use it as a weapon.

Sometimes, you just have to forget about embarrassment, awkwardness, and potential misunderstandings and "go for it", as Michal always says. "Michal has party at work. She invite me and tell me, 'Bring date.' So, I think, 'Who will be fun for go with me…?'" Even I knew that sentence was an English nightmare. "Is wrong words. Um…"

"I got the gist."

"Good. So I see Andre walk by the window. I remember fun time at StoryLand. So… would you go with me to the party?" I remembered the theme just as she opened her mouth to answer. "There is—how you say? Um…" The idiom monster struck again. "I forget. Is not important. Party is for the ugly sweaters." The words sounded wrong again. This time, I didn't know why. "I buy one at thrift store—what you call the thing that is have horns and red nose?"

Blushing cheeks on a woman with darker skin is a beautiful thing. Not too red—not blotchy. Just beautiful color. Lavonne concentrated on stirring chocolate bits into the dough and said, "I think you mean Rudolph—the red-nosed reindeer."

"Yes! Is the reindeer. Why his nose is red and is light up?"

Inside ten minutes, I sat on a couch watching a strange film about a little reindeer who felt ostracized and unwelcome. Inside three-quarters of an hour, the little reindeer saved Christmas—the underdog, as Lavonne called him—and made friends. I identified with the little guy. I hadn't saved Christmas, but thanks to Michal, I got to help provide one this year.

As the credits rolled, Lavonne came in and sat opposite me. "Why me?"

"Huh?"

"Why did you ask me? You've been out on dates with some seriously gorgeous girls. I've seen them on your Instagram account. Why did you ask *me*?"

"I have fun with you. You make me laugh. I think, 'She will make this fun, this looking foolish in sweater.' And..."

"And what?"

Something in her eyes made me add words I didn't want to say. "And I know for you is not serious date. You can go for fun?"

Her laughter rang out just as Andre burst through the door. He froze and stared. "Aw, man! You're gettin' all hot on my mom. That's just gross."

Andre said the words, but his face and even the tone of his voice showed that he was excited. Lavonne just laughed harder. I had to go—to leave before I said anything else embarrassing.

Before I even got into Ralph's house, her text came.

HOPE I DIDN'T OFFEND U. IF I CAN GET SOMEONE 2 LET ANDRE STAY WITH THEM, I'D LOVE 2 GO. HAVE THE PERFECT SWEATER.

25

Carol—

Michal was with a client when I arrived that Thursday. Papers in my lap—printouts from Ioan—showed the greatest needs of the orphanage, the costs of each, and his personal recommendation. So many needs—so little money. Ralph had added a thousand dollar check to the total. Seven thousand. Michal didn't know about it yet.

I just hadn't decided if I'd tell her up front or just before she made her decision. Draw out the surprise? Don't waste time? It was hard to decide.

But the client exited before I knew what I'd do. A woman, probably closer to forty, stepped from the office and smiled at me—flirted with me, I think. "Sorry to keep you waiting. It's such a good cause, isn't it? There's something pathetic in orphans that tugs at your heartstrings, isn't there?"

"I would not know. Is different maybe when you are orphan. Excuse me."

Yes, it was probably rude, but sometimes people's attempts at compassion cut deep. Michal met me halfway across the room, hugged me, and moved to shut the door. "We won't be able to hear ourselves think once people start heading out for lunch or delivery folks show up with their lunches."

Though she took the papers I offered, she didn't look at them. Instead, she pulled out the planner—the one she said held all the plans for the wedding. "We have flowers! And think we found someone who might do the catering. We have to test the food, of course, but the price is right, and the man said he's about seventy-five percent certain that his client for that day is going to cancel. So... maybe!"

She pulled out a stack of magazines. "Now... want to help me pick out a dress? I want ideas before I go into any stores, you know?"

How could I know? Half of what she said I didn't understand, and the other half I didn't want to. But we poured over those magazines, each dress more amazing than the last—or more ridiculous. It seemed that some wedding dresses were just beautiful dresses and others did their best to be so unique that they ended up looking hideous. Then the page turned once more and there it was—the perfect dress for her.

"This one. This is the dress."

She sighed, and in that sigh I heard longing—desire. Michal loved the dress. "I can't. Lloyd wants white—and elegant."

It's not polite to argue—to say that someone's fiancé is wrong. But I couldn't help it. She should wear that dress. "Is your wedding, too. If this is what you want, is what you should wear."

"Oh, Lloyd wouldn't say anything, Carol! I didn't mean that. He'd tell me I was beautiful and that it was perfect. And he'd mean it. But if he could choose..."

Arguing once is maybe forgivable. Arguing again—I couldn't do it no matter how strong the desire. So I did the only other thing I could think of. I asked if she'd looked at the dresses with him. She hadn't. "Maybe you can go to him with pictures, and there you will see what he want."

Lunch arrived before she could answer—pasta with sauces that melted in your mouth and garlic bread. Salad. Carbonated tea. I'd never heard of such a thing, but she had it and it was good. Delicious. "I am more hunger than I think. Is good."

"Isn't it? Lloyd and I discovered it a couple of months ago by accident, and then last week I learned that they deliver! How awesome is that?" She pulled the papers I'd given her closer and flipped through them as she ate. "So... Ioan thinks we should do the mattresses. We could get about sixty if we used all the money. But I really wanted to do something nice for each kid, you know? A meal... a gift..."

It seemed the best time. I pulled the check from my pocket and passed it across the desk. "Maybe this..."

She cried—happy tears, of course. Her bread dropped to the floor as she pushed her chair back from the desk and bolted around it to my side. She pulled to my feet and squeezed the breath out of me. "I can't believe it! We can give them a nice dinner and maybe a... five or ten dollar gift each?"

For a thousand dollars? You're optimistic. I couldn't say it, though. Instead, I thought of asking the folks at HearthLand to donate—even twenty dollars a family might be enough to cover the meal. And five dollars apiece for a gift could give a notebook and colored pencils—maybe a small stuffed animal or a ball. I'd have to ask Mirela if she could find a storeowner who might give us these things close to cost.

The words came out of my mouth before I could consider the wisdom of them. I couldn't help myself. "I will pay all what we need if there is not money for gift and meal and mattresses. Ioan say he maybe find better price for them since we buy so many."

"Oh, Carol..." Tears fell again. One dropped onto her collar before she could brush it away.

Have you ever had such an ache in your throat that you didn't know if you'd ever be able to breathe or speak again? Have you ever looked at someone and wondered how she could be more beautiful every time you saw her? Have you realized, at that moment, that her beauty had everything to do with who she *is* rather than her hair or makeup or clothes? Have you ever had to pray for the strength not to wish harm to the person who held her heart out of your reach?

I held her while she wept her tears of gratitude, compassion, and joy. And when my heart overtook my soul, I allowed myself a moment to imagine a kiss that could never be. In my heart, I saw her eyes—still glistening with unshed tears. They gazed at me with the kind of love I've never felt. Who am I kidding? I haven't felt any kind of love for so many years. Her eyes dropped to my lips and with the dizzying speed of a slug on a sidewalk, traveled back up to meet my gaze once more. And God forgive me, I lost myself in a kiss so perfect, no book or movie could hope to capture its wonder.

If only I didn't need to find a priest and confess before my conscience became further seared.

If only it had been real.

Michal—

The ugly Christmas sweater party is my work baby. I started it back when I first went to work for the foundation, and I've been in charge ever since. See, most people think that the point is to mock fashion choices, and for some, I'm sure it is. But I decided on it for us because people spend a fortune on holiday attire. And when you move in the same social circles and go to a couple of parties a week over the six weeks of Christmas frivolity, well... most women are going to want a different outfit for each one. Cha-ching!

Ugly Christmas sweater parties allow people to make the decision to spend as little or as much as they like. Some will wear pretty sweaters—others ugly. Sure, there are a few of these floating around—likely in those same circles. But, here's the thing. No one thinks a thing about it if you wear the same sweater to a party like that. Weird, right?

And, a party like that is understandably casual. You can just do finger foods and punch. It doesn't have to be real hors d'oeuvres or an open bar or anything. Well, foundations like ours rarely do that anyway. Our contributors are pretty much fifty-fifty pro and con the alcohol thing.

So, I spend the day running myself ragged, trying to get everything just perfect. It's supposed to be an "office" party, but when your job is to raise money for Christian causes, every occasion is a fundraiser. Forget that, walking to the mailbox can be a fundraiser if someone even looks the least bit interested in what you do. Give us half a chance and we can do serious shame to any direct sales marketer out there.

That hurts to admit. With an ornament in one hand and a string of fake evergreen garland in the other, I stared at the wall just thinking about it. Had we become *that* charity? Had we reduced ourselves to the level of seeing people as potential dollar signs? It sickened me to admit that even if our hearts didn't go there, our actions did. Garland and ornament landed in a pile on an abandoned table of random stuff, and I went in search of my boss.

"Greg?" He sat at his desk, likely finishing up the last of the day's emails.

"Hey, Michal. Need me?" The guy was on his feet and around the desk before I could stop him. That's just the kind of guy he is. If he were about thirty years younger and unmarried, I'd probably have fallen in love with him the day he hired me. Lloyd always joked that he was jealous of Greg. Then again, I hadn't heard that for a while.

Just further proof of how committed we are. It's beautiful. I waved him back to his seat and sat before him, pouring out my heart about the attitude I'd sensed. "What do you think? Have we become *that* group?"

"Well, not in mission, anyway, but it's a good thing to bring before the board at the January meeting. I love your sensitivity to it, Michal. That's why I was so keen to hire you in the first place. We needed your drive, but I knew your compassion would temper it."

"I'm not sure it has—not enough." It's hard to admit that you're wrong. Well, it's hard for me to admit, anyway. "The thing with the orphanage project…"

Again, Greg demonstrated another reason I love him to bits. He always sees the best side of people. His hands reached across the desk and waited for me to reach out to him, too. "Michal, we all have those things that are so dear to us that we become single-minded in our pursuit of them. This is yours, for understandable and obvious reasons, and I for one am pleased to be a part of it." He leaned back in his chair, swirled his mouse, and looked back up at me. "Now, is there anything else or…"

"That's it. Thanks. I'm almost done with the decor, the caterer will be here in half an hour, so that gives me maybe twenty minutes to get ready. Perfect."

"See you out there. Barbara got me a new one for this year. I think it has Jimmy Stewart and 'ZuZu' on it."

By the time I returned to the conference room where we hold our parties, everything was done—I mean, *done*. The boxes—gone. The garland in place. Music played through the sound system, and even the temperature had finally moderated between half-frozen and sauna. Just as I went to find him, the maintenance supervisor walked through with a trashcan on wheels, searching for anything he might have missed. "This what you wanted, Miss Hargrave?"

"Perfect, Jimmy! Thanks. You're awesome, as usual. I'm going to go put my cute on before the caterer arrives."

"Like you need that. Why, if my wife wouldn't have something to say about it, I'd be scooping you up for our Dennis."

"Isn't he about sixteen?"

"Yeah..." Jimmy grinned. "But he can drive, and you could train him to be the right kind of husband."

It's good for a girl's ego to hear that someone thinks that well of her. It is. But it's also just a tad creepy to think of yourself as some dad's ideal cougar for his son—at *thirty-four!* Ugh. "Why don't we leave him for Greg's granddaughter? She's a sweet girl, pretty, and a year *younger.*"

With that as a parting shot, I dashed for my office, grabbed my duffel bag, and hurried to the restroom. Whoever designs bathroom stalls designed them for skinny women who wear skirts or something. I'm not a large woman, and I sometimes have a hard enough time pulling up a pair of pants without "funny business" with my elbows on the sides of the stalls. *Changing* clothes? Insanity. I instantly regretted not using the handicapped stall. I mean, there you have sufficient room... to *maneuver.* But, to me, those are kind of like handicapped parking spaces. You just don't use them. Now, in an emergency, I'll do it. I'm no legalist on that score, but otherwise, it's a no-go. And, well, changing into a stupid sweater isn't an emergency in my book.

I also gave up. Thank the Lord we live in North America.—in the Midwest, no less. It's *cold* here. So that means I wear camis under *everything* I possibly can. Sometimes silk thermals. So, when I hit that same funny bone for the second time, I gave up and stepped out to put on the sweater. I mean, why not? I was covered, and the odds of anyone walking into that restroom right then—slim to none.

The sweater barely fit the criteria. It was a sweater, and it was Christmassy. I'd found it in a yard sale at one of the condos in my complex last June and promptly forgot about it until last night. It hit mid-thigh, so it was really supposed to be a sweater *dress,* but I don't wear stuff that short. Not that Lloyd would mind. I think he hinted when I got it that it would be perfect with a pair of black knee boots—just as it was. Yeah. Maybe next Christmas—just for him. I could do that. But there is no way I could hope to walk around a party in this thing without flashing panties—or at least making people think I would.

Still, over black slacks, that white, fuzzy trim around the hem and arms looked great. A touch to makeup, a twist of my hair into a knot, a few bobby pins, and I was set to go. *Show time.*

Okay, have you ever found yourself jealous with no idea of why? Seriously? What's with that? But I was. Man, was I ever. Carol walked into the office party wearing the cutest, most ridiculous, most "Elf-like" reindeer sweater ever. And on his arm was Lavonne, looking particularly gorgeous in a Grinch sweater. No joke. No one should look that good in Grinch green, but she did. And an ugly part of me I didn't know existed reared up and snarled.

Why did I ask you to invite someone, anyway? Lloyd's not coming. We could have been each other's date.

Of course, I'd be a lousy date that night, and honesty demanded I admit it—to myself, if no one else. This was work. And work meant, well, *work.* I couldn't just hang on some guy's arm and laugh with him all night.

219

I had to mingle, make sure people were comfortable, make sure the few employees and independent contractors we have were all having a good time. I needed to do anything but be someone other than my fiancé's date. And it doesn't get any simpler than that.

Well, unless you count the, "this stinks" factor. That's definitely simpler.

Carol brought her to me before I could get over there. "Michal! Is sweater good—bad—ugly? Is ugly enough?"

"It's perfect! And wow, Lavonne! That one is perfect, too!"

He turned to Lavonne. "Yay! You are ugly, too!" Carol frowned as his words registered. "This is not what I think to say."

Lavonne, man, the woman has a great sense of humor. She handled him with just the right blend of teasing and reassurance. I'm pretty sure I've never been so glad and so *mad* that I am a Christian in my life. Glad because I couldn't hate her like I wanted to. And mad for the same reason, of course. It made no sense. Maybe it was just the green of her sweater reflecting in my eyes or something. Maybe it soaked through into my heart. Yeah. That makes as much sense as anything else.

But then he turned to me with a mock scold in his voice. "Your sweater is not ugly. You make fail—no, that is wrong. You are fail...*ure?*"

Look, it's just a sweater, okay? It shouldn't have mattered. But it stung. I felt like I really had failed him. Just at that moment, though, I saw Lloyd walk through the door. He wore a brown sweater with a sprig of mistletoe pinned at the neck with a red bow. A pinecone.

And I totally overreacted. There should have been a trail of rolling people like bowling pins after a strike the way I barreled through there. "Lloyd!!!"

Lloyd's kind of a reserved guy in public. He's not afraid to show affection, but he's not... *exuberant* with it. He was that night. By the time I reached him and threw my arms around him, he picked me up and swung me around—didn't let me go. "Sorry I'm late."

"Late! Are you kidding? You're almost right on time, and you *came!* I can't believe you came!"

His eyes—Lloyd has the most expressive eyes. The rest of him isn't, you know. He's hard to read sometimes, but you look into those eyes and you see what he feels. At that moment, he felt love and insecurity. I just didn't know why the insecurity. Hands on his cheeks, my eyes fixated on his until the moment our lips met. My heart flopped—in all the wrong ways. Seriously the *worst* kiss in my life. And I'd had a few dussies in junior high. This one was just...*there.* No swirl of emotions knitting our hearts together further. No electric zings to my lips or my toes.

You know what it was like? Have you ever met someone for the first time, offered your hand, and gotten one of those fish-like, dishcloth handshakes that leave you feeling icky and dissatisfied? That is the perfect equivalent of that so-called kiss.

The air in the whole room grew awkward. I mean, it was like they could all *feel* what had been lacking or something. Lloyd cleared his throat, I volunteered to get us punch, and the room went back to a quiet buzz of conversation.

After that, everything improved. Well, it did until we played this game I'd found online. You had to do this scavenger hunt thing by buying stuff off the guests or anyone in the building, on the street—anything. But you couldn't use anything of yours, and you couldn't spend more than 5.00. Then you had to wrap it for a Yankee swap. I even had a pile of five-dollar bills so that those who didn't have cash would be able to play.

I grabbed Lloyd's hand and hissed, "C'mon. I cheated. I talked to the guy at the bakery down the street. He'll sell me a dozen mini cupcakes for five dollars."

"Cheated is right," Lloyd groused. "What am I supposed to do?"

That brought out the snippy in me. Yeah, it wasn't right, and I'm not proud of it, but man, sometimes you just lose your cool. I lost mine. "Well, they *were* for you so you wouldn't have to do all this. I know how you hate these things. But you know what? Forget it. Just figure it out on your own."

"You didn't even know I was coming, Michal!"

"I meant *now*. Like when I saw you come in. I thought, 'I'm so glad I got those cupcakes now. Lloyd will be so relieved.' Now, you can just deal with it."

Waving a five over my head, I took off out of the room and down the elevator to the street. I ignored Lloyd's call—both the vocal and the phone versions. Inside ten minutes, I returned with my box of cupcakes and ran to wrap them. Lloyd stood there wrapping something himself. Lavonne arrived a minute later.

"This is fun! What a cool idea, Michal!"

"You think so?" Lloyd's tone told everyone in the room exactly what he thought of the game.

"Well, yeah. I mean, everyone overthinks that whole white elephant thing. This gives you a limited budget and time, and everyone is on a level playing field."

The muttered, "Not everyone," that barely reached my ear managed to boil my blood.

I don't know what made me do it. I usually have impressive self-control, if I do say so myself. But man, he'd pushed every button I have with that incessant jab of an impatient man in an elevator. The words tumbled out before I could consider just how rude and demeaning they were. "Oh, don't mind him. He's just being nasty because he lost the chance at the easiest and best gift here." I met his shocked gaze and tied another barb on the high wire I'd pulled us up onto. "It's what you get for having so little faith in me. Deal with it."

Dead silence—I mean stone cold dead. Lavonne fumbled for the tape. Lloyd stared at me in utter disgust, and movement behind me hinted that perhaps someone else had overheard. I started to apologize, really I did. It's like my dad always says, "Be the better person." And well, I hadn't been. Lloyd's mistake didn't mean I had the right to be a jerk. He *had* made an effort to come. Probably had to reschedule a few patients even.

You have no idea how much I wish I hadn't turned around right then. If I hadn't, I'd have apologized. But when Carol's face filled my vision as I turned, I absolutely lost it. "Did you hear that? The guy is ruining everything!" At that point, mortification overrode any hint of common sense I had left. I wanted to run. Almost did, too.

But then Lloyd pulled out his fangs. I've only seen them once—when someone was being rude to me, in fact. This time he turned to Lavonne, and in the most charming tone he possessed, he said, "So, how do you like being one of Carol's Belles?"

Lavonne's gasp. The pain in Carol's eyes. The triumph in Lloyd's. Pain consumed me until I turned to Lloyd and brought out my, "Don't mess with me" tone. With each word carefully enunciated, I gave the order. "Go home, Lloyd."

"Yeah?"

"Now."

If I'd expected an argument, I'd have been disappointed. He turned on his heel and left. I turned to Lavonne and found her dragging Carol from the room. I raced after them, desperate to apologize, but when I reached the door to the hall and heard her hiss, "I am not 'one of your belles.' I'm a human with feelings and I'm not—"

"Is not my words." Carol's face. The pain and confusion in it cut deep. He looked at me over his shoulder and the pain in his eyes... Can I just say I've never been so ashamed of myself in my life? Yeah.

The tremble in Lavonne's voice ripped through me all over again. I made arm movements, urging him to hug her. He patted her shoulder instead.

"Please forgive." Just two words—that's all he said. But her entire posture changed. Again, I urged him to hug her. This time he took a step forward when he touched her. That's all it took.

Of course, I'd have a harder time fixing the breach with Lloyd—and I couldn't even start until the party was over. Yeah. Don't pick a fight when you're at work. If that guy on that Navy criminal investigation show had another rule, that'd be it. "Don't pick a fight when you're at work." It's a good one.

26

Carol—

Michal's call came late that night. She apologized at the party, but I wasn't surprised when I got the call almost at midnight. The sniffles came over the airwaves in semi-regular bouts. "I can't believe I did that, Carol. Poor Lavonne. And you—how could I have let him drag you into that? If I'd kept my mouth shut, I would have been fine."

At least, that's what I think she said. Between the hiccoughs, the sniffles, and the odd breaks in sentences, it was difficult to determine. But when I found a break in her rambling, I tried to calm her. "Is forgiven, Michal. Is time for you to forgive you now."

"Why are you being so nice about it, Carol? I was rude to Lloyd, embarrassed you and Lavonne, and in the process she was hurt and insulted. You should be furious with me."

"Is because I know you. This is not surprise me. This you have told me. 'When I really get mad, I can get nasty.' How many times you say this in your letter? How many times you write about friend who insult other friend and you are unkind. You say, 'I knew I should keep shut my mouth, but I say it anyway.'"

"But at *work!* I *have* to be professional at work, and I wasn't. Greg is so going to kill me on Monday."

"Call tomorrow. Say, 'Mr. Greg, I am behave badly last night. I have apologize to everyone else. Now I apologize for you."

"*To* you, but yeah. I should do that." Even before her voice grew quiet, even before she spoke the words, I knew what she'd ask next. "Why did I let him get to me, Carol? Why? I'm still so mad at him."

Sometimes people ask questions when they really just want the chance to answer them themselves. So, I listened as she rambled about the strangest thing—something missing in a kiss, the way he didn't like games, and how she wanted to apologize but he kept egging her on. Egging... some idioms I don't think I want to understand. That might be one of them. It sounds messy.

But something happened as she rehashed the night—her words. I relived them, and as I did, the look in Lavonne's eyes wounded my heart. Disappointment in Michal grew. By the time I hung up with her, I'd grown angry. My Michal really did have a blemish on her—one I hated to acknowledge. *My* Michal was caring, sensitive, compassionate, loving. She fought fiercely for orphans and single mothers in inner cities. She worked long hours trying to raise funds for wells in places with no clean water. She tried to find homes for thousands of Syrian refugees. This was *my* Michal.

Knowing someone has an ugly side, and *seeing* it play out before your eyes—seeing it *hurt* someone who has done nothing to deserve it, those are very different things.

Lavonne's eyes... the way she promised me she was fine—promised with a catch in her throat and an urgency to go in the house before I saw the tears that would fall. A now familiar ache filled me all over again. *Why can I not love* her? *I am so angry with Michal. The more I think about it, the angrier I get. I want to lash out at her—make her feel the sting of her tongue. It's wrong. It's horrible. But I want to. And yet, I love her.*

The question I'd asked almost daily—sometimes hourly—since arriving in America resurfaced. *Why can't I love someone like Lavonne? Someone who needs the support. Someone who is free to love and be loved. That boy—he needs someone to help him learn how to be a man—a good man. He could so easily be like I was.*

That thought chilled me. Seeing Andre in a drunken stupor—fighting with another drunk for cash to buy more alcohol—for drugs. Oh, my heart squeezed at the thought of it—that confused little boy who so thought he was a man already. Would he do despicable things to feed a habit? His mother would feed him. He wouldn't be reduced to selling himself to eat, but what about drugs? Rockland was full of them—in the places she'd moved from. She'd shown me on the way to the party. Horrible, dirty places with intimidating men on street corners.

She needs someone to help. Moving here—moving away from temptation isn't enough. It's not enough. I could...

As much as I wanted to finish that thought, I couldn't let myself. I didn't know. I didn't *want* to even consider it. I wanted Michal. Of course, I wanted to shake her right then, but I also wanted *her*.

Michal—

The clock rolled over to eight o'clock. I punched the numbers for Lavonne so fast, I'm surprised I didn't wake up some old lady in Hawaii. "Lavonne? It's Michal. I just called to apologize."

"Again."

Okay, right there, I swallowed hard enough to force down a golf ball. "Um, well, yeah. I'm just so—"

"Michal? Can I just interrupt you right here?"

Between the tone of voice that said, "You are seriously ticking me off, lady" and the fact that interrupting to ask if she could interrupt just made no sense, well... what could I do but say, "Sure!" I even tried to sound like I meant it.

"I'm going to tell you something I always tell my son. So, if it sounds condescending, well, I've kind of had to use it a lot on him, and it's taken on a certain... air."

Already I relaxed a bit. "Let me have it, Mama."

It worked. She laughed, I laughed, all felt good. Then she lit into me.

227

"Michal, you apologized last night. I forgave you. Asking *again* just cheapens that first apology—like I lied when I said I forgave you or something. So take it from me when I say that if I *hadn't* forgiven you when you asked, I would *not* have said I did. I've dealt with enough fake 'forgiveness' to know I never want anyone to have to wonder about mine."

Okay, so I did have to send a text to find out if I'd hung up on her at that point, because her words rocked my world. I kept thinking of all the times I asked God to forgive me for the exact same execution of a particular sin. "January 1, 1999. I screamed an obscenity; remember? I am still so mad at myself for that. Please forgive me."

Can you imagine God up on that great white throne going, "Kind of can't forgive you for something that is already wiped clean. Sorry. Forgive yourself and move on!"

Okay, I don't know what God really says or thinks, but that's how I saw it play out in my mind, and it unsettled me.

Lloyd proved to be another problem. You see, I *was* going to ask for and offer forgiveness—an apology I didn't mean and forgiveness I didn't truly feel. Because it's what you do when you blow it. It's what you do when someone else blows it too.

So I waited until just after noon and called him. "Can we talk?"

"It's probably not a good idea. I'm still angry."

"So am I. But I think we should deal with this before it gets worse." How on earth did I managed to say that so calmly? When he said, 'I'm still angry,' I wanted to punch him through the phone.

"Fine. I'll come over at dinnertime. I'll bring Chinese."

Well, thanks for asking. It took every ounce of something for me not to say it. I so wanted to. "See you then." The words "I love you" welled up in my throat, but the whole situation choked the life out of them. Instead, I just said, "Bye."

Routines and systems exist to help us keep from letting these kinds of things consume us. So, I spent my Saturday ignoring the need to go dress shopping and cleaned my house. I scrubbed every bit of it. Then, because that's not self-flagellation enough, I went for an eight-mile run. By the time

I returned, it was nearly six. I was hot, sweaty, cold, stinky, and did I say sweaty? Not exactly the poised, attractive version of myself that I wanted to portray in the upcoming, likely-to-be-heated debate.

No joke, I'd just reinserted the mascara wand when I heard Lloyd's key in the lock. I considered lipstick and opted for biting my lips instead. Why waste perfectly good lipstick when I suspected it would just end up transferred to Lloyd inside an hour. Isn't that what they say? People fight for the joy of making out—er, up?

Oh, the awkwardness. We'd never had a fight—not like this. Our arguments were usually civil affairs that were just slightly overwarm disagreements. This, on the other hand, had been particularly nasty, and I suspected neither of us thought we were the "at fault" party. Lloyd filled plates and took them to the table. I filled glasses and got silverware—so far, all was normal. Normal and oh, so miserable. He prayed over the food. Never had I heard Lloyd pray in an utter monotone. I did that day.

He passed the soy sauce. I passed the spicy mustard. Fortune cookies sat on a plate in the middle, almost the only words between us the entire meal. Lloyd collected our plates and dumped them in the sink. He gripped the counter, and I saw the anger ripple through his shoulders.

"You hurt me, Michal—deliberately mocked me."

"You were being difficult and petty. I'm not proud of how I behaved. We both know it was wrong. But, c'mon. You were off almost from the moment you walked in. That *kiss!*"

"It wasn't so great from my end either."

You know, I shouldn't have been surprised. And actually, I really wasn't. But it still felt like a kick in the gut. The Lloyd I knew didn't ever even hint that I could be lacking in physical appeal—even if I sometimes suspected it. But curiosity overrode it, and I sort of mused aloud as my brain tried to work things out. "I wonder why it was so weird."

He whirled in place. "Seriously? You have to ask that question?" His entire demeanor shifted from impatience to incredulity as he saw that I really didn't know.

"What?"

"You were *trying* to put on some kind of show when I got there—like you had something to prove to yourself. That kiss alone—since when do we make out in the middle of a room full of people?"

It started again—that welling of anger and justification. How I kept from lashing out again, I can only attribute to the merciful hand of a gracious God—or one Who was just fed up with my nonsense. Or both. Probably both.

But I didn't control the flow of sarcasm I drizzled over my retort. "Well, you certainly were all for it the *last* time we were at a work affair. And *you* instigated that one."

"People kiss when they get engaged. They don't make out like that sailor in the parade at the end of WWII just because they haven't seen each other in eight hours!"

"*Ten!*" Yeah. I was that petty. I went there.

"I should go."

Oh, you don't *know* how much I wanted to snap, "Yes, you should." Could anything have been more satisfying? I don't think so. But relationships don't mend by ignoring problems. I'd learned that by watching a friend or twenty.

"Lloyd?" It took until he reached the door before I could say his name.

Without looking back, he just sighed and said, "I don't want to fight anymore, Michal. I hate it."

Finally. Something we could agree on. "I do too."

He turned to look at me. "Can we keep it civil?"

Okay, I deserved that. And he put "we" in there, too. He didn't have to. I nodded. "If I can get a hug."

You know, there are people who say they aren't "huggers." You know what? I don't get that. Not at all. When everything is all wrong, a good, long hug can drain all the ugliness right out of you. By the time one of us finally pulled back a bit—and I never did know who did that—I could see how I'd blown everything he said out of proportion. He made one, semi-predictable and honest statement about something that makes him uncomfortable, and I'd egged him on until he insulted someone. Sure, his mistakes were his own, but few people can resist responding to a deliberate egging.

"I'm sorry, Lloyd. I was so ugly, and I kept blaming you for it."

"I called Lavonne—wasn't easy. They're pretty protective over at HearthLand, but Carol finally decided I meant it."

Melted heart... right there. One tear... Two... Fifty. By the time his lips found mine, I was a soppy, slippery mess. It should have been reminiscent of those junior high kisses I mentioned—you know, where the guy has no clue what he's doing and manages to leave your face wetter than a Great Dane?

Tender, gentle—such depth and intimacy in that kiss. My stomach did flops—the good kind. I felt the moment when he realized he'd have to break away—felt the resistance. The disappointment. His eyes—oh, so close to mine. They told me just how much he loved me as his lips told me just how much he *didn't* want to stop. "I think it's a very good thing we decided on January."

Oh, my speeding heart. If it were on the highway, they'd do a pit maneuver and put me in jail.

"Yeah... I agree."

And of course, that was the worst part of all. We finally got to a good place—a place where we could talk about what happened—could work it out. We got there and he had to go. I could see it in his eyes. If my mom knew just how tempted I was to tell him to stay, I think she might have hauled our butts down to city hall right then and there.

He started to say it—started to complain that he had to go. I knew it, too. He really *did* have to go. But I wanted anything to keep him there—to solder our fractured relationship just a little better so it could weather the distance until we could try again. So, I did the only thing I could think of. It wouldn't work—it never did. The only thing that would work would be if I touched his face—if I pulled him close again. Still, I had to try.

"The cookies! We forgot the fortune cookies."

Shocker to beat all shockers, Lloyd followed me to the table with that indulgent smile that said, *"I know exactly what you're doing, and you're cute when you do it."* And I'll take that.

"You spin."

He hesitated, knowing how much I love our silly little ritual. But his hand reached out and gave the little plate a gentle spin. He started to reach for his when Mr. Miniver rubbed against his leg. In that distracted moment, I panicked and grabbed his cookie. I wanted to be sure I got the right one, and fate seemed against us.

He scratched the cat's ear, reached for the remaining cookie, and broke it. He'd never eat it, of course. Can't really blame him. They're pretty tasteless. Why waste the calories?

"'An old friend will make new conflict.'"

I nearly choked just listening. But when I unrolled my fortune and read, "'Hold fast to love or it will slip away,'" my voice shook. "Weird, isn't it?"

Lloyd tossed his on the table. "Well, I'm just glad we each got the one we did. Otherwise, that could have been ominous." He pulled me close again, and I sensed something different this time. He really didn't care if he should go anymore. His lips found mine, and I don't think they left again for an hour.

But the moment that door shut behind him, my eyes flew to the table and my conscience whipped at my heart. *Why does it seem so awful? They're just silly, meaningless fortunes!*

My conscience mocked me. *And you cheated.*

Carol—

I didn't go to mass. It's a long drive, I didn't sleep much, and my priest couldn't take the time on a busy Sunday morning to hold one parishioner's hands and talk him through his issues. Instead, I wandered HearthLand, praying. Derek found me out by a giant tree and offered to make me breakfast. Rory invited me up to his "tree-ler." Who hoists a travel trailer up in a tree for a tree house anyway?

So when footsteps alerted me to the presence of yet another HearthLander, I just wanted to scream, "Leave me *alone!*"

"Carol?"

Lavonne—it *would* be the last person I should talk to. Michal had talked about somebody's law. I didn't remember the name, but it basically said that whatever can go wrong, will. I felt like I was his latest target—an innocent victim of a law designed to ensure humanity stays evil.

The water rippled over some stones and splashed against others. Occasionally, one of the remaining leaves on the trees would flutter down and sail to distant lands far out of my sight. I followed one leaf even as I spoke. "You are well? Michal called?"

"She called—woke me *up*, but she called." If Lavonne wanted to sound annoyed, she'd failed. She sounded amused to me. "Poor girl is eating herself up for something her fiancé did. And even he wasn't trying to be nasty to *me.*" She sat down beside me and reached for a small twig. "Why did Lloyd want to hurt you, Carol?"

That did it. My head whipped around to look at her. "Hurt *me?* I think he was try to hurt Michal."

Her head shook, but something in her face changed as well. "Perhaps. I don't think so, though. He seemed more put out at you than me. I think he's jealous."

"Why? He is engage to Michal." Nothing about what Lavonne said made sense to me, so I tried to change the subject. "I am want to buy the presents for everyone, but I have... how you say...?" Shrugged shoulders and a confused expression go a long way in helping people understand you.

"Limited funds? You want to provide gifts, but you need to be frugal. This I know how to do."

"I am think I will make gifts—pendants for ladies, tie pin for men. I cannot have the time, now. This I make in January for next year."

Her laughter—beautiful. I wanted to ask her to sing for me. When she sang with the others, everyone's voice grew just a little quieter to hear her. The words tumbled from me before I could stop them. "You should be on TV show—sing. You win million dollars, and we hear on radio in car."

Again, she laughed, but this time she touched my arm as she did. I should have felt something—some thrill of electricity from the touch of a beautiful woman. I felt nothing but compassion for someone who should not have to walk this life alone. And that thought made up my mind.

"You are good for me. You make me think. I am talk to Ralph."

Without another word, or even a thought to how rude it was to get up and walk away from her, I hurried back to Ralph's house. He wasn't there. I tried the greenhouse, Annie's trailer, the new milking sheds. His truck sat where it always does, but he wasn't even in the general store.

And, because of that guy's law, the moment it occurred to me to *call* him and ask if he was available to talk, Ralph appeared on Janie's porch and jogged down the porch steps as he answered the call. I waved. "Is me. I cannot find you, so I call."

We pocketed our mobiles and met in the middle of the road. "So, what can I do you for?"

Just when you think you understand a language, someone says something like that and you think there's no hope. And then, just as you decide there's no hope, he apologizes for mixing up the words. "Sorry. I think I'm channeling my inner hick or something. What can I do for you?"

We wandered down the road in the direction of that strange tree house, but I couldn't bring myself to ask. That's when Ralph said that things are usually easier and less ominous once you just say it. "Lavonne is good woman. We could be happy. I think she is attracting me?"

Ralph put up a hand. "Wait. Do you mean that you find her attractive or that she finds *you* attractive?"

"She is attractive, yes, but I think she maybe think I am..."

"Okay, you think she's interested in you. And you don't sound averse to her, so what—oh!" Ralph laughed and dropped an arm around my shoulder. "Carol, you don't have to get permission to date anyone here. Go for it!"

My heart fluttered to the ground. The wind caught it and tossed it in lazy flips and slides along the road until I didn't know where it would end up. "This I wish is true. I wish I see her as the woman I wish to love."

"Well... then I'm lost."

We stood at the end of the road, not stepping into the meadow, not returning either. "I could be happy with her. I think I can make her happy. Andre needs man to show him difference—" When Ralph's head snapped up, I faltered. Maybe it wasn't a good idea.

"What difference?"

"Between acting like man and *being* man." At his smile, I continued. "But is wrong? Is wrong to try to start relationship with someone when someone else..."

There were so many things he could say. I imagined things like, "It's not fair to be with someone when you love someone else" or "You'd have to tell her so she knows what she's getting into." But, instead, his eyes filled with compassion and a pained mask covered his face. "Carol, if you try to spend your life with someone you didn't choose, I imagine it will feel more like a life sentence than a life*time.*"

"But I am choose her. I am say, 'This is woman I will commit to.'" The words choked me. "If I do it, I mean. I maybe not think is good idea. This is why I ask."

Oh, the confidence I felt as I spoke those words. They felt honorable, true, a little self-sacrificial, but I imagined that doing the right and honorable thing would provide me with a true love that would make me see how silly my little "infatuation" with Michal had really been. I fear I overheard too many of the period movies that Ralph's nieces and sister had been watching. They are probably where I got the idea in the first place.

Ralph brought me down to earth with a simple reminder. "No, you would be choosing to *help* her, not choosing *her*. It's not the same thing. Lavonne deserves a man who wants her for her own sake, not as a filler for an empty heart. And Carol..." He waited until I met his gaze. "You can be the influence Andre needs without being married to his mom. I sure intend to!"

A car rounded the corner—one carrying that young couple with the little homestead—and beeped as it whizzed past. "They go to church?"

Ralph nodded. "Yeah. I see you're not on your way."

"I need to think. So, I do. Then I come up with brilliant plan to save boy from himself."

Laughter—I think the ability to laugh at one's own foolishnesses is a good sign of healing. Unfortunately, the text I sent Michal—the one about how I wasn't doing any more dates—just proved that I hadn't healed as much as I wanted to think.

Michal—

Once in a while, taking a day off from church to focus solely on you and the Lord really helps reground you. I took a "personal" day with the Lord and worshiped at home. I'd just bought this new Indie album. The artists had taken old hymns and remixed the tunes just enough to keep them recognizable but still modernized in a fresh, light, Indie vibe.

I decorated for Christmas while I listened to Luke chapters one and two. Maybe I should have waited for Lloyd, but I didn't. He's a guy. He doesn't get into those things like I do anyway. Of course, when I laid out ornaments on the table to plan the grouping—yeah, I'm anal like that—I found our fortunes again.

Oh, the guilt. Fortunes are just funny things that occasionally fit a situation in your life in ways that amuse you. Okay? That's just what they are. But this time it ripped a hole in my heart. Carol had done that. He was an old friend who I had allowed to create conflict in my relationship with Lloyd. It wasn't his fault. He hadn't *meant* to do it. He'd been *supportive* of my relationship with Lloyd. He always asked about Lloyd and tried to include him—Lloyd, that is—in anything we did. It's just the kind of guy he is.

But something had happened at that party, and I didn't know what to think of it. Even now, just the memory of him walking in with Lavonne, it felt strange. They looked awkward and unnatural together, even while they'd been talking and laughing.

Perhaps it felt strange because it seemed so familiar.

When life shoves something uncomfortable at you, stuff it in your pocket and move on. I did, too. Ornament by ornament, that white frosted pre-lit tree with its tiny pinecones that I'd fallen love with last year, on clearance, of course, looked amazing. Candles, Christmas runners, my little nutcracker collection in the center of my dining table, a bowl of glass ornament balls on the entry table. I keep them there because Mr. Miniver has a particular aversion to glass ornaments on a tree. He won't touch mine unless there's anything glass on it. Then he makes it his mission to eradicate the tree of the dangerous bombs. Two vet bills to remove fragments—it took two for me to learn. Won't do *that* again. But I love those ornaments, so they sit in a bowl and look festive with lights shining beneath them.

At the bottom of my ornament box laid a handmade card a friend had sent to all of us last year. So simple—but so sweet. Keys in hand, I dashed out to Walmart for supplies. Card stock, ribbons, glue runner, star buttons. I put those back and found puffy star stickers. Little kids might choke on buttons. When I couldn't find envelopes the right size, I bought a package of copy paper as well. A roll of washi tape could seal 'em up. Done.

My first attempts were kind of pathetic, but once I made one that I liked the proportions of, I copied the lengths so I could do them assembly style. Long bottom…next, next—stacked up those ribbons five-high, slapped that star on top and a vertical, brown skinny ribbon on bottom. Voilà! A tree. Too cute, if I do say so myself. I had twenty cards done inside an hour—well, once I got the ribbons cut. I cut enough for a hundred.

Of course, by the time I got all them made, my dining table was trashed, glue stuck to everything, and there were still envelopes to assemble. Mr. Miniver watched the proceeding with a bored eye. "So, what do you think? Will they do?" The copy paper mocked me. "And, do orphans care about envelopes? Maybe I could skip those?"

If I told you he coughed up a hairball right then, would you believe me? Yeah, I wouldn't either. But he did. Right on one of the cards. The only saving grace was that it was one of the ugly ones. So, with ninety-nine cards, leftover Chinese nuked to perfect rubberiness, and a free translation site, I began writing.

Each card had a sticky note saying something like, "Boy: age 9" or "Girl: age 15" The messages, I tried to vary between different genders and ages.

Oh, the hand cramps. I wrote, flexed fingers, wrote, prayed. Oh, yeah. It was like the Hargrave day of prayer or something. The weird thing is I really don't know what I actually prayed about. So much came out with me saying stuff like, "God, what? What am I even saying? Help me. I don't know what to do."

And that was the biggest problem of all. Sometimes you know there's a problem. You can sense it deep in your gut. But just because you pray about it, just because you study it, just because you wrestle with it until there's nothing left of it, that doesn't mean you've actually solved anything.

So, when nothing else worked, I ordered Mr. Miniver to leave my enormous stack of cards alone and went for a jog.

A dark canopy had covered the world. That's when I realized it had to be after five o'clock already—probably closer to six or seven. Stars twinkled between cloudy patches. The moon, in a bashful mood I guess, ducked behind a cloud, almost like a little kid hiding behind his mom at church. I sound like Carol, don't I? He does that to you. You start seeing the world through his eyes. Here I had the idyllic life and I was the pragmatist. He'd been almost tortured, half-starved, and left alone to fend for himself. He saw the world as beautiful, rich—as a poem.

With each footfall, the sky above darkened. The wind whipped up and pushed me back. I pressed forward. Oh, but it felt good when I rounded a corner and the wind suddenly propelled me down the street. Right up to when the first snowflake fell. Another—five—ten. At twenty, counting became futile.

By the time the condo came into view, I'd gotten cold—wet and very cold. Still, I stood out front and watched the snowflakes fall, faster and faster. The ground seemed to grow white before my eyes. Exaggerated? Probably. Sometimes things just seem exaggerated.

That night, my whole life seemed exaggerated, but nothing could explain *why* it felt that way.

28

Michal—

How is it that December flies by faster every year? Yet, this December dragged slower than a root canal. So many reasons—it's easy to blame it on any of them. But all of them merely mask the real one. Lloyd.

After that night, days passed where we talked about everything *but* what happened. We talked music for the wedding, honeymoon destinations, and birth control. I found out he loves my hair up in a chopstick bun or a messy one—because then he can take it out himself without much hassle. I'd always thought he preferred it down. Now I knew why.

I also learned that the reason he barely tolerates Micaiah is because my punk kid brother told him he'd never be good enough for me. And Lloyd, being the great guy he is, agreed. So, if he agreed to something that flattering, why did it tick me off?

Lloyd bumped up our marriage counseling. It wasn't supposed to start until after Christmas. We now had our first one scheduled for—you got it. Christmas Eve. It might have been cutting things a bit close, but considering we'd had a lot of couple counseling as we dated, the elders were taking that into consideration. So, I kind of assumed we'd be focusing primarily on strictly marriage related issues.

Carol and I talked too—every day after the party, although I only saw him a couple of times. While one or the other of us shopped for a gift or volunteered to ring a kettle bell, we talked. He told me about the gift wrap making party—invited me to it. I didn't go. I couldn't. I was supposed to have lunch with Lloyd. He had to cancel for something with Malinda.

I was on the phone to him the whole way to the marriage counseling session. "Who does this, Carol? I mean, was it that necessary to interrupt someone's family time for this? Mom says he's just afraid of more damage to our relationship since we can't seem to talk about the thing at the party. What do you think?"

"I think I do not know what is right thought. I think he loves you. He wishes to make you happy—to make relationship strong."

"You know, sometimes I hate it when you're right."

His laughter—man I loved that laughter. It filled my car and warmed my heart. He was right. Everything would be fine. That's what marriage counseling is for, right? But Carol said something so brilliant. He said, "Michal, marriage is worth the trouble, yes?"

My mom says something similar. She says, "Anything worth having is worth sacrifice. If it's too easy, you don't appreciate it." I think they have a point.

But it was hard to recognize that as I pulled into the church parking lot and saw Lloyd's Scirocco already there. Somehow, him arriving first just filled me with dread. Honestly, the way my heart raced and my breathing went all shallow, I thought I was going to have some kind of anxiety attack. Kind of funny, if you ask me, because I was in an actual attack of some kind—mild, but definitely something—and half of it was because I was freaking out about having one. That's got to be some kind of irony, there.

The Welks are the coolest couple. And that sounds so weird to say. But it's true. Frank Welk is this small, serious guy. He's stern and looks like a hard, cold dude. I mean, the first time he approached me "as my shepherd," I expected to be a blubbering mess by the time I left the elders' office.

I was, too—but totally in a different way. He'd seen me heading toward spiritual compromise and stepped in before I was too steeped in it. I don't even know how he saw it. It's not like we talked much, you know? I kind of avoided him because he was so… stern.

Instead, with his wife, Pat, sitting in one corner of the room, just knitting away as if she weren't even there, he took my hands, he prayed with me—man that guy is a scary dude, okay? But when he prays, you see just how tender a man of God he is. Tender—but totally fierce. He showed me where I was allowing sentiment and compassion to take precedence over Scripture. He offered to meet with me every Thursday at lunch for a couple of months until I felt confident in "rightly dividing" the Word again. That's some seriously amazing shepherding.

I found the Welks and Lloyd in the elders' office. All four elders shared one office, and sometimes scheduling got difficult, but I suppose they don't usually use it much on Christmas Eve. Pat, Frank, and Lloyd were already deep in prayer. Hearing that man praying for our upcoming marriage, for strength to fight against all that would seek to destroy our relationship, and then in the very next breath the wisdom to know if it was the *right* relationship while that question remained a valid one—heartwarmingly terrifying. Just sayin'.

"There's our Michal!" Pat jumped up, hugged me, and led me to one of the chairs. Four chairs always sat in a semi-circle of that office—four wing-backed chairs. As a little kid, I thought they were like thrones where the kings of the church proclaimed the truths of God. I'll never forget being totally devastated to find out that they were just men who served the Lord by serving the church.

After a prayer, the rest of the meeting was just a blur. Personality tests, maybe? The only thing I remember at all was a question about what we considered our biggest relational issue was—something like that. That's about when my brain went blurry and I couldn't concentrate on the discussion.

Words rolled through my mind—words and thoughts that I'd heard so many times. "*You're just so used to each other that you see it as love. You guys are more like old friends. There's no passion—just familiarity and comfort.*"

Our kiss as we left felt hollow—empty. Lloyd pulled out and turned left. I went right. Symbolic—that's the only word I could think of—symbolic. The familiar pang at him leaving didn't come. I always hated to hear the door shut, the car start. I watched those tail lights disappear without the slightest hint of disappointment or loss.

I don't love him—not like I should. I can't marry him. Even the thoughts forming into cohesive strings of words didn't snap me out of it. All I could think of was, *I have to call him. I have to follow him. I have to tell him.*

Carol—

Mid-afternoon on Christmas Eve, Michal called. Hysterical is the only word I can think of to describe her, but her tone was calm—deadly calm, almost. "I just got out of our first marriage counseling session. Did you know Lloyd is jealous of you? Why, I can't imagine, but it just hit me that he said something like that. I really wasn't paying attention."

A horn blared and I heard the distinct sound of a turn signal clicking. "You are drive the car?"

"Yeah. I've got you on speaker—hands-free."

"Is good." Silence. I felt as though I had to say something about the Lloyd jealousy thing. I couldn't imagine why a man like him could be jealous of me. "I am sorry for Lloyd. Maybe if we talk?" Those words hurt to say—hurt more than I could ever have imagined.

"I don't think it'll do any good, Carol. I've made a decision. I think. I'll talk to Lloyd about it first, of course, but…" It felt like I should hear her sniffle. I didn't. Instead, she cleared her throat and said, "I know I asked you to be my man of honor, and you've worked so hard to help me get this wedding together fast, but I don't think I can go through with it."

Disappointment. Relief. Dismay. Pain. They swirled in a slow-churned mixture in my heart. "If is what you wish, you must do what is best for you. You must think of Lloyd."

"He's going to be so hurt, but it's for the best."

Why would Lloyd care if he's jealous of me? I don't understand. Despite my confusion, somehow the right words formed in my mind and heart and told me two things. First, I needed to help her repair her relationship. And then I needed to leave. I needed to go home, spend the winter there maybe. Come back after the wedding was over and when I would no longer be tempted to beg her not to do it.

"Let the heart lead you, Michal. Do what is make you happy. Have the Happy Christmas—*Merry* Christmas. I will talk with you later."

The mobile rang again after I disconnected. Her face flashed on the screen. I turned it off and set it on the desk. Ideas swirled in my mind, but one pushed me forward. Clothes piled into my duffel bag as fast as I could dump them. Razor, deodorant, brush, toothpaste, toothbrush. Bible. Everything I'd brought to America. My journal, the framed "selfie" of Michal and me. I wrapped that and popped it in the bag as well. If they wouldn't let me carry it on, I'd remove the glass.

With my passport stuffed in my jacket pocket, I raced down the stairs two at a time. Ralph and Annie sat in the office going over some kind of numbers. I'd forgotten about that—something about doing them now so they could take that night through New Year's Day off.

New Year's. We'd planned a party. I was supposed to cook. The thought nearly made me change my mind. I could go after New Year's. There was no reason to do it *right* now. No reason other than knowing, if I didn't go now, I'd drive over to her house and beg her not to marry Lloyd. I'd tell her everything. *It's not right, Carol. Be a man. She loves him. Let her be happy.*

Annie looked up first. "Car—wait. Where are you going?"

"Home."

She began to protest, but Ralph put a hand on her shoulder as he moved around her and led me from the room. "What's going on?"

"I can't watch her marry him. I can't."

"You're the 'man of hon—'"

"Not anymore. Lloyd is the jealousy. Jealous. Lloyd *is* jealous?"

Ralph's smile broke my heart. That man's smile would make anyone feel reassured, loved. But here he looked pained. "I'm going to miss you. Tell me you're coming back." I couldn't answer, but at my nod, he gave me a hug. "Probably sometime in early February, I imagine. What'll this do to your visa application?"

I didn't know. As irresponsible as it may seem, I didn't even care. I just wanted—no, *needed*—to go home. "I will ask when I talk to embassy at home. You are good friend, Ralph. I will come back if—"

Another hug, another smile, promises that I was not only welcome but expected. "We love you, Stefan—"

That's when I had to say something. "Ralph?"

"Yeah?"

"What is name your mother call you when he wants you come to her?"

He looked at me so strangely. "Um... Ralph."

"My mother, he call me Carol. When they take me to orphanage, the old woman next door does not know the other name..."

"Your last name? Wait... your name is Carol Stefan? It's not Stefan Carol?"

"In first beginning, I do not know why I am Stefan when you are Ralph and Zain is Zain—not Kadir. But then I think is nickname. Some of men use other name. I hear the work mens say last name not first. They say, 'Ford will be soon here. Get this done.' So I think is... how you say...?"

"Normal."

"I tell Ramiro, but he say nothing, so..." A shrug and a smile—they seemed enough.

Ralph walked me to the rental. "Yeah. It is. I just... Wow. Sorry. I didn't know."

Gertie rushed up to me and climbed up in the car and on my lap just as I sat down. She licked my face and put her paws up on my shoulder, just as she always did when Ralph tried to leave. "She is like me now that I am go." As Ralph pulled the dog from me, I had to reassure him. "I am coming back. I am. Soon. I send list of those who can come for demonstrations. If you are sure is worth expense."

"It's worth it. We're sold out. I mean, is there even anything *in* that store?"

There were still things on the shelves—not much, but some. Still, he made an excellent point. "We will come. Thank you for the belief in us. I go home. I eat with orphans and watch them with their new presents from Michal. Is make me happy again."

"I think it's likely to hurt you again, but you're probably right."

A flutter at the window and a flash of red showed that Annie watched from the living room. Maybe it was wrong, maybe I shouldn't have done it. I think my own hurt and loss drove me to meddle in someone else's heartstrings instead. "Annie's in there—watching."

"She doesn't want you to go any more than I or the rest of us do."

Even as he spoke, a protest welled up inside. "That's not why I tell you this. I say this because I know your hurt. I know her pain. She is amazing woman. Tell her."

His confused expression followed me as I pulled away from the house and drove down Hearthfield Way and toward the highway.

Oh, God, please let me return. I need this place. I think.

Michal—

When Carol just hung up, I wanted to throw my phone through the windshield. Instead, squealing tires and burning rubber filled the intersection as I did a one-eighty and sped toward Lloyd's place. Rehearsed apologies, explanations, and even rebuttals to imagined arguments filled the car until I pulled up out front. As much as I wanted to call my mom for moral support, I zipped a text telling her I was calling off the wedding and hit Crystal's contact button instead.

"I'm going in."

"Where? Why? And do you need backup?"

That's my best friend I know and love. Look, I might as well admit it. I half shook, half-cried as I tried to tell her what I was about to do. "I'm at Lloyd's place."

"What happened?"

"Nothing, yet. But I'm about to go in and call it off. He'll probably call you." Those words echoed in the car. "He does, doesn't he?"

Crystal sounded strangled as she asked, "Does what?"

"Call you—anytime we have any trouble—little that it's been—he calls. Wow. How did I not notice that?"

"Probably the same way I didn't." Her voice dropped to that soft, low tone that men loved so much. "Michal, are you sure? You—"

The last thing I needed was my best friend talking me out of this. I needed to do it while I had the courage. Look, I'm not a spontaneous person. I make a decision very slowly and change it even slower. I plan, plan, plan, and then execute. So breaking up with Lloyd on what most people would think of as a whim isn't really in my profile. But it was right. I knew it. Deep down in my gut, I knew it. I also knew if I didn't do it, we'd be married with three kids and trapped inside ten years. He'd never leave me—not after one failed marriage already. I'd never do that to kids. I'd stick it out for a nice, pleasant, cordial life.

"I can't do it, Crystal. I can't marry him. It's all wrong. I'm going in, so pray for me, okay?"

"Praying... Love you, Mickey."

She rarely calls me Mickey—not really. Micaiah does—Lloyd too. Mom and Dad do once in a long while, but Crystal saves it for those rare moments when she knows I need to know just how much she cares about me. I needed to hear it right then. "Thanks."

Snow crunched, the wind whipped at my scarf, and shocker of all shockers, my nose stung as the cold air bit it. Stepping into Lloyd's building undid me all over again, though. It was like the warmth of the place fed me a false sense of comfort. So help me, I almost ran.

Doorbells—the pause button to entrances. You arrive, pause, and continue. And that pause takes as long as the person on the other side needs. Lloyd took forever. I almost went out to see if he was still in his car. I mean, I'd seen it as I pulled up, but he wasn't answering.

Once the door finally opened and red-eyed, red-nosed Lloyd stood there, I almost couldn't do it. "Who died? Are you okay?"

His arms wrapped around me right there in the doorway. He held me so tight and so close that I almost couldn't breathe. That wasn't new. He always took my breath away when he held me in his arms, but this time I felt smothered, not cherished. Oh, to have been able to run right then. I wanted nothing more. "I can't believe you came. I wanted you so... but you were so distant at the church. I—" Lloyd's lips brushed my forehead before he added, "Thank you."

"Wha—"

At that point, he seemed to realize where we stood and pulled us inside. He shoved folded piles of clothes aside and sat down. Me, I stared at those piles with a heart breaking at the sight of them. "You messed up your laundry!"

"I can refold. Come sit with me."

Have you ever stood frozen, knowing that if you take a single step, your life will be irrevocably changed? That's what it was like. I couldn't speak, couldn't explain, couldn't cry, couldn't comfort. I couldn't hope to understand what was going on in my messed up head. Instead, I wriggled the ring off my finger. Oh, how my heart cracked and crumbled as Lloyd's eyes widened and filled with tears.

He closed them, refused to look at me as I held it out and tried to explain. "Lloyd, I'm sorry. You know I love you but—"

"If you love me, we work this out. It's what people in love do."

"I'm not *in* love with you, though." Honesty made me qualify that. "I don't think."

He jumped up and tried to hold me but stumbled back as my hands shot out to stop him. "We'll work this out, Michal. We will. It's just a blip—probably those pre-wedding jitters. People get those."

"I don't think that's it. I keep remembering that kiss at the party."

Everything changed with those words. He spat out a response that showed more honesty since the wretched event. "Party. I wish I'd never gone to that thing. It ruined everything." Then, under his breath, so quietly that I didn't know if I'd actually heard it or not, he whispered, "I wish he'd never come here."

"What? Who—Carol?"

When you've been with a man for four years, you get to know him really well. I knew Lloyd better than he knew himself sometimes. I suspect the reverse is true as well. And well, he was fighting not saying something ugly. I could see it in the way his jaw clenched, his teeth ground, a particular vein in his temple throbbed. I tried to reassure him, but he preempted me. "You have no idea how jealous I've been of him. I tried so hard to hide it. I tried to stifle it—kill it. I just 'knew' it was unreasonable." Once he got going, he couldn't stop. "At first, I wasn't. At first, he seemed like the Carol you've always talked about—just as a guy."

Look, interrupting is always rude. I just want to put that out there. But sometimes rudeness is a kindness. I chose kind over polite that day. "He is just a guy—just a guy who has been there for me through every major joy and sorrow of my life. He helped me over Grandpa Colbert's death like no one else could. Everyone tried. *You* tried. Carol succeeded. But he's *just* my friend. This isn't about me choosing my lifelong pen pal over you. This is about me realizing we're a habit—not a couple."

"That's ridiculous!"

Again with the interrupting thing, but I had to while the words flowed. "No, we are. My friends—all of whom really like you, by the way—all have said, 'You guys seem so perfect for each other' in one breath and 'but there's no passion with you. You're just *there*' in the next. Well, I don't want fifty or more years of 'just a habit' with anyone. I'm sorry. You need to find someone who lights up and tingles at the thought of you." My eyes dropped to my feet. "I don't."

"But Michal, that's not you. It's not how we're wired." Lloyd reached for me, but when I didn't meet him halfway, he grew almost desperate sounding. "We have passion, Michal. You can't tell me you felt nothing when we've kissed. We've barely avoided crossing a few lines more than once."

I've never been so confident of anything as I became of my decision right then. I heard myself saying things I'd probably felt for years but didn't know how to articulate or even if I should. "Hormones, Lloyd. I get it now. I confused hormones for passion—for love. And I *do* love you. But not enough to spend the rest of my life with you. I want…*more.*"

"That's just—"

I couldn't let him continue. "I keep thinking of Grace, of my parents. I keep thinking of that couple from Fairbury—Richard and Ruth. They waited a *decade* for each other out of love. I'd wait a decade out of commitment." My voice cracked as I added, "I don't want to be that person. I want the kind of love they have." Lloyd looked as if he'd been sucker-punched. Maybe I shouldn't have kept talking, but I did. A memory hit me—one of Crystal trying to convince me that my apathy to Lloyd comforting Malinda wasn't normal, and I ran with that.

"Okay, remember that day in your office? I went all over town to get the perfect picnic lunch for us. And when I arrived, you were there holding Malinda, remember?"

"If you're jealous—"

"That's just it!" Suddenly I felt like a woman I'd seen in a movie. I always thought she was so stupid for being upset that she wasn't upset when her boyfriend was out with another woman. She thought she should be jealous. I'd always said she should be glad she had such a strong relationship that she had no concerns. Now I got it. I understood.

Lloyd tried to hold me again, but I shoved the ring in his hand and backed away once more. "Michal!" He sounded like he'd cry. "Don't do this!"

"No, listen. I wasn't jealous. I knew exactly what was going on. I knew she'd lost a patient or something—"

"Got rejected again, actually."

"Right! I knew it wasn't you making out with her or anything. You didn't even startle when I walked in and found you. You apologized. And you went right on comforting her—*as you should have.*" He tried to interject, but once you're on a roll with a guy who has been able to talk you out of cats, dogs, bad car and bad hair choices, you don't let him get a word in edgewise when you're talking him out of marriage. "I don't want to be that woman who flips out at something like that. But I think I want to feel just a twinge of something before I talk myself into reason again. And I didn't."

"Michal…"

Shaking my head, I backed away further. "And I won't. I just know it. I won't. Look, I'll take care of everything. I'll let everyone know it's my fault. I—" When he stepped closer again, I decided to try a different tack. I wrapped my arms around him, kissed his cheek, whispered goodbye, and then bolted. He didn't know what hit him.

In my car, I imagined him standing there, door open, ring in his hand, and shock on his face. Then I bawled.

29

Michal—

Mom, for all her complaints about him, yelled at me for twenty-minutes straight—right up to the moment when I hung up the phone. I didn't want to spend Christmas Eve with the famous Barb Hargrave glare boring holes in me. My heart bled enough without that too. I called Micaiah. He didn't answer, but I knew he'd be glad. Then I took a shower, put on fuzzy sleep pants, fuzzy socks, and a long-sleeved t-shirt.

I thought about calling Crystal, but I wasn't ready to talk about it yet. So, instead, I sent a quick text. IT'S DONE. CAN YOU CALL HIM? I THOUGHT HE'D GET IT. I THOUGHT HE'D AGREE. HE ACTS DEVASTATED. I'LL TALK TO YOU TOMORROW.

Mr. Miniver is a great comfort when life swallows you whole and spits you out. We cuddled together on the couch for at least an hour—you know, until I soaked his fur with tears, and he'd had enough of me. Then he batted his paw at my hand, stalked to the other end of the couch, curled up, and glared at me. I could read his thoughts as if he spoke human instead of Superiorese. *Snap out of it! Get yourself together. You made this bed, now lie in it.* I'm pretty sure if he knew any other clichés he'd have used them too. He's a little short on clichés.

So, without him to talk me down from calling Lloyd to talk again, I tried Carol. It went straight to voice mail. For an hour. I left exactly sixty voice mails. At the sixty-one mark, Ralph answered. Right then, my heart dropped to my stomach. "What's wrong? Why do you have his phone? I should have known—"

"Michal, he's gone."

"Gone?" Ice in my heart spread through my veins until the shivers sent me scrambling for the throw blanket. "What do you mean, gone?"

The pain in his voice surprised me. I could hear it in every word. "Michal, he went home to Romania for the holidays. I think he was a bit homesick, and he said something about wanting to give you and Lloyd space."

Ralph hadn't finished saying "Romania for the holidays" before I jumped up and grabbed my keys. The lock to my firebox, of course, acted up again. Lloyd had told me a thousand times to buy a new one. Here I was wishing I'd listened to him even as I was running away—from him. How stupid is that?

"Michal? You still there?"

"Yeah! Sorry. Look, I gotta go. You have a Merry Christmas."

"Are you sure you're okay?"

Confidence overflowed just then. I'd never been more okay in my life. "Yeah. I'm going."

"Where?"

"To Romania. I'm going to bring him back. Bye."

He may have tried to say more. I don't know. I just tossed my phone on the bed as I wrestled with that stupid fire box until it finally opened. Passport. Birth certificate. Emergency cash. *Here I come.*

My phone did flight searches from Rockland to NYC and from NYC to Constanţa. I had an hour and a half in the airport at JFK. I could do it. Before I could talk myself out of it, and I'd already begun, I bought the non-refundable tickets. Clothes—threw them in the suitcase. Toiletries, hair stuff, makeup, the Christmas present that had been sitting under my tree for weeks—it all piled in in a jumbled mess. I could have put ten times more in that stupid thing if I hadn't just thrown it all in there, but I zipped it shut, grabbed my purse, coat, and scarf, and bolted for the door.

Mr. Miniver sat there yowling at me. Dinner time. Oh, yeah. And I was about to take off for who knew how long without contacting my boss or anyone to feed my cat. "Hang on. I'll get your dinner."

The sound of kibble hitting his bowl filled the phone as I tried to tell Crystal what was up. "—going to Consta—yeah. Going to talk to him."

"Good! That's awesome!"

"—care of Mr. Miniver? He's already ticked at me for almost leaving without feeding him." A stack of note cards on the counter gave me an idea. I shoved them in my purse as we talked.

"Sure! Sure! I'll get your mail—whatever. Just *go!*"

Have you ever felt like nothing you did was right? That if you just kept doing stuff long enough, you'd completely mess up every aspect of your life? Yeah—that was me as I dumped my suitcase in the back of my car and whizzed off toward the highway.

I also got a ticket before I got out of the city limits.

A flight from Rockland to NYC on Christmas Eve with zero turbulence—unheard of. But I had one. Out of fifty notes I wrote, only one got spoiled with any bump at all—thanks to the guy who just *had* to get into his suitcase for a book that he promptly sat down and *didn't* read.

One after another, the words flowed onto the cards. Family members, my boss, my coworkers, people at church, oh... and Grace. I wrote a long one to Grace, begging for her wisdom and prayers. I just knew she'd understand and agree. Odd... less than twenty-four hours earlier, I would have been convinced of the opposite.

The woman next to me snored through the first half of the flight. I'd worn my earbuds to try to drown her out, but it's like my nerves knew it was happening regardless of what my ears could hear. So when she woke up and asked what I was doing, I pulled them out and answered. Conversation beats sawn logs any day.

"They're... apology notes? I don't know how to describe it. I just called off my wedding, so I'm letting people know. We even have a few gifts to return, so I'm promising to take care of those right away, telling my wedding party—everything. Lloyd shouldn't have to do any of it."

She didn't speak at first. Her eyes watched me, but I could tell she wasn't trying to read the words. She wanted something—what, I couldn't tell. The airplane hummed along in the night air—the soundtrack of my journey. Then she smiled and stuck out her hand just as I popped the next one in its envelope. "I'm Joyce…"

"Michal."

"Aaah… King David's wife." Her lips stretched into a smile that both hid wrinkles and added more.

I couldn't help but smile at the picture. "You know, you're a beautiful woman. I hope I am as lovely when I'm older."

"Ancient is a better word, my dear." Her eyes traveled back to the cards. "Michal, are you sure?" When I didn't respond, she continued as if I'd begged for more. "Are you sure—really sure. Girls these days, if you'll pardon an unflattering observation. You just expect everything to be movie perfect. Life isn't."

"I—"

But Joyce held her hand to her chest and shook her head. "If you don't mind, I'd like to continue. You see, life is messy and complicated and full of one stumble after the next."

"Isn't that the truth?" My hand covered her other one without me realizing I'd done it at first.

"I just mean," she continued with true concern and almost affection in her eyes. "It's not a bad thing if things get messy. You'll hold each other up." Then she took my hand between both of hers and pleaded earnestly with me. "Don't throw away something real for an ideal. I don't know if that's what you're doing, but I have to beg you to reconsider."

Usually, I would have given her a dozen explanations for why I had made the right decision, went back to writing, and ignored her until she left me alone. I'd have been polite, but quite clear in my meaning. *Don't interfere where it's none of your business.* I'm not proud of that.

This time I listened, I thought. I even prayed a bit, and then shook my head. "I wish that was it. I really do. But it's not. We're not messy. We don't *do* messy. We've had almost no arguments, and even disagreements are few and far between."

"That's a rare thing—beautiful. So, if you don't mind my interference, why did you decide against it, then?"

"Habit. I think we'd become a habit—a very lovely, very comfortable, couldn't ask for a better... *habit.*" My hand shook as I closed my pen and put it away. The cards followed. Once I'd re-stowed my tray, I turned back to her. "I want more than habit. My friends warned me—kept saying, 'there's no spark'. I didn't listen until we'd already half-planned the wedding." My face flushed. "I confused natural desire for personal passion. Does that make sense?"

Joyce listened with the kind of understanding I think Grace would have. She challenged me. She comforted me.

"When I showed up to call it off, I really expected him to say, 'That's probably a good idea.' I mean, I love him. He loves me. We love our best friends, but we wouldn't want to marry them." Carol's face filled my mind, and I said before I could stop myself, "Although, I could probably marry my best friend and be perfectly happy."

"Your best friend?" Joyce sat up and looked a little alarmed.

It was kind of cruel, really. Here was this sweet old lady who probably felt scandalized over the way the world kept changing and accepting things that had once been *illegal.* But I did it. "Yeah, Carol. We've been pen pals since I was a kid." I wanted to laugh but I couldn't. Shame filled me as the woman swallowed hard and nodded. "He's such a great guy, and now he's gone."

"Who is gone, and where did he go?"

"Carol—my pen pal. I kept calling him, but his friend said he's on his way home to Romania, so I just packed up and here I am." The words shook me. "Wow. I just *packed and went.* I don't *do* stuff like that. Wow. Just...wow!"

Joyce listened as I rambled. She asked questions that I didn't realize

I'd answered until she asked the next. And when she'd finished, I was ready to cry. But her words sucked the tears from my eyes and ripped my heart out through my throat. "Sounds to me like you said yes to the wrong man."

Denial spilled from my lips faster than a kid with her hand in a cookie jar. "Carol? Naw... we're..." I couldn't finish that thought as the truth of her words shoved my heart right back to where it belonged, and it flopped to my stomach. She had a way with organs, that Joyce.

"I thought you'd see it." Joyce pulled her neck pillow off and passed it to me. "Get some sleep, dear Michal. You are going to need all the rest you can get."

Michal—

An hour and a half is plenty of time to get from terminal seven to terminal one at JFK. It is. But that didn't stop me from bolting down the jet way and snagging the first train that rolled through five minutes later. Others flooded in behind me. The chances of Carol being on that flight were so slim it wasn't even funny, but I watched every face that got on and every face that raced up and tried to get on after the doors closed and we were whisked away to terminal one.

A full hour. I had a full hour before the flight took off. There hadn't been any first-class tickets, which my budget and credit card both praised the Lord for, and I couldn't stop whining to myself about. This meant one thing. They'd begin boarding in forty minutes. I'd have to wait until the last second to get on. With a nine-hour flight, a *twenty-hour* layover in Istanbul, and just over an hour from Istanbul to Constanța, I wanted to be sitting as little as possible on that plane. Yeah... as little time as possible cramped, wedged, squeezed between people who would probably sleep and drool on me on the plane. Who wouldn't? Want to wait till the last second, I mean.

Once in the terminal, I made a long, slow sweep of every gate, every restaurant-slash-store—everything. But there was no sign of Carol anywhere. *He probably got another flight.*

After a woman gave me a once-over that clearly was not flattering, I bolted to a bathroom to assess the damage. Let's just say it was bad. Actually, I'd say that the fact they let me through customs looking as I did is proof enough of miracles. Brush. Hair. Voilà. Not gorgeous. Not by a long shot, but I was just grateful Carol wouldn't be waiting for me when I landed. I'd probably have to wait twenty-four hours or so before I could see him. He'd be dead. I'd be dead. Jet lag is real, and the only complements or direct objects—never remember the rules for those things—that I can find to go with that are words that my mother would wash my mouth out with soap for using, even at my age.

Makeup—I had none on. *None.* I'm not the most vain woman on the planet, but seriously. What was I *not* thinking? It took ten minutes to get a look that wouldn't end up more on the neck pillow I intended to buy than on my face. I suppose I might as well admit that this is when I saw that I hadn't gotten dressed before I bolted out that front door. Yep. I stood there in my charcoal gray pea coat, my cool cranberry scarf tucked inside the collar, a long-sleeved t-shirt, fuzzy sleep pants, and my comfy Sketchers walkers.

I wore these shoes? Why? But the vague memory of thinking, "Those'll be easy to take on and off at security" flooded my mind and grew stronger. I could see my pants in my memory as I'd pulled on socks. Why didn't they register back at home when I could have done something about them?

Then came the decision… to change or not to change? I had my carry-on. Jeans were in there. But suddenly the idea of nine hours on a flight in jeans versus fuzzy, buttery soft, comfy sleep pants seemed unbearable. *It's not like he's going to see them. Vanity—all is vanity. Just go find that pillow.*

The obnoxious beeping of a cart carrying a disabled passenger to her gate greeted me as I stepped outside the bathroom door. A few people milled about, but one man walked straight in the path of that stupid cart. I screamed for him to stop. The cart nearly ran into him, which only made him stumble and fall. People rushed forward. But the moment I saw the man get up and insist he was fine, I turned toward the nearest store and went in search of a good flight pillow. And a book. I definitely would need a book.

Carol—

A scream rang out, drowning out the incessant beeping of one of those carts that drives people through the airport. Something about the voice reminded me of Michal. *Don't let yourself go there. You must learn to be happy for her. You must.*

After another glance, I heard someone say, "Excuse me." Another man wanted to enter the restrooms—the ones I blocked as I watched the melee surrounding that cart.

"Sorry."

It's easy to acclimate to a new environment. America had taught me to love coffee with chocolate, whipped cream, and "sprinkles." So, with almost an hour to kill, I wandered off looking for a coffee cart or store. A woman stopped me—asked if I knew where the restrooms were. I pointed at the sign less than ten feet away. "Is there. Merry Christmas."

"Happy Holidays to you too."

The overt flirtation—no one could miss it—not even me. But I pretended not to notice and strolled away again, determined to get that coffee. There is an advantage to a midnight flight to Istanbul from JFK on Christmas Eve—there isn't a mile-long line for coffee. And how American I sound using their acronyms.

Cup in hand, that amazing aroma filling the air—it was time to shuffle down to the gate. I slung my duffel bag over one shoulder and took off. A Muslim family filled the corridor as we strolled past gate after gate, to gate eleven—Turkish Airlines. Once there, it wasn't difficult to find a spot to sit in—sit and wait. Wait and watch.

The husband went to the gate to speak to the attendant before settling just out of sight with his family. *They are nice children—well behaved for so late tonight.* That thought struck a chord of pain. I'd miss the children of HearthLand—even for the short time I planned to be gone. Rory and

Andre, Emma and Ida Jo. Those little girls I imagined as great friends someday—and maybe even Rory and Andre.

Twice I pulled out my mobile to read or play a game. I didn't have it, of course. That made up my mind. With cup in hand and a glance at the clock behind the gate counter, I headed back up the concourse to the shops. Maybe if I read a book in English it would help my language skills. It would also make the long flight and even longer layover more interesting.

A voice rang out over the loudspeaker as I stood and made my way out of the gate area to the concourse. "Flight 1249 to Istanbul with connections to Constanța will begin boarding in twenty minutes. We ask that all passengers be ready to board as your group is called. Thank you and happy holidays from Turkish Airlines."

Michal—

Airport prices are the retail equivalent to usury. Only cinemas can top them for excessive markup. I paid twenty bucks for a six dollar pillow. Twenty. My only consolation is that if cinemas sold them they'd be thirty. At least the paperback was "only" retail. Okay, so I'm used to buying at Costco where I get them for like half price or something like that. Sue me.

I leaned against a pillar and pulled out the book. No matter how badly I wanted to crawl into one of the chairs at the gate, it wasn't going to happen. No way. No how. Nuh uh. It's a kindness to your legs, you know. I read a study once where it said that you lose a ton of the electrical activity to your legs in just minutes of sitting down. The flight was nine and a half or so hours. I'd stand until the last second.

Why don't people teach children to read standing up? Why didn't someone teach kids that standing with their backs to the furnace or the fireplace while reading is the most comforting, cozy feeling ever? They'd have bought it—or I would have, anyway. Then standing in an airport wouldn't feel weird at all. It'd be *normal.*

The attendant at the gate called for those on flight 1249 to Istanbul to be ready to board. I was in zone 4. I thought about asking if Carol Stefan was on the flight, but I figured they couldn't tell me. So, after a good glance around me, I flipped open the book to the first page and began reading. A little girl came around the pole and stared up at me.

"Whatcha reading?"

"It's a book about a girl who goes back to her family's homeland to understand it better." Kneeling isn't sitting, right? I knelt down so she could see better. "See? She grew up in America, but her family is originally from Pakistan. So she's going there."

A man's voice called to her, admonishing her not to bother the lady—that'd be me. She dashed away, but not before I saw the disappointed look in her eyes. You know, before Grace had kids, I would have argued with him—insisted she wasn't bothering me at all. Thanks to her teaching all of us how hard that is on parents and kids alike, that mistake was averted. Instead, I peered around the pole and met the mother's gaze. "I don't mind," I mouthed. "She's not bothering me."

The woman nodded and then murmured something to her husband. When the girl reached his side, he nodded in my direction. "The lady says you can talk to her. Just don't leave our sight."

Little braids flopped as she skipped back to me. "I like to read, too. But I've never read a book that big."

"Someday you will." At the longing she showed, I couldn't help but add, "Or maybe you'll *write* one."

"Me? What would I write about?"

Why is it so easy to answer a child's questions rather than helping them think the questions through? "Well... you're going somewhere now, aren't you?"

"I'm going to visit my *Dede* in Istanbul."

"Is *Dede* Turkish for grandmother?"

A giggle escaped as wide, dark, sparkling eyes met mine again. "No... grand*father*. We will stay a whole month!" A funny expression came over her face. "I have to go now."

The child ran to her mother, whispered something, and they took off in the direction of the restrooms. Me, I gave the area one more sweep of my eyes and then went back to reading. *He had to have taken another flight. He's still not here.*

Carol—

The words swam together in nonsensical jumbles on the page. No matter how hard I tried to rearrange them into proper lines and meaningful words, I failed—miserably. Each second that passed felt an eternity. A mobile would have been a great distraction, not to mention a likely disaster. With a mobile nothing could have prevented me from calling Michal. It would have happened, and that wasn't a good idea. A little girl skipped past with her mother—the Muslim family. Her eyes caught mine before she saw the book I carried. That stopped her in her tracks. She tugged free of her mother's hand and pointed at it.

"That's a book about a girl who grew up in America and went back to Pakistan to see her family there."

"Yes! Have you read it?"

She shook her head. "No…"

"Is very good book, I think." I showed her the back. "Here people say why they like. I think, 'If is this good, I should read. So I buy."

Her finger pointed to a pillar across the gate lounge area. "There's a lady over there with that book. She says it's good. You should talk to her."

Words tumbled forth without me thinking of who I spoke to or what I said. "Can I tell you secret?"

"Yes…" The little girl's eyes lit up.

Her mother stared at me with a look that said, "Don't make me hurt you." Aloud she just said, "Come on, Ayla. Leave the poor man alone."

"Is fine," I assured her. Ayla—such a beautiful name. Another glance at her mother told me to stick to my secret and keep the compliments to myself. "I just left my friend to go home. I am sad. So I like to make the friends, but not today. I think for me it would be sad even more."

"Maybe if you make a new friend, you won't miss the other one so much."

The pain that filled my heart made it impossible to speak. Tears came before any hope of stopping them, and I bolted from the place without even saying goodbye. Conscience accused, but I ignored it. Nine and a half hours on a plane would be plenty of time to apologize, when I could speak again. Right then, I needed to walk—walk and pray for wisdom and relief.

Michal—

The moment they called the first class and other "elite" passengers, I realized just where I was and what I was doing. You just don't wake up one day, decide to call off your wedding, hop on a couple of planes, and fly to places unknown. What sane person does that? Not *me!* It's like I decided I had to make up for a lifetime of lack of spontaneity all at once or something. Then again, I'd been more spontaneous in the three months I'd spent with Carol than I had in my whole life. What about Carol inspired that, anyway?

Knuckles white from gripping the suitcase handle, hand protesting as the leather strap of my purse dug into it, I stood staring at the boarding pass as passenger after passenger boarded that plane. *I'll stand here. I'll watch every single person. If Carol is in the group, I'll get on the plane. If not, I'll go home.*

My latent frugal side protested. Nine hundred dollars for a ticket. *Nine hundred.* I'd just toss it away for nothing? Not hardly. But Christmas! I'd decided to just *chuck* Christmas with my family. And, of course, that's when the text came through. Mom.

WHAT IS THIS ABOUT GOING TO ROMANIA? FIRST YOU CALL OFF THE WEDDING, THEN YOU CHASE CAROL ACROSS THE WORLD? ON CHRISTMAS? GET YOUR BUTT BACK HERE, MISSY.

That's Mom-speak for, "You've got me worried sick."

They called for zone one. Zone two. That one took forever—forever in which my two selves warred within me. If I could have done one of those stupid sci-fi body split things, it would have happened right there. Half of me running back to the air train and over to terminal seven again. Half of me bolting onto the plane without stopping for them to scan that boarding pass.

Row forty-two. I've got a long way to go. A lot of time to panic and bolt. I wonder if they'd let me on early.

Before I could talk myself out of it, I joined the line at the desk— people asking for seat changes, upgrades—the works. When the woman reached out for my ticket, the story poured out before I could stop myself. "I'm terrified that I won't get on this plane. I need to get on this plane. Can I go now? I usually wait, like, forever. But I *need* to get on. Please."

"Have you taken a motion-sickness—"

"I'm not afraid of flying, and I don't get air sick. I just am afraid I won't go. And I need to go." Her eyes met mine just as I begged. "*Please...*"

With a marker, she scratched out the four and scrawled a two with her initials. "Go ahead. Hope you have a pleasant flight. Next!"

Hands shaking, body quaking, just standing in the line now, waiting to board and sit for the next half hour. *What's gotten into you? This is so insane. Go home while you can!*

Two more people moved forward. Two more. I stood there with a gap forming as the attendant called out again. "We're continuing our boarding for flight 1249 to Istanbul. First class passengers, club members, and zones one and two are free to board. Zone three boarding in just a moment. Zone three, prepare to board."

A man's voice asking if I'd planned to move forward sent me scurrying to the gate. The attendant who had moved me through smiled. "Glad you'll be joining us."

I think I am, too. I think.

Carol—

Airports were designed to confuse passengers and sell more plane tickets when people miss their flight. I didn't know that before I found myself standing in the middle of shops and food places feeling as though I'd completely lost all sense of space and time. I stopped a passing man.

"Where to gate eleven, please?"

"I think that's the next terminal. Just get on the train and get off at the next stop."

Fear, panic, frustration boiled over as I bolted to the train. The clock said boarding had already begun. How did I get into the wrong terminal? A woman mopping the floor saw me and smiled.

"Late for your flight?"

"Wasn't... but I must have gotten to wrong terminal. I lose the gate. I should not have leave gate."

Her forehead furrowed. "Wait... you were at the right one, but now you have to go to another terminal?" She held out her hand. "Let me see your boarding pass."

Part of me screamed not to do it. She could take it and run. Then what would I do? I couldn't remember the flight number. I couldn't remember anything. But I pulled it from my pocket and passed it to her. "Turkish Airlines to Istanbul. Is boarding."

Eyes flashing and tongue rattling faster than any translator could hope to follow, much less me, the woman pointed back the way I'd come. "You're in the right terminal. It's way down there at the end. Run. You don't have much time."

"Thank you!" Just as I'd made it almost out of sight or hearing, I think she called back, "Good luck." At least, someone did.

People grumbled as I tried to weave in and out without hitting anyone with the duffel. Had it not been so late at night, there's no way I could have made it. Just as I neared gate eleven, I heard a final call for flight 1249. Gasping for air, I passed the boarding pass and tried to smile as the woman welcomed me aboard. "You just made it. We're closing the doors in two minutes."

"Thank you."

Only half a dozen people stood ahead in the jet way. They moved through with reasonable speed. My ticket said I belonged in row thirty-one. With the duffel stowed, jacket off, and book in hand, I seated myself and prepared for the long flight.

Michal—

The worst part of buying tickets just hours before a flight? You don't get a window seat. The neck pillow helped me sleep for the first couple of hours or so, but after the drink cart went through, I was wide awake.

You know that crazy excitement you get on Christmas Eve or just before you leave for vacation? You're so ready to go that you can't sleep? That's it exactly. They should have a name for that. Well, I think they do. I heard someone say something once, but it made no sense to me. They need one that makes sense—something like PEDS... pre-excitement stress disorder. But that's PESD. I like PEDS better. Maybe they'd go for pre-excitement disorder of stress. Yeah. Like that's not stupid.

My attention span was shot. Maybe it was pre-jet lag, or maybe it was just PEDS. Whatever it was, I couldn't read more than a couple of pages without looking up and around me. People got up and down all the time, but sometimes it's just best to hold out until you can't stand it anymore. Then make a lap or two of the airplane and you're good to sit for another hour—give or take.

But every time someone did get up, I watched. I mean, Carol hadn't been planning to go home, so he couldn't have bought a ticket *that* much sooner than me. So, that meant if somehow he was on this plane, he shouldn't be up front unless he'd gotten the comfort economy or something. Oh, how I wished I had.

Then again, it wasn't bad. The seat next to me was free, so there was room to plop a purse to dig through or whatever. Gotta take what you can get, right? Look on the bright side. All that jazz.

Movement in my peripheral vision sent my eyes forward. Heart racing, skipping, jumping—*Carol.*

Carol—

I understand why airplanes don't have lavish lavatories. I understand why they must be small. It seems wrong to complain, but do they have to be *that* small? How do overweight people manage? My shoulders nearly have to fit in sideways.

This is why I waited for a good forty minutes after the first twinge of discomfort before I got up. Of course, the fact that the *four* lavatories two rows ahead of me stayed occupied every time I looked up didn't help.

Eventually, waiting ceases to be an option. A queue formed, and I started to join when I noticed someone exiting at the back of the plane— and no one waited to get in. Running isn't recommended on planes, or so the attendant told me, but I imagine that those sorts of accidents aren't either. I ran.

A queue had formed by the time I exited—one that blocked the aisle I needed to use to get to my seat without climbing over everyone. Half a dozen rows down, I heard someone—*Michal*—call my name. *This is proof that you needed to go home. You're hearing her voice now.*

"Carol... are you that mad at me?" If she hadn't giggled, I'd have run.

Now I know why movies have those scenes where everything is in slow motion. Now I understand why everything spins and light bubbles go everywhere. It's real. It really happens.

At first she didn't move. She just sat there with one of those pillows for your neck making her hair stick out all over and looking ready for Christmas morning. No, really. She wore red and white snowflake pajama bottoms—that fuzzy fabric that looks so soft and warm that it's nearly impossible not to stroke it like a cat. An irrational thought made me order myself *not* to do that. I wanted to believe it wasn't even possible. I knew better.

"Michal?"

That's another thing that happens in movies. It takes time to register things, and well, it took time for me to really trust that the woman sitting there was *my* Michal. Well, *Lloyd's* Michal, technically. But whatever.

She scrambled to pull her purse off the seat beside her and somehow shoved it—a purse the size of a carry-on suitcase—under the seat in front of her. "Sit with me? No one is sitting here."

In a daze, I did—sat down, hugged her, stared at her, laughed with her. She teased me about being an unwelcome surprise. Only God kept me from kissing her. "Why are you here? I thought you have Christmas with family. I thought you have—"

"My family is pretty ticked at me right now."

I started to ask why, when I realized it must be because she decided against having me in the wedding. *Why would they care?* Some questions you can only think and never ask. Asking them sounds like you're fishing for compliments—I think that's the phrase. But asking a simple "why" seemed safe enough. "Why?"

"Because I've invested four years in a relationship with Lloyd. I 'led him on.' I 'practically lived with him.' And then I 'just dumped him' over a few 'pre-wedding jitters.'" Her hands did enough air quotes for me to wonder if I had misunderstood what those meant. "I can't make them under—"

"Wait. You dump. What is this mean?" It's disconcerting when you think you understand an idiom and someone uses it in a way that implies that you don't. Sitting there waiting for an explanation took longer than the rest of the flight. I'm sure of it.

"You know, because I called off the wedding."

Of course, movies are not perfect examples of life. In a movie, at that point, I would have kissed her. I would have cradled her face in my hands and lost myself in the wonder of her eyes, her smile, her lips. I would have told her how much I loved her. I would have captured her hand, held it to my heart, and never let it go again.

Sometimes, a conscience well-trained by a priest who is determined to keep you from going back down a terrible path, is an incredibly inconvenient thing. My heart bled as I spoke the words I knew I should and ignored the ones that pleaded for a chance to win her heart. "Is right that you do this? You are certain this is what you wish?"

The hurt in her eyes ripped at me all over again. "I thought, of all people, you might understand. I thought—" She tried to search my face, but the tears must have blinded her. "Never mind."

"Michal—I..."

"Carol, I needed support right now, okay? I didn't need yet *another* person telling me how wrong I am to make a decision for *my* life!"

We both glanced around us as the man beside me snorted half-awake before dropping back to sleep. Then we giggled. Yes, I did as well, I think. It's embarrassing.

Sometimes, despite all resolve, you find yourself listening to your heart instead of your mind. It's also usually a bad thing—for me anyway. Still, seeing the distress I'd caused overrode any cautions I might otherwise have heeded.

It must be a difficult thing for any man to try to show affection for the first time to the woman he loves. And, it would seem that if it was too easy, there might be a bit of pride or arrogance driving it—over-confidence in its reception. But, when your world has just been sent spinning backwards, it just... at that moment, it seems like it's the hardest thing you'll ever do.

Fingers clenched and released. Arm muscles nearly snapped from the strain of restraint. Prayers, every one I could remember, or at least snippets of them, filled my heart as I struggled to do something as simple as taking her hand. *It's a long flight. If this is wrong, it could be even more awkward.*

Never have I felt such instant and overwhelming peace. One moment I cried out for strength and wisdom. The next, I had peace and a small measure of confidence—not in how she'd respond, but in what I should do regardless. That's when I understood how men might not struggle. It doesn't have to be arrogance. Sometimes it may just be the quiet confidence of a man listening to his Heavenly Father.

The touch of our hands melted all tension faster than the finest chocolate on a summer's day. Her eyes met mine. I suspect my smile was just as awkward as hers. And the only words I could think of to say were, "It will be well. God will control this."

Michal—

The moment his hand touched mine, something crazy happened in my heart. I've never felt anything like it. You know, Lloyd and I had chemistry. I don't care what anyone wants to say. Crystal can think we had no passion all she likes, but she didn't live through kisses so dizzying that they tempted me to rethink my determination to remain a virgin until marriage. I'd barely made it to thirty-four. Barely.

I'll take that one step further. Thanks to Lloyd's ability to turn my stomach to mush and fuel fires I shouldn't have even kindled, some might say I'm not. I'm clinging to semantics on this one, but Jesus had strong words to say about lustful thoughts, and well... Ouch. It may have *just* been chemistry. Or maybe it really was love that had just fizzled. Maybe those slow embers I thought we had had been real. Maybe I had been in love with him, but if so, something doused it. Something smothered it until those embers went cold. I'm just grateful that the Lord let it happen *before* I promised to love and be faithful to him for life.

So with that in mind, when I say that the touch of Carol's hands did amazing things to my heart, I do not exaggerate. I couldn't *breathe*. I didn't *want* to breathe. Fingers tingling, heart dancing—never have I been so *content* just at the touch of a guy's hand. And yet, I could sense it. I also wanted more. But this desire for more was also patient. I'd never imagined First Corinthians 13 meaning *eros* when it says love is patient, but at that moment, I understood how it could.

It would wait for the right time. Just then, though, with his fingers laced with mine, his hand covering mine, the touch of his arm on my leg—I could revel in it for days. A glance at his eyes corrected that. *Weeks even. How cute are you, looking all adorably awkward?*

"It will be well. God will control this."

Strange words from a man who had just turned me into a puddle of mush. Then I got it. *God is in control. That's what you mean. Do you have any idea what you just did to me? Did you feel it too?*

I maybe shouldn't have asked, but I did. "Why did you leave, Carol?"

Tears filled his eyes. His Adam's apple rose and fell until it felt like watching a kid at a party bobbing for apples. Did he realize he squeezed my hand so tight I couldn't feel it any longer? He must have, his hand relaxed and his thumb stroked the back of mine. Of course, my heart zinged again.

"You ask me to be man of honor. Is hard for me to say yes, but I cannot say no to my friend. Is difficult to see the ring on the finger. You talk of the wedding and your first dance with husband. I suggest song and cry on the way home." His eyes dropped. "I want to say no. This I cannot do." Once more, he tried to look at me—tried and failed. "I cannot tell Michal I will not help."

Until that moment, I'd dismissed every time a friend said he was falling for me. I really didn't believe it. Maybe I was blind or maybe he was just that good at hiding it. But you'd have to be a fool not to sense what he'd say next. Of course, he didn't *say* anymore. He gripped the arm of the seat and stared ahead as if preparing to do some horrible feat.

"Carol? That's really sad, and I'm so sorry I hurt you by asking, but that doesn't tell me why you left." Call me cruel. I deserve it. But I had to ask.

As if he hadn't stopped, as if I hadn't pressed, he continued talking. "Then you call. You say, 'I am sorry for all what we plan, but you do not be the man of honor now.' I am relief. Then picture is in the mind. It show you saying vows. It show you kissing Lloyd. It show me and I cry. So I leave. I go home until is over. Is easier for me, I think. I do not know you say, 'I will not marry Lloyd.'"

Oh, we humans can be cruel, selfish creatures. Despite everything in me that said, "Don't do it," I started to ask anyway. "But why—"

At that moment, the plane jumped. The fasten seatbelt signs glowed. The captain assured us all would be well, but we'd hit a bit of "mild" turbulence, and he asked if we would please stay in our seats until we'd gotten through it.

So, instead, I wrapped my other hand around his arm, leaned against him, and prayed. I think I felt his lips brush my hair. No… that's not right. I choose to *believe* I felt it. Honesty forces me to admit that it could have been wistful dreaming.

31

Michal—

Snow on the ground—*snow* in Constanța. Carol admitted that, over the last few years, it had become more common. Even the Black Sea froze sometimes. They blamed it on climate change.

We stumbled through the airport and climbed into a taxi. Carol gave directions in Romanian, and I think I swooned. That's a lie. I totally swooned. He noticed, too.

In the past twenty years, we'd become the best of friends. Seriously, whenever asked who my best friend was, I always said, "My pen pal Carol from Romania." But in the past twenty hours, we'd taken that friendship to a whole new level.

He flirted with me—deliberately, masterfully, unforgettably, and a million other adverbs flirted with me. A new side of him emerged, one that I would have told you I hated if you'd warned me.

Carol the gentle and somewhat submissive to others became Carol the leader—the confident. I hadn't realized how much he had stamped down his own personality to honor me. I hadn't realized just how intimidating a new culture can be. Whizzing through the streets of Constanța to Ioan's apartment, I learned. Fast.

For the thousandth time, he kissed my hand. His eyes kissed my lips, but he wouldn't let his anywhere near them. I'd even tried to initiate one, but he was either too obtuse to notice or wasn't ready. Then again, from the looks he gave me, maybe he was *too* ready. Either way, it's probably best that this leader side came out right about then. I thought I was ready to explore these new feelings, but my more mature side realized that I just might be in a vulnerable state. You don't break up with the "love of your life" without needing some time to regroup and be sure that the guy who probably sparked that decision is really who you want after all.

At Ioan's apartment, he threw his duffel bag over one shoulder, hiked my suitcase under an arm, and grabbed my hand. "Come! Ioan is up there. I see him at window. He wave; do you see?"

Up two flights of stairs, people peered out of doors and stepped into the hall as we rushed past. He pounded on the door. But the man who opened it—how had I not realized how old he was? Romanian flowed like wine in Napa. No joke. Ioan said something like, "Pleased I am to meet you." His accent though. It was so thick he could have said something completely different.

Buried somewhere in my phone is a picture of what we ate. Ioan fed us almost immediately, but I was so exhausted that whatever it was didn't register. At some point, I slumped to the table—man, I hope I didn't drool—and Carol carried me to a bed. Ioan says we both slept for hours.

Carol—

Darkness filled the apartment by the time I woke at Ioan's. Even before my eyes opened, the familiar sounds of home welcomed me. There's a raw beauty found when you lie in bed, eyes closed, and absorb the scents and sounds of the place you know as home. Perhaps what makes it so meaningful is that no one could describe those moments to adequately reflect that feeling.

Ioan was gone—likely working at the guild workshop to give us a quiet place to sleep. Michal lay curled on the bed still, a soft snore escaping every now and then, just as it had in the Istanbul airport. For just a moment, I could imagine what life might be like if she lived here with me.

No! This is a terrible idea! She has friends and family. She has an important job—one that helps thousands of people every year. This is selfish of you. And Ralph has promised such a wonderful life for you in HearthLand. She might live there, but you will never consider asking her to live in Romania so far from her family and friends.

So, with the sounds of the night filling my ears, I planned. Going home shouldn't hurt my plans to stay in America if I only visited for a few days. I had to return quickly—very quickly. But there were so many things I wanted to show her. The orphanage, of course. She'd want to see that the children had their mattresses and hear how they liked their Christmas dinner.

The guild would want to meet her. The few friends I had outside the guild—all three of them—we would go to dinner somewhere. I'd take her around the city—show her The Casino. Somehow, I knew she'd love that. The beautiful art nouveau architecture and the rich opulence that once filled the rooms would appeal to her sense of beauty. We'd wear safety hats—they hand them out at the door. She would post a picture for her friends on Instagram.

Will they blame me for the broken wedding? Crystal won't. She'll be glad, I think. She didn't want Michal to marry Lloyd. He will blame me, I think. She said he'd become jealous.

It's a terrible thing when knowing you've hurt someone gives you a sense of joy. Guilt choked me and drove me to grab a glass of water. It choked me again as the sound woke Michal and my heart raced at the thought of her being up. *She needs her rest,* one part of me argued. But even as I moved to turn on a light, another side insisted, *She needs to be awake for the next four or five hours, or we'll be awake all night and sleep during the day.*

"Carol?"

Her hair frizzed around her head—likely in knots. Sleepy eyes blinked up at me as I sat beside her. One thought consumed me, though. I could tell her I loved her. It wasn't wrong anymore. I could do it. I wouldn't—not yet. She needed time. But I wouldn't have to try to hide it either.

"Sleep well?"

"Woke up and freaked out! I heard that guy shouting in Romanian and couldn't figure out why he wasn't speaking English!"

I hadn't even noticed. It would be Luca down the hall. He always railed at his family when he got home from work. Then he ate, mellowed, and laughed the rest of the night. "Luca is have bite worse—no. Bark worse than the bite."

"It was the language more than anything." She tried to stand, swayed, and held onto my shoulder until she was steady, and glanced around her. "Where's the bathroom?"

I pointed to a door across the hall. "Just there."

At the door, she smiled back at me. "I can't believe we're here! For years I've imagined coming, and now I'm really here."

The entire time she was in there, I prayed prayers of thanksgiving. *She is really here.*

Michal—

The words blurred together. How many times that day had I heard the same thing? I knew what they meant, "This is Michal from America— the 'boy' I wrote to all those years. No, she's not my girlfriend." He introduced me to the entire guild, to three friends, and to the director of the orphanage.

When you've done as much research on the Romanian orphan crisis as I have, you think you know—that you really get it. It's a lie. I still don't know if Carol's assurances that things are "so much the better now" is reassuring or horrifying. If this is better, my American sensibilities can't fathom the worse.

The children didn't come to us or try to talk to us. They didn't make friends. I'd imagined falling in love with some little boy or girl who latched onto us and being allowed to adopt because Carol is Romanian—because he's a Romanian *orphan.*

Two problems rose with that idea. Of course, the first was that I didn't become deeply attached to a beautiful little girl with deep brown eyes and shining black hair who tried to practice the half dozen English words she knew on me. The girls hid and watched from afar as the director explained who we were and that we had arranged for the new mattresses. No little boy with a crooked nose from fighting and bad teeth that would need braces wormed his way into my heart and pleaded with me to call him son.

Don't get me wrong, I wanted to take every last one of them *home.* I wanted to start a group home for them in HearthLand—a place where they would grow and thrive. I wanted to be the director and teach them how to give and receive affection. Oh, how I longed to teach them that humanity isn't all cruel, life isn't all cold, and hunger, and neglect! But the deep, personal connection I'd imagined in my naive idealism never materialized.

The director followed us as Carol led me upstairs to a small window where he'd written his letters by moonlight. "Is here. I look out over city and write to the boy who has 'two dogs, a cat, and a goldfish that the cat thinks is toy—a cat name Sylvester, because he is boy cat. Girl cat is lame.'"

"Did I really say that? I guess so. I really hated anything to do with being a girl then. Girls were dumb. Boys had all the fun." Sometimes, curiosity is a painful disease. "Where did you sleep?"

Instant, raw pain filled his eyes. "You will not wish to see." Rapid words in Romanian produced a decided "No!" from the director. Carol pulled me away again. "We must go."

He showed me where he hid all the letters—where someone had found them and destroyed them. We walked the path from the orphanage, through the edge of town and down to where his school had been. As he walked, he pulled sunflower seeds from his pocket and offered me some. How many times had he done that on a long walk? Even Crystal had mentioned it after one of their dates. Ioan did it as well. These Romanians—they loved their sunflower seeds.

He pointed to an enormous concrete slab. "There I play with

Constantin when other boys go home after school. There he beat me up when one come back to find lost pencil."

Hearing things like this when I could see where they happened brought a reality to them that did horrible things to my heart. I held him and wept—odd dichotomy there, but I did. At times like that, I really thought he loved me, but then something would happen, and I'd doubt again.

Carol—

Never had hiding my feelings been harder. Even as a child, I didn't have to be so careful. People asked about her. *"Is she your girlfriend?"* I *ached* to say yes, but I couldn't.

Sometimes she looked at me exactly as I'd dreamed of her doing—almost from the day I met her. She'd tried to kiss me once, but I pretended not to notice. If there was any part of her still hurting over Lloyd, I wanted her to heal before I told her—*showed her*—how I felt.

Every introduction followed the same pattern. I'd introduce her, they'd ask if she was my girlfriend, I'd tell them no, and I'd say "She is the 'boy' I have been writing almost all my life." But when I took her to meet my priest and introduced her just as I had a dozen times, he turned to me and rebuked me. "She's hurting, Carol. She knows you say she's not your girlfriend. She feels rejected. I think she cares for you."

A glance at her didn't give me any answers—only a fake smile that could mean anything. Father Florian didn't say any more, but his words rooted in my heart. Instead, he asked about her trip. "What brings you to Romania?"

"Carol. He came and I followed." She blushed. "That sounds so needy and desperate. But you know him. I didn't know why he was leaving, he left his phone behind, I'd just broken up with my fiancé, and I just *came*."

They talked about the orphanage, about her church. She asked questions about our faith—intelligent, respectful, loving questions. I could see she didn't agree with something Father Florian said, but I don't think he noticed. As she turned to go, he pulled me aside. "She's a beautiful woman—kind. I think you should tell her how you feel."

"She is not orthodox, Father."

"If it is God's will, He will make a way. Pray, Carol. Pray and talk to her."

This I had already planned. But Father Florian wouldn't like the decision I'd made. I would convert. I liked the faith of her friends in Brunswick. I liked the faith of the people in HearthLand. Maybe if I had grown up in the church, I might have been more loyal. I probably would have been. As I hugged the man who had mentored me—taught me how to *be* a man—I realized that it might be the last time I ever saw him. And then I cried.

We didn't talk on the way back to Ioan's. I held her hand again, but it seemed to make things worse. She wouldn't let it go. Even as we entered the house, she held fast to me. But when she saw Ioan's room empty and the bed free, she dropped it and rushed forward. I reached for her. "What is wrong?"

"Nothing." The anguish in her voice mocked her words.

I pulled her close, held her. "Michal, tell me. You are the upset. What is wrong?"

Why are women so stubborn? Why do they hide behind words rather than using them to communicate? I don't understand. She still refused—and refused to step away. With her hair tickling my neck she murmured, "I can't, Carol. It's humiliating—too personal. I just... *can't.*"

I almost told her right there. Not saying something felt like it would cost me everything, but I had to do it. I didn't ever want her to wonder if I meant it or if they had *only* been words to comfort. I didn't know how to tell her I'd had to stuff them down for the past two months at least. I didn't know how to tell her that I'd cried over feelings I couldn't share. Truth be told, I didn't *want* to tell her that. The men she knew—the man she'd *loved*—wouldn't cry.

But I loved her enough not to do it. I loved her enough to wait so she would know when I said I loved her that it was because I chose to say it, not because she needed to hear it.

Michal—

Two days we wandered Constanța. He showed me amazing sights—the freezing Black Sea and The Casino. Oh, that place is beautiful. It's supposed to be renovated, but the project keeps falling through. There are times like that when I wish I were independently wealthy so I could do it. At night, when he thought I was sleeping, Carol worked. And that's when I realized how expensive coming home must have been for him. He left because of me—because he hurt to see me marry Lloyd.

We'd walked the city, froze our butts off, and then got on a train to go north—up closer to Brașov, where we'd go cross-country skiing. He slept at first, but when he woke, his eyes met mine, and he smiled. I had to say words that would likely cause him more pain. But after two days, I couldn't delay anymore.

"I have to make plans to go home. I can't keep Ioan from his bed indefinitely, and I have a job." Tears splashed on my cheeks—tears I hadn't felt form. "I don't want to leave you here."

Carol reached for the phone I'd set on the seat beside me. "We find tickets. Embassy say I should go home to HearthLand. I call. They say visa paperwork is important questions."

I think that meant that they had to have him answer questions. I was so excited that he'd go back with me that I forgot to ask. "Really?"

"Yes. I am buy more suitcases to take my things to America."

Inside fifteen minutes, with the help of Carol's Romanian and my wicked search skills, we found great tickets—tickets that had us flying home in three days. "Are you sure?" I searched his face for any trace of hesitation, but there was none.

"Ralph, he give me mortgage in HearthLand. This he does not do very much, but he say I pay back house as I work for store. He say, 'You need

282

your own place, Stefan. You need a home. We want you here, so I will do this.'"

"You know, if you had told me a year ago that I'd ever even think of living in a place like HearthLand, I would have laughed at you. But it's really an amazing place—expensive, but amazing. I can't believe Ralph is doing that for you!"

Carol's eyes lit up as he talked. "I am having the chickens and a dog. I want dog like Gertie that likes me *before* I go away."

"Oh, that's rich. She didn't want you to go?"

Laughter filled the car as he described the parting. "I think, 'You are just happy that I am gone. You pretend to be sad, but I know the better.'"

Sometimes you can communicate more by what you don't say than by what you do. Carol taught me that on that trip. The restraint he showed. My heart knew that he loved me, but Lloyd would never have taken so long to kiss me. He'd never have held himself back from those little touches that had characterized our relationship. Carol did. I think it's because my breakup was still so fresh. He thought I needed time. Well, he *acted* like that, anyway. All it did was strengthen my respect for him—deepen love I was just beginning to acknowledge.

Somewhere between Constanța and Brașov, it became obvious to me that I'd begun to fall in love with Carol weeks before. Things became clearer so far removed from home—removed from the guilt that probably fueled my determination to stay with Lloyd for so long. My arguments about our relationship rang hollow now that I could recall them with some measure of objectivity.

A glance at Carol sent fresh flutters through my heart followed by a sickening wave of guilt. *Lord, forgive me. I didn't know. I really don't think I knew. Lloyd deserved better.* Another glance at Carol sent my eyes skittering away again. *Carol did too. He cared about me—loved me. And I in my self-absorbed, stubborn determination just clung to the ideal of the perfect relationship. Carol shouldn't have had to endure that.*

The train slowed. Carol's eyes widened with anticipation and excitement, and like a twit, I asked the obvious question. "Are we here?"

Carol nodded. "We are here."

Carol—

In my pocket, a small circlet of silver with a tiny diamond burned against my leg. Ioan had tried to talk me out of it—told me to use the credit card and buy a *real* ring. *"The one you described must have cost thousands of Euros. Why would you give her silver and a diamond you need a microscope to see?"*

I'd thought, of all people, he would understand how much I *needed* to give her something that held a part of me in it. He's an artist. It's the only reason I hesitated. But I had to be true to myself.

At the top of a little rise, Michal pulled off her skis and tossed the poles on the ground beside them. Trees surrounded us. The snow sparkled and glistened—much like her eyes. The way they looked at me. I knew it was real. She loved me and didn't know how to tell me. *She's probably afraid you'll think it's just reciprocation of your obvious feelings. She's probably embarrassed about Lloyd.*

But being able to speak first—to tell *her*—had become important to me. I had to say something while I had the courage. "I have want to say something for long time. For very long time. I hide very well what I feel because you have the boyfriend, and he is good man."

"Lloyd is a good man. You're right. Thanks for reminding me. I have a feeling it would become easy for me to demonize him as a way to justify breaking up with someone so wonderful."

By the time I'd translated what I thought she said, it could have meant regret or relief. I didn't know. What I did know is I couldn't second-guess myself. "I have fall in love with you—almost from first day." Tears filled her eyes, and she wrapped her arms around me as I made the speech I'd rehearsed for days. "It scare me—the realize that I am fall for you. I cannot tell you the feelings. I have to be only the friend. The love of brother is not enough, but I must only have that. I don't like it."

Michal snickered. "Funny thing… looking back, I didn't like it either.

I think I wanted more, too. I just hid behind the protection of my relationship with Lloyd. I really believed I saw you only as a friend. I lied to myself, I think. But I believed that lie."

"That lie break my heart." Though my heart screamed that it was too soon, I couldn't help myself. "I have gift for you. Is can mean whatever is what you want." The ring sat in my palm, but Michal didn't take it. A lump welled up in my throat.

"Did you make that?"

"Yes." Explanations, jumbled and half-spoken in Romanian, tumbled from my lips as I tried to justify why I'd chosen what I had. "I think to self, 'What is only gift you can give—no one else. Silver is pretty but is not have big cost.'"

"I don't care about that, Carol. I love that you made it." She took the ring from my hand, turned it over in hers, and her eyes met mine. "It's a pen!"

I traced the pen barrel with my finger and smoothed the little ridge where the point of the nib overlapped the other end. "I think, 'What is something special for us? I want stamps, but pretty they are not—too big and flat. I try the letter opener, but is look like knife. Not pleasant image."

Michal's laughter tickled my heart. "I'd say not!"

"I search the Internet with your mobile. I find pen pal website and is have the fountain pen. The little hole in the nib is perfect setting for my little diamond. Then I know."

Her eyes widened, and her lips trembled. "You've been working on this at night while I slept, haven't you?"

"*Da.*" When she gave it back to me, my heart constricted.

"Will you put it on?"

A lump nearly choked me as I took it. She held out her left hand. Our eyes met. She nodded at my unspoken question. Heart pounding, soaring, singing, I slid it on that ring finger. How did I not cry? It fit, too. The dental floss measurement that took me half an hour to get so I wouldn't wake her up had worked. I wanted to kiss her, but she wouldn't look up at me. She wouldn't stop staring at the ring.

"Is good?"

A nod. A sigh. "It's perfect. The most beautiful thing I've ever owned."

That did it. Her eyes met mine. I'd waited, dreamed, hoped for a kiss since I'd realized how much I cared about her. I'd relived a dozen ways to show her the love in my heart, but I needed to tell her too. "I love you." In a whisper, I added, "*Te iubesc*" as well.

When our lips met—when I felt the silky brush of her hair on my cheek—nothing could hope to describe it. I'd imagined her lips clinging to mine—such a hollow, weak, meaningless dream compared to the moment when they truly did. It wasn't my first kiss, but it might as well have been. I think it could have been my last. Then I almost cried at the thought.

When did it end? I'll never know. Her breath caught, her hand touched my face. "You are such a handsome man. Seriously, you are one hot dude."

"I am to blush if you say that more."

So she did. Compliment after compliment flew at me—most I understood. Every single one I tried to give her turned out almost inappropriate until finally I quit trying. "I love you. This is enough for me."

"It's just perfect for me, too. I'd begun to wonder what was wrong—if you'd come back here and decided you didn't want to go back." Her forehead dropped to my chest. Michal inhaled deeply. "Man, you smell good."

"I cannot stay—not if I love you. I do not have the family. You cannot leave yours. Answer is for me to move to HearthLand. I will have chickens and the garden. You will eat many, many salads."

Don't ask me what she said then. A kiss followed and wiped my memory of anything but the realization that she really did love me. But once we turned to go, she asked, "So... when's the chapel in HearthLand going to be done?"

I'd told her the ring could mean whatever she wanted. That question gave me the courage to try to make it what I wanted. "I think Ralph say is in May or June." I slid my finger around the ring and tilted her chin to watch her eyes as I said, "When you are ready, *vrei sa te casatoresti cu mine?*"

"That sounds like a question, but I can only guess what it is."

"Guess—answer your guess." She protested, but I pressed her. "Is mean much to me, Michal."

Our lips met for just a second before she whispered, "I think I'm ready now, but yes, when I'm ready, I'll marry you."

"You understand very well the Romanian." A memory, one I'd treasured so many times in the past months, resurfaced. "Do you remember the star that fall? The wish I make?"

"Yeah… I always wondered what you said. I even tried to look it up in a translator thing, but I couldn't remember it right or I spelled it wrong—one of those."

"I say then, '*Va doresc numai bucurie si fericire.*' Is mean, 'I only wish you joy and happiness.' When you say you are marry Lloyd, I think, 'That wish is come true. I wish I not *make* that wish!'" My throat constricted as I tried to find the words to say what my heart felt. "Now I pray God helps me make this wish come true."

It took twice as long to return to the train as it had taken to get up that hill. Stopping every few minutes to enjoy the moment—to steal just *one* more kiss—that might be why. We missed the train home to Constanța. So, we sat up all night, talking and planning in the train station. We slept in each other's arms. We kissed under imaginary mistletoe.

It was a belated Christmas, but I doubted I'd ever have a more magical one.

Epilogue

Carol—

Snow crunched, and a cold, biting wind whipped at my back as I trudged the long way up Hearthfield Way to the mailbox. Ralph's truck wouldn't start, and I never felt comfortable driving anyone else's car. The rental had gone back when we returned from Constanța six weeks ago. I'd buy a car when I found one I could afford and Mac said was worth driving. So far, every time we found one, he insisted it would need repairs inside six months. So I waited.

Gertie had started off with me, but a hundred yards from the house, she'd whined, whimpered, whined again, and then trudged back with a betrayed look in her eye. That dog…

The mail truck drove off just as I reached the highway. A stack of mail sat at the bottom of the bin, bundled and waiting, and as usual, I flipped through in hopes of word on my visa. Nothing from the State Department, but a letter from Michal sat right on top.

With the others shoved in the letter bag slung over one shoulder, I opened the envelope and smiled at the letter and tiny envelope within. A picture of her—never had I seen anything so beautiful—dropped to the snow. Am I foolish that I snapped a picture of it with my mobile before picking it up? Probably.

But that envelope, the letter—those captured my attention even more.

How many years had I received a letter in March with that same tiny envelope with a letter? So familiar—so Michal.

February 12, 2016

Dear Carol in HearthLand,

Happy Valentine's Day! This is the twenty-sixth? time I've written those words. When I was a kid, everyone brought these little valentines to school to give out. I always put one of those little conversation hearts in mine, but the mail machines just chew them up, so I never did send you one. I'll have to give you one when I see you on Sunday. This year, almost every single one of the valentines boxes were some kind of cartoon thing. I had to order these online so it could be just simple and normal.

I love you. Thank you for asking me to be your valentine—forever. Thank you for making me "Carol's one and only 'belle.'"

All those years ago when I was just writing to my Romanian friend and wondering what she looked like, I could never have imagined an outcome like this. After that first picture, where I totally looked like a boy, I never could send another picture. Stringy hair that looked awful no matter what I did, braces on my teeth that I hated so much—no matter what, I looked awful. I couldn't do it. Vanity is very ugly and very real. I justified it by reminding myself that you didn't have one to send, and it was rude to make you feel bad. Yeah. I did that.

I debated sending you this picture. When I talked to a wedding photographer for Lloyd's and my engagement pictures, I had her snap a couple to get a feel for how her style would work with me. I'd planned to give it to you. Then everything ended, and I didn't. But I ran across them today and thought, "This was supposed to be his. No one has ever seen it. I am doing it." So here you go. I only have two copies—this one and one I'm putting in my firebox in case something happens to this. It's my way of making up for never sending one before.

We had no way of knowing, all those years ago, that we were writing to the one we'd spend the rest of our lives with. We grew up together. We had that "boy and girl next door" romance, but ours was the continent next door.

290

Funny how I'd gotten my heart set on a special story to tell my children about how I got my engagement ring. You gave me that. You gave me a romantic tale that only happens in sappy Christmas movies and in young girls' daydreams.

In three months, I'm going to walk down that aisle in that sweet little church and become Mrs. Carol Stefan. Can I tell you a secret? I keep writing my married name on sticky notes and the backs of receipts, and on envelopes. Michal Stefan.

Did you know girls do silly things like that? Life is full of a series of silly nothings that God weaves into a rich tapestry that tells His story of our lives. I can't help but laugh when I read that. It sounds like something you'd say. You've rubbed off on me, Dulceață.

Happy Valentine's Day. Just three months. Three long, delightful months. I love you,

Michal in Brunswick

Chautona Havig's Books

The Rockland Chronicles

Aggie's Inheritance Series
- Ready or Not
- For Keeps
- Here We Come
- Ante Up! (Coming 2016)

Past Forward: A Serial Novel (Six Volumes)
- Volume One
- Volume Two
- Volume Three
- Volume Four
- Volume Five
- Volume Six

HearthLand Series: A Serial Novel (4-8 Volumes—in progress 2015)
- Volume One
- Volume Two
- Volume Three
- Volume Four
- Volume Five

The Hartfield Mysteries
- Manuscript for Murder

- Crime of Fashion
- Two o'Clock Slump
- Front Window (coming 2016)

Noble Pursuits
Argosy Junction
Discovering Hope
Not a Word
Speak Now
A Bird Died
Thirty Days Hath...
Confessions of a De-cluttering Junkie
Corner Booth
Rockland Chronicles Collection One
(Contains *Noble Pursuits, Argosy Junction,* and *Discovering Hope)*

The Agency Files
- Justified Means
- Mismatched
- Effective Immediately
- A Forgotten Truth

Sight Unseen Series
- None So Blind

Christmas Fiction
- Advent
- 31 Kisses
- Tarnished Silver
- The Matchmakers of Holly Circle
- Carol and the Belles

* * *

Legacy of the Vines
- <u>Deepest Roots of the Heart</u>

Journey of Dreams Series
- <u>Prairie</u>
- <u>Highlands</u>

Heart of Warwickshire Series
- <u>Allerednic</u>
- Bullfinch's Methodology

* * *

The Annals of Wynnewood
- <u>Shadows & Secrets</u>
- <u>Cloaked in Secrets</u>
- <u>Beneath the Cloak</u>

Not-So-Fairy Tales
- <u>Princess Paisley</u>
- <u>Everard</u>

Legends of the Vengeance
- <u>The First Adventure</u>